Flame of the Oracle: A Mythic Ancient Roman Romantasy
D. Amon Hume

ORACLE
PUBLISHING LLC

Oracle Publishing LLC

Flame of the Oracle

Written by D. Amon Hume

ISBN: 979-8-9945607-1-6

(Hard cover)

Published by Oracle Publishing LLC

Contents

To my wife,
Carla.
The love of my life.

Preface

From the Archivum Montis Caelorum

(Translated from Late Latin fragments; provenance disputed)

In the winter of the Year of Our Lord 1137, during the clearing of collapsed stone galleries beneath the Monastery of Saint Aurelius in the Apennine foothills east of Rome, a sealed cedar chest was uncovered behind a walled recess near the old scriptorium.

Within lay three incomplete codices and twelve bundles of brittle papyrus, many scorched at the edges, others darkened by resin and ash. The handwriting varies across centuries, suggesting repeated copying and preservation by unknown orders. Several leaves bear marginal warnings in a later hand: Do not copy further and let this name sleep.

One point remains uncontested: the Monastery of Saint Aurelius was financed and erected under the authority of Pope Leo I (440–461). A surviving charter fragment reads, "...a foundation ratified in the pontificate of Leo, upon land conveyed by the heirs of an ancient eastern house." The final clause, partially effaced in all known copies, appears to allude to familial ties between donor and pontiff, though no extant registry confirms the claim.

The texts themselves describe a foreign priestess, a Roman officer of unusual prominence, and a sequence of public rites, military commands, executions, and fires within the city. Dates appear deliberately altered. Personal names fade into erasures. In one fragment, the emblem of a crescent moon appears in black ink beside a passage scraped almost entirely away.

Scholars remain divided. Some argue medieval fabrication. Others note linguistic structures inconsistent with contemporary monastic Latin, suggesting older sources filtered through Christian scribes who neither understood nor trusted what they preserved.

What survives forms no continuous chronicle, only a lattice of testimony, rumor, and fear.

This volume presents the most coherent reconstruction yet attempted.

It Begins with a Curse

An Omen for the Reader

Be Warned.

These words are not safe.

They are ancient... These letters are fire disguised as ink.

Each line you read stirs what should have slept.

Ink carries breath. Breath feeds flame.

With every page, The Goddess of the Flame wakes again

The foreign goddess who crossed the sea in Albina's blood.

She does not bless. She takes.

Read long enough and you may feel her nearby.

You may walk in another body.

You may bleed in another century.

You may not escape the binding.

Know this: she marks all who call her.

She remembers. She waits.

Once you begin, the offering is made.

Turn the page, and the bond is sealed.

If you see the Goddess...

do not ask her name.

-Nisaya, the Witch in Black

Chapter 1
DANCE OF THE ORACLE

E ast shore of the Caspian Sea - Temple at Valbena - 64 B.C.
Thunder shook the roof of the old temple just before dawn.

The lamps trembled. Smoke bent in the wind.

Albina froze mid-dance at the center of the floor, bare feet gripping the cold stone.

Something secret moved inside her.

A storm behind her ribs trying to rip its way out.

Lightning flared through the open door. White fire burned a man's face into her mind.

Tall. Light skin. Broad shoulders. Red cloak. Twin blades drawn.

Rufus.

Albina knew the name without hearing it. She knew it for years.

And she knew what it meant.

Death.

He walked toward her and her remaining people.

Her muscles jerked. Cold climbed her spine, locking her knees and throat. Breath caught, held.

Her dancers pressed close, a ring of silk and skin. The eunuch guards lifted their spears in the vision. Zarmina and Nisaya, the red and black witches, raised their hands, lips moving, old words scraping the air as if they could cage what she saw.

Every sound in the temple hit too hard, thunder, wind, the scrape of sandals, her own heart slamming.

The world hardened. Cracked.

She wasn't in her temple anymore.

Polished marble rolled under her feet. Red-veined walls loomed high. Carved fountains spilled clear water. Mosaic floors gleamed wet under the falling rain. The air sat thick with mint, citrus, crushed roses. All of it... wrong.

Leaves skidded across the tiles. Rain hammered the roof.

He turned the corner.

Rufus. Real now. Alive.

His scent hit her first; leather, olive oil, warm skin, male sweat.

A scent from a man she had never met.

A scent that should not have crossed a vision.

But behind that scent, fainter, unexpected, something else rode the storm.

A second presence.

Dry dust. Pine resin. A leaner warmth. A different Roman.

Someone linked to Rufus by blood, not blade.

She didn't know the name yet, but the scent struck her like a whispered omen.

Rufus's boots struck marble in a steady beat. Gavel blows. Verdict already passed.

No fear in his eyes. No mercy. No doubt.

Two short swords, bright as sunrise.

Her guards surged forward.

They died before their next breath. Six heartbeats. Six thrusts. Bodies falling, clean as cut rope.

The witches lunged behind them, spells half-formed on their lips.

Steel ended both.

Nisaya's knife hit the floor, smoking beside her hand, spell uncompleted. Zarmina fell back over the mosaic, eyes wide, desperation caught like a trapped flame.

Silk blurred red. Anklets rang. Dancers scattered like startled birds. Their cries blended into the storm. Their blood, and lives flowed down the drain.

She stood alone, the last of her people.

He kept coming.

Albina spat at him. Hate struck his cheek. Dripped down his face and mixed with the rain. He didn't even blink. Nothing would stop him.

He caught her by the throat. Lifted her against the wall. Stone and rough mortar bit her spine. His grip held her steady, measured, and inevitable.

Cold steel pressed under her ribs. His blade.

"I curse you," she forced out.

He leaned close.

Her face turning red, eyes tearing.

She smelled leather again, the faint bite of oil, and the killers sweat. A scent she would never forget.

"You are a curse."

The blade drove in.

His calloused thumb brushed her pulse. One slow, deliberate second too long.

"Steady, little witch," he murmured. "Close your eyes now. Rome doesn't tolerate fire goddesses."

Light tore her apart.

Drums thundered beneath the world, her drums.

Heat. Smoke. Pain. Home.

She fell through marble into limestone.

The palace shattered.

The Temple at Valbena formed around her, cracked and stubborn, alive with firelight.

Bells screamed at her ankles as she danced. The trance took her fully, spine arched, breath gone thin, body shaking with the goddess's grip.

Her blood pumped with smoke. Resin. Burned roots. The old mixtures. Intoxicants.

Albina was dancing. The thing she did best.

Drums hammered through her head.

Her hips rolled slowly. Silk blew around her like a flame around a wick. Sweat turned the crimson cloth translucent against her ribs, hips, thighs. Anklets chimed.

The Flame Goddess climbed her bones. She whispered;

"Move."

Three steps forward. Each heavier than granite, as if stone pulled at her ankles.

Sweat burned down her spine. Cloth dragged across skin with every breath.

Her people watched in silence.

None knew what she had seen.

The goddess rose hotter.

He comes. And next time, you'll hold the knife.

Her hips caught the rhythm. Breath smoked.

Three steps forward. One back. Bells kissed stone.

"Why me?"

Because no one else can.

She struck each beat; hips, ribs, shoulders. Sharp. Defiant.

Rufus's scent clung to the vision; leather, oil, heat. It clung to her skin as if he'd passed through her. Desire?... Yes.

Shame burned her. Rage burned hotter.

"He'll destroy us."

Yes, the Flame answered.

And from that ruin will rise your children. And we will rise again.

Changed. Stronger. Fire unending.

Spears slammed against stone. Iron rain. The sound shook the rafters.

She spun with it. Sweat flew.

He cannot be beaten by man or beast, the goddess whispered, invulnerable to all... except himself.

Albina slowed. Heat bit her palms as she reached over the brazier. A drop of sweat hissed.

"I hate him," she breathed. "I don't want him. I don't want Rome."

Your wants mean nothing, child. Your hate, even less.

You are mine.

And he is marked.

But another Roman approaches your path.

A shadow of his fire.

Remember the scent.

The last drumbeat hung.

The flame stretched tall, thin, then tall again.

Silence closed on her skin like a grip.

Another roar hit her.

Doors.

Wood. Iron. Men.

A second vision slammed into her.

The temple doors exploded inward.

Men shouted. Iron smashed iron. Sweat. Horses. Male musk. Heat. Burned leather.

Red Ring himself stormed through, a giant in black armor, a red serpent painted across his shield.

He had chased her people across deserts. Poisoned wells. Burned villages. Looted their temples and homes. Enslaved the women and children.

Torches flew. Cloth caught. Oil flashed.

Screams and foul smoke filled the air.

Fire raced up the curtains, leaping like a living thing.

"Protect the Twelve!" Albina cried, but her voice drowned in the roar.

Red Ring kicked the brazier.

Coals scattered like dark pearls.

The Eternal Flame flared once, bright as noon.

Then died.

A sound tore out of Albina that did not belong to any human throat.

She lunged for the coals. Heat blistered her palms. Hair singed. She clawed the ash until smoke filled her lungs.

Over five hundred years the sacred flame burned. Murdered in three seconds.

You will wait in this temple for three months, whispered the goddess.

The King of Kings will wait for a message from Red Ring. The scroll won't make its way to him.

By a fluke or by design, that message will make its way to Rome.

The great Caesar will read it, and order a rescue.

A fighter, an opportunist will obey.

Two Romans move toward you, one to end you, one to save you.

And both will change our world.

Albina watched the ashes grow cold and screamed until her voice broke.

Stone closed in around her.

Real. Cold.

She lay on the temple floor. Zarmina bent over her. Nisaya's thin hands hovered above trembling water.

"The Parthian comes," Albina rasped. "He'll burn the temple. Hide the Twelve. Take charred wood from the sacred fire. The spirit sleeps in it."

They vanished at once.

Albina dragged herself to her knees before the brazier.

Ash glowed faint red.

"He'll love me before he kills me," she whispered. "And when he does, Rome will burn."

Her hand tightened on warm stone.

"But first," softer, "the King of Kings will suffer."

Outside, the wind howled in from the sea.

Her ankle bells chimed once.

The Flame pressed hard under her ribs, trying to break through.

The vision had warned her.

It had named two debts.

Two Romans.

Two fates.

One she would love.

One she would break.

Both she would face.

And Albina whispered into the dark,

"Then let them come... I'm ready."

Chapter 2
A GLOW

East shore of the Caspian Sea - Temple at Valbena - 64 B.C.
As always, the trance spat her out like surf breaking against a rocky shore. The trances, brought on by smoke and dance, left her breathing deeply and drenched in sweat.

Albina leaned against the nearest column. Cold slid into her palm. Lichen smeared green. Soot left a witches thumbmark on her skin. The bells at her ankles trembled once, little ghost chimes releasing her body. The air smelled of salt, burned resin, and faint oil. Around her, the priestesses bowed low but kept their distance. No one touched what the goddess had used.

She drew breath in thin strips, ribs still bruised by prophecy. Sweat cooled on her back. The crimson silk clung where it touched her ribs and hips, sheer as breath, heavy against her thighs. Her heartbeat pulsed through the cloth. The stone beneath her feet thrummed with the old quiet of her temple.

Behind her, the Eternal Flame settled to a thin blue thread. Resin smoke twisted in slow, tired spirals. Incense bowls collapsed into chalk. At the doorway, her guards stood motionless, bronze rings winking in the dim light. She passed between them. Her bare feet left damp prints on the stone.

Grooves, paths ran from altar to threshold. Centuries of Sibyls had carved them with their steps. She followed the scars, a daughter of the line, the next in the blood of fire. A shawl slid from her shoulders. Wool surrendered to dust.

Wind met her at the outer wall. Not land wind, sea wind. Wide, cold, metallic. It carried wet earth and storms from the far Caspian. She filled her lungs.

The vision's memory struck again.

A lion sprawled in blood-dark sand.

A man stood over it, bare arms slick, the sun burning gold on his shoulders. He raised steel. He lowered steel. No flourish. No cruelty. Just clean death. The lion shuddered once, then stilled. The sand swallowed its blood with a thirsty hiss.

Her pulse named him.

Rufus.

The name felt foreign, minted from another empire. Hard. Sharp. Dangerous. Yet it warmed her tongue before fading. She saw him again, the efficiency of his motion, the clarity, the balance in his hips. Recognition locked her chest like armor.

She reached the basin. Water quivered. Lamp fire carved gold stripes across it. Her reflection drifted: loose black hair, flushed cheeks, wide eyes. Something glowed behind them, knowledge, destiny, desire?

Love?

The word rose and died.

A Sibyl kept no heart for herself.

The oaths had taken that away long ago.

Still, her pulse thrashed like something new-born. She cupped water but didn't drink. Metal scent rose from it.

Blood lived everywhere tonight.

Footsteps echoed.

Zarmina the Red arrived first, tall, grave, wrapped in blood-red wool, her mortar heavy in one arm. The pestle ground roots to paste, steady rhythm, no haste. Nisaya the Black followed, a small shadow in black, wrists ink-stained, eyes too bright. Her smile flickered and vanished.

They didn't speak. They watched her the way healers watch a wound close.

Albina touched her pulse points, throat, wrists. The scent of his memory lingered. She breathed slow: four counts in, hold, eight out. The shaking eased. The crescent moon mark on her wrist cooled.

"I heard a name," Nisaya said, voice like a reed over water. "Your face spoke before your mouth did."

"Faces betray," Zarmina murmured. "The body tattles first." The pestle never stopped.

"The goddess put a boy's name on my tongue," Albina said.

Nisaya's grin sharpened. "The goddess has taste."

Zarmina handed her a clay cup, vinegar, water, bruised leaf, pinch of salt. "Drink. A throat lies after trance."

Albina sipped. Sour bit. Salt burned. Breath returned deeper.

"Describe him," Nisaya said.

"Heat," Albina said softly. "Blaze. Balance. His sword worked like a craftsman's tool. Quiet. No waste."

"Then he's no boy," Zarmina said.

"Yes... no," Albina whispered. "He's young. A few years older."

"And the feeling?" Nisaya asked.

Albina studied the basin. Gold light broke over the water. "It sits here." She touched the bone between her breasts. "Want without hunger. Pain without harm."

Nisaya's smile was gentle. "We have a word for that."

"Keep it," Zarmina said. "Sibyl can't be distracted."

Albina's eyes drifted toward the sanctum. Smoke leaked beneath the door. The scent of oiled olivewood breathed out, the Twelve waited inside, relics older than memory, stones that hummed like sleeping hearts.

Duty pulled from that shadow.

Desire pulled from the basin.

One body between two fates.

"Speak the first law of the Sibyl," Zarmina said.

Albina straightened. "A Sibyl bound to the goddess cannot yield to desire." Silence held.

Then Albina's mouth betrayed her with a sliver of a smile.

"Still," she said, "I desire to see him bleed and beg."

Laughter cracked the heaviness. They were women again, alive, amused, unholy.

"You were born under smoke," Zarmina said.

"She solved the Trader's Riddle at four," Nisaya added.

"She speaks seven tongues."

"She's the most skilled dancer alive, the eastern dance master claimed."

"She crushed a man's arm with her thighs."

"She escaped a war camp with fire and cunning."

"Enough," Albina said, though her lips curved.

She looked again into the basin.

A scent ghosted across her memory, leather, olive oil, warm skin. Rufus. The man that fate tied to her throat. The man who might one day kill her. The man she must one day make love her.

Another scent followed.

Dust. Pine. Iron. Horses.

Matineus. The fox.

A different Roman. A different shape of danger. His presence brushed her vision like a shadow seen from behind a curtain, faint, unfinished, but real. He did not blaze like Rufus. He smoldered.

Two men.

Two futures.

Two blades pointed at her life.

She shut her eyes. The relics hummed louder. The flame in her chest matched it.

She moved to the sanctum door. The bronze latch bit her palm. The stones beyond leaned toward her. The air thickened with ancient expectation.

Not tonight.

Tonight, she stood between exhaustion and awakening.

"At dawn," she said. "We begin the hiding. Prepare the crates. Burn the rest."

The witches vanished into the dark.

Albina sat alone by the lamp. Its wick spat blue. The sea wind pressed at the shutters like a creature wanting in.

Her hand pulled a silver coin from a fold of her dress. She rolled it between her fingers.

She rested her forehead on her knees. The temple hummed through her bones. The Twelve. The guards. The surf on the cliff. The storm crawling west. Everything waiting.

A fifteen-year-old oracle.

A child of smoke and blood.

A goddess in her veins.

Two Romans now lived on her tongue.

One smelled of leather and olive oil.

One smelled of dust and pine.

One would rescue her.

One may try to kill her.

Both would change her.

The Romans were different sides of the same coin.

The lamp hissed and went out.

Deep in the sanctum, stone shifted, one of the Twelve turning in its sleep.

She held up the coin.

She turned and looked west, toward Rome.

Albina whispered into the dark:

"Which side of the coin will land face up?"

She flipped the coin.

Chapter 3
THE GIRL BEHIND THE LATTICE

The Latinus Compound, Rome - Years Earlier

Fulvia had slipped away from her mother's house on the Quirinal Hill so many afternoons the guards stopped pretending surprise.

A litter carried her at first, silk curtains drawn, slaves sweating under the poles. Then she made them stop at the last corner before the Subura, where the slope dropped and the smell changed. She always stepped out there, sandals on dirty stone, leaving the litter under an awning.

"Three streets," she told her bodyguard the first time. "Just three. Then we go back."

He'd grunted. "Your father..."

"Won't hear a word," she said. "Unless you shout it."

He never did.

After that, the route lived in her bones: past the shrine with the chipped Victory, left at the fig seller, right by the cracked fountain where children hit each other with reeds. Garlic, smoke, spilled wine. Voices thick with exhaustion or drink. Her nurse muttered disapproval every third step.

Fulvia walked faster.

Today she came with only one guard, the old soldier with the scar across his wrist. The Quirinal already lay behind them, its polished stone, its perfect order. Here, laundry drooped like surrender flags. Windows gaped. People stared at her hair.

The white always drew looks.

White hair, white brows, white lashes. Eyes bright blue. Skin pale as fresh plaster. Roman, yes, yet uncanny enough that children pointed, women crossed themselves, men stared twice.

On the Quirinal they called it a gift from the gods. Down here, it looked like trouble.

She didn't come to be admired or feared.

She came for him.

The Latinus compound took up the whole block; stone walls, iron-banded gates, no garlands, no carved beasts. Just the name LATINUS cut into the arch. Men read it, rubbed the scar on their chins, and chose another street.

Fulvia loved that.

The certainty. The earned respect.

The door slave nodded. They knew her by now, the pale patrician girl who came for the spoiled red-haired one. The gate opened without announcement. If you made it through the Subura to this door, you had earned your place or a beating. Sometimes both.

Inside, the air sharpened, cement, sweat, river water, cut wood. The courtyard stretched wide, shaded by olives and pines. Workers shouted numbers, not curses. Children hauled bricks with the seriousness of old men. Women sewed under an awning. Forge smoke rose clean and straight.

Fulvia breathed in the order.

The guard peeled toward the shade. Visitors stayed at the edges unless invited.

"Fulvia!" A voice like laughter against stone. "You're late."

Latina barreled across the courtyard, hair a blaze of red, plait swinging down her back, tunic hitched above dusty ankles. No jewels. No paint. No softness.

Fulvia's opposite.

"I had lessons," Fulvia said. "Greek terms for grain laws. I nearly died."

Latina grabbed her hand. "You'll live. Come on. He's already out."

He.

Fulvia didn't ask which. Latina tugged her past the trough where boys dunked their heads, past the small household shrine cluttered with faded offerings. Through the noise came the rhythm of impact, thud, thud, wood on wood, flesh on sand.

Fulvia's pulse followed.

"Your father doesn't mind?" she asked.

"He minds everything," Latina said. "But I'm his favorite. And you're with me. That helps."

"Or makes us twice the trouble."

Latina grinned. "Both."

They slipped under a low beam and climbed a narrow stair. At the top, a walkway looked down into the square training yard, packed earth, stone benches, racks of weapons, buckets of water.

Voices. Sweat. Sun. Training.

Fulvia pressed her palms to the lattice and looked through the slats.

And saw him.

Rufus.

Fifteen. Taller than most men. Broad shoulders, heavy arms, narrow waist. Hair short, red catching sunlight until it burned like gold-dusted flame. A pale scar cut one eyebrow. Dust streaked his chest; sweat shone along his spine.

He moved with absolute purpose. He moved with gravity.

Other boys orbited him without meaning to, measuring themselves by him. Trainers shouted, but their eyes stayed on him longer.

He held a wooden gladius, shield strapped tight. Both weighted. Heavier than the real thing. His stance spoke discipline; shoulders set, jaw locked, breath controlled.

Fulvia couldn't look away.

"You stare," Latina whispered.

"I'm watching."

"Same thing."

Below, a taller boy charged him. Rufus stepped into the blow. Shields cracked. Sand jumped. Rufus turned his hips, rolled the force off, struck twice, rib, knee. The boy collapsed.

Rufus stepped back. Guard up. Breathing steady.

Fulvia felt it in her ribs.

"He could've broken his leg," Latina said. "He held back."

"How do you know?"

"I've seen him when he didn't." Latina smirked. "Age thirteen."

Fulvia tried to imagine him smaller.

She couldn't.

He still hadn't smiled.

She caught herself imagining what that smile might look like.

A flicker of motion brushed her eye.

Across the yard, tucked under the colonnade shade, sat a thin boy on a low stool. Leg stiff at an odd angle, braced with a carved stick. Tunic hanging loose on a narrow frame. Dark hair hiding one eye. Wax tablet balanced against his thigh.

He wasn't watching the drills.

He was drawing.

Lines. Arcs. Angles. Curves.

Symmetry born of instinct, not lessons.

"Who is that?" Fulvia asked.

Latina didn't even glance. "Lucius. My older brother. Two years above Rufus."

Fulvia frowned. "I thought you had only two brothers."

"I have too many," Latina said. "That one doesn't count the same. He belongs to the tablet."

"Why is his leg..."

"Fever when he was small. It changed him." Latina lowered her voice. "He doesn't like being touched. Not by anyone but Rufus. Head works differently. He sees things. Bridges. Ships. Tunnels. Construction machines. Angles. He's smarter than architects twice his age."

Fulvia looked again.

Lucius's fingers trembled only when he lifted his stylus to think. When he drew, they stilled, precise, sure, delicate. The wax glowed with shapes that made sense to no one but him.

"What is he drawing?" she whispered.

"Something for Rufus," Latina said. "Always is."

On cue, Lucius glanced toward the center of the yard.

Not at the fighters.

At Rufus.

A quick look, pride, fear, devotion, love, then back to his tablet, working faster now, lines sharpening.

Fulvia's heart tugged.

Rufus had someone who adored him already. Someone he protected.

She wondered if he knew how fiercely he was loved.

Latina continued, softer, "Rufus would tear out a man's throat for him."

Fulvia believed it.

Rufus strode to the trough. A slave offered a ladle; he ignored it. He plunged his hands in cold water, dragged handfuls over his face and hair. Water cut through dust, leaving shining lines down his chest.

Fulvia gripped the lattice.

Latina muttered, "You stopped breathing."

"No I..."

"You breathe like him now." Latina grinned. "You mirror him. Like a dancer."

Heat climbed Fulvia's throat. But she didn't look away.

"What does he want?" she asked.

Latina shrugged. "To be a centurion. To die well. To honor our family line."

"That's all?"

"It's enough."

Down below, Rufus reset his stance as the trainer called for javelins. Boys lined up. Spears rose.

Lucius watched him again, quick, furtive, as if checking whether the design on his tablet would help Rufus one day.

Fulvia felt her breath catch.

Here was a family forged by pain, discipline, and loyalty so deep it bordered on worship.

She understood suddenly: choosing Rufus meant choosing all of them.

And she did not hesitate.

Rufus cast the first spear. It flew truer, farther than any other, striking the post with a dull, absolute sound.

Something inside her answered.

"Yes," she whispered to no one. "He will matter."

Latina nudged her. "Come. Before your nurse faints."

"She never faints."

"She will today."

Fulvia took one last look:

Rufus resetting for another throw.

Lucius drawing a new shape, quick and bright.

Dust rising around both, two brothers, two worlds, bound by blood and strange brilliance.

She followed Latina down the stairs.

On the walk back to the Quirinal, Rome pressed in, loud and alive. None of it reached her.

She carried a new secret now.

A red-haired fighter.

A quiet genius in the shade.

A family that shook the earth with its presence.

And a certainty blooming sharp as a blade:

One day he will look up and see me.

When he does, she thought, Rome will change.

Because she had already chosen him.

And she did not change her mind.

Chapter 4
THE BOY THAT DREW

T he Latinus Compound, Rome

The workshop smelled of wet clay, sawdust, and lamp oil.

Lucius sat where he always did, on the low stool by the long table, one leg braced straight with a leather support, the other tucked close. Morning light spilled through the high window, catching the curls around his ears and the thin lines of concentration on his face.

This room's walls were covered with his drawings, both detailed and strange, a close up of a bee's head, a snake's skeleton, the dissected belly of a fish. Among those hung portraits of his mother, aunt, and sister. Accurate and beautiful.

A block of wax rested before him. Two knives. A reed. A bowl of water.

He didn't look up when Rufus stepped inside.

"Father wants the bridge plan," Rufus said.

Lucius dipped his reed in the water. Drew a steady line through the wax. Another. Two more. The beginnings of a span.

"It's wrong," Lucius murmured.

Rufus came closer. "What is?"

"The river." Lucius tapped the wax. "The current shifts twice before noon. Sandbar forms here." He pointed with the reed, precise as a surgeon. "It'll eat the left support by the first storm."

Rufus blinked. "You haven't been to the river today."

Lucius shrugged, knife sliding. A curl of wax curled onto the table like thin shavings of bone.

"Did you go?" Rufus asked.

"No."

"Then how do you know?"

Lucius gave the reed a small turn between his fingers. "It's what rivers do."

Rufus laughed under his breath, soft, proud. He loved that answer. He loved every strange part of the brother the gods had marked as fragile and brilliant all at once.

Outside, the drills clattered, shields, shouted cadence, spear shafts striking sand. Rufus's world. Not Lucius's. But Rufus always stepped away from it for this room.

Lucius's hands moved again, carving supports, adjusting the span, cutting a channel on the model's underside.

"You're favoring your leg," Rufus said quietly.

Lucius paused. His jaw tightened before he answered. "It's a bad morning."

Rufus crouched beside him, large hand resting briefly on the back of Lucius's chair. A small gesture. Protective. Grounding.

"You should rest," Rufus said.

"No." Lucius didn't look away from the wax. "If I stop now, the shape leaves my head."

A simple sentence. But Rufus heard what others missed:

Lucius's mind burned hot, fast, fragile. Sparks that needed catching before they disappeared.

He watched the bridge emerge under the younger brother's hands, arches forming from nothing, supports thickening, a channel deepening in the wax as though the river itself had whispered to him where it wanted freedom.

Lucius murmured to himself sometimes. Soft. Almost singing. Numbers, Rufus realized. Ratios. Lines. Weight. Breath.

Not magic, but something close.

When Lucius finished, he sat back, sweat at his temples. His thin chest rose and fell like he'd run a hill.

Rufus touched the edge of the model. "This will hold the carts?"

"Yes."

"And the cattle?"

"Yes."

"And if the flood comes?"

Lucius traced a small arc above the wax. "The water lifts here. Breaks here. Flows under the arch. You let the river win where it wants to win. Then it leaves you alone."

Rufus smiled. "You think like a general."

Lucius shook his head. "I think like water."

Rufus felt a knot grow in his throat, sudden, sharp. Not pity. Pride. A love so fierce it scared him more than battle.

"You know," Rufus said, "Father says our company grows because of you."

Lucius's ears pinked. "Father talks too much."

"He's right." Rufus tapped the wax. "Nobody in Rome builds like this."

Lucius swallowed. Hard. "I can't fight, Rufus."

"No," Rufus said. "But I can't see what you see. Together we are the whole."

Lucius blinked fast, eyes shimmering for a breath before he stared back at the model.

He pushed the wax model toward Rufus.

"Take it," he said. "Build it right."

Rufus lifted the bridge. It weighed almost nothing. But it felt like holding the whole future in his hands.

Lucius picked up the reed again.

"Come back tonight," he said. "I want to show you a ship."

Rufus grinned. "Another one?"

"This one will sail faster than wind."

Rufus shook his head. "God's help us."

Lucius didn't look up, but Rufus caught the faintest smile at the corner of his mouth.

Outside, the soldiers kept drilling.

Inside, a boy drew bridges and temples the world hadn't dreamed of yet.

Chapter 5
THE TWELVE

Temple at Valbena, Hyrcania - 64 B.C.

The air behind the altar carried weight. Pressure.

As if the goddess still stood there, unseen.

Albina braced a hand against the stone. It drank her sweat like an old animal tasting salt. Her ankles quivered; the bells at her feet gave a single tired shiver before falling quiet. The trance hadn't left her bones yet. Her breath came thin, sharp, sliced into pieces by whatever power had ridden her.

She was fifteen, too young to bear a goddess, too old to run from one.

The crimson robe clung where trance-heat had soaked it, sheer against ribs, heavy at her hips, reminding her she was both girl and blade. Sibyl wasn't supposed to blush, but warmth crept up her throat anyway. Rufus's face still lived behind her eyes, bronze skin, that impossible strength, the clean violence of his hands.

Zarmina struck flint to wick. A thin flame opened like an eye.

Nisaya hummed from the corner, grinding herbs with her sharp little wrists.

Neither asked if the vision hurt. They already knew.

Albina turned to the olivewood chest.

Centuries of palms had polished it dark. The carved lid bore grooves made by women who came before her, each one marking fear, devotion, or hunger. She lifted the lid. Lamplight slid across what history should have lost long ago.

The Twelve.

Older than kings. Older than empires. Older than sin.

They breathed faintly in the light, pulsing like tiny hearts.

She touched each in turn.

The Mother of Fire, warm through the shadow. A carved belly swelling with birth or destruction.

The Sibyl's Chariot, pale granite, mica catching sparks. A lion dragging the ghost of a wheel. Her fingertip found a heartbeat in the stone.

The Twins of Water, serpentine slick as river skin. Amphorae on tiny shoulders. Mist clung to her palm.

The Moon-Maid, ivory, crescent-faced, cool as chalk after rain.

The Black Dog, basalt ribs deep and hollow. Cold shot through her wrist.

The Bird King, ochre-striped sandstone; grit broke under her thumb.

The Womb, smooth gray river stone, patient as winter.

The Blade, thin black slate that sang when her nail slid across it.

The Old Child, a boy's face carved with a man's jaw, eyes deep enough to drown memory.

The Thirteenth, rough granite, half-made, half-born.

The Empty One, white marble. Her own face reflected where no face was carved.

Then she touched the Eye.

Dark. Veined in gold.

Something in her chest answered with a slow, terrible pulse.

Zarmina spoke without looking up.

"They predate cities."

"They outlast mortals," Nisaya whispered.

"Made by the first woman," Zarmina said, "and fed by the Flame."

Albina closed the lid. The sound was small but final.

"They bind me now. They demand flight. Pursuit. Rome. Into the house of a boy, I fear... and hate."

A beat.

"And can't stop foreseeing."

Neither witch spoke.

Smoke curled in lazy spirals, tasting of resin and omen. The eternal flame wavered, then steadied, like it listened through the stone.

Albina knelt. "If the Flame commands west, we go. We hide the Twelve. We carry them until Rome learns their name."

Zarmina studied her. "You saw the boy again."

"Yes."

"The Roman."

Albina's fingers tightened on her knees. "He kills clean. He doesn't gloat. But he frightens me."

"Fear teaches faster than prayer," Zarmina murmured. "And you'll need both."

Nisaya held her pestle still. "What else?"

"Fire," Albina whispered. "Our temple burning. Bells melting. Smoke swallowing the sky."

"That's not a vision," Zarmina said. "That's a promise."

Albina pressed a word between her teeth, older than Rome, older than the Flame. The air thickened. The temple fire leaned toward her hand, bowing like a beast chained by devotion.

"She binds us all," Nisaya said quietly.

Albina nodded. "Then help me carry her burden."

"We always have," Zarmina said. "Since the day they painted your forehead with ash."

A gust pushed through the cracks. Lamps trembled. Shadows stretched like reaching hands. Herbs hissed on the coals, filling the chamber with a bitter, medicinal sweetness.

Albina stood. Her knees complained, small reminders she was mortal, even if the goddess inside her wasn't. She stepped into the corridor. Cool night air met her face. Beyond the wall the reeds whispered, bending with a rhythm too heavy for wind alone.

She listened.

Again.

Again.

Other sounds mixed with the wind, marching and the clanking of metal.

Zarmina joined her. "Hear it?"

"Yes."

"Parthians," Zarmina breathed. "Or worse."

"Worse," Albina said. "Him."

Nisaya approached from behind. "We have hours... maybe less."

Albina moved back to the chest. "Then we use them. Wrap each stone in cloth. Layer linen between. If we lose even one..."

"We won't," Zarmina said, already gathering cloth.

Nisaya's hands shook as she collected jars and wax. "The Twelve must travel as flesh travels. Hidden beneath breath."

Albina set both palms on the chest. Heat pulsed faint under the wood.

"The Flame never sleeps," she whispered. "It only waits."

Thunder rolled from the sea. The rhythm outside grew louder, footsteps or hooves, echoing off sand and stone. Grit blew through the doorway, tasting like the edge of prophecy made real.

Albina closed her eyes.

Red banners. A serpent crest. A conqueror in black armor.

Red Ring.

The one her dreams hadn't finished with. The one the goddess had already marked.

She breathed deep, until salt drowned smoke.

"Hide the Twelve," she said. "And whatever happens, don't let the Flame see fear."

The witches obeyed.

Outside, marching tightened into a single pulse.

Albina looked east, where dawn and danger would meet. Dust rose on the horizon, shaped like a serpent uncoiling through the reeds.

"The wind carries him," she whispered. "And tomorrow, it will carry me."

The wind answered through the cracks, whispering her name into the dark.

Albina.

Chapter 6
FOLLOW THE WIND

East Caspian Coast - Before Dawn

The wind woke first.

Not the tame kind that flirted with reeds or teased fishing boats, this one crawled up from the black ribs of the Caspian, built in pressure, darkness, and the crush of places where no sun had ever lived. It clawed upward through miles of water, gathering cold and salt and memory. Bubbles spiraled like drowned prayers.

Then the sea exhaled. A single heave. A tremor. A birth.

The newborn gale hit open water with a hunter's hunger. It learned speed. It tasted foam. Gulls scattered in shrieking panic, wings snapped sideways. Waves bowed, whitecaps slashed to ribbons.

When the wind reached land, it broke its first law: it accelerated.

Sand lifted like thrown knives. Grass bent flat. Seashells whipped across the stones, bone-colored meteors. The cliffs shook. Caves older than the world itself screamed their hollow notes. Moss peeled away in sheets. Cracks spidered across rock.

Still, the wind climbed.

It scaled the temple hill as easily as a thief climbing a rope, slipping through goats' paths, sucking grit into its belly, spitting it back out as needles.

Inside the Temple of Valbena, the air shifted.

Albina's body caught the first tremor. Her toes curled against cold stone. Sweat from the trance still dampened the crimson silk pasted to her skin; the cloth clung to her ribs, hips, thighs, goddess-marked, storm-marked. Her breath fought her chest.

The wind reached the doors.

They groaned. Wood shuddered. Hinges complained. Bells at her ankles gave a single, involuntary cry.

Albina lifted her head.

Not storm. Not tide.

A presence.

The name struck her mind like iron:

Red Ring.

Her jaw tightened, but her face stayed calm. She crossed the floor, bare feet leaving faint prints in the marble dust. She closed the shutters; her hair lifted in the draft like black flame.

Her hand found the chest.

Found the black iron hilt.

Found Zarakar.

The meteor blade drank what little light the lamps offered. Its weight steadied the tremor in her wrist. The goddess inside her ribs uncoiled and tasted the air.

Behind her, Zarmina rose from sleep without a word; tall, spectral, shawl tangled around her waist. She didn't need explanation; the wind told the story.

Nisaya followed, tiny, quick, eyes bright as coals. "The wind carries men," she whispered.

Albina nodded once.

Zarmina listened at the door. "Not yet dawn."

"Then dawn is late," Nisaya said.

The wind climbed higher.

Up the ridge. Past olive trees bending like old widows. It ripped dust from the path and arranged it into a long serpent's trail.

And there, waiting on the highest ledge, stood the man who made children fear shadows:

Red Ring.

Black beard. Bull shoulders. Eyes like cooled pitch.

His cloak hung heavy with miles of dust.

The wind grabbed it, jerked it upward, spread it like wings.

He didn't resist.

He let the wind uncover him.

Below, the temple sat pale against the stone, smoke curling like stubborn life.

He hated that place.

Those bells.

Those women.

That girl.

Especially the girl.

He had watched her dance once, the small one in crimson, hips moving like flame had muscle and will. She had moved without fear. She had looked him in the eye without shaking.

Worse, she had spoken a Roman name in trance.

A foreign name.

A threat.

His second approached, armor rattling softly. "They say she's a goddess."

"She bleeds like a girl," Red Ring said.

"They say she sees the future."

"She won't after tomorrow."

The second hesitated. "The King said..."

Red Ring sliced a hand through the air. "I heard the King. She lives. The witches live. The dancers live. The eunuchs... untouched." He smiled. "The rest die confused."

He pictured heads on stakes outside the gate. Eyes frozen wide. Mouths half-open. The boy in the back always died pissing himself. That one he would remember.

Albina's head, though no. The King forbade it.

He spat. The wind carried it away.

Inside the temple, the eunuchs stirred. Their hands tightened on their short swords. Armor chimed. The wind whispered warnings none of them could decode.

The dancers slept in a tangle of limbs and silk. The youngest clutched a bell in her fist.

Albina walked between them, soft as smoke. She didn't wake them. Dreams were the last mercy she could offer.

She stepped into the courtyard. Zarmina and Nisaya flanked her.

The eternal flame flickered sideways from the force of the wind, thin, blue, frightened.

Albina lifted Zarakar.

"The King sends him," she said.

Zarmina's voice was low. "Then the King fears you."

"Or wants what you guard," Nisaya murmured.

"Both," Albina said.

The wind hit the outer gate like a battering ram.

Albina closed her eyes for a heartbeat. In that dark space behind her lids, a different figure appeared; bronze skin, red cloak, twin blades, sunlight striking bronze shoulders like a benediction and a curse.

Rufus.

She tried to push him from her mind. The goddess refused.

Prophecy sharpened when danger closed in.

He will find me.

I will go to him.

Blood will follow.

Fire after that.

On the ridge, Red Ring crouched. His men gathered close. No torches. No horns. Not yet.

One boy tightened a strap with shaking fingers. Another sharpened a blade to calm his nerves. Two wrestled quietly for warmth.

Children tonight.

Killers tomorrow.

The sound of whetstone on steel blended with the rising wind, a rough hymn for the slaughter to come.

Red Ring watched the temple glow. It flickered once, as though blinking at him.

Soon.

Inside, Albina gripped the nearest pillar. The trance had burned her hollow, but the goddess's heat still simmered in her chest.

Zarmina touched her shoulder. "You are not the first Sibyl they hunted."

"And not the last," Nisaya added.

Albina's voice was steady. "They will not take the Twelve. And they will not take me alive."

Zarmina bowed her head. "Every Sibyl says those words."

Nisaya whispered, "Not every Sibyl dies saying them."

Albina took her place at the center. The blade across her palms. Breath low. Shoulders squared.

The wind screamed through the cracks, a beast trying to enter.

Horses snorted outside. Feet moved. Shields knocked. One last shuffle of men awaiting the order.

The smell hit next:

Blood.

Sweat.

Oiled leather.

An army's breath.

The doors shuddered.

Albina whispered a prayer, not for mercy, but for aim.

Zarmina fed the coals. Nisaya drew a circle of salt.

Outside, a horn blared a long, broken note, carried and torn by the gale.

Albina lifted the blade.

Dawn crouched at the world's edge.

So did blood.

The wind surged with murderous joy, slamming the doors wide.

Light. Ash. Heat. Pressure.

Everything burst inward at once.

Albina's bells rang once, clear, sharp, final.

Then the world inhaled.

And held its breath.

Chapter 7
THE BREACH

Temple at Valbena - Hyrcania, 64 B.C. - The Next Morning

The last of the night clung to the stones.

Albina knelt beside the brazier, cross-legged, body small in the wide hush. The coals glowed a dull, defiant red, breath still alive inside them. Her hair hung loose, damp with trance-sweat, catching the new dawn in black strands. Every inhale dragged the bruise of prophecy deeper inside her ribs.

The crate that hid the Twelve sat close enough for her fingertips to touch. Even through the wood she felt the faint pulse of the relics, old as creation, stubborn as gods. They hummed slow, like hearts that refused to die.

The silence felt wrong. No gull cries. No wave slap. No temple mice scurrying under grain baskets. Only breath. Her own. Nisaya's. Zarmina's. Then nothing.

She touched her throat. Heat lived there still, a thin line of fire the goddess had left behind. Or fear. She refused to name which.

Zarmina stepped from shadow, hood thrown back, her broad shoulders stiff with omen. "They come."

She didn't whisper. She didn't need to.

Witch was the name the world gave women who knew too much. But before fear turned them into myths, they had been healers. Midwives. Herb-binders. Bone-setters. They learned from blood, not scrolls. From women in labor. From men dying badly. Their power grew from the places Rome and Parthia pretended not to see.

Witch was a shield. Witch was teeth.

Zarmina smelled of smoke and crushed roots, certainty wrapped in scar and silence. Nisaya was the opposite: small, quick, fingers stained blue from ink and berries. She hummed softly, a broken-lute rhythm threaded with nerves.

Albina rose. The crimson robe clung where trance-heat had soaked it, shaping ribs and hips, reminding her she was both vessel and weapon. Her ankles trembled. The bells gave one faint cry... then stilled.

Nisaya gathered herbs into her skirts. Zarmina lifted the black-lacquer box of linen strips. They worked without speech. They had done this before. Too many times.

The dancers assembled behind them. Seven girls, five blood kin, two apprentices. Barefoot, hair braided with charms. Eyes wide, bodies straight. They breathed like one creature. Anklets rested like gold rings waiting for a wedding they'd never have.

The six eunuchs knelt closest to the door. Small men with scarred chests and strong arms. Albina's cousins. Her brothers in the only way that mattered. They bowed their shorn heads and rested their blades across their thighs.

Albina moved to the youngest attendant, thin, limping, her braid uneven. "Listen," Albina said, voice low. "You run when the path opens."

The girl's breath hitched. "High One..."

"You hide with the stones. Food. Water. Cloth. All there. Stay until the world forgets your scent. Come out only after Red Ring leads us away. Tell the Romans that come what you saw."

The girl trembled. Albina pressed her forehead to hers. "The relics matter more than I do. Say it."

The girl swallowed. "They matter more than you."

Albina nodded once. Zarmina pressed her palm to a seam in the wall. Stone shifted. A narrow crack yawned open. The air inside tasted of cold earth.

"Go."

The child pulled the crate into the dark. The wall sealed behind her with a whisper.

The temple exhaled.

Outside, the enemy spread like ink on sand.

Parthian scouts crawled through reed beds. Two men slipped toward goat pens. One climbed the rear wall, fingers quiet as spiders. The rest approached the gate with no torches, no horns, no prayer.

The first temple guard blinked. A wet choke followed. His knees buckled. The second guard lifted his spear, saw nothing, then steel flashed and cut his voice in half.

Red Ring's men moved like practiced sin. Efficient. Wordless. Their fear was a taught thing, hammered into bone by their master.

The cedar doors groaned under the first axe strike.

Albina inhaled once. The coals shivered. The floor trembled under her bare feet. She tightened her braid and slid Zarakar, the meteor-blade, into it. The iron kissed her scalp. Heat pooled at her spine as if the goddess pressed a palm there.

Zarmina wrapped relic-stones in linen. Nisaya drew white dust in a circle, chanting old words that bent the smoke sideways.

The dancers clasped hands.

The eunuchs rose to their feet as the second axe blow cracked the lintel. Dust rained. Wood splintered.

A third blow. The door screamed.

Then silence.

Twelve archers slipped inside first, faces painted, bows raised. Their eyes were pits of hunger. Behind them, filling the doorway like a shadow that learned to kill, stepped Red Ring.

Black armor. Red serpent painted across his shield. Beard braided with copper. Eyes like pits of hot tar. His presence ate the morning light.

He raised his hand. The archers froze mid-step.

Albina lifted her chin.

Her witches stood on either side, shoulders squared, jaws set. The dancers tightened their circle. The eunuchs drew blades.

Red Ring smiled. He liked rules. Especially the ones he could twist. The King forbade killing the Sibyl or her holy women. Forbidden blood meant deeper cruelty.

He stepped forward.

Albina met his stare. Her stomach tightened, but she did not bow.

Smoke gathered low along the floor, curling around ankles like warning serpents.

The nearest eunuch braced his small body into a shield. Red Ring stopped inches from the man, and their eyes locked, warrior to warrior, predator to guardian.

A gust blasted through the broken doorway. Rain-scent. Iron. Sand. Dawn.

Red Ring's voice cut the hush. "So. The goddess wakes."

Albina answered without flinching. "She never slept."

The wind rattled the broken doors.

A single bell, hidden somewhere behind the altar, struck one clear, crystalline note.

The sound hung like a final heartbeat.

And the temple held its breath for the first cut of the day.

Chapter 8
THE MEMORY

Temple at Valbena - Hyrcania, 64 B.C.

The bell had rung.

Albina felt it in her ribs, a single missed beat, then stillness.

The Twelve lived. Hidden. Moving. That was enough. For now.

The temple held its breath with her.

The Temple at Valbena had no beauty from the outside, only defiance. Stone stacked on stone, eight centuries of wind-carved scars, its face leaning back as if daring storms to break themselves upon it. No banners. No marble. Only a narrow stair climbing from the sea, steep enough to make pilgrims bleed. The goddess demanded pain before she gave anything back.

Inside, the cold owned everything. Dawn's light reached only in thin strips. Smoke pressed low to the floor. The air tasted of resin and salt, and the walls sweated like living skin. Silence wrapped the chamber in slow, patient coils.

The niches built into the stone, hundreds, held pieces of women long dead: hair, teeth, bowls, bones, charms. Some sealed with wax, some stained with dried blood, some marked with languages no one spoke anymore. The temple remembered every hand that left an offering. Nothing was forgotten here. Not even fear.

At the center lay the black pool. Perfectly round. Perfectly still. No reflection. No birds dared near it. No insects crossed its lip. The old women said the first Sibyl had carved open her chest above that water, giving her voice to the Flame. No one questioned the story. All truth left scars.

Behind the pool: the shrine.

Twelve small statues once stood there: obsidian, bone, river stone, ash. Each older than the Republic, older than empire, older than names. Albina had learned them by touch long before she learned them by sight.

Now the shelves sat empty.

Dust scattered on the stone like a promise broken.

She felt their absence the way a body feels a missing limb.

She had once danced before them until her heels split open and blood streaked the floor. Zarmina had dragged her back before she pitched into the pool. The goddess had spared her. Or claimed her. The two things were the same.

Stone shifted. Not a sound a man could hear, only someone bound to the Flame.

Red Ring had crossed the threshold.

He stepped past his archers, past the kneeling men outside, and into the sanctum where even kings felt their breath shorten. His boots hit stone with heavy finality. His cloak trailed dust and salt. His hands were bare.

Albina waited at the center, still as a stone.

He stopped three paces from her.

Something in her presence pressed against him, heat without fire, the hum of power that had no visible source. He hated that it unsettled him.

A memory rose before he could force it down.

Another shrine. Another girl.

His daughter, six years old, hair wild from running, eyes bright as fresh bronze. She had danced in offering, laughing, proud of the rhythm she had learned. Her feet had slapped stone like a heartbeat.

A priest, heavy with jewels, had seized her arm and screamed blasphemy.

The punishment came fast. Fire.

A child's scream. His own legs refusing to move.

He had watched her burn.

Two winters later, he found that priest and cut his throat in silence.

Too late.

Now he looked at Albina and saw the same spark, the same fearless defiance, and fury tightened his jaw until his teeth hurt.

He said nothing.

She did not lower her gaze.

Zarmina stood near the wall, sleeves hiding her hands, eyes dark and certain. Nisaya's fingers traced the cracks along a clay bowl, the whisper of movement barely audible. Both witches waited for the moment the sanctum would choose its side.

Red Ring broke the silence first.

"This is where your goddess hides?"

Albina's voice slipped through the cold.

"She hides nowhere. She waits."

"She waits for Parthia?"

"For judgment."

His smile was thin, sharp. "You believe I am judgment?"

"You are what she sent to test me."

He almost laughed. The sound scraped out of him, humorless. "Then you'll fail her before dawn."

"The wind disagrees."

As if summoned, a gust curled through the broken gate. Salt. Cold. The faint cry of a gull carried miles inland. The braziers' flames bent left, straining toward the pool.

Both of them watched the fire settle again.

Something ancient stirred in the stone, an old awareness waking.

He wanted to grab her throat. Shake the calm from her face. But a warning thrummed beneath his skin, as if the temple itself whispered caution.

Instead, he stepped closer.

"You fear me."

Albina's mouth curved, barely. "I fear prophecy, not its tools."

Her calm struck him harder than defiance.

He smelled incense on her skin, the heat of her trance, the clean metallic tang of the blade braided into her hair.

His daughter's ash-scent drifted through memory again. He stiffened and looked away.

From the hall outside came a hiss, steel unsheathed. His men growing restless. Hungry for orders.

He lifted a hand. Wait.

Albina's gaze dropped to the pool. The water stayed black, empty, absorbing everything.

"The stones are gone," he said.

"I know."

"You sent them."

"Yes."

The muscle in his jaw worked once.

"The King wanted them."

"Then he should have come himself."

He stepped so close the pool's edge gleamed between them like a threat.

"If he wanted you dead, you would be."

"I already am."

The truth in her voice cut into him.

The air thickened. The wind moaned through the cracks. Light slid across the walls like a living thing.

He reached for the hilt at his waist, not a threat, a reminder of power. "Come with me. Peacefully."

"Peace died before you reached the gate."

He almost admired her. Almost.

Outside, the horn called one long note. A summons. A sentence.

Albina's bells answered from the shadows, three short rings.

Zarmina the Red's chant rose first, low and sharp. Nisaya the Black joined, higher, faster, weaving the sound into a thread that wrapped the chamber.

The braziers flared.

Red Ring raised his hand for his men, but the doors slammed shut.

Hard. Final.

The wind howled through the cracks, a scream with weight behind it. Every flame bent sideways at once.

Smoke twisted. Light fractured.

A single bubble rose from the black pool. Then another. Then stillness.

Red Ring turned back.

Albina stood unchanged, eyes hollow, reflections swallowed.

The wind brought the scent of decay.

And far beneath the temple, beneath stone, beneath memory...

something began to breathe.

Chapter 9
THE MOCKING

Temple at Valbena - Hyrcania, 64 B.C.

The Eternal Flame had died.

Not faded. Not flickered out.

Died. Murdered.

The hiss still clung to the air, a ghost burning in a room with no fire.

Albina stood at the center of the sanctum, robe clinging to her ribs, breath tight in her throat. Her dancers huddled before her; bare feet pale against the ash-dark stone. The witches knelt behind them. The eunuchs knelt in front of her, six small walls of flesh ready to die again.

None breathed loud. None moved.

The temple itself felt stunned, stone holding its breath, walls recoiling from a wound eight centuries deep.

Red Ring stepped into that silence.

He didn't enter like a conqueror or a soldier.

He entered like a man walking into a pen to inspect animals.

His boots crushed the ash.

His shadow reached her before his body did.

"This?" he said, sweeping a hand across the chamber. "This is the heart of your goddess. A pile of rot and superstition?"

He kicked a bronze bowl across the floor.

It spun, clattered, cracked.

The sound felt like a bone breaking in the dark.

"You think this place protects you," he said. "You think these girls, these eunuchs, these old women," he flicked his fingers at Zarmina and Nisaya "mean anything?"

A soldier behind him seized the nearest eunuch by the wrists. Metal scraped raw skin. The blade pulled from the man's hands screamed louder than the wind outside.

Albina didn't flinch.

She held her ground as Red Ring circled.

Slow. Predatory. Too confident.

"You're not sacred," he said. "You're a child who learned how to dance and call it prophecy."

He stepped close, so close she felt the heat of his breath on her cheek.

"You smell like fear," he murmured. "And piss."

Her jaw tightened.

She didn't raise her chin. She didn't back away.

Stillness was her weapon.

"A stupid little girl with dirty feet without a coin to her name."

He circled again, cloak dragging, boots whispering threats.

"The King of Kings knows what you are," he continued. "A womb wearing silk. A little flame pretending to be a fire."

His voice dropped lower, meant for her alone, meant to burrow and rot.

"He will decide your fate. He will take what he wants. He will mark you. Break you. Fill you. Again, and again until you forget your goddess's name and learn his."

Behind her, a dancer sobbed.

Red Ring smiled with his teeth.

Albina said nothing.

Not yet.

Two soldiers dragged forward a bucket of cistern water. The metal sloshed, cold and heavy. Red Ring snatched it without looking at them.

He walked to the Eternal Flame's ancient brazier.

The bowl that had burned since before cities had names.

Before kings had crowns.

Before the sea had maps.

He paused.

Looked back at her.

"You live because he commands it," he said. "Not because you matter."

Then he tipped the bucket.

The water struck the coals.

The scream that followed did not belong to any living creature.

It belonged to history being murdered.

A roar of steam exploded upward, white, violent, final.

The chamber shook.

The walls echoed the loss like a wound torn down their spine.

The flame died with a hiss sharp enough to cut the ears.

Albina screamed.

Her witches screamed.

Her dancers cried out like children seeing their mother fall.

And then there was nothing. No light. No smoke.

Only the smell:

Old resin. Wet ash. Death.

Red Ring turned for the door, pleased with the silence he left behind.

At the threshold, he paused, his outline framed in pale morning glare.

"You'll forget who you were," he said. "All prisoners do."

He left without waiting for an answer.

The broken doors groaned shut behind him.

For a long while the room didn't breathe.

Then the crying began, soft, choking, mournful, human.

Albina crouched among her people.

Not comforting, not speaking, just being the center they revolved around, grief orbiting her like moons.

Soot coated her tongue.

Her skin smelled of smoke and sweat and humiliation.

The place where his breath touched her cheek still burned.

Red Ring.

She hated the name.

She hated how it clung to her ribs like a bruise.

After a time she stood.

The dancers pressed against the walls, their anklets tangled.

The witches bowed over their knees.

The eunuchs stared at the dead fire as if their god had fallen.

The quiet felt wrong. Not empty. Expectant.

Albina crossed the floor. Her bells didn't ring; even the metal seemed stunned. She knelt where Red Ring's boots had left soot and pressed her fingertips into the black prints.

The stone pulsed warm beneath her hand.

Her breath steadied. Her jaw set. Not in anger... in purpose.

Something ancient moved inside her chest, slow as a creature waking from ages of sleep.

She stood and turned toward the doorway where sunrise cut a blade of gold across the floor.

Smoke curled in the beam. Dust lifted.

A single white feather drifted down from the rafters, its tip charred black.

She caught it.

Behind her, Zarmina whispered, "He killed the fire."

Albina didn't look back.

Her voice was quiet but sharp as Zarakar's edge.

"No," she said. "He reminded it why it burns."

The witches lifted their heads.

The dancers straightened.

The eunuchs bowed their foreheads to the floor; the old vow renewed without sound.

Albina placed her palm on the altar.

It felt cold. Then warmer. Then alive.

"The temple endures," she said. "So will we."

Outside, gulls began to cry again.

Wind pushed through the doorway, lifting her hair, tugging her ankle bells until they gave a faint, trembling chime.

Just one note. Sharp. Defiant. Alive. A promise and a warning.

And Albina whispered to the Feather, the altar, the ashes, the goddess inside her:

"Let him come."

Chapter 10
THE MESSENGER

Parthian Controlled Lands

They chose a small man for the long road.

They called him Gnat, thin face, quick hands, quicker mouth.

Obedient when watched. Clever when not. He rode better than anyone else Red Ring had.

He took the scroll. Leather dry, seal hard as chalk. He pressed it flat against his chest, slid it under the tunic, laced the throat. A captain leaned close.

"No stops."

Another touched the horse's neck. "If you fall, burn the message first."

Gnat nodded, mounted, and rode east without a word.

Hooves struck the cliff road, iron on stone. Dust coiled behind him, a pale ghost. The black temple shrank, swallowed by rock, then by heat, then by distance itself. Ravens rose from the ledges and followed his shadow until even the shadow broke.

By the second mile he slowed. No one watched. No one counted. The gorge widened; the horse eased to a jog.

"We're deep enough," he muttered. "The king's eyes don't see this far."

He touched the scroll through cloth, felt its edge. Sun bit the cliff face. A lizard ran across the track and vanished into dust.

At the first village he stopped for food, goat stew, flat bread crusted with salt.

A girl poured wine. Henna on her fingers. Scar near her lip. Eyes that weighed him.

He smiled back. She laughed low.

He left a copper under the bowl.

He rode an hour, turned back, said the horse needed water. Found her again by the door at dusk. She held the jug. He held the cup.

He stayed the night.

At dawn he told himself the world still held its shape. Kings still ruled, temples still burned, dawn still rose. He rode late and sang to the horse.

Three days brought him to a river bend.

He let the mare rest under fig trees. The water slid brown over stones, slow and certain.

Swifts cut the air and stitched silence behind them.

He slept with the bridle in his hand, woke to wind that smelled of iron and dust.

He drank. He stretched. He whistled. The king would hear, someday.

Markets blurred together, salt, wine, meat, sweat.

He bought a new cloak, undyed wool, clean hem. Tried it on in a bronze mirror, warped and honest. He liked the hang.

He stole a ring from a drunk, silver with a chipped green stone. Sold it cheap to a man with a scarred ear.

New sandals. Soft leather.

The old pair he burned in a pit with fennel stems, watched the smoke curl, spat once for luck.

Road after road. Dust after dust.

At night he sat by strangers' fires, told half-stories, listened to worse ones.

Men liked him because he was small. Women liked him because he laughed.

He never touched the seal, only the leather above it. "Tomorrow," he whispered. "Tomorrow I deliver."

Between two hills he hunted with a merchant's boy who carried a spear too long for his arm. A lean boar burst from the reeds. The spear struck ribs. Gnat cut the throat.

They ate crisp fat and bread. The merchant's wife sang. The boy fell asleep on the table.

Gnat slept indoors and dreamed of gold halls.

Five days crossed the valley, white dust, wind like a song.

He bought raisins, a whistle shaped like a fish, gave it to a staring child.

He took slower roads. Less watch. More shade.

A dog found him there: old, brown, half-tail, sore footed. Gnat shared gristle. Never named him. The dog stayed.

Morning changed on the plain. The wind smelled of long grass and river dust. Heat rose in tight waves.

The capital shimmered behind the haze.

By noon the dog vanished.

A cry from the reeds, short and final. Gnat called once. Rode on.

He checked the seal, dry, warm from his chest. He liked that.

It meant the message had a pulse. His own. He smiled at the thought, then spat it out.

He found a barber. Bronze razor, dull from use.

Took a nick on the jaw, dabbed it with salt water. Nails cleaned. Hair cropped.

The barber burned the sweepings with thyme and laughed at his own smoke.

Gnat bought dates and wine. Practiced the words until they fit his mouth.

I carry word from Red Ring. The temple fallen. The girl seized.

He rolled the lines like dice, each one falling clean.

He pictured the king's nod. The hall of gold cloth.

He saw himself reflected in bronze, taller, finer. Handsome, maybe.

He practiced not smiling.

At a roadside shrine he tied a thread to a nail and left three dates on the stone. A bribe for luck, or silence.

He thought of turning north, narrow roads, easier to hold. Turned south instead, better wine.

He passed a village where every door gaped and no voice answered. Pots cooled on low fires. Grain scattered.

He said Plague once, under breath, and did not breathe again until the far field.

A day later he saw a rider behind him.

Green cloak. No banner. No pack mule.

Just a man on a mare that moved like thought.

Gnat watched through heat shimmer.

Every road has riders, he told himself. Every color has its cloth.

He drank. He rode.

That night he dreamed the temple groaned and bent, the girl in red cutting the moon into shards.

He woke with the scroll hot against his chest.

Two more days, he told himself.

Two more.

Poplars lined the horizon, gate trees for the king's road. Dust already tasted royal.

He rehearsed the bow he'd give the guard. The pace of his step. The tone of his report.

At a farmstead, three girls pounded grain, their song a hammer on the skull.

An old man bragged about an ox that never stopped walking.

Gnat smiled, overpaid, and thought: Men remember coins; roads remember names.

He cut across a meadow to shave a mile.

Tamarisk hid the ditch. Birds rose, dropped, rose again.

The mare walked easy. He smoothed the tunic, checked the knot at his throat, loosened his jaw.

A messenger should enter a city like a man who slept in silk.

He never saw the arrow.

One breath: teeth worrying a date pit.

Next breath: white light, red light, then dirt.

He slid from the saddle. Dust lifted, settled. The mare stood waiting, reins slack.

The man in green moved from the tamarisk.

No sound.

No pause.

He knelt beside the body, turned the head with two fingers.

Clean pass. No splinter. Good draw. Good wind.

He searched the corpse; purse, knife, ring. Took the silver. Left the charm shaped like a hook.

He cut the laces of the tunic, slid the scroll free.

Seal unbroken. Dry. Still warm.

He touched the wax with his nail, felt the brittle snap waiting under it, and smiled.

He did not open it. He didn't need words to know worth.

He tucked the message under his own vest.

He buried Gnat face-down in the ditch so the first rain would turn him to earth.

Two stones over the head. Not prayer... warning.

If anyone came searching, they would read it right: Too late.

He took the mare. Left the cloak. Left the sandals.

Dust's now.

He mounted and turned west.

The bow rode high on his back. The green cloak hid nothing.

He rode like a man who'd been riding forever.

Villagers saw him pass and said nothing.

A boy on a wall counted hoofbeats, lost the number when a dog barked. A woman lifting water from a well watched him go and did not blink until the dust covered him.

By dusk, the man in green crossed the royal road and turned away from the capital.

He watered the mare at a pool where reeds clicked, and frogs whispered their tiny psalms.

Ate flat bread, dried meat, drank once. Slept sitting up with the reins across his thigh and the scroll warm against his ribs.

At midnight he rode again.

Stars spread a pale net.

He moved inside it like a fish that knew each knot.

He did not lose time. He harvested it.

Back on the meadow, flies found the ditch and sang their slow hymn.

Jackals paused, listened, moved on.

The mare that had carried Gnat now carried silence.

The road that had stretched ahead for him folded behind another.

Far west, the black temple waited. Wind combed its broken grass. Stone breathed. Ash settled. No candles. No drums. No prayers. Forgotten.

Only the sun rising and falling. Only the wind against the stone.

And one rider, westbound, with a sealed truth burning against his heart.

Chapter 11
HOUSE OF CAESAR - PONIFEX MAXIMUS

Rome, Caesar's House on the Forum - 64 B.C.

The messenger rode through Rome's eastern gate at dusk.

Heat still hung from the stones. Donkeys brayed. Bakers shouted prices that drifted with the smoke. The air reeked of olives, sweat, and dust ground fine as flour. He hadn't eaten since dawn. His lips cracked when he tried to swallow. The seal against his chest burned with every breath.

He had dreamed of this moment, arrival, duty done, but the city dwarfed him. Hills stacked with temples, columns red as blood under the setting sun. Even the gutters glittered with broken pottery. He passed soldiers in line for pay, a woman washing her child with river water from a bronze bowl, and an old man singing to an empty cage. All of it Rome. All of it deaf to him.

By the time he reached the Palatine rise his thighs trembled from the climb. The horse blew foam. He dismounted, stumbling once before catching the reins. The guards at the marble arch watched but did not speak. Their spears glinted in the dying light.

"I bring word," he said.

"From whom?"

"For Caesar's ears only."

"Code word?"

"Saturn's delivery."

That name pulled silence tight. One guard vanished inside. The other took the horse.

The messenger stood alone, dust dripping from his cloak. The seal under his tunic felt heavier than lead.

The guard returned. "Follow."

Caesar's house rose half-temple, half-fortress. Columns flanked the portico, carved wolves crouching at their bases. The air inside cooled to stone temperature. Torches hissed. Mosaic floors mirrored firelight: gods, lovers, beasts locked in struggle. The messenger's boots sounded too loud.

He crossed an atrium where water trickled from a bronze lion's mouth. Two priestesses passed, heads veiled, faces pale from fasting. One looked at him and looked away, the way one looks at a condemned man.

A lictor barred the inner door, axe-shaft across his knees. The scar along his jaw gleamed like a river scar in moonlight. He studied the messenger, then lifted his chin toward the hall. "He waits."

The messenger entered.

Caesar sat behind a cedar table forearms tanned from field sun. No crown, no armor, just a plain linen tunic belted high. He had the sort of stillness that made air lean toward him. His eyes were dark, one shade short of black, steady, intelligent, impossible to read. Lines carved around the mouth hinted at both laughter and contempt.

The messenger dropped to one knee and extended the scroll. "From the lands of Parthia, Dominus. Sealed under lion's mane."

Caesar took it without speaking. His hands were square, long-fingered, built for grip, not show. The man's beauty lay not in symmetry but in precision; everything in him served function. He could be cruel. He could be kind. Both would look the same.

"You rode alone?"

"Yes, lord."

"You stopped where?"

"Straight here from the Ostia piers."

His voice rasped; dust broke loose from his throat. Caesar nodded once and gestured to the cupbearer. "Wine. Meat. Bread."

Caesar asked of the man's adventures to get this Parthian Message to Rome. Caesar praised the young man's skill and endurance.

When the messenger finished eating, Caesar said, "Sleep below. First a hot bath. My steward will see to you."

The man bowed, but Caesar had already turned back to the scroll.

He rolled the wax between finger and thumb. Parthian seal, lion's mane pressed deep, edges cracked. The smell of desert still clung to the leather. He broke the seal with a clean twist. The sound reminded him of crusty bread.

He read once. Then again slower. The corners of his mouth thinned, but the eyes brightened. The message was clear enough: a temple burned, a goddess taken, a prophecy undone.

Footsteps behind him.

"You smile," a woman said. "That usually means blood."

He didn't turn. "Mother."

Aurelia stood framed by the curtain, tall despite her years. Her gown of dark blue silk barely moved when she did. No paint, no jewels. A face of order and quiet command, the kind men obeyed without knowing why.

She reached for the parchment, and he let her take it. She read aloud softly, voice even as she parsed the foreign script. "An oracle captured... an eastern priestess... Red Ring's doing." Her thumb brushed the lion emblem. "And you smile."

Caesar folded his arms. "The Parthians never waste breath. If they wrote, it's a challenge."

"Or an invitation." She handed the scroll back. "She's not Roman."

"No."

"She's sacred. We women know of her, and her twelve stones, even here in Rome."

"Yes."

Aurelia looked toward the forum through the open shutters. The last of the sunlight struck her hair like iron. "The women will care... deeply," she said.

"They care for bread."

"Yes, but they care for miracles more."

He waited. She went on, tone almost tender. "Rescue her, and Rome's women will whisper your name every time they light a lamp. They will teach their sons who saved the oracle at Valbena. They will remember."

"And if I fail?"

"Then you never tried."

The words held no softness. They were command wrapped in mother's silk. She touched the scroll, and the candlelight caught the line of her wrist, strong still, veins blue under translucent skin. "Bring her and those stones here."

When she was gone, he stood by the table a long while. The smell of the parchment lingered. Outside, the city's hum pressed at the shutters: wheels on cobblestone, vendors calling figs, the distant argument of dogs.

He unfolded a map of the East. Ink lines wove like veins from the Caspian to the Tigris. He traced them with a stylus until it clicked on the edge of Hyrcania. Red Ring's mark there. Too close to Armenia for comfort.

Not a war, he thought. Not yet. But a spark.

He imagined the priestess: small, foreign, dangerous because she commanded loyalty without legions. A young girl, barely a teenager. The kind of girl who could move a people with dance instead of decree. Rome feared that kind more than armies.

He touched his chin with the stylus tip, half-smile returning. "A priestess who makes men kneel," he murmured. "Let's see how Rome kneels back."

He turned to the centurion waiting in shadow near the door. "Send to the Latinus compound. Have that boy sent to me. The younger Latinus. Matineus."

The centurion hesitated. "The pillager?"

"The same. Bring him before noon tomorrow."

"Yes, General."

When the man left, Caesar crossed to the open casement. Night had cooled the marble; it breathed faintly against his bare feet. He could smell the Tiber, faint, metallic, carrying the city's filth and glory alike. Torches flared along the streets, a thousand small suns burning against the dark.

A slave entered to collect the scrolls. Caesar waved him away. He poured wine, thick and red, and drank without dilution. A very rare treat. The taste bit back. He liked that. He stared at the map again and imagined Rufus, tall, disciplined, dangerous, the kind of soldier who obeyed until death. Already a hero. The kind that left a mark.

Then there was Rufus's half-brother, Matineus, same quality but more crafty, less direct, a ravager, a border line criminal. Certainly not a hero.

If anyone could cross that desert and return with the girl alive, it would be him.

Caesar rolled the scroll again, tighter this time, and pressed his thumb over the broken seal. Wax flaked away like old skin. He thought of Aurelia's voice, Bring her here.

He imagined the priestess stepping into his atrium, firelight on her crimson silk, eyes that didn't lower when men spoke. He wondered if she would curse him, thank him, or try to kill him. He wondered which would thrill him more.

The thing that truly motivated Caesar to send a rescue crew after this girl priestess was the pleasure he would get from reaching deep into the Parthian kings territory and taking something of importance from him.

Yeah, that made him smile.

He blew out the candle.

Outside, Rome exhaled. Wind moved through the cypress along the forum walls. Somewhere far down the hill, a bell from Vesta's shrine chimed the hour.

Caesar's silhouette lingered by the casement, broad-shouldered, bare-armed, the lean form of a man carved by war and sharpened by ambition. His reflection in the dark window looked both younger and older, as if time itself had paused to watch him decide.

He spoke once, low enough the night could keep the secret.

"This is my city. This is my world."

The candle's last thread of smoke curled toward the ceiling and vanished.

The map remained open, one red dot glowing in the lamplight, the edge of the world where a flame waited to be rescued.

And beyond Rome's sleeping roofs, a wind from the east began to stir.

Chapter 12
THE ORDER

Rome, Caesar's House on the Forum - 64 B.C.

The flame had burned low by the time he returned.

Caesar crossed the study and sat behind the cedar table again. The scroll still lay open; its edges curled from the heat. Beside it, the broken seal, black and cracked, caught a last fleck of lamplight before rolling to stillness. He stared at it a long time.

He had seen that mark before.

Not here. Not in Rome.

In another life. Another world.

Twenty-five years old, sailing off Phaselis when the Cilician pirates took him. The sea then smelled of rot and olive oil, their black ships sliding from fog like sharks. They'd swarmed his deck shouting for ransom. Twenty talents, they said. He laughed and told them to ask for fifty. They thought him mad. He was... a little.

They bound his ankles, wrists, and throat. Dragged him ashore. The sand cut like glass. He remembered the captain's teeth, gold, cracked, reeking of garlic, and stained by wine. He remembered the ropes biting through skin, the salt grinding in. And the scroll he glimpsed in the captain's hand, bound in wax so dark it swallowed light. The Parthian lion. He never forgot.

The camp had reeked of fish guts and fear. He'd watched them drink, gamble, argue in three languages, half of them children. Yet one among them, tall and quiet, wore rings and read by firelight. That one handled the scroll. Fingers clean. Nails trimmed. Educated hands. The kind that signed decrees, not swung oars.

Caesar studied him for nights. When he stepped out to piss, he saw the same man later, sprawled beneath a cedar, throat black, flies humming where the eyes had been. The scroll clutched to his chest. The seal intact.

He had memorized it then, the curve of the mane, the cut of the claws, the faint nick in the wax.

Parthian black. Lion crowned. Message undelivered.

After his ransom was paid, after his release, after he raised ships and hunted those same pirates down and nailed them to crosses along the coast, he'd looked again at that memory. At the seal. He'd told himself he'd forgotten. He hadn't. The sea had buried the messenger, but not the message.

Now the same mark sat before him again, ten years or so later, carried across deserts and empires, still whispering through the cracks of empire.

Not ransom. Not tribute.

Warning.

The oil lamp fluttered. Its flame leaned east, as if listening. Shadows swam across the map wall, the Black Sea, Armenia, Pontus, the edge of the Caspian. The old lion had come west again.

Caesar poured more wine and let it breathe. The scent; rose, smoke, plum, oak. He drank deep, wiped his mouth with the back of his wrist, and looked down at his own reflection in the wine. The face that stared back bore little of the boy from Phaselis. Lines ran deep now from mouth to jaw; a scar near the temple caught every glint of light. His body had stayed strong, but the eyes had changed. They measured distance faster. They trusted slower.

He leaned back, elbows on the chair's carved arms, eyes half-closed, and the ghosts came easy.

The campfire smoke. The wolves in Spain. The slave's scream that had split night from morning. The girl, Lusita, her laughter low and her wrists too thin. The smell of her hair when he'd buried his face there before marching to another revolt. Gone now. All gone. Yet memory returned like a tide, salt and relentless.

The map crackled when he opened his eyes. He looked down and spoke to the dark. "Everything repeats."

He raised two fingers.

A shadow filled the doorway, not a soldier, not a slave. The clerk. Gray tunic, chain at the throat, ink smudge on the thumb. The man, having been sent by the centurion, bowed once, waiting.

"Send for a runner," Caesar said. His voice came steady, measured. "A message for Matineus Latinus. Brother to Rufus."

The clerk nodded.

"Find him at their compound in the morning," Caesar added. "I want him here before noon."

The clerk hesitated. "Yes, Dominus."

Not a question. Just precision. The kind of servant a man like Caesar needed: invisible, exact, gone before the air cooled behind him.

When the curtain fell again, Caesar sat motionless. Two paths spread before him, both bloody, both sure. One he would walk himself. The other he would hand to another man: a soldier born from the same dust he once crawled through.

Rufus Latinus. The name fit the rhythm of war. Hard start, clean stop.

Matineus Latinus. The shadow brother. The quiet one.

Yes, the gods had sent him men who still believed in silence.

He poured the last of the wine. The liquid caught the lamplight and painted the maps red. A small, cruel smile touched his mouth, the kind Aurelia would have recognized from his boyhood, the one that came before he did something unforgivable.

"Tomorrow," he said to no one. "We start the climb."

The curtain stirred. Wind from the east again, the same that had haunted him all night. It pressed against the marble as if seeking entry. Rome's torches guttered below, sparks carried upward on the drafts that ran between columns. Far off, thunder rolled over the hills.

He looked once more at the broken seal on the table. "Your lion sleeps in the wrong empire," he murmured. Then he crushed the wax between thumb and forefinger until it crumbled into dust.

Below, the Forum murmured. Wheels on stone. A drunk singing. A child calling for her mother.

The sound reached his ear and steadied him. Rome... stubborn, filthy, immortal... still breathed.

He closed his eyes. The flame leaned toward him. For an instant it seemed the light bent in acknowledgment, as though recognizing its own reflection in the man who never stayed still. Then it steadied.

He opened them again. "Bring her here," Aurelia had said.

He could still hear her.

He would.

Chapter 13
THE RUNNER

Rome

The first sound was sandals on marble.

Shortly after dawn, the runner moved fast through Caesar's house.

Past scribes bent under lamplight. Past statues whose eyes caught firelight and seemed awake. He passed corners still half-dark, where servants whispered prayers to household gods. A brazier hissed. The smell of warm bronze and wax followed him out the gate.

The air outside bit with the last chill of night. He breathed once, sharp, steady, and started downhill.

Rome opened beneath him, tiered and gleaming. The Palatine bathed in early gold. Roof tiles flashed wet from dew. Lions carved in stone watched him pass. A sentry shifted his spear, nodded, said nothing. Far off, temple bells rang for morning sacrifices, three tones, slow and pure.

He crossed the Sacred Way at a run.

The Forum spread like a sea of white fire. Columns blazed. Bronze doors shone dull green. Vendors unrolled linen from their carts. A woman swept petals from the temple of Venus with a reed broom. Priests shook out incense, sparks clinging to their sleeves. The smell of wet limestone, olive oil, and crushed mint filled the air.

A child clapped stones near Saturn's statue. Doves scattered upward. A chained debtor knelt by the courthouse steps, cheek swollen purple. He mouthed the same line again and again: "Mercy, mercy." No one stopped.

The runner did not pause. He had no eyes for pity. Few Romans did.

He turned off the Sacred Way, boots striking sparks on stone. Down. Always down. The street narrowed, walls leaning closer, light thinning to dust and smoke. He passed under a terrace where women hung laundry. White sheets billowing like ghosts. The smell changed. Less incense, more people.

Subura.

It hit like breath from a furnace. Urine in the gutters. Vinegar wine in the air. A pig screamed beneath a cart, wheels still turning. Dogs snarled over a fish spine. Steam poured from bread ovens and carried the scent of yeast, sweat, and burned oil.

A drunk laughed. A boy pissed against a wall. Two women shouted over onions. A thief ran past clutching bread; behind him, a baker threw a peel like a spear and missed. The runner kept pace, eyes fixed ahead.

He passed the butcher. Blood on stone, flies thick.

The flower witch with dyed fingers muttering to her jars.

The fishmonger scraping scales that flashed silver before they fell dull.

He turned another corner. The noise fell away. The stones grew uneven, cracked from old fires. Fewer balconies above, fewer voices. Smoke lingered low and sour.

The air smelled of salt and rot.

Rome's breath in its sleep.

He saw bones stacked by a tanner's door. Saw a woman cutting the hide from a mule. Saw two foreigners kneeling before a tree wrapped with blue cloth, whispering in tongues he did not know. Coins glinted among the roots.

He stepped over a broken jug and a child's sandal half-buried in ash. Pigeons fluttered from the rafters, wings brushing his shoulder like breath.

The ground widened.

Space at last.

Here stood the edge, not wild, not safe. The city's last heartbeat before silence. Bark sellers, bone sellers, rag pickers. A girl hawked eels from a bowl, her wrists raw from cold water. A goat bleated behind a gate that hadn't been shut in years.

The runner adjusted the strap at his shoulder. Sweat slicked the back of his neck. He could taste iron in the air now, forge smoke from the workshops below the hill.

Ahead, a broken arch. He passed beneath it.

Graves spread beyond, half-swallowed by weeds. Stones leaned. Names faded. Coins glimmered on one slab, offerings to the forgotten. Others had been pried loose and taken. The dead no longer cared.

A wind swept the grass, heavy with ash. It carried the sea's faint salt though the sea lay miles away. Rome's ghosts breathed through that wind, smelling of damp wool and old rain.

Then walls.

The Latinus compound rose out of the smoke like a fortress left behind by a vanished army.

Three stories of brick, blackened at the edges, fireproofed by hands that expected attack. Iron bolts thick as a man's arm sealed the main doors. No statues. No wreaths. No marble.

Only one word carved deep above the arch:

LATINUS.

No color filled the cuts. No paint softened them.

Just the name. Raw. Permanent.

The runner slowed. He'd heard of this place. Everyone in Rome had. The family didn't rule from marble halls. They built them. They didn't buy senators. They buried them when needed. Their fortune came not from gold, but from work, and blood.

Men of war.

Thick-necked, scarred, quiet.

Centurions, builders, farmers. Killers.

Every branch bred soldiers.

Even bastards were trained.

Born of slaves, yes, but fed, taught, punished the same. Never weak. Never second. Not by their own code.

They trained in packs. Moved like wolves.

Built bridges, laid roads, crushed rebellions.

When called, they came fast, silent, prepared, unflinching.

Rome respected them. Or feared them. Often both.

The runner stopped before the gate. His chest lifted and fell, slow and deliberate. He could hear his pulse in his ears, smell the dust baked into the door seams. A crow perched on the lintel, one eye white from age, the other black as pitch. It watched him.

He knocked twice.

Wood thudded like stone.

He breathed in a deep breath and waited.

Footsteps stirred inside, heavy, measured, close.

A hinge groaned.

The crow let out one hoarse caw and took flight, its wings scraping the arch.

The runner looked up at the empty space it left behind.

Wind pressed against his back, warm now, carrying the scent of rain and iron from the east.

He swallowed once.

The door began to open.

Chapter 14
BLOOD OF LATINUS

Rome, The Latinus Compound

The compound filled the whole block. Every stone fused by sweat.

Every course laid straight, every door lined with the sun.

Generations had worked here, died here, left their heat inside the walls.

Morning light slid across the façade, clean, severe.

No graffiti scarred it. No piss smell lingered between the stones.

If someone dared defile it, the mark vanished before dawn. Punishment quickly followed.

Four entrances cut the block: one for clients, one for slaves, one for family, and a wide iron gate for wagons and material.

Shops clung to the outer walls like vines; an armor-polisher, a cobbler, a butcher, an herbalist whose jars gleamed green in the gloom.

Every merchant paid rent in coin or blood.

Cheating meant disappearance.

The city whispered about it, but never near the gate.

Inside, the air cooled and thickened.

A courtyard opened beneath olive trees older than the Republic.

Water ran cold through a stone trough carved by hand and banded in iron.

The scent was earth and lime and a faint trace of forge smoke.

Statues watched from the corners. Tall broad-shouldered ancestors in tunics, veiled women with solemn mouths, a few foreign figures with eyes like hawks.

Each base bore the same single word, chiseled shallow: Latinus.

Rufus had trained here.

His father and uncles before him.

Every child born to the blood, legitimate, bastard, slave-sired, had all sweated on these stones.

The grandfathers poured their own blood into the mortar when they built it.

Not myth. Fact.

Roof tiles came from Sicily, iron hinges from Spain, marble steps pried out of a ruined temple.

A cousin had died beneath one of those slabs, ribs crushed, lungs burst. The crack in the stone still showed his shape. They left it as part of the design.

The runner crossed the threshold and felt the quiet weight that comes from discipline, not fear.

Women worked under the awning, hemming tunics with neat, fast hands.

Two half-grown boys hauled logs to the forge.

Steel rang behind them, measured, never frantic. No one shouted. Every movement spoke training.

A man and his partner sparred against the north wall in subligacula, bare chests shining with sweat.

Wood blades smacked forearms, ribs, thighs.

Neither grunted.

Blood trickled, ignored. Their breathing timed to the hammer striking iron behind them.

The runner's heart quickened.

He'd carried orders through battlefields, through Parthian dust storms, but nothing unnerved him like this stillness.

He felt Rome's power here, unpolished, unspoken.

The Latinus blood carried a kind of gravity that bent strangers smaller.

A woman swept the doorway for the third time, broom rasping against stone. A smile on her face.

Amazingly beautiful, dark hair coiled high, eyes fixed on her work.

She did not look up.

He did not speak.

To pause here without purpose invited questions best unanswered.

The runner smelled resin from the forge and roasted barley from the kitchen.

Voices drifted low, men talking in the clipped rhythm of command.

He followed the sound through the open court until the light dimmed and the heat thickened.

Matineus stood near the forge, stripped to his subligaculum, muscles etched in soot.

Lime dust whitened his chest, sweat cutting dark rivers through it. A hammer hung loose in his hand, its head scarred and blackened.

When he struck, sparks crawled up his arm like living things. Each blow landed exact, no waste, no anger. A man who understood pressure and release, who knew when to stop.

He looked up.

The runner froze mid-step.

Matineus Latinus. Rufus's half-brother.

Tall, broad-shouldered, yet not the blunt kind of strength. More sinew than mass.

His eyes caught light the way wet stone catches dawn, dark, sharp, reflective.

His mother's blood had shifted something in him, added shadow where the others carried heat.

"Message," the runner said, and his voice came out smaller than he meant.

Matineus didn't move.

The hammer stayed balanced against his shoulder.

Only his head tilted, fraction by fraction.

The runner stepped forward, held the scroll out.

"From Caesar's house," he managed.

A beat of silence stretched thin between them.

Then Matineus descended the scaffold, deliberate, each rung creaking. He wiped his hands on the belt, took the scroll, and weighed it as if testing an enemy blade.

The wax seal caught a vein of sunlight, purple, flawless.

He broke it clean, eyes scanning the words.

Once. Again.

He read like a man measuring danger by heartbeat.

The runner tried not to stare.

The Latinus men were legends, but this one... this one carried something else, something quieter and worse.

Rumors said he vanished for months at a time with ten followers. Men who were loyal, spoke little, killed fast, and returned richer.

One story told of a coastal village burned to cinder, its people gone, the survivors whispering of shadows with Roman tongues.

No one proved it. No one asked.

Now that same stillness hummed in the air around him.

Matineus lowered the scroll.

His lips formed a word the runner didn't catch, maybe a name, maybe a curse. Whatever it was, it chilled the courtyard.

He turned toward the house.

The hammer thudded once on the anvil, a sound like a door closing.

The runner waited.

Matineus disappeared inside without another glance, swallowed by the shadowed hall.

The forge light dimmed, smoke twisting upward.

The workers had gone silent. Even the boys at the cart stood frozen.

The runner exhaled, shallow. Sweat cooled on his back.

He had delivered messages to kings and killers, but never to a man who felt less human than stone. He turned toward the gate, steps light.

Behind him the compound breathed, hammers ringing again, women murmuring, life resuming as if nothing had happened. But he knew the air had changed.

Something had begun to move under the surface, quiet and certain, like magma finding a new path.

Outside, the street sunlight struck his face.

He wiped grit from his palm and realized it trembled. He thought of Caesar's order, of the seal's weight, of the name he'd heard whispered... Matineus.

If this was the man Caesar wanted, Rome would soon tremble too.

He started down the alley, breath quickening, pulse in his ears. Behind him, the compound's iron gate closed with a dull, final sound... not warning, not threat... promise.

And above the arch, the single word caught the light again:

LATINUS.

Chapter 15
THE OLD BLOOD

Before Sulla.

Before Caesar.

Before the lion's son drew breath, there were two men.

Veterans. Propertied. Proven.

They had marched through the dust of Numidia, under suns that blistered bronze and bone alike.

They had watched the Cimbri come screaming out of the north and had not broken.

They were the kind of soldiers Marius needed when he remade the legions. Men whose scars told him what orders words could not.

Marcus Latinus came from the hills south of the city, lean, deliberate, a man whose silence carried weight.

Titus Sertorius traced his blood to Alba Longa, broad-shouldered, rough-voiced, half wolf, half craftsman.

Not patricians, not gutter men, but farmers who could fight, fighters who could build.

When they returned, their coin purses clinked with more than pay.

Land. Silver. Tools. Mules. Slaves. Spoils earned the hard way and kept harder.

They built on what their fathers had left, fields, workshops, slaves, debts already paid.

They added stone to stone until wealth had a shape.

Then they made the pact.

Your sons. My daughters.

They marry. They build. They fight.

No dowry. No bride price. Only trust and calloused hands.

Two lines became one.

The name Latinus rose from that union, not pride but statement.

Builders, fighters, men who stood in the dust and made Rome larger by will alone.

They bought a burnt down city block near the Subura, with blood and silver, close enough to hear the Senate's speeches yet far enough to smell sweat and steel.

From foundation to roof they built it themselves; workshops below, tenements above, a courtyard and a small shrine in the corner.

Running water. Sewer access. Brick marked with the thumbprints of their own blood.

Every course set straight. Every beam stamped with discipline.

They trained everyone who carried their name.

Sons. Daughters. Bastards. No difference.

Knives by twelve.

Run, climb, wrestle, shoot.

Half-siblings slept under the same roof and rose at the same trumpet.

No shame. Only work.

The children called the old men Avus. Grandfather. Never General. Never Lord.

When one of them walked into the yard, every back straightened.

Pride did that, not fear.

Marcus Latinus and Titus Sertorius would pace the yard after drills, hands clasped behind them, faces carved from stone.

Marcus, the taller, had held the line at Aquae Sextiae when the Teutones broke against it like surf.

Titus had stood at Cirta beside Marius, Jugurtha's banner in the dirt.

Both had earned land. Both had learned regret.

They remembered the gladiators Marius brought into the camps to teach single combat, the arena killers who showed legionaries the value of speed and cruelty.

Marcus and Titus had trained against them, learned what soldiers never should forget: the difference between order and survival.

The legion fought in ranks.

The gladiator fought to kill.

The old men blended both and called it balance.

Sometimes, even in winter, they called the grandsons into the yard.

Wooden swords. Bare feet on stone. Sweat darkening cheap tunics.

Marcus corrected the guard, slow, patient.

Titus barked about footwork, faster.

Then a scarred ex-gladiator would appear. One eye white, scars thick across his ribs.

He showed a lunge, a net throw, a curve of the blade meant to spill guts in one sweep.

Marcus stopped him before the flourish.

"Enough," he said. "The army doesn't need pretty."

Titus grinned. "But learn it anyway. A man in the dark might."

The boys learned both.

Years later, those lessons shaped a dynasty.

Marcus and Titus built their homes side by side above the Tiber and tore down the wall between them.

Their children married by torchlight, no priest, no audience, just witnesses who bled if they lied.

They dug the foundation with their own spades, set the beams with their own backs.

The family business grew: roads, villas, warehouses, walls.

Latinus boys hauled sand before they learned to sign their names.

Sertorius girls ran accounts that made senators sweat.

Even slaves read numbers. Everyone earned food by effort.

When Sulla's army marched on Rome, Marcus kept his trowel sharp and his mouth shut, but his sons marched under the red cloaks.

They fought through Greece, through blood and salt, and stood among those who placed the Grass Crown on Sulla's head.

They spoke little of it afterward.

The Latinus block remained whole.

Reward followed. Land. Contracts. Silver.

Respect harder than all three.

Even at seventy, the two old men rose before dawn.

They sharpened blades they no longer used.

Breakfast was bread, figs, oil, goat meat.

No one sat until sweat touched the floor.

They taught without speeches. Discipline was their language.

"Names are earned," Marcus told a circle of children once, pressing bricks into small palms.

"You carry this one. You don't drop it."

Titus unwrapped his tunic and showed them a spear scar, puckered and pale.

"Pain teaches," he said. "But you have to listen."

They still walked the construction sites together... slow steps, straight backs, eyes that missed nothing.

Laborers bowed their heads as the old centurions passed, not from fear, but from the weight of earned things.

At night, they sat by the brazier and drank watered wine, speaking of walls yet to build, sons yet to bury, debts yet to pay.

When one coughed blood, the other caught it in his palm and said, "Still red. Good."

They laughed until the coughing stopped.

Their bloodline kept the habit.

Each generation afterward mixed soldier and builder until the two were one craft.

Tools and weapons hung on the same wall.

The hammer that forged a hinge could crush a skull; the sword that killed could cut limestone.

Their descendants learned both uses and forgot which mattered more.

By the time Rufus was born, the Latinus name had hardened into something beyond lineage.

A warning. A promise. A banner without cloth.

People spoke it softly in taverns and louder in barracks.

Latinus meant competence; it meant a job done fast and quiet; it meant a contract kept.

Not noble blood... iron blood.

The kind that stains but never dries.

Even the bastards carried themselves like soldiers.

Half-sons in the courtyard still bore the same shoulders, the same watchful silence.

A whip was rare. Shame sharper. Laziness unforgiven.

The house that Marcus and Titus built had never fallen, not to fire, not to debt, not to neglect, not to envy.

Its walls still hummed with the rhythm of tools, the grind of stone, the ring of discipline.

Every child knew the stories. Every child repeated the oath whispered at dusk:

Build. Fight. Protect. Endure.

That was the true inheritance.

Not gold. Not land. The creed.

When the torches burned low and the yard emptied, Matineus often stood alone in the same spot where the grandfathers had drilled the boys centuries earlier.

He could still smell the lime dust, hear the scrape of wooden swords, feel the ghosts counting his breath.

Sometimes he thought he heard them speak, not in words, but in the shift of wind through olive leaves:

Hold the line. Keep the name.

He always answered the same way, quietly, almost a prayer:

"I will."

And from the forge nearby, sparks rose like a century's heartbeat.

Chapter 16
ORDERS FROM THE PALATINE

R ome
Matineus bathed fast, the cold water biting every bruise he never acknowledged. He dried with rough cloth, dressed without ceremony. Dark wool tunic. Boots strapped tight. Belt straight over narrow hips. No rings. No crest. Nothing that shone in daylight.

Nothing that could be grabbed in a fight.

His long black hair lay slicked back with oil. He tied it once at the nape. A soldier's knot. His own knot. The kind that stayed put even in blood or seawater.

He stepped out into the courtyard alone.

The Latinus compound breathed morning heat. Smoke drifted from the forge. Women swept the stones for the third time. Boys hauled buckets, wood, stone. Two cousins sparred bare-chested under the awning, wooden practice blades cracking against each other's ribs.

No one laughed.

No one wasted breath.

He didn't look at them. They didn't look at him. Not disrespect, something sharper.

Recognition.

Matineus walked like the fight had already been decided. Shoulders loose. Chin high. Hands easy. One calloused thumb rested near the hilt under his tunic. A habit, not a fear.

The runner who had delivered Caesar's summons still lingered near the gate, trying not to be noticed and failing. He stepped aside as Matineus passed, eyes lowered, pulse jumping in his throat. Everyone felt something when Matineus moved.

Not a soldier's weight.

Not a noble's power.

Something older. Something quieter. The kind of danger that didn't brag.

Matineus crossed through the gate and out into Rome.

The Subura opened in front of him: smoke, heat, piss running between the stones. Vendors called from stalls, fingers stained with onion juice and dye. A drunk slept against a pillar, mouth open like a wound. A dog dragged a pig's hide. A girl with bare feet and a chipped tooth tried to sell figs, then shrank back when she saw him.

He didn't slow.

Even the thieves stepped aside for Latinus' blood.

He climbed the slope toward the Forum, leaving the slum behind. The air changed first, thinner, less heavy with sweat. Then the stones brightened. Chalk dust. Marble chips. Voices that echoed instead of muffled.

He reached the Palatine.

Guards straightened. They didn't challenge him. They knew the summons came from inside, and a man called by Caesar walked with a different rhythm.

Matineus entered through bronze doors etched with wolves and laurel. Water trickled from carved mouths into marble basins. Fruit trees stood in tiled courts. Birds perched in manicured branches like jewels set in green.

A servant bowed low.

"Follow me."

Matineus followed, silent. His steps were swallowed by expensive floors.

They reached the upper chamber, Caesar's study.

The room held its breath: marble, gold light, long shadows. A map sprawled across the central table, inked with red lines that ran across seas and mountains. A bronze lamp burned low, its flame sharpened by the early sun.

Caesar stood with his back to the window. He looked younger in morning light, sharp cheekbones, a strong jaw, the faintest shadow of stubble. Bare feet on cold stone. A plain tunic. No wreath. No rings. Power didn't need decoration; it needed a pulse.

He didn't turn when Matineus entered. He waited.

A test.

When he finally faced him, his gaze cut straight through the space between them.

"You favor your brother," he said.

Matineus met his eyes. "Everyone says that."

Caesar nodded, as if confirming his own choice. "Sit."

Matineus sat.

"Water?" Caesar asked.

A servant poured. Matineus drank with one hand, eyes steady on Caesar, waiting.

The scroll lay between them, the Parthian message. Black seal cracked. Lion's mane pressed into wax. Caesar rested his palm over it, tapping once, a signal, or a warning.

He raised two fingers.

The clerk from earlier slipped in. Ink-stained tunic. Calm eyes.

"Fetch my mother."

The man bowed and vanished.

Matineus said nothing. Caesar liked silence more than flattery. Matineus understood that.

Minutes passed like measured breath.

Then Aurelia entered.

Blue silk. Gray hair braided back. No scent except clean oil. She carried herself like the Republic itself walked in behind her. Grace. Warning. Authority.

Her eyes met Matineus's. One look. One judgment.

"You look like your brother," she said.

He stood, bowed, kissed her hand. "I hear that a lot."

A hint of approval softened her mouth. "You belong to the Latinus. A stout house."

She moved beside Caesar, folding herself into the room's brightness as if she had always belonged to the sun.

Caesar began.

"You go east," he said, the order sharp as flint.

A breeze pushed the curtain; dust motes floated like tiny omens.

"You'll take five of your own. Or ten, if they still follow you."

Matineus inclined his head once.

"I'll send ten of mine," Caesar went on. "Men who travel light. Men who ask nothing."

Aurelia stood behind him, listening, weaving the political thread behind the military one.

"You go beyond Antioch," Caesar continued. "Past Pontus. Past the Black Sea's shadow. To the Caspian's edge. A priestess has been seized. A foreign temple holds her."

He let that sink in. The weight of it. The distance.

"Rescue her."

No flourish. No permission for doubt.

Matineus didn't blink. "I'll see it done."

Caesar laid three scrolls on the table.

"This," he said, sliding the first forward, "gets you aboard a ship at Ostia. One Rufus left for my use. The captain owes me his life."

He tapped the second. "This goes to Antioch. Hand it to Rufus. He'll provide maps, coin, allies, and whatever shadow work you need."

He held the third longer, the sealed one. "This stays sealed. Leave it where they will find it after the rescue. Not for your eyes. For theirs."

Aurelia added quietly, "There are votive stones. Twelve. Small. Carved. Sacred. Bring them home. Even if the girl dies, bring those back to Rome."

Caesar resumed:

"Move fast. Parthians are slow to bargain but swift to anger. If the captives remain in that temple, you'll find them. If not, the trail runs short."

He stepped closer.

"Chase. Cut. Kill those who stand in the way. Bring the priestess, her witches, dancers, eunuchs, attendants, and those rocks. All of them. Then run as if the Furies ride your heels."

He slid the sealed scroll across the table. Its weight might as well have been an anvil.

"When the King of Parthia reads this," Caesar said, "everything east of Armenia will turn toward you."

Matineus took the scrolls. The mission clicked into place behind his eyes.

Aurelia studied him, her voice soft but exact. "You understand the cost," she said.

He met her gaze. "Yes."

Caesar's eyes sharpened. "Then prove you are the right brother."

The air tightened.

Matineus bowed once, short, deep, absolute.

He turned and left, scrolls tucked close, the scent of foreign embers clinging to his tongue.

Outside, Rome breathed fire and dust. Inside, the map still showed one red dot at the world's far edge.

Caesar and Aurelia looked at each other.

The road east had begun.

Chapter 17
THE RIDE TO OSTIA

D awn broke.

Matineus rode at full gallop.

Twenty riders behind him: ten of his own, boys he had hardened from alleys and stables, and ten from Caesar's household, clean men with the sure gait of palace training. Another five had slipped ahead in the dark to hold the ship. They passed the gate without slackening; the guard saw the seal, one raised a fist, then lowered it. Matineus touched the bronze post under the arch; ritual, not thought.

Hooves struck stone like a clock. The Via Ostiensis curved; the Tiber slid beside them, brown and wide, carrying branches, oil, dead fish toward the sea. A grain barge drifted; a boy at the helm watched as if he had already lost the habit of hope. Matineus noted him and rode on.

Warehouses and graves marched the roadside. The air tasted of swamp mud, smoke, pig fat, and horse shit. A dog barked once behind a cracked wall. Two half-starved curs fought over a rotten carcass; men passing did not glance. At the crossroads, a shrine held fresh blood on its altar; ravens circled above and dropped; no one slowed.

They rode like shadows. No banners. No drums. Each man folded his silence around his weapons. Signals moved between them, short pulls on a rein, two fingers raised, less language than muscle memory. The road unrolled damp with dew; sea birds lifted in a scattering of sound. Salt reached their nostrils before the docks came into view.

Masts cropped the horizon. Ropes sang. Men shouted. Matineus counted ships as a habit; the numbers told the harbor's mood: twelve to the left, nine right; no purple sails. One hull lay apart from the rest: black, low, narrow, gangplank down, oars tied and waiting. No name carved, no crest. Tar sealed the planks; iron rings sharpened the prow. The bow knifed forward like a wolf's snout.

He read design as others read faces. The rudder's slope; the braces; the tight, forward set of the benches: a ship built to bite. Function the sole purpose of design. This was Rufus. Matineus felt the recognition as surely as his hand felt the bit; the craft bore the same hard angles he had seen on the man's face. No paint, no show; only motion planned. The Sea Wolf.

Off the quay, a Roman officer stepped and stated duty. "Orders came last night. You're expected." Matineus inclined once and boarded. The men followed.

The crew took them without ceremony. Ropes creaked; the gangplank sighed as it rose. Matineus walked along the rail next to the captain: his uncle, a hand callused from oar and rope. He nodded. The ship breathed black beneath his palm.

Rowers stripped to subligacula sat like a muscle; their oars raised in unison, fell in perfect rhythm. Thirty strokes; fifteen a side; no wasted motion. No song, no shout; just wood, sweat, and a single steady breath. The tiller groaned once; the black nose turned east.

On deck the two tens arrayed themselves by habit: Matineus's men clustered loose, eyes sharp, hands traveling to hilts; Caesar's men stood ordered, faces trained into polite indifference. The difference read like years: one group learned in blood and hunger, the other forged in palace courts and parade grounds. Each measured the other with a glance.

A man from Caesar's ten stepped forward, broad shoulder, clean wrist, and addressed Matineus in a voice that held instruction. "You handle fighters from the street? Interesting."

Matineus did not answer. He watched the man's mouth move and read the small truths lying under the politeness: confidence, the sense of being taught to be brave rather than forced into it. He watched how the man's eyes slid to Matineus's hands and then to his belt. He read contempt there for dirt-earned skill; the man could not hide the gap between his training and the taste of blood. Matineus let him learn that lesson slowly.

One of Matineus's boys, Toles, a lean thing with knuckles split wide, stepped close to the rail and spat into the sea. The action was small, the message large. The palace man's jaw tightened, a policeman's reflex, not a fighter's.

Aurelia's ten watched all of this like an audience; they kept their faces still. Their swords were polished; their boots shone; their bearing said they might lace a toga as easily as take a life. Yet when Matineus moved toward the rail to help unlash an oar, two of Caesar's men followed by habit: a shared task made kin of them for the width of a deck.

Rufus's ship cut water as if killing prey. Men shifted to the work with the quiet of those who had expected this since birth: hour after hour of pull and burn, repeated until motion matched thought. The black hull slid through foam; gulls wheeled and screamed; the shore fell away into an old map of rooftops and thin smoke.

Matineus walked among his men, noting small things: a thin scar across a knuckle; a loose tooth held by an old stitch of rope; the way a youngster's hand trembled when he held the oar. He checked packs: mutton, hard bread, a flask of vinegar, ropes with knots known to the hands that made them. He tucked a scrap of the sealed scroll into his tunic, near rib and heart, not for secrecy; to feel the paper there like a hot coal.

Across the deck Caesar's ten polished a bit of brass, joked in clipped tones, tested each other's mettle with words that never turned to blows. The boys from Matineus answered only by glance, by the small tightening of a fist. Neither pride surrendered. Neither offered courtesy.

By noon the land fell away, and the sea rolled flat, the horizon a single thread. The ship prowed east, the wolf-bow parting swell and sun. Matineus stood with one hand on the rail, feeling the motion and the breath of men behind him. The two tens had met; they had not yet become one. That was the point. There would be time for that, on a shore, in a fight, when the long run of oars finished and swords took the sound.

The ship cut on. Sun slid across the polished planks. Men trimmed lines. Sea spray ghosted the faces. Matineus looked at his hands and thought of Rufus: of the ship shaped like the man, lean and forward and without show. He tipped his head once toward the horizon. Somewhere beyond it, a quiet temple stood with a priestess held under foreign stones. The scroll in his breast burned the promise and the order; the men behind him readied their hunger into a thing that would carry them to the next blood.

The wolf moved through the water; the two tens found their rhythm; the sea kept its own counsel.

Chapter 18
SILENT WAR

Hyrcania, 64 B.C.

The temple held its breath.

Heat crawled down the walls in slow beads, darkening stone the way fear darkened skin. Outside, the sun baked the steps until lizards avoided them. Inside, Albina sat with her spine straight, legs folded beneath her, palms open on her knees. Stillness armored her more than bronze ever could.

Her people mirrored her quiet.

The witches. The dancers. The eunuchs. The two apprentices clutching each other like sparrows in smoke.

They waited.

And watching became their warfare.

They measured time by guard rotations and the shape of shadows crawling over the floor. By the scrape of sandals at the gate. By the grunt of a bored soldier, the cough of a tired one, the shift of metal on skin. They memorized who stared too long at the curtain, who drifted, who sharpened his spear with anger instead of duty.

The youngest dancer, fifteen, amber-eyed, chain bruising her ankle, was the first piece placed on the board.

Albina didn't speak. She didn't need to.

A tilt of chin. A flick of fingers.

A breath-thin command.

The girl understood.

She shifted just enough to let the chain sing. She turned her head the slow way, letting her hair slide across her shoulder like poured honey. A smile touched her mouth, there, gone, leaving heat where innocence used to be.

By sunset, one guard checked the curtain each hour.

By sunrise, two more drifted closer than their posts required.

By the third day, they lingered even after their replacements arrived, leaning on stone with lazy, stupid grins.

Zarmina fed the brazier in the corner.

Not firewood.

Not herbs meant for prayers. Black roots, brittle with bitterness. Seeds that numbed the tongue. Yellow leaves that had been banned in three kingdoms.

She crushed everything with a stone worn smooth by deathbed offerings.

The smoke that rose was not smoke.

It was silk.

It was a hand stroking the mind.

It curled low, clung to the floor, tasted of incense, honey, and the edge of dreams.

Albina's people breathed it like air.

The guards breathed it like fools.

At first it softened them.

A heaviness behind the eyes. A warmth in the limbs.

By the second day, shoulders slumped. By the third, thoughts wandered.

Commands arrived late and were obeyed slower.

The smoke did not kill. That was never its purpose.

It unraveled men, thread by thread, until belts loosened, spears dropped without flinch, helmets sat crooked, and discipline sagged like rope left in the rain.

The first guard scratched his chest every time the young dancer passed him, not knowing why his skin burned.

The second laughed at jokes she never told.

The third leaned so close his shoulder touched the curtain, breath catching on the scent of her hair.

Hunters, thinking they stalked prey.

Never noticing the leash at their own throats.

The witches burned more.

The smoke thickened, sweet and bitter at once, sliding into lungs, coating tongues, clinging to cloth like perfume from a forbidden chamber.

Red Ring stayed outside.

The smoke made his thoughts slow, muddied logic, turned memory thick. He paced instead, boots grinding dust, muttering curses. The King's command kept him out. So he remained on the steps, hungry and irritated, never understanding how close he stood to losing control of his own men.

He had sent a messenger west weeks ago, slow rider, slower thinker. That man stopped at inns, drank, bragged, dallied, believed no empire would cross deserts and mountains for a handful of dancers and witches.

He died for that belief. The scroll he carried was already in Rome.

Inside, Albina steadied her breath.

No prayers. No chant. Just waiting.

Her people whispered in corners, soft, urgent scraps of strategy. They counted footsteps. Watched sway of spear shafts. Mapped the fatigue rising in the guards' eyes.

Albina saw all of it. Her golden eyes missed nothing.

But her face stayed smooth.

Calm. Unreadable.

Her heartbeat lived in her throat, heavy but controlled.

Every day could be the last. One mistake, one slip, one poorly timed whisper, and the storm would tear through the temple like a knife through lace.

She knew the King of Kings could send for her at any hour.

Knew Red Ring's patience was a wolf on a chain.

Knew the men outside wanted her dead or broken or both.

But none of that touched her posture.

When she spoke, her voice came high, deliberate, sweet as honey poured over steel.

Stillness remained her weapon.

A dancer shifted her chain.

A guard smirked, pupils too wide.

Zarmina fed another blackened root to the flame.

The smoke deepened to a low blue haze.

Hour by hour, thread by thread, Albina tightened the rope around her captors' throats. They never felt it.

She rested her hands on her knees, palms open to the stone.

Her breath shallow, controlled.

Her eyes half-lidded.

Inside, her mind moved like a blade across plans.

The King had not summoned her.

No envoy.

No executioner.

That meant time.

And time was life.

She would turn every breath into a weapon.

Outside the curtain, a guard startled awake from standing still. Another laughed at nothing. A third dropped his spear, blinked at it, left it lying for someone else.

None of the girls spoke.

They didn't need to.

Their silence carried more threat than screams.

Albina did not curse.

Did not bless.

She breathed.

She listened.

She waited.

The goddess warmed her ribs like a hidden flame in winter.

A pulse, ancient and patient, running through her veins.

The witches smiled as the smoke thickened. Their smiles meant war.

Albina closed her eyes, just once, and listened to the faint drag of sandals outside the curtain.

Her thought was quiet, sharp:

The war has already begun.

And no sword has yet been drawn.

Chapter 19
RUFUS

Latinus Compound, Near the Subura - 65 B.C.

Heat lay low over the Latinus block.

Hammers rang in the yards. Slaves hauled stone. Smoke from the forges crawled along the roofline and drifted toward the Subura like a warning. Lime dust floated in thin veils. The whole block smelled of iron, sweat, wet wool, and fresh-cut timber.

In the middle of the training court, a red-haired boy moved through drills.

No helmet. No armor. Just a leather belt and a rough tunic clinging to his back, dark with sweat. Bare legs braced wide. Forearms roped with muscle. Hands wrapped in striped linen.

Rufus.

Sixteen years old. Already taller than most men in the yard. Shoulders thick from years under shield weight. Neck like a short pillar. Clean-shaven jaw set hard. Steel-blue eyes narrowed against the light.

He shifted his grip on the wooden gladius. The blade snapped against a padded shield, turned, and drove in again. Each strike landed where a throat or heart might live. No flourish. No shout.

Breath left him slow, measured. Heat rolled off his skin; salt and iron and crushed grass. When he twisted at the waist, light slid along the muscles in his back like water.

Under the awning, girls pretended to sew.

Needles paused. Thread tangled. Eyes drifted.

A younger cousin in the shadow of a column whispered, "He never misses."

"Shut up and stitch," her aunt muttered, but even she watched when he pivoted and drove his shoulder into the post. The old wood groaned, straps creaking.

Rufus saw them in the corner of his vision. The flicker of heads. The way hands stilled at the loom when he walked past. The way voices dropped when he stripped his tunic off after drills.

Once, that attention had felt strange. Now he treated it like rain. Noted. Ignored.

He slammed the shield again. Felt the give. Read the weakness the way other boys read letters.

"Enough," the trainer called.

Rufus lowered his weapons, chest rising. Sweat slicked his neck. The tunic clung to him like a second skin.

A slave boy hurried over with a clay jug. Twelve, maybe. Narrow shoulders, ribs sharp under a torn tunic. He held the jug with both hands; it shook against Rufus's forearm.

"Dominus," the boy murmured, eyes down.

"Ah, did you make my brother, Lucius, drink?"

"Yes Dominus, he drank deeply and then went inside."

Rufus took the jug. The clay felt cool in his grip. He drank deep, throat working, water spilling over his bottom lip and down his chest. The slave swallowed hard, watching the drops track along the muscle. His arms trembled from the weight.

Rufus lowered the jug halfway. The boy reached for it, expecting it back.

"Drink," Rufus said.

The boy blinked. "For you, master."

Rufus tipped the jug toward his mouth. "If you drop, I drop. Drink."

The boy hesitated, then lifted it with both hands. Rufus kept one palm under the base to steady it. The boy drank too quickly, coughed, water splashing his chin. Rufus waited, hand still firm under the jug.

"Slow," he said. "You carry stone for my walls. I need your legs under you."

The boy nodded, cheeks flushed. Water dripped from his nose. When he tried to wipe his face on his shoulder, Rufus handed him a scrap of cloth from his belt.

"Eat when you leave the yard," Rufus said. "Bread, not scraps."

"I will," the boy whispered.

Rufus watched him go. Thin back. Bare feet slapping stone.

He knew that boy's name. He tried to know all of them. Stone stayed loyal when you treated it well. So did flesh.

He rolled his shoulders once. Picked up the wooden gladius again.

They said he stood at that training post by age four.

By five he drilled every dawn, small fists tight around a child's sword, striking until his arms refused to lift. The old men let him fall once. Only once. After that, he learned to stand no matter how his muscles burned.

By six, he bled.

Not from some street brawl. From training. A misjudged block split his lip to the gum. Blood filled his mouth, hot and copper. He swallowed it and kept swinging. His grandfather watched from the wall and nodded once. Approval, not praise.

Rufus grew inside stone and work.

The Latinus compound filled a whole city block near the Subura. Walls higher than three men. Corners braced against fire. Inside: workshops, school-rooms, stables, barracks, kitchens, a shrine. A private world. A fortress that never fully slept.

Every child learned letters and numbers. Every child learned to cut stone and mix concrete. Every child learned to fight. Sons, daughters, bastards, slave-born. All carried knives by twelve. All ran the roof lines at night. All tied sandals in the dark without thinking.

Rufus stood as the youngest legitimate son of the elder Latinus. Status without claim. Two older brothers ahead of him. Two older male cousins. All strong. All trained. All certain of their place.

He had none. That was freedom.

So he carved one.

Not by shouting. Not by sulking. He simply trained harder. Hit cleaner. Endured longer. Watched more.

When he walked through the yard, boys stepped aside without knowing why. The old men saw that and talked in low voices over bread and lentils. "That one," they said. "If he lives long enough."

At thirteen he killed for the first time.

The family gathered in the inner court. No guests. No music. No wine. Just the old men, his father, his uncles, his mother, several aunts, and the boy himself. In the center, chained to a post, a Thracian slave. Thick arms. Tattoos curling around his neck like blue snakes. Eyes full of hate, not fear.

The man had killed another slave in the yard. No trial. No appeal.

The grandfather put a real gladius in Rufus's hand.

"Fast," the old man said. "Clean."

No speech. No blessing.

Rufus stepped forward. His heart knocked once, twice. His fingers tightened around the leather grip. The slave smiled, lips splitting around broken teeth, then lunged as far as the chain allowed.

Rufus did not jump back.

He drove the blade up under the ribs, just left of center, exactly where he had drilled a hundred times on straw dummies. Steel met flesh, then bone, then the wet slide of organs. Heat spilled over his hand, thick and slick.

The man shuddered. Breath left him in a ragged gust. Knees hit stone. Blood spread across the floor, hot around Rufus's bare feet. Steam rose.

He did not step away.

He knelt with the body as it sagged. Hands still on the hilt. Head bowed.

The old men watched his face, his knuckles, the line of his back. They searched for a tremor, for tears, for the flinch that meant softness.

He gave them nothing.

Inside, something shifted. Not guilt exactly. Not triumph. A heavy knowledge settled behind his ribs:

This is real now. No backing away. This is my road.

He pulled the blade free when they told him. Wiped it on the dead man's tunic. Handed it back. His fingers shook only once, later, when he washed his feet alone.

He told no one.

He had passed.

By fourteen, the Sons of Centurions began to watch.

They never sent letters. They arrived. Old veterans with one eye, half ears, twisted fingers. Men who knew the weight of Roman eagles and the taste of Germanic blood. They leaned on spear shafts at the edge of the yard and watched Rufus run rope courses, haul sandbags, fight three boys at once in shield drill. They watched him fall, rise, drive forward.

One winter morning he woke with frost on his blanket and a red mark painted on his door: two slanting strokes, chevrons, like a bird in flight.

His mother saw it. Her eyes shone once, then cooled.

"Breakfast first," she said. "Then destiny."

Sons of Centurions did not take boys for names alone.

They tested them in mud and smoke. Rope courses strung over pits. Knife runs through screaming crowds. Fire carries with burning logs on bare shoulders. Marches until toenails ripped free. Nights without sleep until dreams came with open eyes. Lessons in how long a man might live with a lung pierced, how fast blood fled from a cut at the inner thigh.

If a boy cried, he walked.

If he begged, he walked.

If he bragged, he walked.

Rufus stayed.

He fought through blisters until his boots filled with blood. He climbed until his arms felt carved from stone. He ran beside boys already breaking, steadied them with his presence, then left them when they fell behind. Pity had no place in that circle. He learned to break noses with the heel of his hand, to crush a windpipe with one precise blow, to move in the dark by scent and breath alone. To listen for the exact change in a crowd when fear turned to panic.

The Sons of Centurions often rode the roads outside the city hunting escaped slaves, fugitives, kidnappers, and armed robbers. The Sons captured a few, but most of them were killed. The bodies nailed to trees as a warning.

One night, after a forced march that left half the boys vomiting in the ditch, he lay awake under thin blankets, eyes open to the dark.

Around him, others whimpered. Cursed. Prayed.

He stared up, chest aching, legs on fire, and thought of his family courtyard. Of his brothers, already promised command in some future legion. Of his father's glance when counting heirs. The quick measure. The unspoken "extra."

If I earn the vine staff, they can never set me aside.

Not for lack of birth. Not for lack of courage. Not for being third or fourth in the line.

Centurion meant a place that no cousin could take. A right to stand in the front rank, voice carrying over a hundred men. A right to die for something clean.

He closed his eyes and let that want burn through the pain. It tasted sharper than any laurel.

Each surviving boy received two blood-red chevrons sewn over the heart.

Rufus wore his under his tunic, close to skin.

He didn't parade them. He trained in them.

By sixteen he towered over most men. Six feet three, maybe more. Two hundred twenty, all solid. The drills stripped away every softness. His body held the same spare logic as the Latinus walls: nothing decorative, everything built to stand.

His hair burned red in the sun, cropped short at the sides, longer on top, pushed back out of his eyes. His skin carried the bronze of outdoor labor, not scented oil. His jaw stayed clean-shaven; the old men cursed beards on a fighting man. His mouth rarely curved, but when it did, it knocked years from his face and made girls look away too slow.

He drank little wine. Thick stew, meat, olives, bread: those he took in full measure. Beef from the family farms. Goat, lamb, pork. Game from the hills. Food that built bodies that could break walls.

He carried himself like a threat he had leashed.

No swagger. No loud talk. Danger in him spoke through how he walked, the way other boys shifted a step aside without thinking, the quick hush when he lifted a bow.

Archery came late.

One spring an old Briton appeared at the Latinus yard. Hair like winter straw. Face carved by wind and years. Hands that treated yew like sacred wood. Maccus. A prisoner once, then a craftsman. His Latin clipped, his eyes bright and amused.

He carved a longbow thicker than a man's wrist, taller than Rufus's shoulder, heavy as sin. Most men failed to draw it past their chest. Their faces reddened; their arms shook.

Rufus stepped up when his turn came. He wrapped his hand around the grip.

The string kissed his ear. No shake.

The first arrow thudded deep into the post at sixty paces. The second shaved a knot off the first. The third sank between the two, splitting grain.

Maccus's mouth twitched. "Again," he said.

Soon Rufus shot from walls, from roofs, from moving carts. He hit tossed jugs, swinging sacks, boars in full run. He split shafts already in the target wood. He learned to loose in storm wind, at dusk, through smoke stinging his eyes.

Word ran across the Campus Martius: the red-haired Latinus boy never missed.

Boys who might test him at wrestling stayed silent when he walked past with a bow. Trainers watched his form and made the sign for good fortune. Girls carrying water lingered in doorways, pitchers heavy on hips, pretending to fuss with their veils while watching the play of muscle under his tunic.

Rufus noticed more than he let on.

The way one slave girl's breath hitched when he wiped sweat from his chest. How a patrician cousin of his sister looked away, then back, then away again as he strung the bow, cheeks flushed. Once he caught their eyes together, saw the wide-open hunger there, and had to look away first.

Not because he disliked it.

Because he liked it too much.

Pleasure meant distraction. Distraction meant weakness. Weakness meant death, for him or for the men he meant to lead one day.

He chose the bow.

After drills he washed his hands and arms at the family fountain, cool water stripping sweat and dust from his skin. He ducked into the shrine room, where lamps burned low on a small altar. The air smelled of soot and oil. He left offerings there: a strip of cured meat, a sprig of laurel pilfered from the training ground, a broken arrowhead that had still struck true.

He prayed little.

He lived as if the gods already watched and expected proof.

Outside, Rome breathed. The Subura smoked and yawned. Men cursed. Women shouted at children. Chickens scattered under cart wheels. The Latinus block sat orderly at the edge, a square of control against the sprawl.

Inside that square, the boy sharpened into a man who wanted one thing.

Not gold. Not a senator's robe. Not a garland.

A place in the front line. A centurion's vine staff in his hand. The right to stand between Rome and whatever came at her with teeth, to decide who held and who ran.

He finished another set of shield drills, sweat darkening the stone at his feet.

From the gate, a shout: "Visitor. From Pompey the Younger!"

Heads turned.

A young man in a fine tunic stepped into the yard. Sandal straps clean. Hair carefully curled. Rings bright on his fingers. He walked like someone more used to polished floors than scarred stone, but his eyes took in the yard with quick, sharp sweeps.

Gnaeus Pompeius. Eldest son and heir of Pompey Magnus.

His gaze found Rufus and stayed there.

Once, years before, he had watched Rufus on the Campus Martius, watched the red-haired boy break a bigger youth in the shield ring, take three cuts, win anyway. That day he had walked over, offered bread and questions, asked to train with him.

One boy born from war merchants and generals.

One from builders and centurions.

Somehow, they fit.

Now Gnaeus watched Rufus fit an arrow to the string of the longest war bow he'd ever seen.

He saw the easy balance. The bare, dirty feet set firm on stone. The long line of the boy's back as the bow bent, muscles sliding under sun-burned skin. The way Rufus's face went utterly calm in that last breath before release, as if nothing else in the world mattered but distance and wind.

In that still moment, two futures shifted.

One in Rome.

One far off, at the edge of a sea a girl on the Caspian cliffs had already dreamed of.

Rufus loosed.

The bow snapped. The arrow flew, a hard, fast line against the light.

The yard fell silent.

And Gnaeus Pompey, heir to the most powerful men in the Republic, thought without saying it:

I'm going to need him.

Chapter 20
WARBOW

The lake lay black under a bruised sky.

Wind pushed from the north, sharp enough to wrinkle the surface into silver teeth. Reeds hissed at the edges. Somewhere in the gloom, a frog croaked once, then thought better of it.

Rufus stood barefoot in the boat.

His toes gripped wet planks; his stance anchored the hull the way a seasoned fighter anchors a shield, without thought. Thighs taut beneath a soaked tunic. Shoulders broad. Skin salted by spray. The breeze lifted the copper in his hair and pushed it off his forehead.

The longbow rested in his left hand. Yew. Heavy. Sacred.

He drew a slow breath. Damp leather. River mud. Old pitch on the oars. His heartbeat followed the boat's sway, a tight rhythm sunk deep in muscle.

The oarsman, an old farm slave, bent-backed, arms cut like roots, rowed without a word. Each stroke steady. Water parted clean around the hull.

On the far side waited a second boat, unmanned, tied to a stake. At its bow a thin pole held a strip of red cloth snapping hard in the wind.

On the shore stood Rufus's uncle, arms folded, cloak pulled close. Beside him: Gnaeus Pompey, sixteen, wearing new sandals he didn't want dirty, curls neatly combed but already losing the battle against the gusts.

Gnaeus squinted. "No one hits that."

The uncle's mouth twitched. "He tied it himself."

Rufus checked the quiver. His fingers brushed fletching. He selected one arrow by touch, chose it the way he chose everything important: without hesitation, without doubt.

He nocked.

He drew.

The boat dipped. The sky tilted. Wind shoved the hull sideways.

Rufus shifted with it. Hips absorbing the sway. Back tightening. Shoulders rolling. The bow creaked under the strain as the string reached his ear.

His eyes narrowed. That still, steel-blue calm, the look girls on the compound pretended not to watch.

Release.

The string snapped like bone.

The arrow vanished.

Gnaeus lost sight halfway across the lake. For a heartbeat, nothing.

Then the cloth jerked, ripped sideways in a clean, brutal tear.

Rufus did not grin. Did not bow. Just reached for another arrow with the same quiet certainty that made older men step out of his path.

He nocked again.

"Mother of..." Gnaeus cut himself off.

Rufus ignored him. Drew. Released.

Another strike. Clean. The strip twisted tighter around the pole.

"Push us farther," Rufus said.

The oarsman snorted, amused. "Trying to make the gods jealous, boy?"

But he rowed them out, deeper, where the water turned colder and the wind less forgiving.

Rufus wiped his palm on his tunic. The cloth pulled over his abdomen tight enough that the oarsman's granddaughter, waiting onshore with a basket, forgot what she'd been doing. She blushed. Rufus didn't see.

Or pretended not to.

Gnaeus, though... Gnaeus noticed everything.

The oarsman, needing a new target, stripped the belt from his own waist and tied it to a stick. He raised it high. Brown leather snapping in the wind.

Rufus set his feet. Legs steady. Chest rising slow. His bow hand shook out once, habit, not nerves.

He nocked.

He pulled.

The longbow bent under the force, its arc perfect. Most grown men couldn't draw it half this far. But Rufus pulled smooth and silent, spine straight, jaw relaxed.

For a moment, just one, the world narrowed to cloth, wind, weight, angle.

He loosed.

The arrow punched the belt's center dead-on, snapping it backward like a whip strike.

The uncle barked a laugh.

Gnaeus didn't laugh.

He stared.

Long. Hard.

Something in his mind shifted. The way foundations shift before walls change direction.

He saw Rufus, not as a farm block boy, or a fighter, or even his closest friend, but as a weapon waiting for a war no one else had imagined yet.

Rufus lowered the bow. His breath stayed quiet, steady. A drop of water slid down his calf, darkening the plank beneath him.

A sound broke the wind, a soft cough.

The slave boy who carried spare arrows had been watching from the stern, shivering. Too thin. Too young. He steadied the quiver with trembling hands.

Rufus noticed.

He reached for the water-skin, uncorked it, and handed it to the boy without words. Not a gesture for show. Not kindness for approval. Just instinct.

The boy drank. Blinked fast. Bowed his head.

Gnaeus saw that too.

Something softened in the heir of Pompey Magnus. Something dangerous. Something that would matter later.

The oarsman rowed them back.

Rufus leapt from the boat before it touched shore, boots in one hand, longbow in the other. Water slid from his legs. Wind pushed his hair back. Girls at the woodpile stared openly now, flushed, breath shallow, hands frozen mid-task.

He didn't notice. Or refused to.

What he did notice was the field beyond the lake. The open ground. The space where men formed lines. The front of a legion.

His chest tightened, not with fear, but with want.

A centurion's staff.

A hundred lives behind him.

The right to hold a line until the earth shook.

That was the shape inside him. A hunger carved years ago under the Latinus roof. Not glory. Not praise. Duty. The oldest kind. The kind that ate sleep and left iron in the blood.

Gnaeus walked toward him. "Where'd you learn that?"

"Same place I learned to breathe," Rufus said.

Gnaeus studied him, really studied him.

Barefoot archer. Sun-burned shoulders. Bow strong as a horse's spine. Kind hand. Quiet mouth. Deadly focus. A boy who didn't realize how many eyes followed him.

In that moment, Gnaeus Pompey made a decision that would echo across seas.

He would need this boy.

Not as decoration. Not as friend.

As weapon.

As future.

By nightfall, in his tent, he unrolled parchment and sketched lines only he understood.

A cove.

A route.

A single ship.

A plan born quiet.

A danger born red-haired.

Far away, on the Caspian cliffs, a girl of smoke and prophecy would soon name him in a trance. Hatred and awe in the same breath.

But here, on this black lake, everything began with one arrow.

With a sixteen-year-old boy who moved like truth itself.

With a breeze that held still, as if waiting for the next shot.

The arrow waited.

Chapter 21
THE TEEN IDOL

She carved him from memory.

No sketch. No charcoal lines on wax. No model sitting for her.

Just the warm feel of his presence.

The bust stood ten inches tall. Marble cut smooth, cool as creek stone. Straight nose. High cheekbones. The faint scar under his right eye, carved as if her thumb had found it in darkness. The jaw locked tight, caught in that moment right before he spoke, or bit down.

Her father didn't approve. "You carve heroes," he said. "Not ghosts and soldiers."

But the piece sold. Fast.

Then another.

Then ten more.

Girls came first. Patrician daughters. Merchant's nieces. Teenagers clutching veils tight, voices trembling with curiosity. They kept the smaller busts hidden in bedrooms, tucked behind lamps, set on windowsills where the morning light touched his cheek.

But the buyers grew.

A soldier bought one before marching east to join Lucculus's scouts, said the lion-faced boy brought luck.

A baker's widow kept hers by the hearth.

Two matrons from the Palatine ordered matching ones, whispering he looked like Mars returned.

Even a senator's slave came hooded, coin clutched hard, refusing to meet her eyes.

Word moved fast through Rome.

The lion had a face now.

Rufus Latinus.

The red-haired boy from the Campus Martius. The one who never smiled unless he meant it. The one whose eyes carried storms.

She had seen him once. Maybe twice. Never spoke. But his presence stayed with her the way heat stays after a forge is shut.

So she carved.

And then the trouble began.

The Subura filled with cheap clay knockoffs, grinning faces, laurel crowns, silly heroic poses. One counterfeit even showed him lifting a sword overhead like some tavern drunk. She smashed that one herself.

They didn't understand the truth in him.

Worse, they sold the imitations everywhere, markets, alleys, even a stall near the incense shops. Some fakes bore her name scratched underneath.

One vendor bragged openly, "He posed in my workshop! Drank my wine!"

She spit in the dirt when she heard.

Then came the man in the fine robe.

Soft voice. Rings on every finger. Perfumed beard masking something sour.

"I represent a house with refined taste," he said. "We'd like a private commission."

She did not answer.

He slipped a purse onto the table. Heavy. Rich. Wrapped in black cord.

She picked it up. Weighed it. Then dropped it back.

"I don't carve whores," she said.

His smile never changed. "It's business, nothing more."

She turned away.

He left the purse behind anyway.

She tossed it into the gutter before dawn.

The next day, her real busts were smashed.

Her brother was followed home.

Two men lingered outside the shop long after dark.

Then a big man came.

He didn't knock.

He filled the doorway like a wall had stood up and walked in, broad shoulders, red hair damp with heat, blue eyes sharp as cut iron.

Rufus Latinus.

Her mother froze. The ladle dropped from her hand.

Her brother backed up into the shelves.

"Apologies for startling you," his voice deep and his Latin beautiful.

Rufus looked at the broken busts on the table. Looked at the cracked pedestal. Looked at the purse she'd nailed to a beam with a carpenter's spike.

He understood everything in a single breath.

He stepped forward.

"Who carved this?" he asked.

She came out from the back room, apron dusted white, a bit of marble stuck to her palm.

"I did."

He studied her. Quiet. Curious.

"You remember my face that clearly?"

"I remember things that matter."

He didn't smile.

He reached for a broken shard, just big enough to fill his fist. He lifted it, turned it once, feeling the weight, then set it back down with the care a man gives a living thing.

He turned to leave.

At the door, he paused.

"Next time someone copies it," he said without raising his voice, "tell them this..."

His eyes met hers, steady.

"I'm still alive."

Then he looked at the smashed stool. The purse on the beam. The fear in her mother's breathing.

"My family owns this block," he added. "You pay no rent for a year. The counterfeiters will be dealt with."

Rufus looked around again.

"You will receive compensation for this damage. You will not be harassed again. My family offers our deepest apologies."

He left.

No swagger.

No threat spoken.

Just finality.

Her family stayed silent long after.

That night, Rome whispered.

A dozen men, some said fewer, some more, moved through the alleys without torches. No shouting. No metal on stone. Just one crash of a lantern, a chicken screaming, then nothing.

In the morning, the stall by the tannery was abandoned.

No bodies.

Just blood in the dust.

The neighbors swept without speaking.

By noon, the Latinus family held the deed to the empty space.

By evening, the girl carved again.

Not a face this time.

A hand.

Large. Strong. Fingers curled, not in a fist, but in control. A promise of violence held back by choice. She placed it behind the counter. No one touched it.

The Subura learned fast.

You didn't copy the lion.

You didn't sell his face without permission.

You didn't threaten the girl who carved him.

Rome remembered.

Her father sat outside every night now, hammer across his knees, watching the street with a quiet pride.

Her busts sold faster than she could finish them. Not because they were perfect. Because they were true.

One piece remained unfinished, set deep in the workshop where no one saw it. Not because she lacked time.

Her hands couldn't complete it. Not yet.

Years later, her daughter would ask why.

"Who was that one for?" the child whispered.

She touched the rough jawline, the groove of the scar.

"Not for him," she said.

"Then who?"

"For the city," she answered. "So, it remembers what true Romans looked like."

She set a hand on the stone.

"When we still had them."

Chapter 22
THE LEGIONS FORGE

Campanian fields outside Capua - 64 B.C.

Heat rolled off the plain in thick waves. The dust tasted like chalk.

Rufus locked his scutum into the line, left edge tight, right edge braced, body angled for impact. Sweat burned down his ribs. His tunic clung to his back. Sun hammered the metal rim of his shield until it stung his knuckles.

"Testudo!" the decurion bellowed, voice rough as pumice.

The shell formed around him like instinct. Rufus moved first, and the others followed. Shields slammed. Leather groaned. A living wall rose.

Spears crashed against the top layer. The testudo shuddered.

Rufus didn't.

"Advance!"

He drove forward with the line, knees bent, feet digging into baked earth. Five steps. Halt. Five more. Halt. Each command struck through them like a drumbeat. The world smelled of forged iron and scorched grass.

"Break and kill!"

The formation exploded outward.

Rufus dropped into a low stance, body coiled. The straw man ahead of him looked almost human; burlap skin, crude shoulders, ugly face, a throat begging for steel.

He lunged.

Thrust. Retract. Thrust again. No wasted motion. The gladius punched deep enough to shake hay loose. He pivoted, drove another into the throat. The dummy sagged, slit open and spilling.

The decurion stalked over. One eye milk-white. Arms thick from two decades of war.

"Name."

"Gaius Latinus Rufus."

"Good thrust. Again."

Rufus reset. Faster this time. Three strikes in less than a breath, center mass, lower ribs, throat. All fatal. All Roman.

Around him boys gasped, tripped, cursed. Rufus didn't hear them. The blade moved because his muscles remembered what his mind didn't need to consider.

He wasn't fighting straw.

He was fighting the life he wanted.

The rank he needed.

A future where he stood with a vine staff in hand and the right to command men in battle. Every blow was a step toward that future. Every drop of sweat carried him closer.

By midmorning the recruits sagged in the heat. Shoulders caved. Faces burned.

Rufus remained upright.

"Hard boy," one recruit muttered, breathless.

Rufus ignored him. He had learned long ago that men watch strength even when they pretend not to. He felt their eyes now on the line of his back, the way he lifted the shield without strain, the unmoving set of his jaw.

Girls back home had watched like that too.

He hadn't understood it at first: the way they lingered, the way their gaze softened then flicked away too late. Now he recognized it the same way he recognized an incoming strike, the shift of breath, the silent pull.

But women watching him and soldiers following him were two different things.

He wanted the second.

He needed the second.

By the second week, the instructors whispered:

"Latinus blood."

"Oh, so he's the Latinus boy. I see it now."

"Fast hands."

"Watch that one."

"He'll lead before he shaves twice."

That night, the tent glowed with lantern light and the low murmur of tired boys.

Rufus sat bare-chested on his cot, sharpening the practice gladius with slow, even strokes. His shoulders glistened with a sheen of dried sweat. His hair, short at the sides, longer on top, hung forward over his brow.

Lucceius sniffed the air. "Is that... meat?"

"Real meat," Varro confirmed. "I smell pork. Good pork."

Marcus eyed the sizzling pan. "Where'd you steal that from?"

Rufus tossed a coin pouch onto the table. "I bought it."

Lucceius blinked. "With what?"

"Family silver."

A shrug.

"And olive oil. And figs. And wine that hasn't touched a rat."

The boys stared.

"Why feed us?" Varro asked.

"Because you bleed beside me," Rufus said. "And because I'm tired of eating gruel like a mule."

A beat of silence.

Then loud, grateful laughter.

Rufus didn't laugh with them. He simply passed the bread, the posture of a man who had already chosen them as his unit.

Lucceius lifted his cup. "Think we'll survive Asia?"

"Some of us," Rufus answered.

"Which ones?"

"The ones who stay awake," he said.

Then, after a beat:

"And the ones who don't break."

They looked at him as if he'd spoken prophecy.

He didn't. He simply knew.

Sleep claimed the tent one by one.

Rufus remained awake, listening for trouble, as he always did. He could feel the eyes of the boys even in their dreams, trust forming, weight shifting toward him.

He hadn't asked for it.

But he felt it.

And it warmed something buried deep, something he never admitted: the thrill of being followed. The quiet satisfaction of being seen as strong.

It also put a sharper edge on his ambition.

He wanted the centurion's position not for glory, but because he belonged on the front line. His blood demanded it. His father had earned it. His grandfathers had forged it.

He would carry it.

Even if he died young.

Word spread through camp before dawn.

"Optio."

"First century."

"First cohort."

"That's the Latinus boy."

Two thousand men stood in formation as the sun cracked the horizon. Frost still clung to the edges of the stone altar. A black bull snorted, its breath steaming in the morning cold.

Rufus stepped forward barefoot. His clean tunic brushed his knees. His jaw set hard enough to ache.

The priest placed the mallet in his hands.

Rufus swung once.

Skull. Bone. Collapse.

Blood spilled into the trench.

No flinch. No hesitation. A clean Roman kill.

The Optio's crested helmet was brought forward; red plumes, reinforced cheek guards, weight enough to matter.

Then the hastile, smooth polished wood topped with bronze. The symbol of authority. The right to keep order. The right to strike a soldier who failed.

Rufus accepted both.

The legion roared once.

Then silence fell, the kind that changes a man's life.

Of course, coin passed behind closed tent flaps.

Part of the system.

Not bribery. Not really.

Custom.

His father had sent the exact amount. Enough to show respect. Not enough to cheapen the achievement.

Rufus hated the practice.

But he understood it: in Rome, strength opened the door, silver kept it open. Not everyone came from a well-to-do family.

Under moonlight, Rufus trained alone behind the tents, two short curved knives flashing in silence. Latinus blades. Nine inches each. Twin devils balanced for killing.

Illegal in camp.

Sacred to his family.

His grandfather had taught him the footwork:

Step. Cut. Spin.

Throat. Kidney. Inner thigh.

Fast. Clean. Gone before the body hit the ground.

Rufus carried the blades everywhere. Even in sleep, one lay under his palm. Even the girls in his family learned the art. Even the bastards.

People called it a lost style.

It wasn't lost.

It was hidden, kept for the moment a Latinus needed it most.

By the end of training, every cohort whispered his name.

"Doesn't bleed."

"Fast as a wolf."

"Killed a man at thirteen."

"Moves like a shadow."

"Silent."

"Dangerous."

Rufus Latinus, seventeen years old.

Not yet a centurion.

But already feared.

And somewhere, in a distant temple above the Caspian Sea, a girl with fire in her blood would soon kneel, breath shaking, as a vision passed through her:

a red-haired Roman boy rising in dust and sun,

gladius in hand,

walking toward a future that would crash into hers.

Chapter 23
SMOKE THAT HUNTS

Temple at Valbena - Hyrcania, 64 B.C.

The temple breathed slow.

Dawn left no warmth on the stones. The walls sweated with trapped heat from yesterday's sun, but the air itself stayed cold, carrying the faint bite of crushed herbs and burnt resin.

Albina sat with her back to the pillar, hair loose, veil hanging at her throat. She held still; palms open on her knees. Her people moved around her in soft circles.

The witches ground roots into powder.

The dancers tightened anklets until the bells fell silent.

Two attendants swept invisible lines across the floor, tracing patterns older than Parthia.

No orders spoken.

No sound wasted.

Their war was not a loud one.

Zarmina stirred the brazier, dropping another thread of brittle yellow leaf into the coals. Smoke rose, low and heavy. Oily. Sweet. A scent that warped time inside the lungs.

Nisaya whispered, "The guards tire."

Albina didn't answer. She didn't need to.

They had watched the same thing.

Men at the gate blinking too slow.

Hands rubbing at the bridge of the nose.

A spear butt dropped and left lying.

A breath that came uneven, as if the body forgot its own timing.

The smoke never choked.

Never blinded.

It coaxed.

Red Ring knew. That was why he kept his distance. Why he paced outside the courtyard with restless steps, not crossing the threshold. The smoke nudged at him too, the way deep water nudges at a man who cannot swim.

Through the curtain, Albina listened.

Footsteps dragged.

Leather creaked.

A guard muttered something soft, then laughed at nothing. Another shushed him, but the hush came late, sloppy.

The temple swallowed every sound.

One of the dancers, Roksana, oldest, steady as carved stone, passed near Albina. The girl's chain caught the light, flickered. Roksana let it scrape the floor once. A whisper of metal.

Outside, a guard shifted toward it.

Zarmina breathed out slowly. "They bend."

Albina kept her gaze on the smoke. Thick. Slow. Almost alive in how it curled along the floor, touching ankles, whispering up calves like fingers.

"Not enough," Albina said.

"Yet," Nisaya murmured.

The youngest dancer, Zermeh, light as a reed, sat under the window with her knees pulled to her chest. Her amber eyes tracked the shadows by the gate. She didn't speak, but her breathing told the rest. Hope. Fear. Hunger for escape and revenge braided together.

Albina placed her fingertips to the stone beside her. The rock pulsed faintly, the echo of the Twelve carried in memory. The little statues were gone, safe, hidden, close, but the temple still felt their absence like a missing tooth.

"We hold," Albina whispered.

"We hold," the girls echoed, soft as dust.

Outside, a voice cursed. Another snapped back. Shields clattered. Someone stumbled.

The smoke slipped under the curtain and twined upward in a lazy coil.

Albina breathed it in and felt nothing. Her people were raised in its shade. The craft lived in their bones.

Red Ring's men weren't.

They felt everything.

A guard groaned.

Another cursed.

One called for water and slurred the word.

Red Ring barked an order, brief, sharp, angry, and the soldiers stilled. But the edge of discipline had dulled. Albina could hear it. The hesitation. The shaking breath someone tried to hide. The wrong rhythm in the boots.

Another leaf dropped into the coals. Smoke thickened. The air grew sticky, warm against the skin.

Albina lifted her chin.

"Soon," she said.

Zarmina nodded. "He frays."

Red Ring's voice shouted again outside, louder, cracking like something struck too many times.

He was unraveling.

Good.

Albina pressed her palms flat to the floor. The stone felt cool now, holding its breath for what came next.

No prophecy whispered names tonight. No visions flared behind her eyes. But the weight in her chest told her truth.

This was the middle of the war.

The quiet part.

The dangerous part.

The kind that killed a general before a blade ever touched him.

A sandal scraped outside. Then another. A stagger.

The smoke curled toward the doorway like a creature testing the air.

Albina stood. Her dancers rose with her. The witches straightened.

No weapons in hand.

No spells spoken aloud.

Only silence sharpened to a blade.

The curtain shifted. A shadow leaned too close, breathing the wrong way.

Albina said nothing. But her people tensed as one. Even the stones seemed to listen.

Outside, Red Ring snapped: "Away from that door!"

The soldier jerked back. His sandals scuffed the stone.

Albina exhaled slowly.

Nisaya moved to her side and whispered, "He will break soon."

Albina's voice stayed high, soft, deliberate. "Then we breathe and wait."

She closed her eyes for one moment, letting the smoke slide past her throat like a ribbon.

Red Ring paced.

The soldiers sagged.

The temple watched.

And in the quiet, Albina felt the goddess settle inside her again, deeper than breath, steadily growing.

The war had not ended.

It had only learned to whisper.

Chapter 24
PIRATE HUNT

R ome
    Rufus came home a different creature.

Two gold chevrons stitched to his tunic. Optio's staff in his hand. Helmet polished bright enough to catch the noon sun and throw it back across the Latinus block.

When he walked through the gates, the compound shifted.

Slaves straightened. Apprentices quit hammering. His brothers paused mid-argument. Even his father, hard, wide, stone-spined, gave one silent nod that meant more than any embrace.

Rufus had earned this, earned it with blood, grit, crushed bone, and the quiet refusal to ever fall.

He had two weeks before duty claimed him. Eastern Italy. Roads. Bridges. Survey lines. Good Roman work. Honorable. Steady. A slow path toward the legions waiting in Asia nine months from now.

Work that built Rome.

Work that would choke him.

Three days into leave, Gnaeus Pompey found him.

They met in a private marble room above the bathhouse. Steam curled under the door. The wine between them remained untouched.

Gnaeus didn't waste words.

"Come with me instead."

Rufus leaned back. "Where?"

"To the sea."

"For what?"

"To kill pirates."

Rufus said nothing, just watched his friend's face. Gnaeus's eyes held excitement sharpened to fear.

"They're moving treasure," Gnaeus said. "Sicily to the northern routes. Silver. Ivory. Jewels. My father's informants marked the ships. I have a fast hull."

"You have your father's permission?"

"I have my father's name."

A small smile. "And I need you."

Rufus waited.

"You don't miss," Gnaeus said, voice low. "And at sea... missing gets men drowned."

Silence stretched.

Rufus remembered his final test at Capua:

A war bow taller than his shoulder. A hundred-twenty-pound pull.

Five targets moving at different angles.

Wind shearing hard from the right.

Five shots.

Five kills.

No effort.

The instructors had stared at him like he was a thing carved from older stone.

He could stay. Train recruits. March east. Build roads. Wait for destiny to catch him.

Or...

He could choose the wind.

The hunt.

The kind of danger that sharpened a man into what he was meant to be.

That night he walked the yard barefoot, tunic loose, Optio staff tapping once in a while on the stone. The dirt felt cool under his soles. The air smelled of crushed grass and nighttime bread from the lower kitchens.

He thought of roads.

Then he thought of salt wind slamming into his face as he stood at the bow, legs braced, bowstring humming under his fingers.

Of pirates screaming when they realized the arrow that struck them came from the dark, not the gods.

He wasn't born to wait.

He wasn't born to build fucking roads.

At dawn, he stood across from Gnaeus, jaw set, eyes steady.

"I'll go."

Gnaeus exhaled like he'd been holding breath for days. "Good. You'll still join your legion, Legio X Classica. Still be Optio of the First. I'll see to it. I know the boss."

Rufus nodded once. Smiled.

He would fight in Asia soon enough.

But first he'd hunt dangerous men on shifting seas. Hardened marines would teach him how to kill from a rocking deck. He would carve his own legend before Rome even asked it of him.

He turned toward the gate.

Salt. Wind. Blood.

That was the path now.

And he walked toward it without looking back.

He didn't know his first true battle waited on the water.

He didn't know someone across the sea would feel the ripple of this decision.

He only knew the wind had changed.

And that it whispered a name he had never heard.

Chapter 25
MACCUS AND THE YEW

The Family Farm, A Few Miles from Rome

The villa slept under a thin blue pre-dawn. Breath-faint. Shadow-soft.

Rufus stood alone in the lower courtyard, bare arms folded, the longbow slung across his back like a living spine. The wood felt warm against him, even before sunrise. He didn't speak. Didn't shift. Just listened.

A single glow burned down the corridor near the animal stalls.

Ames was already working.

Rufus walked toward the flame. His steps whispered across the stone. The bow never creaked.

He slid into the fletcher's room. Heat swallowed him at once, woodsmoke, pitch, beeswax, boiled sinew. The air held a sweet metallic note, the smell of work that mattered. Rows of arrows sat along the long table, lined like soldiers awaiting review. One leaned slightly. Ames straightened it before Rufus reached him, hands fast and sure.

Ames didn't speak. He rarely did. His left ear split long ago, eyes pale as winter sky, hair tied back in a simple cord. He carved arrows with the patience of prayer.

Rufus set the bow on the stone bench, slowly, almost tender. The yew's pale belly caught the rising lamplight. Grain alive. Back dark as old earth. He brushed one thumb along the curve. Still strong. Still true.

"You used eagle feathers," Rufus said.

Ames nodded.

"They hold in the wind."

Ames bowed, palm to fist.

Rufus took one arrow from the new batch. Broadhead gleamed. Shaft straight. Balance perfect on two fingers. He breathed once. Felt the weight. The quiet promise inside it.

"How many?"

Ames pointed.

Dozens of racks. Hundreds of tubes. Thousands of arrows. Labeled with black, red, blue, green lines. Systems only Ames truly understood, though Rufus could read them at a glance by now.

"Good," Rufus said. "I need thirty black tips. Thirty barbs. And three hundred war arrows. Paint the tubes red."

Ames moved before Rufus finished the sentence. Quick. Precise. Like a blade obeying a hand.

Rufus unstrung the bow. Rolled the line through his fingers, checking each twist, each layer of wax. Then restrung it. Smooth. Clean. Measured. The stave bent like a living creature adjusting its spine.

The first sliver of sun touched the outer court.

Ames returned with two bundles wrapped in cloth. Set them on the bench. Bowed again.

"Go eat," Rufus said. "Then keep making more."

Ames slipped out soundless.

Rufus slung the bow and crossed the courtyard to the east fields. Past orchard. Past vineyard. Past the thin brook where the old buck crossed at dusk. Wind carried the night's last cool breath. His boots left no imprint.

He moved like he had been made for mornings like this.

He passed the shed of old tools. Remembered hauling stone with them as a boy. Remembered the hunts after. The hot baths. The music around the fire. The women's laughter, soft, unforced, warm. Nothing like the tight, hungry city girls in Rome.

The field opened. Oak fringe. Scrub brush. Broken shadows.

He slowed. Felt the shift in wind. Crouched low.

Nocked a black-tipped arrow. It clicked against the string, exact, no wobble. His fingers curled easy around the bow. His breath lined up with the earth beneath him.

The roe buck stepped into the clearing.

Rufus rose. Silent.

Forty paces.

He drew full. Back tight. Shoulders flat. The bow bent almost to breaking, yew singing its quiet note. He loosed.

The arrow didn't hiss.

It whispered.

The buck dropped before its knees gave out.

Rufus lowered the bow. Walked to the kill. No rush. The arrow still whole. Edge still true. He slid it free, wiped it, placed it in the red tube.

"Good arrow," he murmured.

He gutted the buck, then slung it over his shoulder. Blood warmed his back through the hide. He walked home without slowing.

The buck hung by its heels now, dripping into a pit lined with pine ash. A house girl fetched basins. Two guards waited for skin. Rufus stood with the bow across both palms.

Then a shape filled the side passage.

Maccus.

Broader in the shoulder than any man in Rome. Slower now with age, but still carrying the gravity of someone who once commanded fear. Pale gray eyes. Hair braided in the old island tribes' style. Face carved by war and smoke. Hands scarred by a lifetime of shaping death.

He didn't bow.

Rufus respected that.

Maccus held out his hand.

Rufus passed the bow.

Maccus turned it. Examined string. Grip. Curvature. Grain. He pressed a fingertip near the nock. He grunted.

Still sound.

He returned the bow.

"You'll need another by spring," he said. Voice cracked by years and old tongues. "Sap runs early."

Rufus nodded. "Use the southern stave. The one we hung last year."

Maccus didn't answer. He walked away.

The house girl handed Rufus a cloth and the cleaned arrow. He took it, smiled at the girl and said, "Gratitude."

Looked once at the buck. Then at the bow.

"I'll use this one against the pirates," he said.

Maccus paused at the doorway. "It is a war bow. It is ready."

This wasn't a Roman weapon.

It didn't shine.

It didn't roar.

It killed from silence. From shadow. At a distance where prayers couldn't reach.

Maccus's workshop was a stone womb of heat and smoke. The new yew stave hung from leather loops, halfway between ceiling and fire. Maccus walked beneath it. Let the tips brush his knuckles.

Still light. Still dry. Still listening.

Yew lied.

It pretended to bend, but only bent for men worthy enough. It cracked in the hands of fools. It waited to judge you.

He took the stave down. Set it on the shaping rack. Drew the bone scraper low along its belly. Shaved thin curls of pale grain. The wood rose to meet him like something waking.

"You want to twist," he muttered. "But I'll keep you true."

A footstep. He didn't turn. Ames.

Maccus held the stave high.

"Not this one," he said. "This is for the lion."

Ames nodded and vanished.

Maccus bent the stave again. Slow. Listening. Yew never sang. It whispered.

This one would whisper violence.

It would whisper death.

It would whisper Rufus's name long after Maccus was buried.

Rufus ducked into the string-maker's room.

Vitus sat hunched, rawhide turning between his palms. Eyes pale. Hands rough. No expression.

Rufus set the old string down.

"It's thinning."

Vitus lifted it to his mouth. Bit hard. It snapped like bone under pressure.

"Dead."

He tossed it aside and reached into a clay jar packed with ash. Drew a new string. Laid it on the table with both hands.

No explanation.

Rufus nodded. "Good."

Vitus grunted. "Better."

"I'll need several more."

"Yes, Dominus."

Rufus turned to go.

He paused.

"Have you eaten?"

Vitus shrugged. "I eat when the string sleeps."

He was already turning back to his work.

Outside, the sun pushed over the villa roofline. The bow across Rufus's shoulder caught the light, bright along the grain, dark along the back. A weapon waiting for sea wind and blood.

Rufus ran one finger along its length. The wood thrummed once beneath his touch.

Alive.

Ready.

So was he.

Chapter 26
THE MARINES OF OSTIA

Ostia

Ostia smelled of fish guts and warm brine when the tide pulled low. Tar stung the air. Salt crusted the ropes. Gulls screamed overhead like lost spirits. Ships groaned against their moorings, heavy hulls shifting as if restless for sea.

Rufus trained on an old stone dock hidden between warehouses, bare arms tight with work, a ribbon of blood drying on his forearm. The bow lay near his feet. The knives glinted beside it. He faced a circle of men who looked carved out of war.

Pompey's marines. Veterans from the pirate hunts. Scar on scar, sun-baked skin, bodies built for water and swords. One had a single eye. One had teeth filed to points. Another moved like smoke, fast, silent, nowhere at once.

They taught him things no drill field in Rome ever whispered.

How to keep balance when a deck pitched underfoot.

How to strike upward from close quarters without exposing the ribs.

How to kill a man climbing a boarding rope so he never hit the water.

Where to aim when the hull shuddered and the world tilted.

Rufus took every blow they delivered. Returned each twice as hard. He never smiled at a hit or winced at a loss. Never asked for rest. Never broke rank. Never wavered.

The marines noticed.

By the third day they stopped laughing when they called him Umbra Optionis... the Optio's Shadow. By the fifth, the name carried weight.

They trained him brutally.

Wet leather chafed his shoulders. His sandals soaked in brine. Salt stiffened the greaves at his shins. They slammed him in the ribs with wooden clubs. He didn't flinch. They knocked him overboard; he surfaced already moving, knife held in reverse grip, eyes hard, water running off him in sheets.

At night, he practiced alone behind the barracks, torchlight throwing his shadow high across the wall. The twin blades flashed in arcs, nine inches each, thin, curved, fast. Latinus knives. Family blades. Throat, groin, kidney, spine. Step. Pivot. Kill. Again.

Some of the marines tried to track the pattern. None could. He moved too fast.

The bow came next.

He brought the war bow, Maccus's bow, seven feet of yew trained under smoke and winter. Most marines had trouble pulling sixty pounds. Rufus drew double that before his voice changed. Now he pulled more.

When he trained, the sea wind bent the fletching sideways, and still he hit every mark. A swinging bucket at sixty paces on the first shot. A melon tossed from a balcony on the second. Split it clean.

"Not a soldier," a marine muttered. "A gods-damned falcon."

They began planning around him.

Not with him.

Around him.

The black-bearded veteran, the one missing half a hand, drew diagrams in the sand.

"We board after he fires," he said. "Three shots. Three kills. Captain, first mate, signal horn. Pirates lose their head, arm, and eyes. They fall apart."

A younger marine nodded. "Take the voice, the command, and the warning. The rest panic."

Rufus listened from behind them, silent. He'd already marked the weak side of the deck. The loose plank near midship. The drag in the port oar. He'd already spotted the line of escape and the first kill zone.

When they told him where to shoot, he didn't argue.

He simply hit the mark.

Above the docks, in a rented stone room, Gnaeus Pompey stood beside the ship's captain, watching Rufus train through a narrow window.

The captain had hands like old rope and eyes burned by sun. "That boy's a wolf," he said. "You sure he's tame?"

Gnaeus didn't look away from Rufus.

"He's not tame. He's loyal."

"Loyal's enough," the captain muttered. "Long as he kills clean."

They poured wine. Neither drank.

Below them, the sea breathed slow against the pylons. Nets dripped. Chains clanked. The sky shifted to copper as evening crept in.

And on the dock, Rufus sharpened his knives in the dying light, blade whispering against stone, movements precise, patient, silent, as if waiting for someone to deserve them.

Somewhere beyond the horizon, a ship full of silver turned north and its crew had no idea death was already training for them."

Chapter 27
BLOOD ON THE WATER

Tyrrhenian waters

The ship cut the Tyrrhenian Sea like a sharp knife.

Black hull low. Fast. Sinister.

Wind hard from the west. Sails snapping so loud they sounded like bones cracking.

Two days out from Ostia, the sky rolled gray above them.

Gnaeus Pompey stood near the stern, wrapped in a blue cloak.

Rufus stood at the bow, helmet off, eyes forward.

Salt stung his lips. Wind pushed his hair back. Something tugged low in his chest, faint and strange, like a hand he couldn't see closing around a thread he didn't know he carried.

He ignored it.

They spotted the first pirate ship at sunrise, exactly where the informant said it would drift.

Larger. Slower. Heavy with cargo.

The lookout shouted down.

Gnaeus raised a hand.

"Run them down."

The marines erupted into motion.

Oars dug. Sails snapped. The Roman hull lunged toward its prey.

Rufus strapped on the armor Gnaeus had made for him; short greaves, leather breastplate, helmet crested deep-water blue. He tightened the straps, checked both blades, javelin, shield, and his bow.

The pirate ship turned.

Too slow.

Rufus lifted his war bow.

A long breath. Full draw.

His arrow punched through the air and dropped a pirate mid-shout. The man fell backward without even touching the rail.

Two more shots followed.

Two more bodies folded.

The pirates hesitated, fear catching their throats.

But the hesitation didn't last.

These weren't the soft raiders of stories. They were older, leaner, salt-worn, desperate. They fought like men who had already lost everything.

Hull slammed hull.

Iron teeth of Roman grapples clamped onto pirate wood.

Rufus was the first to leap.

He cleared the rail and landed hard, shield absorbing the impact.

A pirate charged him immediately. Rufus stepped into the blow, slid his blade under the ribs, and ripped up. The body sagged, nearly dragging his sword down with it.

A lesson burned through him:

In fast. Out faster.

Another pirate came.

Rufus caught the wrist, twisted, slammed the man's head into the mast. The skull cracked like pottery.

"Stay with the Optio!" someone shouted.

The deck pitched under their feet.

Sea spray mixed with blood.

Tar. Smoke. Sweat. Heat.

Chaos. Screams.

But Romans turned chaos into a fight on the ground. Even on a ship.

A tattooed pirate leader lunged at Rufus, curved sword raised.

They circled once.

Twice.

Rufus didn't wait for three.

He surged forward and smashed his shield into the man's chest. Dropped low. Drove the shield's rim up into the pirate's jaw.

The man dropped. Rufus kicked the sword overboard.

On to the next.

He moved like he'd trained for this his whole life, because he had.

And somewhere far away, across mountains and desert, Albina's breath caught in the middle of a dance movement. She tasted salt on her tongue. A strange pressure curled under her ribs. A whisper of warning or recognition, she didn't know which.

The fight ended fast.

Blood pooled. Smoke drifted. The sea swallowed the last shouts.

Marines dragged cargo from the hold, silver, ivory, spices, silks. And two chained girls, barely conscious.

Gnaeus said nothing.

He looked at Rufus.

Rufus leaned on his shield, breathing slow, eyes unreadable.

Blood speckled his cheek. His beautiful blue-and-silver armor gleamed wet under the breaking sun.

The armor was naval-forged, silver hammered for movement, blue enamel deep as stormwater, sea-beasts etched along the plates. Crafted by Pompey the Greats best armourers. When Rufus walked, the blue shifted like waves.

Rufus didn't notice any of it.

He didn't smile.

Didn't boast.

Didn't clean the blood.

He looked only at the horizon, jaw tight, pulse too loud in his ears for reasons he couldn't name.

A wind tightened.

Rufus stiffened, not from danger, but from something else.

Something pulling at him across the sea.

He touched his chest once.

One heartbeat, too strong.

Far away, Albina staggered.

A flash of blue armor hit her mind like lightning.

A man at the bow of a ship, turning toward her.

Salt wind.

A voice she didn't know yet.

A fate she wanted no part of.

Her dancers grabbed her arms.

She tore free.

The Flame whispered:

He moves toward you, child. Even now. Even from the sea.

Albina's pulse raced.

Her breath shortened.

"No," she whispered.

"Not him. Not again."

But Rufus, miles away, still staring at the horizon, felt the pull tighten.

A connection he didn't understand.

A direction he didn't choose.

A truth he couldn't shake:

Someone out there waited for him.

And he would find her.

Even if it ruined them both.

Chapter 28
AFTER THE KILL

Tyrrhenian waters

Tyrrhenian Waters

The sun sank lower.

The pirate ship burned slow behind them, black smoke trailing across the sea like a torn banner.

Rufus sat on a coil of rope, cleaning his knife with an oil-soaked rag. He worked in steady strokes. No hurry. No wasted motion.

Below deck, the two freed girls slept wrapped in wool cloaks. One with broken fingers. The other silent, staring into nothing. The marines moved around them with quiet purpose. No laughter. No boasting. Just work.

The haul was enormous. Enough silver and carved ivory to make every man aboard rich. Richer than any fresh soldier had a right to be.

The pirate leader had refused to die on deck. Hard man. Heavy-boned, tattooed, teeth cracked from the fight. He'd clung to life with one good eye and a mouth full of curses.

Rufus found him near the mast, trembling, breath caught in a wet rattle. He dragged him by the matted hair to the rail. Salt wind hit both their faces.

The pirate looked up with his one eye, wide and shining, blood filling his teeth.

Rufus leaned in.

Smiled.

"You should die by the hands of Neptune in the deep."

Then threw him overboard.

The splash echoed. The man thrashed weakly in the red water. Sharks circled. The sea swallowed the noise.

Gnaeus Pompey stood at the stern, cloak snapping in the breeze. Watching the horizon. Thinking, always thinking.

He didn't speak at first.

Rufus waited.

"You were made for this," Gnaeus said finally.

Rufus kept his gaze on the water. The knife dangled loose in his hand.

"They never touched you."

"They weren't ready," Rufus said. "They had no chance. Your choice of ship, your crew...it was perfect. And my bow didn't hurt."

Gnaeus snorted. "Perfect? No. But you," He shook his head. "I've seen men fight. Good men. Veterans. But I've never seen anyone move like you. You didn't hesitate. You didn't waste a step. You cut through them like you'd trained for this since birth."

Rufus didn't smile.

He didn't deny it.

He simply wiped the blade, slow and sure.

"We'll hunt more," Gnaeus said. "Three ships. Four. Maybe more."

Rufus stood, the armor flashing sea-blue and silver. The blood on it had dried to dark rust. He sheathed the knife.

"I'll sharpen the blades."

Gnaeus nodded, satisfied.

The crew worked in silence. Ropes creaked. The hull breathed. The men moved like a pack, scarred, confident, hungry.

They had tasted victory.

They would hunt again.

They had become wolves.

And wolves hunted.

Far away in the east, in a cracked stone temple lit by fire and smoke,

Albina jerked upright.

Not a vision.

Not a trance.

A scent.

Leather.

Olive oil.

Salt wind.

Him.

Her breath caught.

Her pulse stuttered.

The goddess inside her stirred like waking flame.

Rufus was still alive.

Still killing.

Still moving toward her.

She whispered, "Stay away from me."

But the smoke curled soft against her cheek, warm musk, feminine sweat, the scent he would know, the scent tied to her, rising as if answering him across the sea.

Two scents crossing miles of water and land.

Two fates tightening.

Albina closed her eyes, trembling.

Because somewhere on the Tyrrhenian waves, a Roman boy wiped blood from his blade, and felt something answer him back.

A breath that wasn't wind.

A memory he'd never lived.

A girl who smelled of warm musk and sacred sweat.

And he could not shake it.

The sea rolled.

The ship cut forward.

And the distance between them thinned by the heartbeat.

Chapter 29
FORTUNA

They hunted five more ships.

Some went down fighting. Some tried to flee.

None escaped.

Rufus boarded first every time. Fast. Clean. Brutal.

The marines followed his rhythm without thinking.

Gnaeus gave the orders, but Rufus set the kill-tempo.

They kept the treasure quiet.

Offshore. Night loading. Seals. Silence.

Each man sent his share to a different place.

Rufus sent his to Ostia.

He kept his name off every list. Left no trace.

His share alone:

over 3,000 silver talents, nearly 255 gold talents, crates of jewels and carved ivory. Silk, artwork, spices, relics older than empires.

Seventy-one jewelry sets, each housed in carved rare wooden boxes lined in silk... pieces so ancient the craftsmen were dust and legend.

All his.

No one spoke about what they hauled.

Not one word left that ship.

When he returned to Ostia after the last hunt, he moved carefully, and fast.

He bought a massive warehouse near the river mouth.

Concrete and stone strong room. Steel door. No windows.

He commissioned a beautiful house near the water, with hot baths, mosaic floors, carved fountains, painted ceilings, gardens.

His genius brother, Lucius designed every detail. His family company built it.

Shore wind always in the courtyard.

Office building. Apartment block.

Four more apartment buildings in Rome, built by his family's old crews.

Grain ships... five of them.

Two merchant ships for luxury trade.

Fifteen fast mail carriers, each with a shallow draft and narrow hull for speed.

One held idle at all times for Caesar.

Then he built his pride:

the yacht.

A masterpiece of skill and vanity.

Sleek. Narrow. Long.

Designed by his crippled genius brother, Lucius.

The fastest ship on the sea.

The master cabin paneled in oak and cedar. Ivory trim. Heated water from onboard cisterns.

A carved marble bed. Silk bedding.

Storeroom lined with gold and steel.

Crewed by his own blood: half-brothers, cousins, sons of loyal slaves.

When Rufus first saw it, he stopped on the dock and said nothing.

The hull shone black under tar, trimmed in bronze, sharp as a gladius.

The sail hung deep blue with a silver border, lion mid-leap stitched in thread that caught just enough light.

The prow curved low, wound with etched sea-beasts.

Even the oars gleamed.

No name.

No banner.

Just shape.

Fast. Silent.

Built to move through water like death.

Lucius had delivered.

No Roman under thirty had ever owned a vessel like this.

Not even Crassus.

He kissed his brother, and Lucius tried to wiggle away. Rufus laughed.

And even after all of this, Rufus still held enough silver and gold to match or surpass most senators.

Only the ship's original crew knew the truth.

And they were too busy counting their own fortunes.

Nine months passed.

The pirates died.

The treasure settled into vaults and walls and ships and quiet accounts.

The legion waited.

He and Gnaeus took their time sailing east on Rufus's yacht.

They hugged the coasts, Italy, Sicily, Illyricum, Greece, Anatolia.

They stopped every night.

Some nights burned bright.

Some ended in bruises.

Outside Naples, they stayed at a villa.

Gnaeus charmed the host's daughter.

Rufus beat the household champion in a bare-knuckle fight and left a tooth on the marble floor.

In Corinth, they bathed in stolen perfume, drank with senators' sons, slept aboard the yacht with gold coins under their pillows.

Once, they chased a pirate galley into rocks only to watch it break apart.

Rufus stood on the bow, silent.

Gnaeus shouted curses in Greek until his voice broke.

"Do you ever think of dying?" Gnaeus asked once under the stars.

Rufus didn't answer.

"Me neither."

Gnaeus poured more wine.

By the time they reached Antioch, their bond was sealed, tight as blood, sharper than oath.

They shook hands at the gate.

Rufus didn't speak.

He rarely did.

Gnaeus grinned.

"Try not to kill everyone before I get there."

Then he was gone.

Rufus reported to the legion at dawn.

The bribes had arrived ahead of him.

Optio of the First Century, First Cohort.

His name whispered again.

And the sharpening began.

That night, as Rufus lay on the yacht's wooden bunk, the sea rocking him like a slow breath, a scent he didn't know pulled at him from nowhere, musk and warm feminine sweat, threaded with smoke.

He sat up.

It wasn't on the ship.

Wasn't real.

But it hit him like a memory.

Somewhere, far across land and water, a girl dreamed of leather and olive oil.

Somewhere, a vision linked them for a heartbeat.

Rufus touched the hilt of his gladius, uneasy.

The scent faded.

But not completely.

And he could not sleep.

Chapter 30
THE BROTHERS OF ANTIOCH

Antioch

Antioch smelled of heat, river mud, and old spice.

Matineus reached it at dawn.

His ship slid into Seleucia Pieria under a bruised sky, gulls screaming over the mast. Smoke rolled off the docks. Fish rotted in heaps. Slaves hauled crates under the lash. Sailors fought. Dogs scattered. The air tasted of brine and charcoal.

He rented a horse without a word.

He rode hard through the port district, past shouting crews and grain wagons, past a row of tents where merchants sold stolen armor and half-dead goats. A priest waved incense in his face. A thief tried his saddlebag. Matineus didn't slow.

Antioch opened before him, wide and loud, old as dust.

Stone streets cut through the city like blades. Statues glared from every corner. Vendors pushed figs, dates, bread warm from the oven. Perfume mixed with sewage. Boys wrestled in the mud. A drunk sang in a foreign tongue. A dead man floated face down in a drainage ditch and no one looked twice.

Matineus crossed the river on a Roman bridge, high arches throwing long shadows across the water. Beyond it waited the camps.

Legion tents stretched in rigid lines. Towers rose. Ditches ran deep. Dust blew hard over the drill yards. The clang of wood swords echoed like distant smith-hammers.

He dismounted at the gate.

"Rufus Latinus," he said.

No hesitation.

"Training field. East side."

He walked in.

Rufus stood bare-chested in the yard, skin bronze from months at sea, watching a dozen legionaries run sword drills. Sweat streaked the dirt. Blades flashed dull in the sun.

When Rufus saw him, he smiled. A rare thing. Gone in a heartbeat.

Matineus crossed the yard and handed him the sealed scroll.

"From Caesar."

Rufus broke the wax. Read. His jaw tightened.

"A Sibyl? What is a Sibyl?"

Matineus shrugged. "I have no idea. Just help me get east."

They never talked much. They didn't need to. Blood replaced words.

Rufus stepped forward and gripped his brother's arm.

"You came far."

"I'll go farther."

"How is Lucius?"

"Well, he sends his love."

Rufus nodded once. "You'll need coin, maps, ten good blades, and the best horses in camp. I'll get all of it."

By morning the crates were ready, food, weapons, scrolls, travel maps, sealed gold, saddle bags, ropes, tents, medicines. Three horses. Four mules. A guard detachment waiting with spears grounded.

Rufus leased a local ship for the crossing. Fast. Clean record. No pirate scars. He sent Caesar's courier vessel back with thanks and a gift.

Everything moved quiet. Efficient. Rufus did not wait.

At the dock, the brothers stood side by side while the last packs went aboard. The wind hit sharp off the sea. The ropes creaked. Men called to each other in Greek and Latin.

No dramatic farewell. No long speech.

Just blood between them.

Rufus put a hand on Matineus's shoulder. His voice dropped low.

"I'm proud of you. But this? This is dangerous even for you and your ten."

Matineus met his eyes. Calm. Unshaken. "I know."

A breeze rose off the water, warm, dry, out of the east.

Matineus inhaled without thinking.

A strange scent threaded the salt air.

Not city rot.

Not tar.

Something else.

Smoke.

Musk.

Sweat sweet as crushed petals.

Desert heat wrapped in a woman's skin.

The kind of scent no woman in Antioch wore.

It hit him once, clean and sharp, like a memory he didn't own.

He blinked. Turned. No one stood near him.

The breeze vanished.

Rufus didn't notice a thing.

Matineus forced his breath steady, but the scent clung in his mind, soft, wild, impossible.

Something east waited for him.

Someone.

A strange pulse hit him then, something cold, a weight behind the ribs. As if the road east waited for him with open jaws. As if someone out there was calling him forward.

He didn't speak it.

The ship pushed away from the dock. Sails caught wind. Water foamed along the hull. The sun climbed behind them, burning gold.

Rufus watched until the vessel shrank to a dark shape on the horizon.

Then he turned.

Back to drills.

Back to war.

Back to sharpening.

Chapter 31
SMOKE

The temple on the Caspian Sea

The smoke never rested.

Zarmina fed the coals at dawn. Nisaya at dusk. Bitter roots. Resin that burned sweet. Crushed leaves that carried the smell of old earth and burial pits.

No flame. Only smoke.

It slipped through every crack. Curling under the door. Sliding into lungs.

The guards joked at first. Laughed. Waved it away.

By the third week, none remembered why they laughed.

Shifts blurred. Orders thinned.

One man leaned his spear against the wall and walked off. Never knew he'd laid it down.

Another forgot the word for helmet.

A third forgot his own name until someone slapped him.

Red Ring fared worse.

His skull felt stuffed with wool. His thoughts snapped mid-stride like frayed rope. He barked a question, paused, forgot the question, struck the wrong soldier for answering it.

He walked the ridge at dusk and couldn't recall climbing it.

Inside the temple, the women moved with quiet precision. Like clock gears hidden behind carved stone.

Albina drank goat milk. Ate dates. Slept upright against the warm pillar when her ribs allowed it.

The dancers marked passing hours with soft bells.

Zarmina tracked the sun's slow creep across the floor.

Nisaya counted loyal stars through the roof gaps.

Waiting: their sharpest weapon.

Three months since the first rider vanished.

The second returned with his throat gashed open.

The third never reached the border.

The fourth and fifth dissolved into rumor.

Red Ring wrote messages he no longer understood.

Sealed them. Sent them. Forgot he'd sent them.

His camp sagged under the weight of forgetting.

The older soldiers drank before noon.

The younger ones pressed their faces to the curtain, staring like boys denied a festival. When Albina's dancers fed the garrison bread, one soldier came back with scratches down his spine and a grin stitched across his mouth.

The grin died after Red Ring's whip crossed it.

Still, the edge kept fraying.

Albina hadn't spoken one word to him. Not a single breath spared for the man who butchered her people.

But each time Red Ring turned toward the temple, she sat there. Straight-backed. Still. Silk pooled around her like spilled blood. Golden eyes half-lowered, heavy with judgment.

Her silence carved deeper wounds than curses.

It told him she had already measured him.

It told him she knew the shape of his end.

Her braid hid Zarakar, the black-iron blade forged from a fallen star. The blade that once slept on the altar of the First Temple. She had trained with it since childhood, wrists strengthened on stone, shoulders hardened on desert wind.

Red Ring didn't know. But when her gaze settled on him, his teeth ached. As if the blade pressed under his ribs from thirty paces away.

At night he dreamed of her.

Not as a girl.

Not as a woman.

As a presence.

A weight pressed against his chest. A shadow kneeling on his ribs. Smoke curling under his eyelids.

His men whispered the temple was cursed.

They swore the stone breathed.

They heard bells inside walls where no hand moved.

They begged to move camp before the roots of the mountain swallowed them whole.

He refused.

But he no longer slept.

Not truly.

He paced the ridge. Sword in hand. Breath sharp.

Eyes raw.

And every night, every single night, he watched the smoke roll down the temple steps.

Not drifting.

Not wandering.

Crawling.

Like fingers tightening around his throat.

And that night, when the smoke thickened and the guards shuffled like sleepers, Albina's breath hitched.

A new scent slipped through the trance.

Not Rufus's leather and olive oil.

Another man. Same blood. Same fire.

But sharpened with salt and cold steel.

Matineus.

He sailed east. Fast.

And the sea carried his scent through every god in the wind.

Albina opened her eyes.

"He comes," she whispered. "The brother with the shadowed heart."

Red Ring didn't hear her.

But the smoke did.

And it stirred like something waking.

Chapter 32
SMOKE ROAD

Northern Parthian Territories

The smoke followed them.

Three months of it. Three months of breath turned thick. Three months of guards forgetting their own names.

Red Ring rubbed his temples raw. One morning he snapped.

"Pack everything," he told his officers. "We're leaving."

No permission. No orders. No waiting for the King of Kings.

He would march east, fifty miles, to an old stronghold. Dry. Defensible. Closer to power.

Anything to get away from the walls that whispered.

He stepped into the temple for the first time in weeks.

Boots crushed herbs and ash. The smell clung to him, sweet rot, old blood, charred resin. It dragged memory backward and sideways, never forward.

Albina stood with her witches.

He looked her over once. "I'm done with this place," he said. "No more priestess games. You'll march as prisoners. By the time we reach the King of Kings, you'll know your place."

Albina blinked once, slow.

He left before the room could breathe.

At dawn, they pulled out.

The women walked. No cart. No litter. Bags on shoulders. Hands free but watched by twenty men.

Even the smallest dancer kept pace. Anklets chimed soft over dust.

They left nothing behind.

Except flame.

Red Ring ordered the temple burned.

He laughed that the King of Kings would build a new one, Parthian, proud, proper.

Albina whispered she would find a way to prevent that.

By midday, the roof collapsed.

By nightfall, only smoke. Cracked stone. Black ruin.

Nothing left but ghosts and grit.

They didn't make five miles.

They didn't make three.

The carts broke first. A wheel splintered. An axle snapped. A mule kicked a guard in the thigh.

The witches moved everywhere, quiet, quick, unnoticed.

The apprentices paused mid-step to dance, young bodies swaying like desert reeds. Guards stopped to stare.

One of the older girls feigned a twisted ankle. Two guards rushed to "help."

Each mile softened discipline.

Albina watched all of it. Straight-backed. Silent.

Her braid hung heavy. Zarakar, the sacred black blade, waited inside it.

No man saw it. But the road felt it.

And the road answered.

Red Ring cursed the carts. The heat. The flies. The delays.

But the movement soothed him. Briefly. Almost.

Except for the weight.

A pressure in the wind. In the dust. A sense of something closing the distance.

Something with purpose.

Something that smelled like cold steel and wild earth.

Albina felt it too. She glanced east, into the rising heat shimmer. A faint scent brushed her, iron, cedar, road dust, horses, a man who lived in shadows.

Matineus.

Not the scent of Rufus, leather, oil, sun-warmed bronze.

This one moved darker. Quieter. Sharper.

One was the man fated to kill her.

One would break himself trying to save her.

She felt them both gathering toward her, two threads tightening.

The goddess stirred inside her ribs.

Soon.

Red Ring swore under his breath.

Why did he still smell smoke?

The temple lay miles behind them.

Stone, ash, ruin.

But the smoke rolled down the road anyway, slipping low through dust, curling around their ankles like a slow, patient hand.

Gripping.

Clinging.

Pulling tight.

And Red Ring, who feared nothing, suddenly felt hunted.

Chapter 33
SIBYLS SMILE

Northern Parthian Territories

The march crawled.

Mud gripped wheels. Horses balked. Guards swore at the road, the carts, each other.

Albina walked near the front. Dust dulled her blue dress. Her braid, tight, heavy, hiding Zarakar's iron weight, swung against her spine. She showed nothing. No limp. No slack. No fear. Her calves burned, but her stride never wavered.

The dancers followed her cadence. The witches shadowed her step for step.

The smoke worked.

Hidden herbs. Wrapped roots. Twisted leaves tucked deep in satchels. Zarmina fed slow-burning coils at each halt. Nisaya placed smoldering spirals near the guard tents as dusk fell.

By night, the haze drifted through canvas seams and nostrils.

Men sighed.

Men laughed at nothing.

Men slept too hard, woke too slow.

One boy murmured a dancer's ankle-bell rhythm in his sleep, smiling like a child.

Red Ring shouted more each day. His voice cracked. His grip on the world thinned.

He forgot orders mid-sentence. He swung at shadows. He snapped at men who hadn't spoken.

A salute came late. A spear lifted wrong. A command misheard.

Control slipped from him, thread, thread, thread.

Twice he woke clawing for his sword and found it unsheathed beside him, blade cold, as if someone had placed it there while he slept.

He paced more. Slept less. Sweat salted his armor. Smoke clung to him like judgment.

Albina watched every fracture.

Measured every weakness.

Counted every small victory.

She began to savor this war made of silence and breath, the slow decline of a man who thought he owned her fate.

Her smile came easy now.

Slow.

Soft.

Deliberate.

The Sibyl's smile.

Not joy.

Not mercy.

A warning.

On the fifth day, the column halted.

Zarmina stopped mid-step. The tall witch tilted her chin toward the ridge. Eyes narrowed. Breath held.

Albina turned, gold eyes sharpening like a blade drawn clean.

Zarmina leaned close. Voice thin as smoke in their native tongue.

"A man. Not Parthian. Roman. He watched. Wanted me to notice."

Albina's heart stilled for one beat.

Then another.

Rufus's scent still haunted her, leather, oil, heat.

But this was different.

Drier. Sharper. A trace of desert wind and iron.

The scent of the other one.

The brother-shadow.

Matineus.

Her rescuer. The one her visions had whispered.

The one who walked the line between fate and defiance.

She exhaled once.

And smiled.

Not small.

Not hidden.

A long, certain smile that sent a shiver down every guard's spine without them knowing why.

Wind tugged her braid. Inside it, Zarakar, the black meteor-iron blade, rested against her neck. Warm. Listening.

Ahead, the trees whispered.

Behind her, smoke curled like a hand closing around Red Ring's throat.

Rescue had come.

The world didn't know it yet.

But the Sibyl did.

Chapter 34
THE DAWN

Days crawled like wounded things.

Red Ring's camp sagged further each morning, laughter where discipline should live, patrols cut short, blades left dull in scabbards.

The smoke kept working.

Zarmina fed it at dawn.

Nisaya kept it low at night.

Thin gray threads floated through bedrolls and armor, curled into lungs, softened the men from the inside out. They breathed it without thought. They forgot the day before the day after.

The women moved quiet, always visible, never defiant, yet their eyes tracked everything: loose straps, late salutes, drifting minds, sleeping on watch.

Their war was silence, patience, breath.

Then the sightings began.

First one: a flicker on the ridge.

Then two. Then five. Always watching. Always gone before a guard blinked.

The witches saw them.

The guards never did.

One morning, Albina saw her.

Across a ravine, the attendant she had sent running through fire and smoke on the night the temple fell.

Alive.

Arms raised. Hands trembling underweight.

Cradled against her chest: a stone figure, gray and round, polished smooth by centuries of touch. Belly full, breasts curved, face worn faceless by prayer.

Albina stopped breathing.

The girl lifted the figure high. Sun caught the stone, carved its shadow across the ravine like a god marking its claim.

Albina's throat tightened.

Then came something hotter, victory, clean and pure.

One of the Twelve lived.

If one survived, all had.

They never moved alone. Never separated. Twelve mothers. Twelve watchers. Twelve burdens. Twelve warnings.

Albina closed her eyes. The smile rose before she meant it to.

Not relief. Not hope.

The old joy, shrine-born, blood-deep.

The Twelve still answered.

The world had not broken.

Order held.

By afternoon, a scout failed to return.

The next day, another.

On the third, they found one before dusk.

Hanging upside down from a tamarisk tree.

Belly split.

Intestines dangling like festival garlands.

Eyes glassed.

Mouth stuffed with his own fingers.

Face pulled into a grin that didn't belong to the living.

Red Ring stood beneath the body a long time.

Silent.

Jaw clenched.

No orders. No rage.

That night, he didn't eat.

The men whispered like boys in the dark.

At sundown they stopped.

Fires lit.

The dancers sat in a ring, weaving each other's hair. Bronze combs flashed in the glow. Anklets chimed soft.

The witches brewed their tea, no man dared touch it.

Then a figure stepped from the trees.

Not fast. Not loud.

A shadow returning to firelight.

Roman. Bare feet. A pale scar across his brow. Eyes steady.

Matineus.

He walked straight to Nisaya and placed a leather pack in her hands.

She opened it.

Six blades. Curved. Balanced. Sharp as breath in winter.

He spoke rough Parthian.

"Prepare for dawn."

Then he vanished back into the dark, swallowed by trees.

Nisaya didn't flinch. Zarmina didn't breathe.

Albina felt her heartbeat change... two beats fast, one slow, like the goddess tapping bone.

Albina pressed the pack to her chest.

Iron weight. Iron promise.

She turned to her six guards.

No speech. No chanting. Just a single nod.

They rose together, silent, hungry for the fight they had been denied.

The dawn would not come soft.

It would come knife-first.

And when the sun rose, the world would know:

The Sibyl had not surrendered.

She had only waited.

Chapter 35
SMOKE AND STEEL

Dawn came with smoke.

Not the warm curl of a cookfire, this smoke carried weight.

Bitter, gray, heavy, clinging.

It soaked the canvas. Coated skin.

Hung low and wrong.

Tents sweated. Embers hissed under damp ash. No birds. No morning chatter.

Only silence pressing at the flaps like a hand waiting to close.

Red Ring woke with that pressure in his lungs.

He should have heard men, boots, orders, the scrape of steel. Instead he heard nothing, and the quiet carried teeth.

Then steel whispered.

A throat opened somewhere close, a soft, startled gasp cut short.

A blanket shifted.

A body thudded once.

By the time the camp understood it was under attack, shadows already moved through it, fast, quiet, certain.

Rufus's kin.

The eunuch guards stepped out of smoke like men born from it.

Short Roman blades in hand.

No shouts.

No wasted breath.

They worked the camp as if walking through a familiar ritual: a hand across a mouth, a cut angled clean, a man lowered softly to earth.

Some fell in the dark still dreaming.

Others rose in confusion only to be pressed back down.

Only the sound of canvas brushing canvas carried through the camp.

Albina stood at the center of it all.

Bare feet planted in dirt.

Black dress moving with the faint wind.

Smoke braided through her hair.

Her eyes bright as molten gold.

Her presence steadied the ground.

Her people gathered around her; witches, dancers, the smaller girls, faces set in calm masks. Their silence cut sharper than any blade.

Red Ring stormed from his tent finally, half-armored, rage snapping through him like struck iron.

He saw Matineus first.

Rufus's half-brother stepped out of the thinning smoke, shoulders loose, gaze steady.

No war shout.

No threat.

Just a man who had crossed mountains to stand where he now stood.

Red Ring lunged.

Matineus met him without hurry.

A deflection.

A low cut that buckled the man's stance.

Red Ring staggered, breath torn from him.

He swung again, wide, desperate.

Matineus slipped inside the arc and struck once, a sharp elbow to the jaw.

Red Ring dropped to one knee.

Two loyal soldiers dragged him backward, stumbling into the trees with their commander's curses scattering in the wind.

Around them, the last resistance folded.

The eunuchs worked through the remaining pockets of chaos, efficient, precise.

They moved with the grace of dancers and the discipline of craftsmen.

They disabled men with strikes to the joints, the ribs, the throat, stopping breath, dropping bodies clean, not cruel.

When it ended, the camp sagged in the new quiet.

No woman had a mark on her.

The witches circled, checking the girls, gathering satchels, grounding the air with low murmurs.

The smoke thinned, drifting upward like breath finally released.

Matineus wiped his blade on a fallen cloak.

Pain tightened his jaw, but his eyes held only focus.

Albina stepped toward him.

Her veil hid her mouth, but not her eyes.

Not the spark there, recognition, relief, something deeper she didn't name.

Not yet.

He inclined his head.

Not a bow.

Something older, subtler.

Warrior to oracle.

Her braid shifted with the wind; inside it, Zarakar waited, black iron sleeping against her spine.

Matineus turned to his ten men.

"Gather their gear. Burn what needs burning. Saddle what we can ride. We leave for the river road before the sun climbs. And chase off that ugly camel."

His voice carried calm authority, no strain, no glory-seeking.

Just purpose.

Albina watched the camp reshape itself under his orders; horses collected, tents stripped, supplies sorted, wounded eased aside.

No chaos.

Only movement.

The dancers braided each other's hair and changed into riding clothes.

The witches packed herbs with careful fingers.

The girls moved close to Albina, their steps instinctively matching hers.

Smoke rolled away.

Light crept over the ridge.

Matineus mounted his horse.

He looked down at her once, quiet, steady.

She lifted her chin.

The Sibyl.

Free now.

Not by miracle.

By men who stepped through smoke because a vision had named this dawn long ago.

Matineus nodded once, sharp and sure.

Then he led his men into the pale morning, the women falling in behind him as the Parthian camp died behind them, empty, broken, already turning to rumor.

Albina walked without looking back.

The smoke did that for her. It carried the old world away.

And carried her toward Rome.

Chapter 36

RIDERS ON THE STORM

Northern Parthian Territories

No bodies were touched except to strip.

No graves dug. No prayers given.

The Romans looted what they needed and left the rest to the crows. Horses stood tethered in lines, stamping, snorting, eyes wide from the smell of blood. There were mounts enough for all, with mules besides. One mule bore a special pack: cloth-wrapped, leather-bound, heavier than it looked.

Inside, the twelve stone figures were saved by the attendant girl.

Albina went to her. Placed both hands on her shoulders, steady and warm.

"You did as I asked," she said in her high voice.

The girl blushed, eyes down. When she lifted them again, she smiled.

Albina gave a single nod. That was enough.

Nisaya brushed the girl's cheek with the back of her hand, whisper thin. Zarmina pressed a pouch into her palm, herbs bitter and black, meant to keep evil at bay. Silent thanks. Nothing more.

Albina passed the mule and let her fingers trail across the leather pack. She felt the weight, not of stone, but of lives bound to it. Twelve mothers. Twelve watchers. Twelve guardians. They had survived again.

The girl had hidden near the ruined temple for months, close enough to watch Red Ring's men soften, grow mean, grow careless. She had watched him burn Sibyl's house to char and ruin. She had waited for the last boot to vanish down the eastern road, then ran barefoot from the ruins, ash-smeared, wild-eyed.

She had seen the riders at morning: sixteen Romans, dark and fast, men who rode like they had already spilled blood. She stumbled before them, raised a hand, and pointed toward the road Red Ring had taken. But when the lead rider, quiet-eyed, tall, lean, scarred, asked her what mattered most, she said nothing.

She opened the panniers instead.

Matineus knew at once what the figures were. Aurelia, Caesar's mother, had whispered of them: the Twelve belonged only to the Sibyl. Older than kings. Older than Rome.

He gave one order. Two of his men repacked the mule with reverence. The girl was lifted onto a horse. Only then did they turn east.

There was no cheer after the rescue. No songs. No boasts. Only blood and smoke and the soft scrape of leather.

The eunuchs formed around Albina. Witches checked the tree line. Dancers huddled close on smaller horses, bracelets faint under the straps.

Matineus rode behind them. Blood dried on his sleeve. A cut stung under his ribs. He never fell back. His eyes raked the woods with every step of the horses.

At the edge of the clearing, he tightened a last strap, then looked to Albina.

She sat already mounted, spine straight, golden eyes fixed on the trees ahead. Smoke wrapped her hair. Her braid coiled long over her shoulder, heavy with secrets.

He meant to speak. A simple report. A confirmation. Instead, he stopped.

She turned her face toward him, slow, deliberate. Light caught her cheekbone. Her braid brushed her collarbone. And he breathed her in without meaning to.

Smoke. Spice, cinnamon maybe. Warm skin. And something softer beneath it, feminine musk, heat, salt, life.

Different from other girls he knew. Different from Rome. Something older. Something dangerous.

Her gaze flicked down him, his scar, his jaw, the blood on his sleeve, the weight of his silence, and she felt the pull back. Not want. Not safety. A recognition.

A man who walked the same storm as her, but not toward her. Not yet.

The air tightened between them.

Nisaya stepped forward before either moved.

"None may touch the Sibyl," she said in Greek, quiet, final. "Not now. Not ever. Her guards will not ask questions."

Zarmina stood beside her. The eunuchs leaned in their saddles; hands close to blades.

Matineus didn't look away from Albina, even as he nodded.

"Understood. Now mount. Do what I say when I say it, and we might all live through this."

No one argued.

He pulled a scroll from his pack. Caesar's seal pressed in the leather coil. He drove a Latinus blade through it, pinning the parchment hard into an oak.

"This message," he said, "belongs to the Parthian King."

It would be found. It would sting.

By first light, they were gone.

The field behind them lay stripped and hollow. Blood darkened the grass. Black birds gathered, tearing soft parts from the fallen. Ash drifted from burned wagons. The wind turned smoke into veils.

The forest swallowed the trail.

And the storm, silent and unseen, rode east with them.

Albina's pulse carried two scents now: olive oil and leather from one future, cedar, horses, and warm skin from the other. Two men in her fate. Two blades headed toward her life.

She closed her eyes. Warmth spread through her.

Far across the world, on a field soaked with blood, Rufus raised a shield over fallen men and earned a name that would echo all the way to the Caspian. All the way to Rome.

Chapter 37
BOWS AND BLOOD

Amanus Gates – Orontes River

Rufus smiled as the trumpets called.

Not a grin. Not arrogance.

Just the calm curl of a man who'd dreamed of this moment since boyhood.

Not a pirate raid. Not a skirmish.

This was the legion. Heavy infantry. The eagle. The real war.

The sand itched in his teeth. His knuckles flexed. He held his shield tight, his hand holding the gladius. And he breathed deep and steady.

His first campaign opened in the dust of Syria, cliffs behind, plains ahead, sun straight overhead.

Parthians on fast horses. Syrians with long spears. Loose ranks of hired Greeks. Rebel Jews with curved blades.

Rufus stood in the front line.

The centurion raised his arm. Iron voice.

"Lock shields!"

The line responded without flinch. Hundreds of scuta slammed edge to edge, forming a single wall of curved oak and iron. Boots dug in. Breath held.

"Hold!"

Spears rattled on the far side of the field. The enemy came screaming, loose, wild, swinging blades above their heads.

"Ready pila!"

The second rank reached back, fingers tight around the weighted shafts. Rufus felt his own heartbeat slow. His shield tilted just enough to give him room.

"Wait... Wait..."

Dust kicked up. The ground shook. The enemy closed fast.

"Loose!"

Pila flew. The javelins struck meat. Screams split the line. A rider went down hard. Another fell forward, impaled in the thigh.

"Brace!"

Shields came up. Knees bent. Shoulders leaned in.

The enemy slammed the wall.

Steel scraped wood. Men grunted. The line bowed but did not break.

"Push!"

Rufus dug in. Drove forward. Felt his shoulder drive into a man's chest. Heard bone snap.

"Blades!"

The front line drew short swords. Gladii came out low, tight. They stabbed and sliced into groins, under ribs, through throats. Clean. Fast. Again.

The enemy howled and flailed. The Romans didn't flinch.

This was not a brawl.

This was a slaughter machine.

The enemy turned and ran.

"Hold, handlers, loose the dogs."

The large black and brown war dogs flew past the Romans and went for the fleeing enemy's calves and thighs.

As the enemy fell to the ground the dogs went for the throats.

Rufus called for his bow.

Bow in hand, Rufus let fly.

He didn't miss.

Each arrow flew fast and clean.

One in the throat. One in the eye. Two through shields. One in the back of a fleeing man's skull.

The enemy turned and rushed him.

He dropped six more before the first man reached him.

Then came the sword.

Rufus didn't shout. He didn't roar. He moved, like he'd trained for this day since the cradle.

He slipped through the enemy like a shadow cast in daylight.

His gladius struck in tight arcs, stabbing low, punching high.

He killed with javelins. With the sling. Even with his shield.

A Parthian fell with half his throat crushed by the shield's edge.

Rufus didn't slow.

He was everywhere.

And when the dust cleared, he hadn't taken a scratch.

The stench of death and blood, and sounds of victory and defeat, and the sights of battle, flooded every sense.

He earned his first medals that day.

And again, after the second battle, even bloodier, hotter, harder.

He killed twice as many.

He stood over his legions fallen eagle-bearer. Eyes hard. Hand clenched.

The eagle lay beside the dead Aquilifer, stained red.

The centurions gathered.

Spoke in low voices.

They looked at Rufus.

He didn't ask. He didn't wait. He reached down. Lifted the eagle with both hands.

Rufus held the legions symbol high.

—-

A lion stalked near the mountain villages.

Dragged bodies into the brush. Left bloody bones.

The men of the village had been wiped out in warfare.

The legion needed goodwill. The locals needed hope.

They sent five of the best.

Rufus led them.

He cleaned his blade in silence.

Somewhere, in the stone and dark, the lion waited. And Rufus went to meet his destiny.

Chapter 38
THE LION AND THE EAGLE

Near the Orontes River

The tracks led him to blood.

A torn robe. A broken sandal. What remained of an old woman, more shadow than flesh.

Flies moved slowly in the heat, fat with what they had taken.

Rufus crouched beside the body. Dirt under his nails. Breath held. The ground told its story clean: drag marks; claw rakes; the wide, heavy print of something that hunted without practice.

He had split off from the others hours ago. Four men spread across the river plain, each following a trail. Rufus took the one that felt wrong. The one where the earth looked bruised.

He grew up hunting everything that moved on the Latinus farms, stag, boar, wolf, hawks that tried to pick off chickens. Those years had taught him to read hoof, claw, feather, blood.

The lion he tracked now wasn't young. Wasn't proud. Wasn't practiced.

A rogue.

Driven out by a younger male. Scarred in the face. Pride taken. Sons killed. Desperate. Angry.

A beast that never hunted alone now learned hunger with no lionesses to kill for him. He'd stumbled on a village with no fighting men. Lucky for him. Death for the old woman.

Rufus smelled him a heartbeat before he saw him, rot, musk, dust, and dried blood.

Too close for a bow.

Too fast for a javelin.

He reached for his knives.

The lion charged.

A wall of fur and rage slammed into him, knocking breath and thought sideways. Claws punched into his shoulder. Fangs snapped for the throat. The world spun, dirt, sky, lion rolling under a weight that felt carved from mountains.

Rufus didn't think. He struck.

One knife under the ribs.

Another deep.

A third all the way to the hilt.

A wet, choking roar ripped out of the beast. Its front legs buckled. It slumped heavily across Rufus's chest.

Silence. Except for his breath, jagged, animal, half-broken.

He lay trapped beneath the corpse, ribs screaming. Something inside him popped, sharp as dry wood.

He shoved.

Nothing.

Panic scraped the inside of his throat.

He dug one knee free. He braced both palms. Groaned through the pain. Pushed again.

The lion rolled. Slow, slick. Heavy as sin.

Rufus lay on his back. Blood in his mouth. Wind in his hair. His chest heaved like a kicked bellows.

Tears slipped hot across his temples before he could stop them.

Tears of survival.

He thanked the gods no one saw. The lion killed was glorious. A man crying under one was not.

He spat, rolled to his side, and stood. Breathing hurt. Every rib felt cracked. Every muscle trembled.

Skinning took hours. Blood dried in flakes on his forearms. His hands shook but didn't stop.

At sunrise he limped through the camp gates with the hide across his shoulders, still wet, stinking of death.

Silence hit first.

Then a roar.

Men surged toward him. Centurions. Legionaries. Archers. Even mule drivers stared like they'd seen a god climb out of the river mud.

Aulus Gabinius stepped forward, smug even now. He gave the smallest nod. "Well done."

The army moved too fast for a ceremony. No speeches. No wreath. No time. There were enemies in every canyon, every village, every tree line.

They measured him anyway.

Golden fish-scale armor.

A crested helmet.

A cloak sewn from the hide he carried.

Then came the eagle.

Ashwood shaft. Thick. Dark. Polished by dead men's hands. Bronze rings warm from the sun.

He gripped it and felt the weight all the way through his spine.

The eagle at the top shone dull silver, wings out, claws around lightning. Not pretty. Not gentle. A weapon as much as a symbol. If swung, it would break a skull.

Every aquilifer before him either died holding it or rose to centurion.

He had trained for this. Wanted it. Dreamed it.

But as he lifted the standard, his breath caught.

The eagle didn't feel earned.

It felt given by Rome with one hand and demanded back with the other.

He raised it high. Higher.

A dare.

A promise.

A curse.

Men stared. Word spread. The lion's blood still wet on him. The eagle bright against the rising sun.

Rufus Latinus had stepped out of the ranks and into a story men would tell in deserts and taverns for years.

His ribs hurt with every breath.

But he led the march.

As the line pushed east, dust rising from hundreds of sandals, Rufus felt the eagle shift, heavy, alive, as if Rome itself leaned forward to judge him.

By dusk, scouts returned with whispers.

Villages burned.

Legionaries trapped.

A cohort surrounded and failing.

The kind of fight where men died fast, and one man could turn the tide.

The kind of fight where heroes earned oak leaves or graves.

Rufus tightened his grip on the standard.

The lion had tested his body.

The next battle would test his soul.

And the gods were watching.

Chapter 39
IRON AND OAK

The Battle of Damascus

The enemy crashed against them in waves.

Shields shuddered. The ground shook. The air turned to grit and iron.

Mercenary Parthians on chain-mailed horses. Greeks with long spears. Arab-Nabataeans with axes and hooked blades. All of them screaming for Rome's blood. Javelins cut the sky. Firepots spun. Dust climbed like smoke over the plain.

Rufus stood high on the slope, feet set wide, war bow in hand.

The yew pressed into his palm, slick with sweat. The string bit his fingers through hardened callus. His shoulders burned long before the first charge reached the line. He held the weight anyway. Drew until his ribs creaked. Released.

The first arrow hit a horse through the chest. Impact jarred the beast. Rider toppled, armor ringing against stone.

Rufus found the next target before the first body hit dirt.

Draw. Bite of string. Twist in his spine. Release.

Another man folded over his own saddle, limbs loose.

He shot from the rise, from shallow scrub, from open ground. He shifted his stance to ride each impact, knees flexing, ankles biting into dry soil. The bow kicked back into his hand like a living thing.

He did not miss.

Within minutes his fingers felt flayed raw inside the leather guards. Muscles along his upper back shook with every draw. His breath scraped in and out, hot and sharp, but his arms still moved.

He dropped fifty men before the first enemy blade touched the Roman line.

Then the bow gave him nothing more. Quiver empty. Hands numb.

He slung the yew down. His right hand closed around the gladius grip.

Steel fit into his palm like a second bone.

The crush met him as a physical thing.

Heat of bodies. Slam of shields. Weight of another man's charge along his arm.

Rufus stepped into it.

Short cuts. Heavy blows. His wrist snapped low to open bellies, then rose to punch under chins. Blade met bone again and again, jolting his elbow, sending bright pain up to his shoulder. Blood turned the ground slick; his sandals skidded. His toes clawed for purchase. Calves burned.

He fought near the eagle.

Men reached for it, heads low, shoulders braced, eyes wild. The standard drew them like a lodestone. If they could cut him down, tear the eagle free, Rome's heart would stutter.

Rufus shifted his stance, scutum locked to his left arm. Arrows beat against it in steady, vicious rhythm. Each strike thudded through leather and wood into his forearm. The raw weight grew with every shaft that stuck.

When the dust thinned for a moment, his shield looked like a thornbush. More than a hundred arrow shafts bristled from the hide. Cracks ran through the grain. Bronze boss lay streaked with blood and dust.

So many had tried to reach him.

None had managed it.

Word ran through their ranks. A price sat on his head now, whispered in three tongues.

Silver for the standard bearer. More for the man with the lion's skin. A fortune for the red-haired Roman behind the eagle.

Rufus rolled his shoulders once. The weight of the standard dug into his palm through the leather grip. He set his stance. Let the bounty hunters come.

He saw the wounded as soon as they fell.

One legionary dropped with half a leg left, bone white where the calf had lived. Another on his back, throat cut open, drowning in his own blood. A third whose eyes had lost focus, swinging at enemies who no longer stood there. Panic made him dangerous to his own.

Arms shaking, lungs on fire, Rufus still moved toward them.

He drove his shoulder into an enemy shield, felt the bruise bloom along his collarbone, cut behind the rim, and then heaved the Roman back with his free hand.

He hooked his arm under the man with the missing leg, drag across packed dirt, each step ripping at his thighs. Then the choking one, hand clamped over the wound, hot wetness seeping between Rufus's fingers. Last, the mad one, gripped hard at the back of the neck and forced behind the line.

Steel rained in all around, but his body knew the pattern. Shields glanced off his own. Blades slid along his guard. His boots dug deep ruts. Every joint screamed by the time he dropped the third man into safety.

He ignored the pain.

Romans did not leave Romans to die in the dust.

The left broke first.

Rufus felt the shift through the ground before the shouting started. Dust rolled wider there, darker. The tremble under his heels changed, a different rhythm, unsteady. Men staggered back in clumps, shields turned at the wrong angle.

A hidden swarm spilled over a low rise, infantry that had crawled into position behind rock and scrub, now rushing the exposed flank.

Weight more than fear crushed the line. Too many bodies. Too many blades.

One legionary vanished under a pile of screaming men. Another toppled with a spear through his collar. A section of the wall sagged.

Rufus moved without thought.

He drove the butt end of the eagle deep into the earth. The ash shaft bit into soil hard enough to jar his shoulder. The metal at the top rang, angry and sure.

He felt the pull of it through his hand: Rome anchored there.

He dropped to one knee, bow back in his grip, and drew with torn fingers. Every pull scraped skin to meat; his joints felt full of sand. He still focused on the men who shouted orders. Taller helmets. Arms waving.

First arrow: release, and a captain fell backward, spine arched.

Second: flight, a little left, then correction, a lender of the charge took steel through the eye.

Third: the arrow tore a throat open mid-command. The man's words ended in a cough of blood.

The push slowed. Confusion rippled through the mass.

Not much time bought. Enough.

"On me!" Rufus barked.

Two nearby legionaries dragged themselves to his side. Then three more. Shields closed like a shell locking. They formed a knot around the eagle.

Rufus rose again, gladius red and slick.

He stepped into the mouth of the chaos.

The crush tightened.

Bodies mashed together. Men fought elbow to elbow, ribs grinding against neighbor's armor, breath leaking through clenched teeth. Rufus felt every impact along his bruised forearm, every slide of iron along his shield rim. A blade scraped his ribs, slicing leather, kissing skin beneath. Heat flared, then settled into a hot line.

He did not step back.

He cut through a spine from behind, felt the jar as vertebrae split. He slammed his shoulder into another enemy's chest, felt ribs give under the force, then drove his gladius through the soft meat beneath the sternum. A third man lunged for the eagle; Rufus turned the attack with his own blade and buried steel in the lung, feeling the suction as he pulled free.

"Lock!" he shouted.

Five shields shifted, edges grinding. Their boots dug in. They became the center around which pressure pressed. Rufus worked just outside the rim, striking low at exposed ankles, then high at necks craned forward.

Blood turned soil to paste. Each step tried to slide out from under him. His calves burned from constant adjustment. Arrows hissed overhead, some slamming into shields with bone-bruising force. One stuck deep in a friend's calf, but the man stayed standing, leg shaking.

"Break left!" Rufus drove the words out between breaths.

The wall moved as if one body. A step that crushed shins. Another that shoved. Another that sliced. Inch by inch they ate space, tightening the line, forcing the enemy into a narrow pocket where blades could reach them clean.

Rufus spotted a broken javelin on the ground. Shaft half gone, head still sharp. He scooped it up, feeling splinters bite his palm.

One hard throw, shoulder screaming.

The iron point punched through a charging officer's chest plate. The man took two more steps, then dropped as if someone cut his strings.

The front of the enemy charge wavered. Rhythm lost. Men glanced at each other instead of forward.

"Now!" Rufus roared.

The Roman knot surged.

Shields crashed forward. Feet stamped hard. Steel dug into bellies, backs, eyes. Men toppled under the momentum. The enemy line broke inward on itself, men tripping over the fallen, stepping on hands, slipping in blood.

What had almost rolled the Roman flank now turned to a rout. Those who could still run tried. Many did not get far.

Rufus killed the last spearman himself.

Tall. Scarred. Rage in his gaze. The man jabbed twice in quick succession, hard enough to numb Rufus's forearm. Rufus parried, twisted his hips, and drove his own blade up through the gut and out the back.

The spear slid from nerveless fingers. The body hung for a moment on the steel. Rufus kicked the man free.

Then quiet. The tight, ringing kind.

Then the roar.

The siege of Damascus shuddered. Then cracked.

Later, when command broke the enemy and the survivors pulled back, Rufus walked the field.

His boots sank into mud that had not been mud that morning. Blood clung to his calves, dried in rough patches. Some pools still shone wet and dark. Some had already crusted black.

Buzzards circled overhead, lazy and sure. Crows hopped between corpses, tearing at anything soft. Flies touched every open wound, a hum that sat like a low fever over the ground.

He still carried the eagle. Its weight now felt normal in his grip, a part of him. The shaft dug into his palm. His shoulders ached where the lion's skin dragged across them, hide stiff with old and new blood.

He stepped around broken men, swords still in fists, faces frozen in effort or fear. The stink of opened guts, shit and bile and iron, wrapped him like a cloak. He breathed through it. That smell belonged to his trade.

Then he heard it.

A sound too small for this place. A thin, raw mew.

He turned his head. The mew came again, higher, more desperate. Alive.

Rufus followed the noise to a tangle of bodies. Four men lay heaped together, legs thrown across torsos, arms wrapped around nothing. Blood pooled under them in a slow, thick lake. One man's intestines spilled from a cut belly in coiled ropes.

Rufus stepped closer, gladius loose in hand.

From between a dead man's thighs, out from a split fold of cloth soaked dark, something pale and shaking crawled free.

A kitten.

White and tan fur, slick with blood, paws slipping on the wet cloth as it wriggled forward. Eyes not fully clear yet. Whole body trembling.

The mew came again. Small, stubborn.

Rufus crouched.

The bodies around it made a crude shape: legs forming the sides, that torn cloth in the center. A rent. A mouth. A kind of womb, ripped open by steel.

The kitten dragged itself out of that human wreckage, newborn from the battlefield.

Heat moved along his neck.

A gift, he thought. Mars rarely spoke in words.

He slid his sword away. Reached down with his bare hand. Blood stuck to the kitten's fur and then to his fingers. The tiny ribs fluttered under his touch. Heart a fast drum.

He lifted it into his palm. Its claws pricked his skin, weak but real.

It shivered. Then stilled. Looked up with wet eyes that did not yet know fear.

Rufus wiped it with the cleanest part of his cloak. Blood came away in streaks. The fur under the mess felt soft, warm. Alive.

He uncorked his waterskin. Let a few drops fall into his other hand, then tipped them toward the kitten's mouth. A tiny tongue darted out. Licked. Swallowed.

Nearby, one of his cousins, serving as crew on his yacht, called up as a runner, watched, brow furrowed.

Rufus didn't explain.

"Take this kitten to my ship at Berytus," he told him. The tone left no space for humor. "Find the captain. Keep it warm. Feed it meat and water. If it dies, you die."

The man's face tightened. He nodded. Held out both hands.

Rufus passed the small body over. The kitten curled into the new grip, still trusting.

The cousin wrapped it in what remained of the cloak's clean edge and hurried off the field, cradling the bundle like something sacred.

Rufus watched for a breath. Then heaved the eagle back into his hand, feeling the familiar strain along his forearm.

No priest had raised arms toward the sky for him. No official omen had been declared. No thunderbolt struck the hill at his feet.

Just a small creature pulled from death's mouth.

Something born from blood, not killed by it.

Before any crown. Before the speeches.

Mars had sent a quieter sign.

Rufus accepted it.

Evening found the legions in formation east of Antioch.

Dust still floated in the air, a fine coat that stuck to sweat and leather. The light carried the weight of a long day, thick and amber.

Rufus stood in the front rank. Legs bare. Boots laced tight enough to bite skin. His tunic counted as clean by campaign standards. The lion's pelt lay across his shoulders, mane stiff. Under the fur, bandages wrapped his ribs from the earlier hunt; every breath tugged the healing bone.

His gladius hung low at his side, oil from the hilt tacky on his palm. The eagle's pole rested in his grip. Muscles in his forearm twitched from the day's battle, but he kept the standard steady.

Behind him, two full legions held the line: shields aligned, spearheads a forest of bronze. No murmur. No shuffle. Just breath and the occasional creak of leather.

Drums struck twice. Deep. Sharp.

Officers stepped out. The general walked at their head, flanked by senior centurions, scribes, the aquilifer of another legion. His own lion skin settled over his back, mane dark with old blood that stiffened the hide.

A scribe unrolled a scroll. The parchment crackled in the heat.

"Gaius Latinus Rufus."

His name felt strange in the open air.

Rufus stepped forward. Each pace measured. He planted his feet as if the ground might shift. Chin high. Eyes level. The heat on his face did not make him squint.

Pompey Magnus raised his hand.

The sun hit him from behind, turning the dust around his cloak to gold. Pompey stood broad through the chest, clean-shaven, hair swept forward in the famous curl that looked carved, not grown. A Roman built from oak and oath. His bronze cuirass shone where blood hadn't dried in the seams, griffins hammered along the ribs, the red paludamentum sweeping off one shoulder like a banner that never tired.

Rufus had seen statues of heroes in Rome, broad-shouldered men who looked like they could hold up the sky. Pompey looked like one of them stepped down into heat and dust. His eyes were large and steady, the kind that could quiet a riot or bless a soldier without touching him. As he looked at Rufus, something changed. Recognition. The kind a commander gives a man cut from the same iron.

The wind lifted the cloak. Bronze creaked. Leather straps brushed his legs. He smelled of horse, sweat, oiled armor, and the dry sting of Syrian dust trapped in the folds of his mantle. When he spoke, his voice cracked through the heat like a blade tapping a shield.

Rufus straightened without thinking. Pompey Magnus, Europa's conqueror, Rome's favorite son, first man in Rome, looked at him as if he already belonged beside him.

"For valor," he called, voice carrying like a thrown spear. "For blood. For holding the line when others faltered. For saving Romans under arms. For killing Rome's enemies without pause."

He lifted a crown woven from oak leaves, silver wired through the green.

The civic crown.

The weight of the field pressed into Rufus's shoulders as he watched it.

"The man who wins this crown," Pompey continued, "saves citizens with his own body. Today you did that. But your deeds go beyond it."

He stepped close enough that Rufus could see dust settled in the lines at the corners of his eyes.

The crown settled on Rufus's head.

Cool metal. Scratch of leaves along his scalp. The pressure shaped his skull, light but undeniable. A touch that felt both blessing and mark.

Pompey nodded once. "Rome thanks you."

The legions roared. Steel clanged against shields in rolling thunder.

Rufus held the standard firm. The pole bit into his palm. The crown dug a little deeper.

Pompey's aide stepped forward with a scroll tied in leather.

"My son mentioned you might want this." Pompey handed it over.

Rufus felt the weight as much as the roughness under his fingers.

A deed. Land rich and broad, lying across from his family's own fields in Italy.

"And your rank," Pompey added.

"Centurion."

The word hit with more force than any sword that day.

Rufus's mouth did not move much, but his cheek tightened. The small smile reached his eyes.

He bowed once. The motion pulled on bandaged ribs. Pain shot through his side, sharp and bright. He welcomed it. Pain meant he still belonged to the body that would bear this new load.

Eighteen. Still young enough for some boys to call "kid" in another life.

No one here did.

The primus pilus stepped up, vine staff in hand.

"Take it," he ordered.

Rufus gripped the staff in his left hand. Dry wood rasped against callus. Little knots pressed into his skin. It smelled of old leaves and leather, sweat from a dozen older hands.

A tool for command.

And for punishment.

Pompey leaned in. His voice dropped low, meant only for Rufus.

"You'll serve in the front ranks," he said. "You'll sleep light and eat last. Your failures will cut deeper than your men's. But your victories will outlive your name."

Then, even softer: "By Sulla's laws, you'll sit in the Senate when you return to Rome."

The word formed in Rufus's chest, heavy: senator.

He didn't trust his tongue. He let his body answer. Fist to chest in salute.

Down the line, one centurion after another lifted their own fists. A wave of hard knuckles over harder hearts.

Then the legion's roar came again, sword to shield, sword to shield, sword to shield. Hammer strokes on Rome's anvil.

Rufus turned back to the ranks.

The youngest centurion now. The newest.

Still wrapped tight under the lion's skin. Ribs not yet knit.

Dust blew across his bare knees. The sun pressed heat into his scalp through oak leaves and silver. Sweat stung the slice along his side.

His face did not change.

Inside, something shifted.

This goal had driven him since childhood. Since the first time his father set a blade in his small hand and guided the stroke along a whetstone. Since early mornings on the farm, body training while the rest of the house still slept. Since the day he broke his knuckles on a practice shield and wrapped them tight to keep fighting anyway.

He had wanted this more than food. More than rest.

Now it sat on his head and in his hands.

Too fast.

He had pictured a long climb. Years of blood, decades of battle, a slow scrape up the ladder of rank. Instead, the ground had tilted and thrown him to a peak he hadn't yet seen from below.

The wind at that height hit different. Cold along the back of his neck. Thin in the lungs.

He did not feel ready.

So, he decided not to feel it.

Readiness would come later. Work first.

He had given up the Eagle standard.

He now held the vine staff, and the new crown. Muscle by muscle, he learned the new weight.

Behind him, the sun slid toward the horizon, bleeding gold across helmets and spearpoints.

Rufus stood still. Oak leaves pressed his scalp. Lion fur scratched his neck. The staff dug into his palm.

Iron and oak. Blood and fur.

Somewhere far to the east, a girl who dreamed of lion boys and Roman steel had once misread a vision.

She had thought the crown over his head would belong to her story. Perhaps it would.

For now, it belonged to Rome.

Chapter 40

DAUGHTERS OF ROME

Rome, Palatine Hill

The room hummed with girl-noise, bright laughter, sharp whispers, sandals tapping stone. Sunlight poured through the open arches and warmed the benches. Birds traded calls in the fig trees outside, a loose rhythm under the chatter.

Seven girls formed a circle on the floor, robes gathered neat around their legs, wax tablets in their laps. Their vernae hovered nearby with their own gossip, softer, watching everything.

Julia Caesaris sat with the posture of someone raised to rule. Even at her age she carried her father's steadiness, chin high, eyes quick.

Calpurnia Pisonis traced spirals on her tablet with the flat end of her stylus. A blue ribbon threaded through her pale braid, catching the sun each time she leaned close to hear something scandalous.

Tullia, Cicero's daughter, tapped her stylus on her tablet. "I hear everything," she said. "Better than Calpurnia writes."

Junia Tertia, Tertulla, snapped her fingers. "Enough. Let Fulvia read what she wrote."

Julia Latina, sister of Rufus, watched them all with that quiet half-smirk she carried everywhere. When she spoke, the others always went silent first. Today she watched Fulvia, waiting.

Fulvia pushed hair from her face, white as milk, thick, long, unmistakable. Her blue eyes shined. "I said you're not listening."

"We are," Julia said.

Fulvia sighed, resigned. "Fine. I wrote his name."

Gasps. Laughter. Ink smudges. Someone dropped a stylus.

"Rufus," Calpurnia whispered, delighted.

"Hero Rufus," Julia added, voice musical.

"They say he killed fifty with the bow and fifty with the sword," Tullia said.

"And the lion," Tertulla said. "Everyone forgets the lion."

"And the kitten," Tullia countered. "The kitten decides everything."

Latina covered her mouth to hide a smile.

Fulvia studied her own tablet. The name she'd carved already glimmered where wax met sunlight. "He's different," she said. "Quiet. Strong. Every part of him holds. When he fights..."

"He becomes Mars," Calpurnia murmured.

Fulvia's eyes softened. "First time I saw him, he wrestled three boys on the Campus Martius. All older. He beat them hard. I stared for an hour. Later, during the horse races, he looked right at me. Twice. I was ten."

"You're not the only girl trying," Tullia teased.

Fulvia did not snap back. Her focus settled on the name in front of her, the long lines, the deep grooves. "He will choose me."

The others squealed, delighted by the certainty.

They drifted then, jokes, gossip, talk of shoes, hair, whose brother had embarrassed himself, whose mother schemed most fiercely.

Then Julia quieted them with a look she had learned from her father.

"What about the eastern girl?"

The chatter fell away.

"Albina," Tertulla said.

"The priestess," Tullia confirmed.

Julia tilted her head. "My father says she carries ancient blood. Sibyl blood. Her line stretches to Mithridates and the Ptolemies."

Calpurnia folded her hands. "They say she walks like someone born on a throne."

Latina exchanged a glance with Fulvia.

Fulvia spoke first. "People swear she's the most beautiful woman alive. Even covered in dust. Even in chains."

Tertulla lowered her voice. "My mother says Caesar will place her in a rich home. Someone with influence. Someone Rome trusts."

Fulvia's jaw tightened. Latinas did too.

Fulvia lowered her gaze for a moment, sensing, without knowing why, that the eastern girl would stand in her way someday.

Julia shrugged. "I haven't seen her, but my father's wife believes the Sibyl will change Rome if she lives to reach the city. She says a woman can turn the Republic more than any law."

The girls shared a look that held both fear and excitement, something shifting, something coming.

Then the spell broke. They laughed again, loud and unafraid, as if none of it mattered, as if they were simply girls with ink on their fingers.

They never saw their own shadows stretching long across the marble floor.

They didn't know the truth yet.

The names carved on those wax tablets would one day shape empires.

Chapter 41

KING OF KINGS

Ctesiphon, on the Tigris

The boy with the silver staff pushed the door open.

A tide of firelight rolled into the throne room. Smoke hugged the columns, thick as old grief. Heat pressed down from the high stone vaults. The air tasted of dust, breath, sweat, perfume, an empire's age ground to powder.

Chains dragged behind Red Ring as he stepped inside. Wrists bound. Ankles locked. Three days in a stone cell had stripped him raw. His hair matted. His feet numb. The stink of travel and failure clung to him like a curse.

He passed between two ranks of archers, bows strung, eyes cold. Beyond them waited six executioners, torsos oiled, black steel bars balanced across their shoulders. A priest swayed beside them, voice low, chanting words that sounded older than light.

At the foot of the dais, four men knelt.

His brothers.

Their spines stayed straight from habit alone. Faces swollen from beatings. Eyes blackened. Cuts still weeping. None turned toward him. Shame held their necks stiff.

Red Ring kept moving.

At the top of the black-stone steps sat Artaxes, King of Kings.

He wore no towering crown, only a hammered band of gold set deep in his dark hair. His beard hung long, oiled, threaded with silver like frost trapped in a riverbed. His features were narrow and sun-hardened. His expression fixed, carved more than born. No warmth. No cruelty.

Black robes flowed over him, stitched in red threads that shifted like coals. A wide belt crossed his waist. Soft boots marked no sound. Rings cast dull light along his fingers, iron, ivory, lapis, gold, obsidian, yet his hands didn't twitch. Didn't drum. Didn't acknowledge the world unless he willed it so.

He seemed ageless. A man who had outlasted seasons, wars, dynasties. A man who spoke with his presence before his tongue ever moved.

He watched Red Ring approach.

One blink. Nothing more.

"You chased a girl," Artaxes said.

His voice didn't rise. It didn't need to. The entire throne room leaned toward it.

"You returned with Roman threats and dead men."

A priest stepped forward, offering a scroll impaled on a Latinus blade. Blood dried around the puncture. Wax smeared across torn parchment.

Artaxes slid the knife free. Unrolled the message.

The firelight caught the letters.

Allow the dancing Sibyl to leave your lands and arrive unharmed to Rome.

Or I will burn your kingdom to the ground.

- Gaius Julius Caesar

The scroll fell from his hand. Hit the floor with a wet thud, like an organ dropped on stone.

Rage crawled up the walls.

Artaxes moved one finger. Silence hardened.

"I sent you to end her," he said. "She dances still."

He rose from the throne.

"A stupid dirty little girl."

Each step down the dais landed with a slow thunder. His robe brushed stone like a blade in sand.

"You want fear?" he asked.

He circled Red Ring, gaze heavy as a weight across the shoulders. The chains clicked, the only sound Red Ring owned.

"I knew your father," Artaxes murmured behind him. "He took cities from kings. He carved borders into mountains."

He stepped in front again. Close enough for Red Ring to feel his breath.

"You are none of him. Only smoke left over from his fire."

He didn't shout. The truth didn't need volume.

He pointed at Caesar's blood-soaked scroll.

"That name belongs to Rome now."

His voice sharpened.

"Let the name Barzan rot."

A tremor cut through the kneeling brothers.

"Let your sons learn disgust when they speak it. Let the worms carry it through the earth when your grave splits."

He lifted his hand.

The doors swung open.

Three boys entered, Red Ring's sons, barefoot, tunics clean, hair combed, eyes unsure. The smallest clutched his wrist. The oldest lifted his chin, proud but frightened.

Artaxes did not acknowledge them.

"They stay here," he said. "Until the little girl, this Sibyl lies dead. Or they do."

Two more figures were dragged in then, men Red Ring recognized. His rescuers. The ones who had saved him so he could stand humiliated before his own king.

They staggered, barely held upright. Blood soaked their tunics. One's nose bent sideways. The other could barely breathe.

Artaxes stepped aside with a flick of his hand.

The executioners advanced.

Steel bars swung.

The first blow cracked a skull like a clay pot. Blood sheeted across the tiles. The second bar sank into a ribcage with a sound that made the priest flinch. The third pulped a jaw; teeth scattered like white stones across the floor.

One man screamed as his throat collapsed.

The next blow ended it.

The second man tried to rise. His eye burst when the bar struck. A spray of bone and hair hit a column. Brains slid down the priest's robe. The stink of voided bowels spread.

The bars dripped. The bodies twitched. Then stilled.

The king watched everything. Stood in the blood. Let it touch his sandals. Let it soak into the leather.

The youngest boy gagged. The oldest didn't blink.

Artaxes lowered his hand.

"You failed," he said again. "You will not fail twice."

He turned to the kneeling brothers.

"Rise."

They obeyed.

"You four will follow her trail," he said. "Through rivers, desert, ruin. You will ride until your breath gives out."

He looked back at Red Ring.

"And you will hunt the Sibyl until her throat opens under your blade. No chains. No cages. Only death."

Artaxes flicked two fingers toward the corpses.

"Clean that."

Then he ascended the steps and reclaimed his throne.

Red Ring said nothing. His breath shook once, shallow and low. He stepped forward through the blood, chains scraping the gore. He passed his sons without turning toward them. Passed the mangled bodies of the men who had saved him.

He kept walking.

He never looked back.

The guards unchained him at the door. Barzan stepped into the torchlit hall, blood drying on his ankles. The hunt had already begun. Somewhere beyond the first ridge, a girl of smoke and prophecy turned in her saddle and smiled, as if she had been waiting for him.

Chapter 42
THE CHASE AND THE CAVE

The Lands west of the Caspian Sea

They ran across sand hard as hammered copper.

Through burned-out villages that still smelled of ash.

Over riverbeds cracked to gray stone under a pitiless sky.

Behind them, the world smoldered.

Armies hunted them. Bounty gangs followed in tight packs, silver driving them, rumor sharpening them. Riders carrying Parthian seals. Desert men. Hill men. Half-tamed mercenaries who whispered of a foreign girl with golden eyes, dancers who moved like smoke, and eunuchs who carved throats in silence.

Matineus Latinus broke their trail with the practiced instinct of a wolf bred for long kills.

He drifted ahead, then behind, then vanished into rock or brush, appearing where danger pressed the air thin. Never straight, never predictable. Day travel turned to night travel without warning. Paths bent in maddening arcs. He circled enemies. Slipped behind patrols. Snapped branches in one direction while moving in another. When dogs barked, he froze the entire line with a finger. When wind carried human breath, he folded the group into shadow.

No campfires. No songs. No wasted motion.

Heat thickened until the horizon shook.

Sand blistered hooves and cracked the lips of the mules.

Their sweat dried before it reached the skin.

Still, they pressed north. Then east. Then back south. Then north again.

The desert gave way to pines older than kingdoms. Trunks fat as towers. Bark black as tar. Branches layered so thick the sky shrank to a narrow vein of gray.

The air felt wrong there.

Needles whispered in windless stillness.

The ground breathed sap and rot.

Cold shadows pooled beneath every root.

Zarmina refused to step off the path. She walked rigid, muttering her own childhood charms between her teeth. Nisaya's eyes jumped from trunk to trunk. She whispered in her native tongue, as if arguing with invisible watchers.

They called it the Womb Forest.

In that place, fires hissed and died. Birds avoided the branches. Women bled early. Some bled longer. Every girl from the eastern tribes knew the old tale.

Albina had heard it beside a low fire when she was small, her mother's hand warm on her back.

A nameless queen once ruled there, bone crown, giant blade, women who rode bareback through the high valleys east of the Black Sea. When Alexander came to claim her land, she met him in parley and laughed in his face.

She vowed no man would rule her people.

That night she led her warriors into the forest.

Her entire host.

They vanished.

When Alexander's scouts searched the next morning, they found twelve statues, women carved in perfect detail, all turned westward as if watching the world leave them.

No one touched them.

The trees seemed taller now. Hungrier.

Confusion protected them. Confusion saved them.

One morning they reached a hidden mountain town where old men sold wool and silence. No soldiers. No questions. Smoke rose from chimneys cut low into the hillsides.

An elderly woman crafted furs without flaw, snow fox, wolf, goat, and thick mountain hare. Stitching so tight it kept the wind from slipping through.

Matineus traded silver. The group received gloves, hooded wraps, padded linen underlayers, tall boots lined in wool, and heavy coats that shone in the cold light.

No one lingered.

The old woman watched them leave with eyes like broken slate.

The mountains rose in broken teeth.

Cold struck like a thrown stone.

First the wind. Then the sky.

Gray deepened to iron.

A storm came down the slope without mercy. Snow hit sideways. Boots filled. Hands numbed. Ice climbed their lashes. Breath turned to knives.

Matineus found a slit in the mountainside, a cave big enough to hide, deep enough to shield them. He pulled the riders inside. The mules stamped. Girls huddled. Dancers wrapped their arms around their ribs. Everything shook.

The eunuchs formed a wall at the entrance, broad shoulders blocking the night, knives low, eyes fierce against the white-out beyond.

Zarmina coaxed fire from wet wood, mixing herbs that smoked blue. Nisaya fed thin branches into the flames, chanting to keep the forest from following.

The cave felt alive. Wet stone. Cold breath. Darkness gathered in corners where the snow couldn't reach.

Bodies pressed close. Heat built slowly.

Sleep followed.

Albina settled near the fire.

Fur wrapped her like a second skin, white fox on the outside, deep gray beneath, lined with wool-soft warmth that whispered along her shoulders. The hood framed her golden eyes, catching sparks from the flames. Her breath curled against the fur, leaving tiny drops of meltwater.

The coat carried the scent of earth, hide, cured leather, and faint musk. Beneath that, a trace of something sweet, cinnamon or resin from the craftswoman's hands.

Albina's fingers traced the seams. Each stitch perfect. The pelt thick and rich. The animals had died well; she honored them with every exhale.

Zarakar lay hidden along her spine, warm from her body.

She pressed deeper into the coat. For the first time since fleeing, no male gaze clung to her hips, her legs, her throat. Just warmth. Just the hush of a cave guarded by loyal blades.

Matineus watched from the entrance.

A quick glance. One heartbeat.

It hit him hard.

Even wrapped in fur, she carried the presence of a mountain spirit, ancient, still, magnetic, fierce in quiet.

He faced the storm again, swallowing the breath she stole from him.

The girls wore furs too big for them. Gloves that swallowed their fingers. Boots that creaked. One cursed her hood. Another laughed when she toppled sideways. Mirae tucked charms into her coat. Selka smacked the snow off her sleeves with warrior pride.

Albina's smile spread warmth faster than the fire.

For a moment, one small, fragile moment, they were simply alive.

Zarmina the Red stirred the coals. Smoke crawled up her arm.

Nisaya the Black leaned close to the fire, whispering.

"The wind speaks," she said.

No one answered.

Outside, the blizzard howled. Snow slid in sheets. Something shifted beneath the mountain, stone settling, or a creature older than tribes turning in its sleep.

Matineus didn't blink. His wolf-fur hood stiffened with frost. His breath vanished the moment it left his mouth.

He stood guard, a single man holding the darkness back with nothing but silence and a blade.

The mountain held its secrets.

The storm circled the cave.

Somewhere far below, others hunted their trail.

And the chase had only begun.

Snow shifted somewhere below the cave.

Not wind.

Not stone.

Something following their warmth.

And when Albina opened her eyes, she knew the mountain was no longer the most dangerous thing hunting them.

Chapter 43
ICE COLD HATRED

The Caucasus Mountains, Mountains of the Gods.

The blizzard swallowed everything.

Snow buried trails. Covered hoofprints. Silenced voices.

One by one, the scouts vanished. Bounty hunters. Trackers. Mercenaries. Gone.

Red Ring lost over one hundred thirty men to the white teeth of the mountain. He did not care. He'd send another one hundred and thirty more if he needed to.

Red Ring stood by the fire, lips cracked, jaw tight. His cloak hung heavy with frost. His toes blackened. He could not feel his left thumb.

The last scouts knelt before him. Shivering. Faces bloodied from wind and ice. One's teeth chattered so loud the sound echoed in the tent.

"The priestess is gone," one said. "Vanished. The storm ate them."

"No one lives in that," the other whispered.

Red Ring did not blink. He stepped forward.

"You found no bodies."

"No signs of fire. Of death. Of struggle."

The men said nothing.

"Then dig."

He ordered them back into the cold, back into the mountains. Told them to find every corpse. Bring back every head. He wanted faces. Names. Proof.

They found one scout. Theirs. Kneeling. Frozen solid. Eyes wide. Arms raised toward the sky.

They brought nothing else.

"Some say the storm follows her," one muttered near the edge of camp. "Not the other way around."

Red Ring sat in his tent alone, staring into the coals. They lived. He felt certainty in his bones.

That fox. That Roman bastard. Too clever. Too quiet. The one leading them now, Matineus Latinus, moved like a ghost.

He had not slept in three days. His piss froze before hitting snow. His nose bled every time he breathed deep. The meat they carried had turned grey, burned from exposure to the cold. Still, they climbed.

His brothers stayed silent. Watched. Waited.

Red Ring's hands curled into fists. His eyes burned. He would find them. And they would die screaming under his blade.

He would cut the fox's heart out. He would jar the girl's head in salt and oil. Place the trophy at his son's feet.

Outside, the blizzard screamed.

The snow bit deeper each day. Not just underfoot, but under skin. Under thoughts.

They lost men to cliffs, frost, poison. One to a child's trap, a sharpened stake buried in frozen leaves. They found his tongue thirty feet from his body. Red Ring never asked who made the simple thing. He knew.

The mercenaries had gone silent. The trackers grumbled at night and lied in the morning. Hunters stayed sheltered in warmth at night and pretended to find nothing in the day. One claimed he saw fresh ash near a streambed. Red Ring had him whipped when the proof turned up cold.

Another dropped dead mid-March. No wound. No cry. Just fell forward into the snow and didn't rise. The men didn't stop. Red Ring didn't blink.

He worried for his brothers, though he'd never admit it. The youngest coughed blood now. One brother wrapped his feet each night with lambskin and muttered prayers to gods no one named anymore.

Still, they climbed.

Still, they searched.

He'd send another hundred. Two hundred. He'd burn villages, salt rivers, hang women if it came to that. Whatever Albina was, priestess, witch, ghost, she was his to break.

He no longer cared if she lived. He just wanted to hear her scream.

Inside, Red Ring's hate screamed louder.

Chapter 44
METAMORPHOSIS

High in the Caucasus Mountains

The cave shielded them. But it did not save them.

Stone held the storm back, nothing else.

Food thinned. Fire shrank. Warmth bled away grain by grain. The smoke hung low, clinging to cloaks and throats, but the heat never reached the bones.

Even the mules trembled. Their legs shook as if trying to step out of their own skins.

The girls slept curled against one another, breath shallow, ribs showing in the flicker of dying flame. Their laughter had vanished days ago. Now they whispered only in dreams, soft and frightened.

Matineus kept the vigil.

He stood at the mouth of the cave, hood iced, cloak stiff from frost. Snow swirled around him like ghosts summoned by breath alone.

He never shook. Never shifted.

He waited with the patience of a carved idol.

When dawn came gray and empty, he said one word:

"Move."

They stepped into white.

The wind hit with teeth. Flakes cut skin. Breath froze in beards and lashes. Each step plunged knee-deep. The world behind them vanished under falling snow as if they had never lived at all.

Somewhere above, a ram staggered along the cliffs, thin, slow, doomed. One bodyguard lifted a sling. Lead whistled through the wind. The crack echoed like a bone snapping inside the sky.

They butchered the kill where it fell.

No rites. No spoken thanks.

Just knives slicing hide. Steam rising red and thick. Fat hissing as it hit snow.

They ate with bare hands. Blood warm on their tongues. The meat still shivered with heat from the animal's heart.

Then they walked again.

Too dangerous to ride. Too steep. Too slick. Too exposed.

Tracks of hunters appeared in the drifts, splintered branches, crushed snow, cold ashes. Matineus crouched once, pressed two fingers to a footprint, and pointed ahead.

They found the trackers.

Five men. Then four more.

Steel handled the rest.

The snow swallowed their blood and turned quiet again.

Smoke rose from a ridge, a shelter built of stone, half buried. A Parthian outpost. Five soldiers warmed their hands around a glowing fire.

Matineus lifted his hand. A simple gesture.

The eunuchs slipped out like shadows cast by deeper shadows.

Throats opened. Bodies folded.

No breath wasted.

Inside: a precious pocket of heat. Thick blankets. Grain. Water that didn't freeze before touching the ground.

The girls curled together like kittens around a hearth.

The horses stood close, steam rising off their backs.

The witches stripped wet furs, the air turning white with vapor as it left their bodies.

For two nights, quiet.

On the third, no fire.

Then on again.

Albina's feet bled inside her boots. Wool stuck to skin. Each step left a small warmth that froze before it reached the ground. She never spoke of the pain. And no one asked.

The cold reminded her of another night, long ago, when snow clung to her hair as she walked toward her fate.

She remembered the priestesses climbing the mountain to claim her. Their robes stiff with frost. Their lips cracked from chanting. They laid out the cedar board. Twenty relics. Twenty lives before hers.

She was six.

She touched the comb. Then the one-eyed doll. Then the lion-tooth pendant.

Her hand paused above the shard of glass, smooth on one edge, jagged on the other.

Her fingers closed around it.

The priestesses bowed.

Her father broke.

Her mother fainted.

Albina walked up the mountain that night and learned what cold could carve inside a child.

That was cold.

This was worse.

This cold stripped things from flesh, strength, warmth, hope.

Yet something in her hardened.

Something old.

Something that had waited in her bones.

The storm deepened.

Wind shrieked between the rocks.

Breath turned sharp as blades.

Albina pressed on through the white, her hood crusted with ice, her layered furs thick with frost. The coat hugged her small frame: white fox outside, soft wildcat inside. It carried the scent of earth and hide and something sweet like crushed bark.

Zarakar slept along her spine, warm against her despite the storm.

A promise.

A warning.

Snow crusted her lashes. Her golden eyes did not dim.

She walked as if the cold owed her answers.

The others followed, girls stumbling in oversized furs, witches wrapped in layers that steamed when they exhaled, eunuchs silent and sharp.

Matineus moved just ahead, a shape cut from stone and breath.

He checked the sky. Checked the wind.

Checked her.

Once, Albina faltered. Only a step. Only a heartbeat.

Matineus appeared beside her before she caught the slip. His hand hovered near her arm, close, never touching. His breath fogged the space between them.

Albina lifted her chin and walked on.

Something in her shifted then, quiet, fierce, alive.

The child taken. The priestess shaped. The girl who danced. All of them fading into something leaner. Harder. Sharper.

Not broken.

Changed.

She would not die in the snow.

She would not let her goddess die either.

She would carry fire into Rome herself if she had to drag it mile by mile through the teeth of the world.

Albina's feet bled. Her breath smoked. Her eyes glowed.

The world had taken everything from her.

Now it would learn what came back.

She will leave the mountain smaller than she entered.

The one who steps out will not need warmth again.

Chapter 45
FIRST OVER THE WALL

Temple Mount – July, 63 BCE

The orders had come. Pompey's own seal. His hand. His words.

Rufus was to return to Rome. Wait. Rest. Be seen.

A float was already prepared. His shield, his armor, maybe even the kitten curled beside it, planned to the smallest detail. A gift for the people.

Pompey wanted him alive. Feared the boy would die before Rome could watch him bleed again.

Rufus read the scroll three times. Then lit the edge with a taper and dropped the orders into the brazier.

He packed carefully.

The shield, still bristling with arrows. The kitten, no longer small, but a white predator with gold eyes and silent feet. Loyal only to him. A chest of loot from four kingdoms.

He left everything secured on his yacht, anchored and guarded.

Then turned back toward the siege. He wasn't done bleeding.

Jerusalem stood high and defiant. Stone walls. Fanatics. Smoke.

The siege had dragged for months.

Pompey chose the Sabbath. The city silent in worship. The ladders went up.

Three sections of wall. Rufus positioned near the Roman right.

Faustus Cornelius Sulla, the dictator's son in the middle section.

Rufus didn't wait for orders. He climbed.

Dust caked the leather on his boots. Each rung bit his palms. The wood groaned.

Shield on his back. Gladius tight. Arrows snapped past his ear.

A stone cracked off his helmet. No blood, just fire in the skull.

He climbed anyway.

Rufus reached the top.

He rose with a breath. One leg. One arm. Then he stood.

The courtyard sprawled below, columns cracked, altars scorched, holy ground soaked in fire and dread.

A zealot charged.

Rufus caught the blade on his scutum, arm jolted, he spun low and drove steel behind the thigh.

The man screamed. Dropped. Another came. Rufus met him clean. No noise. No mercy.

Below, someone shouted...

"Rufus is first!"

But he didn't hear those words again.

His men poured up behind him. Formed ranks. Blades tight. Shields locked.

They advanced step by step. Pressing fast before the defenders could regroup.

Blood soaked the stones.

Some leapt from the wall to avoid Roman hands. Some stayed. They died.

He led the century down the stairs. Shields raised. The smoke curled. Zealots screamed prayers their god didn't answer.

A side passage exploded with javelins.

"Testudo!" Rufus barked.

They locked into a living shell. Advanced. Rufus struck through the gap.

A spearman dropped. A club slammed his shoulder. Pain lit the joint. He grunted. Stabbed again.

The line pushed forward. Ten minutes. Then flight.

They breached the Temple Mount. Crossed into Jerusalem.

Barricades burned. Civilians fled. Streets ran with ash and noise.

Twelve men lunged from a doorway.

Rufus caught the first, twisted, drove the gladius deep.

His men finished the rest in seconds.

By dusk, the harsh siege ended.

Two hours from wall to street.

The zealots dead or gone.

Hyrcanus had opened the gate. The city cracked from within.

Rufus stood in the square, sword low, chest rising hard.

Faustus Cornelius Sulla breathing deeply, covered in blood smiled and nodded at Rufus. He had breached a Baris tower on the central section of wall.

The roof of the Temple caught firelight behind him.

Ash drifted down.

Jerusalem lay quiet beneath Rome's iron heel.

And Pompey's messenger came too late.

Too late to stop him. Too late to pull his shadow off the wall.

Chapter 46
OVERSEER

Villa Estates, Near Rome

The overseer rose late, as always. Sunlight crawled through the villa's tall windows, splashing across mosaic floors that hadn't seen a broom in days. He yawned, scratched his belly, and waved off the slave girl asleep at his feet. She stirred, dazed, and crawled from the bed without protest.

He stretched his legs, thick and soft from disuse, then reached for the silver platter by the bed. A wedge of cheese, figs, and a half-finished cup of spiced wine. He ate without sitting up, letting crumbs fall on the linens. The mattress beneath him had once belonged to the owner of the estate. A veteran, a real Roman, a man of order. Now, his name gathered dust in the shrine room, and the estate drifted.

Outside, the fields lay half-tilled. Tools rusted under awnings. The oxen had grown fat and dull-eyed. No schedule. No urgency. The harvest would wait. Everything could wait.

Inside, the overseer lounged. He bathed every three days, sometimes four. He took his meals in the central courtyard, shaded by grapevines, fed by kitchen slaves who feared his moods. Bread was always fresh. Wine always sweet. He'd beaten one boy for bringing olives too cold, another for too few.

His favorites, three girls from the slave quarters, ate with him now and then, curled on cushions, massaging his feet while he gossiped about the local markets. He spoke like a citizen. Acted like one. A cloak hung by the door, dyed red at the hem. A ring on his thumb marked him as 'steward', but no one ever checked. No one came.

He had wine brought to his bath. He had soft slippers and fresh linens every night. The masters' quarters, once solemn, clean, reserved, had turned to a den of ease. He played dice after sunset, slept till midday, and dozed again before dinner. He'd grown thick through the waist. His beard, once neat, had curled wild. He reeked of cumin and oil and sweat.

The estate's ledgers went untouched. The tools unrepaired. He left it all to others. Let them whisper, let them lie. What mattered? No one asked questions. Pompey was far off in Asia, the land changed hands, and he remained. Gold flowed through his fingers. Not much, but enough for indulgence. One day he would worry, but not today.

Even the dogs slept fat by the hearth. They barked only when woken. The overseer had made the place in his image, soft, full, dull.

That morning, he planned to eat, bed one of the girls again, then maybe ride to the far shed to check on the grape press. Or maybe not. He licked juice from his thumb and smiled. The press could wait.

Everything could wait.

He stepped out into the courtyard, barefoot, scratching his chest. The late sun glared off the tile roof. A pair of doves scattered from the fig tree. He yawned, stretched, and spat. Two girls waited by the cistern, one young, one younger. Both smiled when he passed. He said nothing.

The house slave brought figs, goat cheese, and wine. The man waved him off and sat in the shade of the portico. His fat belly rolled over the knot of his tunic. He picked at his food, drank deep, belched. Across the yard, a few field slaves gathered near the gate. One pointed. One laughed. With them, an old man in travel boots leaned on a stick.

The overseer narrowed his eyes.

"Who's that?" he asked, loud enough to be heard.

No one answered.

He shrugged. Didn't matter.

Men were heading to the fields now, late in the day, no summons. No word. No orders. And why should he care? Let them sweat. Let them earn their water tonight. He'd be feasting.

Inside, the villa smelled of roast pork and hot bread. His women had bathed, oiled, and braided their hair. He chose the middle one, the round one, the one who liked dice.

"Tonight," he said, "we drink."

And they did.

Jugs of red wine. Meat falling from the bone. Laughter. The clatter of dice on polished tile. He won, then lost, then won again. At midnight, he shouted for music. Someone found a drum. The girls danced. He threw coins.

He filled his belly and kissed them all. Then kissed the wine again. The dice rolled. He laughed until his face went red.

Sometime after the fourth jug, he slipped sideways, hit the floor, and snored.

One girl tried to rouse him. Another covered him in a cloak.

Outside, the moon turned.

In the villa's far rooms, the hearth burned low. Embers crackled. A pot hissed on the coals. The servants had gone quiet. Too quiet.

He never noticed.

In his dream, he won every throw. He kissed Rome's finest women. He sat at Caesar's side. A crown on his head. A slave at each knee.

The wind shifted. Smoke from the brazier drifted toward the open hall. Something moved past the threshold. Sandals. Heavy steps.

He didn't stir.

The last thing he heard, before morning, was his own laughter echoing off the painted walls.

The sun broke through early. Heat already pressed the shutters.

Inside the villa, the overseer groaned.

His mouth felt packed with wool. Eyes burned. Belly twisted. The wine had gone bitter in his gut. He rolled over, blinked at the light leaking through the wooden slats.

"Water," he croaked. "Cold. And orange juice."

No answer.

He wiped his face with the sheet, stained, damp, reeking of sex and sweat. The girl was gone. He couldn't remember her name. He sat up, muttering. "Clean sheets today. Eggs. Pork. Get the girls to bring fresh bread."

He clutched the edge of the table, stood slowly, legs trembling. The floor rocked under him. He belched, swallowed, and staggered to the basin.

Cold water stung his face.

He felt the hunger then, deep, clawing. "Bring the tray," he barked. "Now!"

His stomach growled.

Moments later, it came. Covered dishes. Steam. A full breakfast: roast pork, spiced eggs, figs, flatbread, fresh-squeezed juice. Silverware clinked as he arranged the plates. His belly gurgled. He grinned as he breathed it in.

Then the door exploded.

Boots thundered. Voices roared. The room filled with men, broad, armed, silent. The tray crashed. Eggs splattered. Juice spilled.

"Hey! I...what is this? Who sent you? This is a mistake!"

They didn't speak.

One grabbed his shoulder. Another yanked him by the arm. They slammed him onto the mosaic floor. His cheek hit hard stone.

He screamed. "Do you know who I am?"

Cold water dumped over his head.

He gasped, choking. "You'll pay for..."

A boot struck his ribs. Sharp sudden pain shocked him into screaming. Large men tore and cut the clothes off his body.

Ungentle hands lifted him by the arms.

He stumbled, naked but for the twisted cloth around his waist, into the courtyard. The light blinded him. The heat seared. He squinted.

Old man. Gray hair. Roman cloak. Watching. No expression.

Dozens of slaves lined the path. Quiet. Cold. Eyes locked on his fall. A few barely hid the joy they felt at his total demise.

He tried to speak. Nothing came. They stripped him completely. Threw his soiled loin cloth in the mud.

Chains clicked. Metal locked.

A whip cracked.

"Move."

He didn't.

Another crack. Fire and pain cut his flesh. His back arched. He staggered forward.

That was the moment. He knew it. The last sun he'd ever stand in free. The last full breath. The last hunger he'd ever answer. What was he thinking? If he had done his job, this would not be. Now it was too late.

He begged the old man. Pleaded for his life. The old man didn't notice his sorrow or hear his pleas and promises. The round woman he had last night openly flirted with the old man. A few workers laughed.

The over seer drowned in the sudden shock of his situation. This had to all be a dream. A nightmare.

No...

The mines waited.

The chain bit into his neck. Iron cuffs rubbed his wrists raw. The sun hadn't risen all the way, but the guards pushed them forward, bare feet, twelve men, silent but for the rattle of links and the labored breath of the weak. The overseer, now stripped of his fine tunic, walked naked. His belly, once proud and full, sagged in front of him. Each step dragged. Blood mixed with dust below his heels. No shoes. No food. No water. Just the road.

A guard shouted. The man to his left stumbled. They didn't stop. One slave died before noon. The guards unchained him, kicked his body into a ditch, and reattached the link to the next man in line.

A few moments later the sound of wild dogs feasting and fighting was clear to hear.

No names were asked. No prayers. Just movement. Onward.

The overseer drooled. He cried. He begged. He explained. His lips cracked. The taste of last night's wine soured in his gut. The pork he had craved now made his stomach twist. He'd pissed himself two hours back. No one cared.

The memories mocked him. His bed, soft. The sheets, clean. The girls, laughing. That second jug of wine, so sweet. That wonderful breakfast on the floor. The dice. His win. His laugh. All gone.

He tried to speak, but no one listened. His throat made a rasping sound. He looked up. The sun blurred. Heat shimmered the road ahead. Someone groaned. A whip cracked.

He whispered her name. The girl from last week. Or was it the one before?

The line turned slightly uphill. His feet scraped stone. His vision dimmed. Just a few more steps. Just a few.

At the crest of the hill, he saw smoke, far off, beyond the haze. The mines. Someone said they would never leave once they entered. Never see daylight again or breathe fresh air. He believed it now.

"Six months in the mines," he whispered as tears wet his cheeks. "If that, then death."

"You won't last that long fat boy," The chain master laughed.

—

Back at the villa, the old man, Rufus's grandfather, stood at the top of the field. A fresh breeze touched his face. Rows had formed again. Slaves moved with purpose. The tool house door stood open. Inside: order, sharp blades, rope coiled tight.

He turned toward the courtyard. A slave girl poured water from the cistern into a bucket. She moved quickly, eyes down. Good.

The master's suite now held no bed, just clean straw and hard benches. The food cellar had been locked. Keys hung from the old man's belt.

A Latinus villa again. He looked to the horizon.

Yes, this would be a nice addition to the Latinus family's collection.

"Back to work," he said.

His grandson deserved a well-run farm and neat estate for his heroics.

By the Gods, he would have just that.

Chapter 47
RIGHT OF
CONQUEST

J erusalem

After the wall fell, the city bled.

Roman boots hammered through smoke; doors cracked open under iron; gold changed hands in shadows. Law had slipped, and predators crawled into the space where order died.

Two locals reached the goldsmith's house first. They strangled the father. Strangled the mother. Dragged the daughter, barely sixteen, into the cellar. Beat her until her breaths hitched. Pressed a heated iron to her arm. Snapped two fingers sideways.

Her screams carried through stone.

Rufus heard them.

He kicked the door once. It flew in.

Blood streaked the stairs. The cellar glowed with flittering lamps, shadows moving like broken limbs.

He spoke no warning.

One man lunged. Rufus cut him down, blade through rib, spine, floor. The second ran for the stairs. Rufus struck clean from behind. Steel punched through lung and heart. The man collapsed face-first into his own gold dust.

The girl crouched under a table. Dress torn. Blood dried on her lip.

Her eyes were hollow, no hope, no fear, the empty stare he'd seen on pirate beaches and in villages sacked before dawn. She sat like someone paused between worlds.

Rufus stripped his cloak off, wrapped her inside it, pulled her close enough for warmth but not enough to frighten.

He turned to the official scribe in the doorway.

"This house is mine. Everything in it. By conquest. The girl as well."

The scribe bowed, ink-stained fingers trembling around the stylus.

Rufus's jaw flexed. Something in her face, quiet strength under shattered edges, cut deep. She deserved more than chains.

He sent for a rabbi.

The bodies received proper rites. Prayers. Names carved on stone. The girl sat wrapped in the cloak while Rufus stood guard over the grave pit until the last shovel of earth fell.

He paid the rabbi and the diggers in gold. Twice the price asked.

In the cellar, beneath a false plank, Rufus pried up the secret the girl's father had died protecting. Bars of gold. Dozens. Rows upon rows, years of labor, maybe lifetimes. The glow lit the stone walls like a small forge.

At dusk, Gnaeus Pompey burst in, breathless.

He took in the bodies. The girl. The treasure. His grin widened.

"You saved her?"

Rufus nodded once.

"And kept the gold?"

Another nod.

"Jupiter's teeth," Gnaeus laughed. "My father will kill us both."

Rufus cracked the smallest smile. Blood still clung to his hands.

They laughed like boys standing in a ruin.

By morning, dust and rubble filled the square. No banners. No triumph calls. Just soldiers waiting with the tense silence of men who'd seen too much.

Pompey Magnus stepped forward, dust on his boots, shadows under his eyes. He held the corona muralis, stone and brass shaped like battlements.

One crown for Faustus Cornelius Sulla. Another for the second man over the far wall. And one held for Rufus.

"My orders were clear," Pompey said. His voice cut across the square. "You were to withdraw."

Rufus stood silent, blood dried under the plates of his armor, ribs bruised, breath tight. No excuse given.

Pompey's frown eased into something warmer.

"I'm glad you disobeyed."

He raised the crown.

"First over your section of the wall. Witnessed by a hundred men. The Wall Crown is yours."

He set it on Rufus's head.

The weight surprised him. Stone and brass pressed down like Rome's hand resting heavy on his skull.

The legion roared. Shields struck in rhythm. Dust shook loose from the roofs.

Pompey leaned close. "Get back to Rome before you die and ruin everything."

Twelve Praetorians formed up for his escort, iron helms, strict eyes, shields big as doors.

The girl rode in a small litter. The gold filled two wagons, wheels groaning under the load. Rufus glanced back at her once. She held his cloak wrapped tight, hands hidden inside, shoulders small in the dim morning light.

Her name was Tirzah.

They moved west.

The road wound through burned huts, broken shrines, shattered stone towers. Scrub trees clung to rock like hands searching for water.

They camped without fire that night. Cold bread. Dry meat. A pot of thin broth passed from palm to palm. Tirzah ate in silence. Rufus didn't ask why she stared at the earth between her knees.

At dawn the sea rose ahead, hard and silver.

His yacht waited in the shallows: low black hull, sails tied tight, anchor sunk deep. A proud eagle at rest.

The gold groaned with every push up the gangplank.

Rufus boarded with Tirzah. The small kitten in its basket blinked once at the light. The ship shoved off.

No trumpets. No cheering crowds. Just the hiss of wind, the strike of oars, the creak of wood under wealth and blood.

Tirzah pulled the cloak tighter. Her eyes stayed hollow. Her lips closed against the wind.

Rufus stood at the prow, memories heavy in his skull, waves below sliding past like slabs of black stone.

Rome would hear of this. Rome would remember.

The right of conquest carried him now, a girl, a fortune, a crown, and the beginning of a bloodline the world could never again ignore.

The price had been paid in full.

Night wrapped the ship in cold and salt. The hull groaned with each swell, a slow, wooden breath that rose and fell beneath her bare feet. Tirzah sat in the dark near the stern, wrapped in the cloak he'd given her, knees drawn tight, rocking with the sea.

The lamps had burned low. Most men slept. Oars hung idle. Above, the stars hid behind a dull smear of cloud.

Rufus slept near the prow, back against the mast, arms folded over his chest. His crown rested in his cabin on a folded cloth, brass catching the faint light like a coiled beast.

She watched him.

His face looked different in sleep. Not softer, nothing soft lived in him. The lines cut by battle eased a little. His breaths came slow, steady. As if nothing haunted him. As if he feared nothing that walked this world.

Tirzah touched the edge of her cloak. His cloak. It still held a trace of his warmth. A trace of smoke. A trace of battle.

Monster, she thought.

Maybe.

He had claimed her. Spoken her fate aloud in front of strangers in beautiful Latin. Wrapped her in his cloak as if she had no will. No name. No choice.

Yet he had buried her parents with honor. Paid for stone. Paid for prayer. Stood over the graves until the earth settled flat. He had done what others would not bother doing for a slave.

She breathed once, thin and sharp.

Fate, she thought.

Maybe.

Wind hissed past the sails. A rope snapped against the mast. Shadows swayed, long and restless. The ship rocked harder, enough to make her brace a hand against the deck.

She looked at the dagger hidden under the cloak. Not hers. Taken from one of the dead men in the cellar. A curved blade. Nicked edge. Short handle. Useful.

If she slid across the deck now, quiet, careful, she could reach him before the next swell hit. She could press the blade under his ribs. She knew where. Her father had taught her that long ago, when lessons were spoken in whispers and life still had warmth.

One thrust. One push. Quick. Clean.

The sea would take him.

The men would wake to chaos. She could slip over the rail. She could swim. Maybe.

Or drown.

But drowning belonged to her. That choice belonged to her.

Tirzah rose to her knees, heart kicking once, hard. She felt the weight of the blade. Felt the cold under her nails. Watched his chest rise. Fall. Rise again.

She waited for hatred to flood her.

It didn't.

Something else stirred, fear, yes, and a thread of heat she couldn't name. She hated him for that. For saving her. For owning her. For giving her warmth she didn't ask for.

The ship rolled. The dagger slipped in her grip. She froze.

Rufus shifted in his sleep, one hand brushing the hilt at his hip. Not waking. Not aware. Even unconscious, he carried battle inside him.

Tirzah sank back into the shadow near the stern. Pulse hammering. Knife pressed under her arm.

She stared at him a long time, breathing slow, letting the storm in her chest settle enough to stand.

Not tonight, she thought.

Not yet.

She wrapped the cloak tight. Leaned her head against the beam. Listened to the sea whisper under the hull.

Her fate sat ten paces away, asleep with a sword at his side.

Her future held a life she didn't want, a road she didn't choose.

Her knife still had a chance to change both.

Sleep didn't come.

Just the question, sharp, unfinished, curling through her mind like smoke.

When the moment comes... will I save him, or end him?

Chapter 48
QUIET SEA

Somewhere at Sea

Rufus didn't rush home.

He had every reason to; honors waited, a senator's seat, a villa on the Caelian Hill with heated floors, painted walls, bedrooms with private baths and toilets, free water for life, even a marble desk from Cicero already set in place. A large farm and estate. Rome had prepared itself for him.

Rufus hadn't.

Not yet.

He stood at the stern while the coastline slid past in long, slow lines. Wind slapped his face. Salt cut his breath.

He'd seen too much. Killed too close. Certain sounds lingered: iron striking stone, a scream swallowed mid-breath, a man exhaling wrong in the dark. They hid under the ribs. Sometimes they woke with him.

He'd rise with fists tight. Or wake with steel already drawn. Near Rhodes he almost struck a cook who touched his shoulder too fast.

Long silences unsettled him. Even at sea.

When the hull rocked the right way, it echoed the wagon crushing bodies outside a burning gate. When the ropes shifted overhead, they carried the weight of a neck breaking. When gulls cried, he heard the wet rattle of a dying man on a cold field.

So he stood in the wind. Let the salt burn what only salt could reach. Let the sea strip the last of the blood that never washed out.

He regretted nothing. But he carried everything.

He ordered the captain to sail south, toward warmer waters.

"Slow," Rufus said. "Stop each night at a port or anchor under a quiet shore."

He needed warmth. Needed days without death. Needed to feel his feet firm under him before Rome swallowed him whole.

Tirzah stayed close. Quiet, but not withdrawn. She smiled more. Small, cautious, real.

She kept the kitten on her lap most afternoons, brushing his fur with slow, careful strokes. The tiny creature stretched, kneaded her dress, curled into her ribs.

Sometimes Rufus watched them both, girl and cat, and felt the noise inside him ease. He hadn't known a kitten could be funny. Or that watching a girl braid her hair could soften the edges of a hard day.

Nights came gentle. No alarms. No scouts. No rain of stones, arrows, or javelins.

They ate simple food on deck: dates, olives, flatbread, roasted fish. The kind of food a man trusted.

He often slept out there, wrapped in wool, the kitten tucked under his arm. Tirzah curled beside the storage chest, cloak tight, eyes half-open at each shift of the sea.

Days blurred. No screams. No orders. No blood.

Just water. Just wind. Just the long road home.

In Crete, a Greek scholar boarded, a gift from Pompey.

Thin. Quick. Always smelling faintly of ink and lemons.

He spoke without pause. Questioned everything. Then questioned the answer.

Lessons twice a day.

Rhetoric. Law. Senate customs. Curses and blessings in rough Homeric Greek.

He made Rufus stand on the stern and shout arguments against the waves. Forced him to take one idea and bend it three ways: with logic, with fire, with laughter.

"You command silence after your words," the scholar snapped. "Or your command is nothing."

He drilled debates: speak as the accuser; speak as the defender; speak without notes; speak as if peasants listened; speak as if senators judged; speak as if gods waited for the last line.

"Truth alone convinces no one," the scholar said. "Give it rhythm. Weight. Inevitable force. Strike like a hammer, end like a chorus. This is how Rome bends."

Rufus hated the drills. But he learned. His voice steadied. His breath sharpened. His mind followed.

In Rhodes, he hired two Egyptian women.

Names unspoken. Faces calm.

One rubbed his shoulders with oil, kneading knots of old pain.

The other worked his feet until the tightness eased.

Neither spoke. They had seen men like him before, men carrying too much war under their skin. He paid double.

He bought Tirzah earrings. A gold bracelet. A black dress. Shoes soft enough for temple floors.

She went to synagogue when she could, stepping inside with bowed head and steady breath.

At night she still wore her old tunic, curled beside the kitten, the cloak pulled up to her chin.

She stood taller now. Her voice carried more weight, even in silence.

In Alexandria, they rented a floor in a small white house near the harbor.

They made love there for the first time.

She lit candles. Warm light spilled over stone and linen. He undressed her slowly, letting each touch speak for him.

Just breath, skin, and hands learning one another.

He didn't ask about her past.

She didn't cry.

She smiled, tiny, brave, real.

Afterward, she pressed her cheek to his chest and whispered against his skin.

"I feel safe."

Rufus fell asleep with her hair under his chin and woke with fewer ghosts.

The night settled warm over Alexandria, a low hum rising from the harbor. Lamps flickered through latticed windows. Spices burned somewhere below, cinnamon carried on a soft wind.

Tirzah stepped onto the balcony wrapped in a thin linen shawl. Candlelight behind her turned the cloth to gold around her shoulders. She rested both hands on the stone rail, watching the city glow.

Rufus stood in the doorway, still half in shadow. He said nothing. Just watched the line of her back as she leaned into the breeze.

"Beautiful," she whispered.

He stepped closer. "The city?"

She shook her head. "The quiet."

He joined her at the railing. Below them, fishermen pushed off from shore. Torches lit their boats like drifting stars. The water moved slowly, heavy, each swell carrying a thin line of fire.

The air tasted of salt and roasted figs. Somewhere, a woman sang to a baby in a minor key, the notes climbing and falling like the tide.

Tirzah closed her eyes. Her hair brushed his forearm. That small touch held more power than battle drums ever did.

"You sleep easier here," she said.

"A little."

"The ghosts are quieter."

He studied her face in the dim light, calm brow, soft jaw, a faint glow on her cheek. "And you?"

She hesitated, then nodded. "Here... I breathe." Her fingers traced the edge of the railing. "When the sea moves like this... nothing chases me."

A long silence swelled between them. A held breath.

Rufus turned slightly, enough to see her profile. "You smile more."

"You laugh less," she answered, but her voice carried warmth.

The kitten ran out, tail high, brushing between their ankles before jumping onto the rail. Tirzah steadied him with a hand, fingers curled under his belly.

Rufus's hand brushed hers by accident, or maybe not. Both of them stilled.

She didn't pull away.

Wind lifted a lock of her hair. The strand drifted across his knuckles. Enough to make something shift inside him.

Below, the harbor shimmered like a bowl of molten bronze. A distant temple bell rang once.

Tirzah looked up at him. "You brought me here."

"You came with me."

"Not the same."

He didn't answer. The truth pressed against his ribs: he had taken her, yes. But something had changed in the slow days, in the soft nights, in the rhythm of waves and breath and silence. He wasn't sure when. He only knew it happened.

Tirzah leaned slightly into his shoulder. She felt cleaner. Trust, maybe. Or rest.

Rufus covered her hand with his.

The city glowed under them, gold, amber, fire.

She watched the horizon as dawn bled over the water. "I don't know what waits in Rome," she murmured.

"Neither do I."

A beat.

"Will you protect me there?"

He didn't look away from the sea. "Yes."

"Even from Rome itself?"

He breathed out, slow. "Especially from Rome."

The kitten crawled into her arms. She held him close, chin sinking into his fur.

Tirzah pressed her shoulder against Rufus again, the faintest weight. "Then... I'm not afraid."

They stood together as the sun climbed over the harbor, her shawl warm against his arm, his hand still on hers, the whole city moving beneath them like one long, living breath.

He felt her lean into him again, soft as breath, and for the first time he didn't know if it meant safety... or surrender.

In the mornings he watched the cat chase dust in the sunbeams. Watched merchants argue over spice prices. Watched young men spar with wooden swords on cracked stone courtyards.

He had nearly died in Jerusalem. He might die in Rome.

But for the first time in a long time, he lived.

Chapter 49
WHERE THE MUD ENDS

Caucasus Mountains

Weeks crawled past.

Snow melted into rivers. Rain punched holes in the earth. The world softened, broke, turned into one endless field of mud.

Mud in boots. Mud in blankets. Mud in the last scraps of food. Mud in their mouths.

Albina hated every step through it. The mire sucked at her stride, pulling her backward, swallowing her ankles. Wet robes clung to her thighs until the skin split open, raw and bright. Blisters burst on her toes. Cloth tore. She never complained. Not once.

The night before, they had slept standing, backs pressed to trees, bodies swaying like storm-bent trunks. Exhaustion dragged them down in slow, shaking waves.

No dry ground. No firewood. A grain sack chewed open by vermin.

Even Zarmina and Nisaya kept their silence.

They moved each dawn without speaking, never resting twice in the same patch of earth. Always watching the tree line. Always hungry. They dodged patrols. Slipped past bounty hunters. Buried their footprints with pine needles and prayer.

They lost weight. Lost shoes. Lost sleep. Lost small pieces of themselves.

But never the path.

The air stank of sweat, wet leather, and fear left too long without breath. Mud clung to ankles like shackles. Each step sent fire up their legs, thighs burning, heels split, shoulders chafed raw under packs heavy with relics, herbs, charms, and memory.

Then came the morning on the ridge.

Matineus halted first, arm raised, shoulders squared against the rising sun.

Albina stepped beside him. Roksana and Yamina crowded close, breath steaming white into cold air. Darak and Samut closed in, their blades half-drawn.

Below, a green valley opened like a held breath.

Grass rolled in waves. Trees swayed in clean wind. A silver river wound through the heart of it.

At the far edge sat a village... Phasis.

Wooden houses. A stone temple. Low shops. Thin trails of smoke curling through calm sky. Greek, Colchian, and Roman voices drifted faint on the breeze. A town still alive. A place that had forgotten war.

Farther out: the Black Sea.

Blue water glittered like a polished shield, bright enough to make Albina blink.

She inhaled. Grass. Warm bread. Sunlight on water. Wind that carried no blood.

Light like that had no right to exist after all they had crossed.

A ship lay anchored in the bay, low, fast, painted in Latinus colors, blood-red and black.

A mail carrier. One of Rufus's.

Waiting. Ready. Exactly where they needed it.

Rome had not forgotten the Sibyl after all.

Albina's chest tightened. For the first time since the temple, she didn't feel hunted.

She felt recognized.

Behind her, Zermeh dropped to her knees, forehead pressed to wet soil.

Nisaya kissed the earth. Zarmina whispered a prayer meant for ancient ears.

Raevan, the youngest eunuch, wiped tears with the back of his hand and tried to hide them.

Matineus looked at the valley. Then at Albina.

A rare smile touched his mouth, sharp, tired, real.

She looked back. Their eyes met.

Exhaustion softened. Something warmer flickered.

A private thing.

A forbidden thing.

His cheek lifted; her breath caught; her lashes lowered just once.

Darak noticed and shifted his stance.

No uncut man touched the Sibyl. Not even a friend.

The bodyguards would carve a man open for less.

But the moment passed through them like a breath. Light. Dangerous. Gone.

They descended the ridge fast.

The witches moved with purpose, robes heavy with mud.

The eunuchs closed in around Albina, a silent wall of steel and muscle.

The dancers whispered prayers, charms, fragments of home.

Smoke rose from village chimneys, thin, steady, calm.

Hot water waited.

Bread.

Wine.

Sleep.

Dry skin. Warm blankets. A bed that didn't shift under ribs. A night without fear. Sleep behind tall, guarded walls.

No one cheered. Misery had taught them caution. Joy vanished quickly in this world.

But that night, in Phasis, they rested.

No songs, no rituals.

Only steam curling from weary bodies.

Feet soaking in warm water.

Wounds cleaned.

Hands unclenching from knives.

Steam rose thicker near the back rooms where hot water simmered in clay tubs. Albina stepped inside alone, the door shut by Zarmina's hand. The heat struck her first, soft, full, alive, wrapping her like a memory of home.

She peeled off the mud-soaked robe. The weight dropped from her shoulders in one wet slap. Beneath it, her skin carried weeks of travel: bruises blooming yellow, lashes from branches, red grooves where straps dug deep.

Albina dipped a hand into the bath. Warmth climbed her wrist, her arm, her throat. Her breath shook once. Not from pain. From release.

When she slid into the water, the surface cupped her hips, her ribs, her spine. Dirt drifted away in thin clouds. The scent of crushed herbs floated up, lavender, wild mint, and something older, something her people kept in pouches for sacred rest.

She leaned back, hair spilling in dark ropes across the water. The heat crawled into her thighs, eased the raw places, loosened the tight grip of fear around her lungs.

For the first time since the temple, she felt her body return to her, piece by piece, breath by breath.

Her eyes closed. The water hummed around her.

She whispered a name under her breath, one of the old names, spoken by priestesses to call back strength.

A low wind slid through the shutter. The flame in the corner bent toward her, as if answering.

When Albina rose from the bath, steam curled around her legs.

She felt clean.

She felt alive.

She felt seen by the goddess who had not abandoned her.

Albina slept first, head on Roksana's lap, hair spread like black silk.

Matineus watched her once before turning away. His smile returned, small, private.

The worst had passed.

For now.

But peace never held long for people chosen by gods.

And the sea waited below them, calling their names.

Chapter 50
MARBLE, MEN, MISCHIEF

Rome

The courtyard school of Domina Aurelia buzzed louder than usual. The day hadn't started, but the gossip had.

Spring sun spilled across the tiled roof. Vines climbed marble columns. Bees hovered at the garden's edge. Inside, six girls lounged on cushions, pretending to study.

None did.

"Have you heard?" Fulvia asked. Her voice quivered with the effort not to shout.

Tullia, Cicero's daughter, rolled her eyes. "Which story this time?"

"The house," Fulvia whispered. "The one Crassus gave him."

Julia Caesaris leaned forward. "The one on the Caelian?"

Fulvia nodded hard. "All marble. Heated floors. A pool with glass tiles. Water from the new aqueduct. Free. For life."

"Of course," said Junia Secunda, Servilia's youngest. "Crassus built the aqueduct."

"Don't forget the mosaic baths," Calpurnia Pisonis added. "With steam rooms. Actual glass windows. And the three main bedrooms with their own baths."

"My mother said the house has fountains that never stop running," Julia said. "And a terrace big enough to hold a dinner for thirty."

Fulvia sighed. "And he hasn't even arrived yet."

"You mean Rufus?" Tullia teased.

Fulvia didn't blink. "Of course I do."

Rufus's sister, Latina Junia, sat in the corner, carving small letters into a wax tablet.

"Everything you said is true," she said.

The others quieted.

Latina glanced up. "And yes. He earned the civic crown. Two crowns actually. First over the wall at Jerusalem, along with Sulla's son."

"That's not all he earned," Calpurnia said. "There's the treasure. And the girl."

"What girl?" Junia asked.

Fulvia's mouth tightened. "A Jewish girl. From the siege. Her family had gold hidden. Lots. She was saved. Claimed."

"She's not Roman," Tullia said.

"She's his slave," Fulvia snapped.

Silence.

Then Julia asked, "And the cat?"

"The cat's real," Latina said. "It sleeps in the sun. Eats bugs. Follows him everywhere."

"A soldier with a kitten," Junia mused.

"And two crowns" Calpurnia said. "Don't forget that."

"He's still not back," Fulvia muttered. "Not yet. I'll be the first to know."

"You mean your father will," Tullia said.

Fulvia ignored her. "Father is in charge of Ostia this year."

Then Julia asked, "What about the priestess?"

They all looked at her.

"Albina," she said. "The one from the east. The one with the amber eyes and the powerful legs."

"The dancer?" Junia asked.

"The witch?" Calpurnia whispered.

"The oracle," Fulvia said. "They say she escaped."

"They say Parthians took her," Julia said. "They burned her temple."

"Then a rescue," Tullia added. "A dozen scouts dead. A madman leading them."

"Our brother, rescued her," Latina said. "Matineus. He's... different."

"A fox," Fulvia said.

The others nodded.

"They're still out there," Julia said. "Running."

"Heading for the Black Sea," Junia guessed.

"With a Parthian army behind them," Calpurnia added.

"Wouldn't it be wild," Tullia grinned, "if she ends up in Rome?"

"Don't be ridiculous," Fulvia snapped.

"She's already here," Latina said.

They turned to her.

"In the minds of every man," she said. "And in the dreams of every woman who's ever wanted to be something more."

"They call this gossip," Julia added, voice soft. "But it's how power moves. First in whispers. Then in law."

Calpurnia smirked. "Let Fulvia have her kitten and her lion. But who gets the Sibyl?"

Julia and Latina exchanged a glance.

Tullia swatted a fly with a scroll. "This is why Cicero mastered Latin. So, his daughter could swat insects."

The young women laughed again.

"Anyway, when I marry Rufus," she teased, "the cat gets my side of the bed. I'm going to be all over his."

"Only if you beat Fulvia to the altar," Julia said.

They all burst into laughter. The scrolls were forgotten again. And the gossip flowed like wine.

Later, in her room, Fulvia sat before a polished silver mirror.

She remembered every rumor. Every name.

Rufus.

She pictured the marble house waiting for him. The fountains. The hot floors. The bed in the western chamber where a woman might sleep, wrapped in wealth, wrapped in him.

Fulvia closed her eyes. She saw herself there.

Then another face rose in the dark.

Amber eyes. Black hair.

A girl from nowhere, carried by whispers and war. A girl who had walked barefoot through fire and mud. A girl the men feared, and the women dreamed about.

Albina.

Fulvia's jaw tightened. She felt her heart thump once, hard, stubborn, jealous.

The Sibyl lived in the world of legends.

Fulvia lived in Rome.

But legends had a habit of stepping into cities.

She pressed a palm to her chest, steadying her breath.

If the priestess ever came here, she thought, Rome will choose sides. And so will he.

The fountain dripped once, sharp as a pin dropping.

Fulvia turned toward the Caelian Hill, the place where Rufus's house waited, empty for now.

She whispered a promise no one heard:

"I'll be there."

And the moon caught her face, bright, determined, dangerous.

Chapter 51
A TIME TO HEAL

The Black Sea

Albina asked Matineus for one thing:

"Tell the captain... no haste. Let the ship stop at every harbor, every village, every inlet, every spring."

She spoke in Greek, her voice calm, firm.

Matineus studied her; he knew the reason before she finished. Her people needed time. The flesh hung from their bones, the hollows under their eyes still carried mountain frost and desert fire. She would not let them arrive in Rome as shadows.

So, the ship slowed. Not much, never long at anchor. Just enough to take on water, trade a bolt of cloth for baskets of figs, a string of fish, flatbread warm from the stone. At first the crew cursed the delays but soon learned to enjoy the cruise. Albina's people healed.

The sea stayed calm for weeks. The days lost their edge of fear.

Albina stood at the rail most mornings, hair knotted by wind, eyes fixed on the horizon. She never forgot the chase behind them, but the distance grew. Each morning of salt and sun carved away the gauntness.

The time of tears had passed.

Pain didn't vanish; pain settled. The ache dropped anchor deep inside her, but it no longer dragged her under. She slept through the night again. Once, she even laughed, when a gull panicked at its own shadow on the sail.

Her body found rhythm again.

One evening, as the moon rose silver, she danced.

Nothing grand. Just enough to breathe.

The girls followed. Barefoot on wood, their bracelets hushed, their hips swaying in time. No incense, no drums, no temple smoke. Only sea and sky. No man watched; the bodyguards turned their backs; swords crossed at their chests.

Matineus stepped down to the lower deck, alone with the night. He knew better than to look.

Albina's body still ached. Her skin was tight from healing; thighs bandaged, red beneath the cloth. Each step tugged something deeper than flesh, but she moved anyway. Anklets rang soft, one bell, then another.

The girls circled her without a word. No one led, no one followed. They moved like shadows, like memory. Albina kept her eyes half-lowered, not trance, never trance. She owned each motion. She turned once, raised her hand, bent her knees. Not deep; not yet. Enough to carry weight heavier than muscle: mountains, blood, mud, fear, silence after screams.

Each breath found rhythm. Each motion became truth.

This dance had no throne, no altar. Only survival.

She danced to remember, to honor the stones that burned, to summon the names of the lost. Each step called up memory, called down strength. It was not joy. It was not kindness.

It was statement:

I live. After everything thrown at me, I live.

Her feet remained swollen, wrapped each night, soaked in saltwater. The witches rubbed pungent paste into her calves. She stretched at dawn, spun barefoot before the others woke. At first, alone, silent.

New dances came. Not inherited; not taught. Born from the march, the cold, the mountain, the mud. They hurt to learn. The younger girls stumbled. The older ones wept when they finished.

Zarmina watched with narrow eyes. Nisaya said nothing. Then Zarmina nodded once. Approval enough.

Albina dropped to one knee, rose, turned three times, left, right, left... like prey hunted but never caught. Her girls followed in broken rhythm. Learning through the ache.

Matineus leaned against the mast, eyes closed. He could feel the power even with lids shut.

Albina had returned. Not the same. Not what she had been. But whole.

Matineus watched her from the mast, the firelight catching her braid, and thought she no longer carried a goddess, she carried a throne.

She knew soon she would dance for Rome. For Rufus. Not for worship. Not for vision. For power. To win him. To hold him. She would give him what he thought he wanted, then what he needed.

The Sibyl of the East now wore linen and leather. No throne behind her. No temple ahead. But her people still followed. That was enough.

She would build again.

The ship touched small ports along the Black Sea.

At one harbor, children ran barefoot along the dock, selling bread still warm in reed baskets. At another, an old Greek poured sour wine from clay jars and muttered about pirates. In a fishing village, the girls tasted honey for the first time since the temple. Their faces brightened; the sweetness clung to their fingers.

The eunuchs sparred on deck, strength slowly returning, blades flashing again with their old rhythm. The witches filled satchels with new herbs, bitter roots, fungi dried in the sun. Albina's people regained color, muscle, laughter.

When they reached Odessa, dawn gilded the coast.

Clay houses lined the shore. Vines climbed cracked walls. An old Greek column jutted near a spring.

The ship pulled in slowly. The crew threw ropes. Locals watched, wary.

Albina stepped off barefoot. Kissed the soil. Stood tall.

They ate full meals. Drank clean water. Bought new clothes, linen, sashes, soft leather, even silk. No one chased them. No one whispered.

The witches walked the marketplace as if they belonged. The girls smiled again, faint but real. The eunuchs sharpened their blades with oil and whetstone, steel ringing steady.

They were alive.

Albina lifted her face to the sky.

When I dance next, she thought, Rome will watch, and Rome will listen.

Chapter 52
NOT MEANT TO BE

Odessa

They stayed longer than planned.

Odessa asked no questions. A quiet town with simple rhythms.

Albina and her girls bathed in the river each morning. The witches climbed the hills to gather herbs. The eunuchs trained at dawn, blades slicing cold air.

Sometimes, Albina, accompanied by her guards, walked the shore with Matineus.

They rarely spoke.

But once, on the third evening, he said...

"Caesar will take you in. He'll care for you. Your people. He sees what you are."

Albina didn't answer. She knew differently. Her eyes followed the sea. She had seen otherwise.

News reached them by a trader's mouth.

Rufus of the Latinus line, first over the wall at Jerusalem.

Lion killer. Hero of Pompey. Civic Crown. Rewarded. A villa on the Caelian. A farm. A girl beside him. Gold. Glory. The senate.

Matineus told the story often, grinning with pride.

Albina overheard him once, outside a bakery, beneath an awning.

"Your brother," she said. "What is his name?"

He turned. "Rufus."

She didn't speak. But something inside her shifted.

A sign. The brother of her rescuer. Rufus. The name fit the shape she'd carried for years. The one in her visions. The man she would give herself to.

The one and only. The father of her son, and of the girls who would carry the line forward.

Later that day, the witches sat in silence. Zarmina poured a line of salt across the floor. Nisaya stared into coals, unmoving. Signs confirmed this was the Rufus.

That night, Albina walked beside Matineus again. They passed a group of young men near the market. The boys stared too long. One licked his lips.

A bodyguard stepped forward. Knife half-drawn. Silent.

Matineus laughed under his breath. "You always draw stares."

Albina stopped. Her voice stayed even. Cold.

"They've looked at me like that since I bled at twelve."

Matineus said nothing.

"At thirteen, I became the Sybil. Reborn."

She met his eyes.

"I am fourteen now. And I hate them for it. Every single one."

Matineus turned toward her.

She kept walking. She didn't raise her voice. Didn't show anger. But her hands closed at her sides.

"They don't see me," she said. "Not really."

"Just the body."

"Not the fire."

"I danced for gods. Not for hunger-eyed boys. They think I was made for them. They don't know they are dust beneath the feet of the old ones."

She stopped again. Faced him.

"I was meant to stay untouched. That was the path. The sacred duty."

"Then the Parthian king's dog took that future from me."

She looked down at her hands. Pale lines crossed her palms, faint, familiar. She remembered holding the sacred knife, the incense bowls, the scrolls burned and blessed by night.

"I was meant to stay within the veil," she said. "To eat only what the old women placed before me. To speak only when the stars aligned. To dance for the goddess, not for kings, not for men or boys. Never to be touched. Never to be claimed."

She stepped away from him, voice steady now.

"I would have died with clean skin. I would have been wrapped in linen, burned beside the black root, my ashes mixed with oil and water and given to the next child to choose."

She turned her head, jaw tight.

"But now... now I walk the mud. I bleed into cloth. I drink from shared cups. I ride under guard. I speak to men who look at me like something already theirs."

Her eyes found his again, hard, dry, gold like molten stone.

"He took that from me. Not just my body. The whole path. The whole thread. And now I must find another."

She paused.

"I go to Rome. I go to a man I have only seen in visions. Not because I want to. I do not. I do so because I must. Because my few remaining people must live. Because the line must not end."

Matineus stayed silent. He glanced at the nearest bodyguard. The knife still half-drawn.

Albina looked to the hills.

"Now I do what I must."

"To protect my goddess."

"To protect what remains."

He felt the anger in her words, and the frustration. He also felt her acceptance of the new reality.

The sun dipped lower. Their shadows stretched into one long shape on the sand.

Neither stepped aside. The blended shadow said more than words ever could.

When the light shifted, the shape broke. They walked on.

He said nothing else. But he knew it then.

He loved her.

She knew it too. She never spoke of it. Some things are not meant to be. Not in this world. Not in this life.

She paused at the edge of the village.

"This life is not the only one," she said softly.

He turned toward her. Just once.

"Then may the next be kinder."

She didn't answer. But her eyes did.

Then they walked on. Not together.

But not apart.

Chapter 53

SHADOW ON THE RIDGE

O dessa

They had rested long enough.

The salt air had done its work. Faces once hollow now carried color. Albina's girls laughed when they thought no one watched, splashing water at the edge of the bay, braiding their hair with ribbons they'd bought at the market. The eunuchs had grown restless; their blades stayed sharp, but their hands twitched for the rhythm of real work. Even the witches, who seldom smiled, hummed soft tunes while they ground herbs at the hearth.

The villagers had not feared them. They had welcomed them. Baskets came daily: eggs warm from the coop, soft goat cheese wrapped in leaves, dried apricots. A fisherman's boy once offered Albina a necklace of shells, rough, uneven, but beautiful and strung with care. She thanked him with a nod and slipped it into her satchel. For weeks, life felt borrowed, almost ordinary.

But peace is a brittle thing.

That morning, the river lost its song. Its bubbling drowned under silence. Birds vanished from the orchard. A stray dog howled once and never again. Nisaya turned her face toward the hills, eyes narrowed, muttering in the tongue of the highlands.

By midmorning, one of Matineus's scouts came pounding down the ridge path, chest heaving, sweat mixing with dust.

"A rider," he said. His voice cut sharp, already stripped of hope. "Above the orchard. Watching."

Matineus's body tightened like a bow. "How long?"

"Long enough to count us. Then he turned west."

A line passed through them, invisible but felt. The witches froze. The girls clutched their satchels. The eunuchs stood taller, hands brushing hilts.

Zarmina stepped forward, her shadow stretched long across the dirt. "They found us." Her voice was flat, a pronouncement, not a guess. "The red shadow rides again."

"Red Ring," Matineus muttered. The name soured in his mouth. "He's close."

Orders followed, quiet, quick, practiced. No shouting. No panic. This was what they had trained for: the moment when shelter shattered.

The villagers watched from doorways, their baskets lowered. No farewells were offered now. No more eggs, no more fruit. They understood what it meant when strangers packed too fast, too silent.

The crew checked ropes. The girls tied bundles with practiced hands. The witches closed their satchels. The eunuchs lifted shields and adjusted straps.

Albina gave one nod. That was all it took.

At the gangplank, she paused. Turned her face inland. The hills rolled away into silence, dark ridges against pale sky. Somewhere up there, a rider galloped toward war with her name in his mouth.

I have given them my back for the last time, she thought. Next time, I will face them.

She stepped aboard.

The ship pushed off mid-afternoon. No coins exchanged. No prayers whispered. Only the whisper of the sea against wood.

The sails filled with clean wind. The oars dipped once, twice, then fell into rhythm.

Behind them, Odessa shrank, a village of smoke and clay, fading into the line of trees. Soon it was a memory, a place that had almost felt like home but never could.

Ahead: open water.

The wind stiffened, pulling them south. Toward the straits. Toward the Republic. Toward Rome. Toward Rufus.

Albina leaned against the rail. The salt stung her cracked lips, but her eyes stayed bright. She thought of the dance she would one day give: not for Parthian guards, not for frightened villagers, but for Rome itself. For him. She would make them listen. She would make him believe.

Matineus stood at the stern, hands tight on the rail. He scanned the horizon, as if he could already see sails of pursuit forming in the distance. He knew this reprieve would not last. Red Ring had her scent. The Parthian King still held his pride. The chase would follow.

But for this day, for this stretch of sea, they had bought themselves time.

The eunuchs stood close to Albina, blades resting but ready. The witches sat cross-legged, eyes on the water, lips moving in soundless prayers. The girls whispered to each other about clean beds, warm food, new dresses, as if those things might come again.

The sea stretched wide and endless. Rome waited at the far end of it.

And somewhere behind them, across ridge and road, the red shadow gathered.

The ship carried her far, yet the hunt clung close, silent as breath on her neck.

Chapter 54
RED RING RIDES

Ridge overlooking Odessa

He arrived at dusk. The sea still kept the last light like a hot coal. Far on the horizon, a black sail slid and thinned; then the mast vanished. Red Ring watched until the sea closed over that dark point. No shout left his throat. No prayer left his mouth. He sat on a stone and let the night set his edges.

Around him men moved: campfires lit with practiced hands, horses fed, blades whet against stone. They made the small noises of survival; measured, efficient. Red Ring did not join them. He sat and spun the ring on his finger: heavy copper red, rim worn soft from blood. After each kill he had dipped that ring into a pool of hot iron and caught the blood on its face. A tally no man could counterfeit; a ledger that wouldn't lie.

Dawn came gray and thin. Hooves broke the silence: four riders; brothers, each carved by a different kind of war. One returned missing an ear; one kept his face still while his mind scanned; one chewed his gums as if chewing the names of the dead; one smiled in the wrong places and at the wrong times, which made the others watch him like a loose thread. They dismounted without words. No fire of welcome rose. Only the flap of capes, the click of buckles.

Red Ring stood. Movement, slow as a blade drawn: a man who had held too many bodies in his hands and had not let one go. He did not ask for loyalty; he produced commands by the shape of his back.

"Join me," he said, and the brothers said nothing, only nodded.

Orders fell like stones. "No more following the army," he said. "No one names her. The king keeps men to the east; we take the west. No more coin for traitors; no more bounties. Men who want to die with pay may walk east; those who want gold go home. We ride north, Danube before the thaw. West along the river's bend; Pannonian valleys; river passes; the Alpine teeth. Cut Roman lines if we must. Then Gaul. Then the Rhine. Then into Italia by the bones of old roads." He drew lines in the dirt with the tip of his blade; the shapes were a map made of promises and long study.

A brother spat. "And after?"

Red Ring's mouth curled; the smile had no warmth. "Rome," he said. "Rome will learn what a priestess costs."

Silence answered. Then motion: men folding packs, remounting. Where the army had been a blunt instrument, chasers, paid men, promises for sack, this group became a blade. Light. Fast. Quiet.

He handed a sealed scroll to a rider who would take the formal notice east to the king. "Tell him we rode," Red Ring said. "Tell him the ritual closed; the gifts lie where we left them. Tell him: find honor in the heat of campfires, not in this chase."

The rider bowed and vanished with a hoofbeat. Red Ring went to the war chest, hands rough, wood more worn than leather. He took what gold remained, locked the lid. "Let the mercenaries rot on the road," he said. "The officers take pay and go home."

Their oath swelled like breath held too long: blood for silence. No more kings. No more markets for heads. No more banners. Only the road, the knife, the necessity of hunger.

They left the camp without fires. No smoke to show the trail; no singing to give them away. The horses moved like shadows, heads low, breath white in the cold air. Red Ring rode at the head, ring bright against the low dawn. Each mile slid into a shape he knew by heart: river, ford, bend, ridge, the small bridges where traders dared, the pines where wolves kept watch.

He thought of the sail he had watched vanish. He thought of the priestess who had been more than a body to sell; she had become an ache. More than pride; the thought of her had seized him like a cold hand and would not let go. He did not want treasure. He wanted the sound after the scream: the silence that proves a man mattered enough to kill for. He craved that silence because she had stolen the sound of his sleep.

The brothers fell into cadence. They spoke little. Strategy lived in short phrases: cross at low flood; avoid the main roads; steal grain where no one would look. Make allies of the small men who hated Rome's reach; take the mountain passes that map forgot. Move like wind, not like armies. Cut the lines of supply; make travel a knife.

Red Ring watched them ride, the four becoming a single shadow that stretched north. He drew the ring across his palm as if to take comfort; the metal left a warm streak on his skin. He imagined the city of Rome under the slow weight of that promise: walls and brass and marble, a people who would not understand why a man with a copper thumb would break the silence he kept.

He rode away from the sea; the salt shrank behind them. Ahead lay forest and river and the long work of removing a god's peace. He had no illusions about the scale: the chase would bend years; men would die for nothing more than a rumor and a ring.

At midday, the youngest brother spoke, breath cold and quick. "She rides safe behind walls," he said.

Red Ring tightened his reins. The line of his jaw cut shadow. "She thinks walls mean safety," he said. "She forgets who has broken walls before. She forgets what men will do for the small sanctuaries of a woman dancing in the dark."

They rode on. The pledge under their mouths tasted like iron. The road swallowed their tracks. The world closed around them: forest and stone and the patient business of revenge. Every mile carried the same truth: he would find her, or he would rot trying. The choice lay clean and simple before him.

No one asked him to forgive. No one asked why. The ring, darkening with each dip, counted the days: one more life stamped into death; one more notch along a rim of blood.

Chapter 55
THE MAN ARRIVES

Ostia Harbor

The ship reached Ostia at dusk: no fanfare, no heralds, just sea wind and the iron silence of men who had fought too long. Rufus stepped onto the dock in a plain tunic, no armor, no red chevrons, no crown. He looked like a laborer, face hard, manner quiet, but every dockhand stepped aside. They knew who he was.

He had built the house before the war, paid in pirate gold. Chose every mosaic, every fresco, every hinge. The stone house wasn't vast like the Caelian villa waiting in Rome, but his first home carried its own beauty: mosaic floors polished to shine, brass gleaming, heated water, a garden court, high walls, and quiet. Peaceful. Designed by his brother, Lucius.

They walked there by torchlight, Rufus, the girl, and the cat. The harbor murmured behind them; ropes creaked, gulls called, water lapped against hulls. Rufus walked steady. Tirzah followed, the kitten tucked into her cloak, purring.

Warehouses lined the road, stacked with amphorae and crates. Laborers lit braziers, orange light spilling across brick streets. The air held olives, salt, butchered meat, and cured fish. A priest swung a censer outside the temple of Mercury. Rufus touched his chest in passing.

Further inland Ostia softened. Less noise, more shadow. Homes leaned into each other. Dogs barked behind doors. Children peeked through shutters. A flute played high and reedy above a courtyard.

They turned at two sycamores arched above a shrine to Fortuna. A woman swept her steps. A man dragged a drunk from the gutter. Nothing had changed. That calmed him. Tirzah stayed quiet, her eyes darting everywhere. The kitten peeked from her arms. Rufus scratched behind its ears, and the growing cat mewed.

At the final street, roasted garlic drifted from a baker's oven. Heat spilled across the stones. Then, the house. Stone, wide, arched, strong. Better than he remembered. Construction completed. Torchlight flickered at the gate. Vines curled along the walls. Bronze hinges gleamed under large umbrella pines.

Home.

He stopped and let the silence hold him. A row of stone pines rose beyond the gate, trunks thick, older than the house. Their canopies formed a green ceiling that whispered in the wind. He had left them standing when he cleared the lot; he liked their sound, their refusal to bow. The house stood apart on a rise, no neighbors, no eavesdropping, no shadows against the glass. Walls of pale Tibur stone. Roof pitched high to take sea winds. He had checked every measurement himself.

The front door, thick oak, bronze studded. The latch fit his hand like a weapon's grip. Not a palace. A soldier's house. A hunter's house. Quiet. Defensible. Waiting.

He needed silence. That was why he told the Greek teacher to stay aboard the ship.

A single servant had kept the place in order. Food waited, lamps lit, everything clean. The man, middle-aged and loyal, cooked simple but fine dishes and welcomed his dominus home with pride in serving such a famous hero. Even Tirzah smiled at the man's warmth.

Rufus had the girl sleep in the guest room. The cat curled at her feet. He stood in the doorway a long time before leaving her to rest.

The atrium fountain splashed. Water whispered into the marble pool. He sat on the bench beside it, letting the wind carry voices only he could hear, the clamor of steel, screams cut short, the wet rasp of men drowning in their blood, cries for mothers. He had not spoken in hours. Salt stripped from his lips; his skin hardened to leather by sun and war. Still, he endured.

This wasn't the life he had trained for, not the glory, not the riches. Not the end he dreamed of as a boy. He should have died already: killed by some enemy champion, death as the Latinus family's final gift, a sacrifice to Rome. But no warrior bested him. No rival earned Fortuna's favor.

And so, he lived.

Suddenly emptiness filled his chest. A hollowness worse than hunger. Failure, not for lack of victories, but for surviving them all. Rufus looked into the pool. Perhaps he had fought too hard, ducked too often, dodged the fate meant for him. His breath caught as a single tear slipped down his cheek. He wiped it away with the back of his hand.

Men do not always die as they wish. The gods do not ask. The gods do not care. The ground opens, and if you are lucky, it closes again.

His face stayed hard, but something shifted inside. He had lived. Now he must decide why and how.

Pompey's gift had not been left behind. The Greek scholar would come ashore at dawn, lean frame wrapped in a travel cloak, ink-stained fingers tightening on his satchel. He spoke little Latin, but his Greek poured like water, relentless, full of questions.

Rufus would allow him into the house. Not for friendship, but for necessity. Rome respected rhetoric as much as scars. Twice each day the man pressed him: repeat the cadence, hold the silence, shape the sentence like a spear. Not enough to speak truth; a senator must also wound with words, then heal with the same breath.

The lessons grated. Rufus preferred steel. But in the pauses, he began to feel the weight of another weapon. One that could kill a man's honor without drawing blood.

Morning would bring order: a bath, a meal, a stop at the warehouse to unload cargos. Then the road to Rome, the walk of heroes. But tonight... no prayers.

He walked to his room. Lay down. Sleep came at once.

Chapter 56
TOGA

Rufus left Tirzah and the cat in the house in Ostia. Made sure they were safe. Warm. Fed.

Rufus knew that several days would pass before he entered the new villa.

He rose before dawn. Dressed in a plain tunic. No armor. No weapons. No insignia. He walked the short distance to his warehouse. Watched his yacht unloaded. Signed papers and contracts. Counted gold and silver.

He even joked with his relatives and slaves there. He toured the large warehouse and was impressed by how well the busy place was kept up and, with its richness. A great investment.

Outside, four black horses waited. Glossy. Strong. Tall for their breed. Gifts from Roman elites. His grandfather held the reins.

Two half-brothers joined them. One carried the family standard.

They rode north. They spoke of many things.

They rode at a steady pace. The road from Ostia to Rome, well-worn by trade and triumph, stretched ahead under the early sun. Rufus rode silent at first, the sea wind still lingering on his cloak. But the voices around him were warm.

"We straightened out that damn farm," the grandfather grumbled, but his tone carried pride. "Your wheat's coming up strong now. New slaves, better ones. Hard workers. No more fat-bellied thieves in the master's bed."

Rufus gave a dry smile. "You sold them to the mines?"

"To the mines, the chain, the lash, whatever they earned."

The half-brother on the left, the one with the tighter jawline, added, "Your house in Rome, she's standing fine."

"Gardens trimmed, floors swept."

The other half-brother, who bore a ring that marked him as one of the family accountants, spoke up. "Your name carries weight, brother. You'll see it when you walk through the Forum. The old ones whisper it now. Your silver's earning. And the tenants, nobody's late."

Rufus gave a short nod. "And Vibia, that old girl?"

"She watches your house. Keeps the fire lit." The horses' hooves beat rhythm into the road. Wind caught the standard as they crested a rise. Rome waited beyond.

His grandfather cleared his throat. "You walk into the Senate tomorrow, not as a boy, not even as a soldier. You walk in as a Latinus."

Rufus looked forward. No fear. No smile.

"I know," he said.

His grandfather said suddenly, "You know, I figured our family would make the senate in a couple more generations, at best. I never expected to see it in my lifetime. I'm very proud of you Rufus."

Rufus gave one of his biggest smiles ever.

And for the first time in months, he felt the world tilt back into place.

The gates of Rome loomed by mid-day. But they did not enter.

Not yet.

On the Campus Martius, just outside the walls, a luxurious tent had been raised. Wood-planked floors. Fine rugs. A bronze brazier. Even a chef.

Caesar waited there. Arms crossed. Smiling.

The two grandfathers entered first. Then his father. Then his uncle. Then his brothers. Then Rufus.

Caesar embraced him. "You came back. I told them you would."

Rufus smiled and nodded once.

"That was good work," Caesar winked. "Better than good. You saved half my legacy. Half of Pompey's too."

The old men beamed.

"I expect you'll surpass us all," Caesar added. "Just not too soon."

That night, they feasted.

Lamb and bitter greens. Soft bread. Hard cheese. Red sauce with anchovy and garlic.

Caesar brought wine. Rufus didn't drink much. Neither did Caesar. They stayed late. Told stories. Even the grandfathers laughed.

Rufus smiled and told stories and listened to more stories.

He rose at dawn.

At the fourth hour, the Walk of Heroes began.

The walk followed a section of the traditional Triumphal Route.

Business paused. Shop doors stayed closed. City slaves had cleaned and scrubbed the path. Flower petals scattered the stones. Crowds lined the walk. Children called his name. Girls and young women flocked to see this Roman idol. This cultural icon. Stalls sold his likeness. These small statues would adorn household shrines for years to come.

Rufus marched with his grandfathers, father, uncle, and kin. Three dozen men of Latinus blood. Led by the family's patron, Caesar.

He walked at the center.

His Civic Crown rode high on his brow.

A younger half-brother proudly carried Rufus's Mural Crown, the golden crown awarded for being first over his section of Jerusalem's wall.

They passed senators. Soldiers. Beggars. Veterans wept. Women cheered.

At the far end, before the Senate steps, the two Censors waited.

Gaius Aurelius Cotta. Quintus Marcius Rex.

Cotta raised both arms.

"People of Rome," he called, "we recognize this man."

"A hero of the Republic. A defender of allies. A commander of men."

He turned to Rufus. "Your shield bore a hundred arrows. Your name carries two dozen honors. The Senate acknowledges your valor."

Marcius Rex held out the new folded senatorial toga. The bright white cloth. The deep red stripe.

"Welcome," he said, "You now bear the burden of Rome's soul. You are a conscript father. Speak with honor, vote with wisdom, and die with your name unblemished."

Rufus stepped forward. Took the garments. Raised them once, high above his head, for the gods to see. He smiled.

The crowd roared.

He bowed slightly to the censors. Then turned. Lifted his chin. And locked eyes with someone in the crowd.

The blonde girl. Pale skin. White-blond hair like polished ivory. Bright white eyebrows. Her unforgettable blue eyes. Wide and bright. Her gaze full of warmth and intelligence. The beautiful girl that he often remembered and thought about in tough times and good. When he was alone.

Beside her stood an older woman. Same features. Hair tied with silver cord. Obviously, her mother. A patrician without a doubt.

The noise faded.

He saw her. She saw him.

No words. Just a shared breath. A smile. The kind that lasts a lifetime.

He lowered his arms. Turned back toward his family. And descended the steps.

The family walked him to their city estate near the Suburra.

Women embraced him. Children screamed. Slaves bowed. Daughters sang.

They laid out olives, nuts, hard bread, goat meat, and milk. He ate standing.

He barely tasted the food. He forgot about war. He truly felt happiness.

The next morning, at the foot of the Caelian Hill, Marcus Crassus waited.

A tall thick man. Dressed in his senatorial toga. A true Roman of the Romans.

A dozen nobles stood with him.

He held a scroll in one hand. A bronze key in the other. Behind him, gates of iron. A villa taller than any on the hill.

White marble. Red tile. Three fountains spraying mist in a large pool. Four full baths, and three bedrooms with private baths. Many shuttered windows. Heated floors. Private shrine. Library. Two dozen slaves already trained.

Crassus stepped forward. "For the man who wears both blade and crown," he said.

"Rome welcomes you to your new home."

He handed Rufus the key.

Rufus took it. Smiled, and shook the great man's hand. No words.

This marked the closest Rufus had ever stood to this man, Crassus, polished, heavy with power, exuding the quiet arrogance of a man who owned half of Rome.

Rufus looked down at Crassus and smiled.

He looked up at the house, awestruck.

Then stepped forward. And claimed the future.

Chapter 57
LAND OF MAGIC

Aegean Sea

The storm passed in the night. Wind ripped the sailcloth. Waves slammed the hull until even the timbers groaned. One of the younger girls vomited until she fainted in her cousin's arms.

Albina stood the whole time, planted at the bow. Salt lashed her face; her robe clung to her legs. She didn't waver. She watched the sea spit blue fire and ghost-white spouts rise like pillars of the old world. She watched lightning rake the sky as if the gods themselves tore at the night.

Then silence.

The sea flattened. A rainbow stretched west to east across the dawn. Oars hung motionless. Men breathed again.

Ahead loomed a wound in the sea. A mountain torn upward, jagged and raw. Green at the crown, white at the base. No shore, not much of a harbor, just rock thrust from blue water like a god's fist.

They landed at sunrise.

Goats clambered across ledges, their hooves clicking like bones. Women waited in the tree line, hips swaying with bronze bells tied at the waist. A boy ran ahead, and soon the drums began. Low, steady, a heartbeat rising from the earth itself.

The island had a name: Kybelon.

A land of magic.

Some whispered it hadn't risen from the sea at all but had been hurled into it. The elders told it as law: long ago, a giant older than cities rose against the gods. In rage he ripped a mountain from the Greek coast, roots and stone and pine clinging to its sides, and hurled it far into the water. The sea boiled where it struck. When it cooled, it rooted again, black and jagged, standing alone in endless blue. Kybelon.

They said the Sibyl herself claimed the rock. She built her first altar there, danced for gods whose names no man remembered. Her voice still echoed on windless nights, carried through the cliffs when the moon was full and the water refused to move. Fishermen swore they heard it. None laughed when the tale was told. No one cast anchor near the rock. They sailed wide, steering clear, in case the gods still listened.

Now the people worshipped the Mountain Mother, Cybele in her island form. They lived in caves carved by waves, called the wind her breath, and trusted her cliffs to keep them safe.

When they saw Albina step onto the beach barefoot, hair braided, eyes unblinking, they dropped to their knees.

—

Her girls were fed until their bellies rounded again. Fish roasted over stone, flatbread brushed with oil, lamb steaming from rock ovens. Honey dripped from fingers, and salt stung their tongues. Wine was pressed into their hands, though Albina waved it away.

The witches sat with the elders in the caves, voices low and steady, herbs exchanged like talismans. They healed many ailments. The eunuchs stood watch at the edge of firelight.

That night the drums grew louder. A fire crackled in the clearing. Old men beat carved sticks against the dirt. The women circled and chanted.

When Albina danced, the air itself stilled.

No incense. No temple walls. Only flame and the pulse of drums. Her bracelets chimed, and the island breathed with her.

—

Days later, she sought out the sacred place spoken of in whispers: a waterfall spilling into a clear basin, rimmed by three smooth stones. Priestesses once bled themselves here, cutting veins to honor the goddess. The air smelled of mint and pine. The water smoked with sunlight.

She knelt. Spread her arms. Danced until the mist soaked her robe. Her cousins joined her, circling in barefoot rhythm. Anklets jingled, skin glowed, hair clung wet to their faces. Each step struck the earth like prayer.

Albina's breath grew sharp. Her thighs ached. Still, she moved. Each motion a call to memory, a command to the gods who once claimed her.

Then she dropped to her knees. Her body twisted to her side. Eyes open.

The vision came.

—

A boy with red hair. A girl on a balcony, white-blond, skin pale as milk. Eyes blue as winter sky. She watched him win a horse race, her hand pressed to the stone rail, lips shaping his name.

The girl grown, strong, patrician, clever. She loved Rufus not as a child dreams, but as a woman plans: to bind her house to his, to breed Roman heirs in fire and blood.

The light turned. A great hall. Marble flashing gold. The king of kings sat on his throne. His son entered, blade drawn. The scream lasted a breath, then died with the light.

A camp. Rufus at war. Matineus stood at the edge of firelight. Arrows rained. Blood sprayed. Matineus fell without sound, silent, beautiful, gone.

Rufus wore the red ring.

Albina saw herself holding a lion cub, arm raised, ordering war on Parthia.

The light snapped shut.

She woke cold and alone. Her body damp against the stones. She staggered to her feet and climbed higher, past thorn and rock, to a ridge above the sea. No guards. No witches.

She curled behind a boulder. And cried until her throat gave out.

—

They stayed a month.

The storms broke. The air warmed. The sea gentled. Wounds closed. Flesh filled back into hollowed cheeks. The girls grew strong again. The eunuchs sparred until the sound of steel echoed off the cliffs. The witches dried herbs over low fires, smoke curling like blessings.

Albina blessed the temple. The villagers wept at her words. They called her the Mountain Mother reborn.

When she danced a final time on the beach, the islanders covered their faces and whispered prayers.

At dawn, without fanfare, they boarded. Oars dipped in calm water. No sails. Just arms pulling them from shore.

The drums followed them to the sea, echoing across the cliffs.

The rocks stood witness. They had seen gods fall, kings rise, and blood wash into the tide. They watched Albina now.

Chapter 58

ALBINA LANDS IN ITALY

Italy

They sailed with the wind behind them. No more stops. Moving fast. Albina stayed below deck, ringed by her people. The witches rarely slept. The girls trained in silence. The eunuchs sharpened blades, cleaned armor, and watched the horizon.

Matineus couldn't relax.

They landed on the southern coast of the Italian peninsula near Locri at dawn. Cold wind. No heralds. No crowds. Just gravel, salt air, and the wind off the sea.

The gangplank dropped. Almost thirty figures came down. Albina stepped last, clothed in gold.

Her feet touched Italian gravel. She looked inland.

She did not kiss the ground of Italy. The ground of Italy kissed her feet.

Matineus led them to a safehouse; a farmhouse owned by one of his contacts. They stayed three nights. Water, chickens, and fresh honey arrived without asking. The girls bathed and trained. The witches found herbs. Their strength came back with their land legs.

Already local women found out that the Sibyl walked among them. They sent gifts.

Albina tried on silk, bracelets, sandals. Tried jars of perfume, combs, brushes, mirrors. Gifts from unknown women. Not one bore a man's name.

The ship and its crew stayed nearby for those three days, then departed quietly after confirming the passengers were safe.

They set out on foot, escorted by Matineus and his crew. Word spread fast.

The crowds started with a handful of women waiting at crossroads, holding bread, kneeling as Albina passed. Then dozens. Then hundreds. They brought gifts: clothes, jewelry, gold rings, carved amulets, and coin. One woman offered a slave boy. Another offered a donkey. Some cried. Some sang. Some fell at Albina's feet and pressed their foreheads to the ground.

Albina would only accept a coin or two from the poor women, who would often give until it hurt. She always gave them more than they gave her.

Soon, a noble widow loaned her a white litter, carried by eight tall German eunuchs with pale eyes and braided hair. From then on, Albina moved like a queen of old, raised high. Unseen hands parting the way.

The twelve carved statuettes, released from their confinement in the large black crate, were displayed on a flat handcart, cushioned in furs and covered with fresh flowers. The wagon train behind them grew longer by the mile.

All gifts were cataloged, packed into wagons, recorded by hand by one of the attendants. They became a holy procession.

Albina blessed women and girls daily, tapping their heads with a myrtle branch dipped in water. Some fainted. Some danced. Some wept. The young girls often followed behind her litter, mimicking her stride, singing the songs they'd heard from her musicians.

Female musicians and singers joined.

She was given dozens of embroidered veils. She wore them all. But always returned to red by evening.

The girls danced at night, always for the women of a town. Rich or poor. Free or slave. No men allowed. The bodyguards stood at the edges, weapons bare.

Sometimes Albina danced too. Wild and unbound. Other times, she entered trance and became the Sybil, speaking of distant lands, a child born in fire, a red-haired man, a blonde girl with eyes like the sea, a kitten wrapped in linen, a boy with a lion's courage, a ring made of bone. Also visions of local women and prophecies related to them.

Crossroads and springs became holy places in her wake.

The women loved her. All classes. All walks. Several noble women left their homes and joined the march.

The very next day a local witch, a woman of power came up to Albina and pressed a small pouch into Albina's hand. No words, only a nod, respectful, unsure. Albina waited until the woman had vanished down the hill before opening the cloth pouch.

Inside lay a ring.

Ivory. Smooth and pale, carved into a spiral band. No jewels. No gold. Just old, bleached matter shaped by hand and fire.

She turned the carved boney thing over in her palm. The thing felt warm.

A whisper touched her ear, though no one stood close. A breeze moved the olive leaves. She closed her eyes.

She saw fire. Snow. A boy standing tall with a lion's pelt across his back. Her son. His eyes like hers, but harder. In his hand, on his finger, this ring.

He wore it not for beauty, but for remembrance. A promise. The pain of her people, worn on his finger like a warning to the world.

Albina opened her eyes.

She held the ring to her lips, kissed the bone, and tucked it into the folds of her dress.

Not for now. Not for Rome. For him. The one not yet born. The one who would carry fire. The boy with lion's courage.

Weeks passed. A month. More.

Word spread and the women came.

Outside the gates of Rome, Albina stopped. She stood amazed at the great walls and repulsed by the stink that reached her nose. Yes, her world had changed.

She would not enter Rome yet. A camp rose, silk and linen, bronze posts, guarded by her own. Her witches circled the center.

The witches burned herbs, roots and incense by the pound. Masking the stink of Rome and leaving passersby with a feeling of holiness, and visitors with a sense of otherworldliness.

Inside a large silk tent and surrounded by the twelve statues, Albina thought about Rufus, combed her hair and waited.

She asked for nothing. The Goddess provided for her needs.
Power came anyway.

Chapter 59
THE WOMEN GATHER

Outside the **Walls of Rome**

The women came first. They brought power

They didn't wait for the Senate; they didn't care what the priests thought, or what their husbands muttered in their porticoes. Fathers grumbled. Brothers threatened. None of that mattered. Word spread faster than joy, faster than fear. The girl from the east had crossed the sea, walked the mountains, sweated through the desert, and bled in the mud. She had reached Italy alive. She camped outside Rome's gates. She had danced through storms. She had survived.

They brought gifts. Gold rings heavy with old engravings. Carved ivory that smelled faintly of cedar. Painted jars from Rhodes, dyes from Phoenicia, perfumes sealed in brittle glass. A necklace once worn by a consul's wife. Incense wrapped in cloth. Wool dyed deep red. Shoes, some too fine for dirt, others plain leather for travel. A few even brought slaves, girls with braided hair and boys barely grown, offered like tokens before a shrine.

Some women brought letters from their daughters, folded in wax-stained packets. Others brought the daughters themselves, veiled, wide-eyed, clutching at their mothers' sleeves. A patrician matron walked with a Syrian freedwoman at her side. A baker's wife carried a wooden box of pastries and a single rose. A Vestal sent a message sealed with ash. Two sisters from Capua brought a clay statue chipped at the base, claiming it wept during storms.

They came veiled, wrapped in cloaks, some barefoot. Patrician women and slave girls. Widows and wet nurses. Seamstresses, fruit sellers, wives of senators.

They bowed. They wept. They sang. One noblewoman abandoned her husband's litter and walked four days to kiss Albina's feet.

They didn't ask her name. They already knew it. They called her what she was.

The Sibyl.

At first, the word passed mouth to mouth like contraband, low, careful. A whisper. A breath. Then louder. Then shouted. The guards standing watch said nothing. The priests turned away, faces tight with unease. But the women pressed closer, their voices lifting the sacred name until it clung to the air like smoke.

She wore no crown, carried no staff, offered no sermon. Still, they gathered. Not for bread, not for coin. For something older, something unnamed.

Some wept as soon as they saw her. Some knelt in the dirt; hands pressed to their bellies. One tore her veil without a word. The oldest pressed trembling fingers to Albina's hands. Albina did not pull away.

The young, asked questions about love, about birth, about omens. The middle-aged, whispered prayers. The broken stared in silence, as if daring her to heal wounds she could not see. None asked for gold. None begged for blessing. Not yet.

She stood still in the red morning light. Her robe plain, her hair braided tight, her skin still pale from hunger. Behind her, the dancers waited in silence. The witches watched the crowd with narrow eyes. Albina's ankles bore bells; they chimed once, faint in the breeze. Even the birds fell quiet.

By the second day, the camp swelled. Tents rose on the hillsides. Cookfires smoked, marking the hours. Women walked barefoot over gravel to stand in line just to glimpse her. Some pressed gifts into the dirt at her feet and left without a word. Others lingered, sleeping under open sky, eating figs and stale bread, brushing dust from their cloaks while they waited for another sight of her.

They watched the dancers when Albina did not dance. They listened to the witches mutter their old tongue. They shared stories at night, stories of husbands who struck too hard, sons lost in war, daughters sold in debt. Some left lighter, as if the act of speaking near her made the burden shift. Some left shaken. And some did not leave at all.

One widow from Tusculum lay down by the fire and died without a cry. Another cut her palm and smeared blood across her own veil, calling it a sign of covenant. The bodyguards carried her away. The women whispered it was holy. And still they came.

The hills filled with voices, sobs, chants, laughter, ululations. Rich silks and plain wool mixed together in the dust. Priests fumed in the temples. Husbands ordered wives' home. Some obeyed. Most did not.

Albina gave no speech. She let silence answer them. She let the sight of her endurance speak louder than any prayer. When one mother placed her infant on the ground before her, Albina bent only long enough to touch the child's brow, then stood. The crowd gasped as if lightning had struck.

The women left changed. Not in body, but in gaze. They had seen her. The Sibyl. Flesh and breath. Not story. Not rumor. Real.

By the third night, the hills glowed with firelight. Songs rose, unfamiliar, many at once. The air smelled of honey, sweat, wool smoke. The stars themselves seemed to bend low, listening.

Albina stood at the edge of her camp and watched the torches burn across the slopes. Her people slept behind her. The witches muttered. The eunuchs sharpened their blades in silence.

She did not smile. She listened to the women below. The voices. The whispers. The prayers not meant for priests.

Rome had not yet spoken. But Rome's women had spoken and they had chosen.

And the Sibyl knew: when women gather, the world shifts.

Chapter 60
ROMAN BROTHERS

At first light, Matineus gave the order.

Albina's camp stirred under gray clouds and city smoke. Her guards moved without sound, ten of his own, hand-picked in silence, and five more from Caesar's household. All fifteen stood watch, faces hard, blades sharp. Her eunuchs trusted no man, but they allowed these. A mutual respect had formed, silent and lethal.

Matineus checked each man. One nodded. Another adjusted a sling. Their eyes scanned the trees, the gate, the hill.

Albina slept beneath thick wool. Her witches did not. Zarmina sat upright, unmoving. Nisaya crouched near the fire, whispering to unseen forces.

He mounted without ceremony. No kiss, no prayer, no glance. He left them like a scout leaves a trail, knowing every root, every stone, every enemy that might follow.

He rode alone, hood drawn, sword under cloak. Rome sprawled ahead, still quiet in its breath between night and day.

The guards at the eastern gate let him pass without question. He had papers, but they never asked. His face, his bearing, the seal of Caesar, they opened the city like a slit throat.

He turned left at the old fountain, then right near the statue of Victory. The slope took him toward the Palatine.

At the top, two soldiers outside a narrow villa stepped forward. One recognized him.

"Matineus?"

He dismounted. "Is he in?"

The soldier nodded. "Alone. This way."

Caesar met him in the inner courtyard, beside a small garden. He wore no adornment, no cloak. A plain white tunic. One arm rested on a fig tree.

"You made it."

Matineus bowed.

Caesar walked closer. "Tell me."

Matineus told him. Not everything. But enough, the escape, the mountains, the near starvation, the dead, the broken temple, the girl.

Caesar listened. One hand gripped the tree harder than it needed to.

At the end, he said, "You did well. You saw the world, walked through fire and came back breathing. Few do ."

Matineus stayed quiet.

"Consider it done, as of now, you're a full free-born citizen and my client. I'll have a bank draft readied tomorrow for ten talents of silver."

Caesar stepped back. "Go now. Find your family. Rest while you can."

Matineus bowed again, smiled, and left without another word. The door closed behind him.

The sky brightened. The city stirred. His boots touched Roman dust again. He turned toward the Forum. He had made his way home to Rome. But the road still waited.

Matineus crossed the Forum with his hood low. No banners flew. No music played. Rome drifted into winter without parade or cheer.

He moved along the edge, past merchants hawking onions and oil, past beggars with pale eyes and open sores. The temples loomed to the right, high, clean, empty. A pair of senators in white togas laughed as they passed. Matineus slipped into the flow of bodies, one more cloak on horseback in the crowd.

He passed through the Subura without pause. The noise swelled there. Children darted under carts. Prostitutes called from painted doors. A man held a rooster by the feet and shouted for wagers.

A pack of dogs barked near a butcher's stall.

Matineus cut through an alley and emerged on a street lined with shrines and bakeries. Two turns, then one sharp right. A slave boy sweeping the steps froze when he saw him.

"Master Matineus?"

He nodded once.

The boy dropped the broom and ran inside.

The family block stood proud, stone walls, tiled roofs, second and third floors with painted shutters. Storefronts ran the edge: a cloth merchant, a toolmaker, a small shrine to Mars. Behind it all: the courtyard, the kitchen, the rooms.

"Young one," he pointed at a girl. "Take care of my horse."

She smiled and took the horse's rein and walked him to the house stables.

Doors opened. His mother's sister stepped out first. Then cousins. Half-siblings. Even the old house steward, gray and bent, but still breathing. They embraced him. The way his people did, arms strong, one breath, then silence. No need for words.

Inside, everything felt the same. The scent of pine from the courtyard tree. The hiss of oil on a brazier. A girl sliced lemons in the kitchen. Another sat cross-legged, sewing up a tear on a tunic.

He ate in silence. Bread. Eggs. A bowl of boiled greens with garlic. The wine tasted sharp and fresh. Someone had remembered what he liked.

They asked about Albina. About the trip. About the march. He spoke little. But he smiled.

When he rose to leave, his mother's sister pressed a satchel into his hands.

"Food for your brother," she said. "And warmth."

He nodded once. Then left through the back gate.

The Caelian Hill waited.

So did Rufus.

The climb up the Caelian Hill felt longer than he thought. Matineus moved alone now, no escort, no gold, no name shouted in the streets. Just boots on stone. Just Rome.

The villa came into view behind a line of umbrella pines, long-limbed, heavy with birds. The walls had been washed. The bronze gate gleamed. A marble lion crouched near the entrance, teeth bared.

He paused there.

The house breathed strength. Not Crassus's anymore. The villa belonged to Rufus now. As every Roman knew.

Two girls raked gravel in the front courtyard. One looked up, startled. She whispered something and darted through the main doors.

Matineus stood still.

A moment later, the door opened. A slave appeared. Maybe twelve. Sharp eyes. Bare feet.

"Who are you?" the boy asked.

"His brother."

The boy vanished. Matineus walked in and gave due respect to the household shrine.

"Would you look at this place," he whispered in awe.

Inside, the house murmured, low voices, clinking cups, the hiss of fire. A cat sped across the floor and vanished behind a column. Matineus stepped into the atrium. Tall ceilings. Clean mosaics. Red and gold trim. A silver bowl of pomegranates sat on a polished table.

Most Roman homes didn't have too much furniture. Each piece was hugely expensive. But this house held more than any Matineus had ever seen. Tables, chairs, couches, and things he had no name for. Gifts from Romans for the crowns.

Matineus laughed because he knew this much furniture wasn't what Rufus wanted.

Soft footsteps.

Then Rufus.

He filled the archway, taller than most, his arms bare, a fine tunic clinging to his frame. His face was calm, unreadable. The red chevrons marked his history. His eyes locked on his brother's.

Neither spoke.

Then:

"You made it."

Matineus nodded.

"I did."

They embraced, kissed cheeks.

Rufus felt relief his half-brother arrived home safely.

"Is the foreigner safe?"

"She is."

"Good."

They stood in silence.

Matineus handed over the satchel. Rufus took it. He knew the smell. Family. Warmth. Garlic. Wine-soaked bread.

"You hungry?" Rufus asked.

"No."

"You clean?"

"I will be."

Rufus turned and led him down the hall, past painted walls and marble lions, past servants who bowed without words. The Jewish girl stood in the garden doorway, watching. Behind her, the white and tan cat curled in the sun near a fig tree.

"You'll stay here tonight," Rufus said.

Matineus nodded.

"And tomorrow?"

The pause hung.

"That depends."

The servant girl led him down the back hall. Thick plaster walls. Oil lamps flickered from bronze hooks. The scent of mint and crushed lemon leaves followed her.

A chamber opened ahead. Steam curled out.

Inside, the bath waited, hot, deep and tiled, its surface trembling. Warm light bounced off water and marble. Two older slaves stepped forward, silent, practiced. They peeled off his tunic. They did not ask his name.

Matineus stepped in.

Heat crawled over old scars. He sank lower, closed his eyes. The room fell quiet except for breath and water. They washed him with firm hands and rough cloth, rinsed him, dried him, rubbed his muscles with pressed oil. One pressed a thumb behind his shoulder. A knot popped. He didn't flinch.

A clean tunic waited, soft and white. They helped him into it. A third girl brought slippers. Her fingers were quick. Her eyes never lifted.

Then came food.

Roast lamb, still steaming. A bowl of salted olives. Flatbread still warm from the stone. Wine dark as ink.

He ate alone at a side table near the garden. The fig tree rustled. Somewhere above, a bird flapped once and settled. The cat slipped past his feet without sound.

Rufus didn't join him.

After the meal, another girl appeared. Younger. Pretty. Barefoot. Spanish maybe. She knelt beside him and poured more wine. She touched his hand, light as breath.

He didn't speak. Neither did she.

When he stood, she followed him. They moved through the villa without words. At the end of the hall, a door opened to a guest room lit by low firelight and a single oil lamp. She entered first. Turned. Undid the sash of her robe.

He stepped inside.

The door shut behind them.

Matineus woke late morning. He lay still and studied the painted ceiling. Clouds and blue sky. He stretched and climbed out of the soft bed. Dressed in a clean tunic and socks. He left the room and went the short distance to the bathroom.

He found his brother finishing up his training.

"You're still training as hard as ever, I see," Matineus said.

"It's the one constant thing in my life," Rufus laughed

"Sit with me, let me catch my breath."

They settled on a bench with a view of a calm section of the long pool in the peristyle.

The white and tan cat sat crouched by the edge of the pool. One paw lifted. Still as a statue. Eyes locked on the water.

Rufus leaned back, arms crossed. Matineus relaxed beside him, chewing a fig.

"He's hunting again," Rufus muttered, nodding at the cat.

"I thought cats only chased birds."

"He's growing ambitious."

They watched.

A shadow flicked below the surface, one of the long-finned fish Rufus had imported from Alexandria. Gold scales. Black spine. Worth more than a fine horse.

The cat didn't blink.

Then, movement.

A flash. A splash. The cat lunged, paws wide, claws out. Water flew. His teeth clamped down hard, just behind the gills. The fish thrashed, tail flailing. The cat's grip held.

"By all the gods," Matineus said.

The cat heaved backward. Wet, soaked, and shaking, he dragged the fish from the pool, slipping once on the tile. It was nearly as long as his own body.

He stopped. Readjusted his bite. Then strutted off, tail high, prize in his mouth.

Rufus raised his eyebrows. "That one cost me three hundred denarii."

"A family of four could live half a year on that," Matineus said.

"Rent, tunics, bread, even sandals."

"She'll eat it raw under the rosemary bush."

Their eyes followed. The cat had vanished into the thick shrubs that grew beside the far wall, low, tight, and green. Something thrashed beneath the leaves. Then went still.

"He's smart," Rufus said. "Waited three days for that fish to get used to him."

"He earned it."

"He'd have made a fine scout."

"Or a senator."

They sat there, laughing.

The bush rustled once more. A wet crunch sounded.

"Guess he's starting with the head," Rufus said.

Matineus chuckled. "Tactician."

Rufus shook his head. "Three hundred denarii."

Matineus smirked. "Let him enjoy his catch. A killer's got to eat."

Rufus grinned.

"Fair enough."

Chapter 61
OUTSIDE THE GATES

The men grew worried. Their priests and augurs watched appalled. This could not be.

Some said she carried plague. Some said she carried prophecies. All waited.

A caged rooster flailed in panic killing itself. Signs and omens were saying everything and nothing at all. An augur's hand trembled. A priest dropped his scroll.

"She's not Roman," someone said. "Not even Greek."

"She walks with bells," another said.

"No, eunuchs. And witches."

Lines of wagons blocked the Appian approach. Her people had built a full camp: silk canopies, armed guards, shrines marked with foreign sigils. The girl and her witches had not tried to enter. She waited. Silent. Perfectly still.

Women poured in from the hills, from towns, from Rome itself. Some walked all night. They brought children, slaves, food, and gifts. Many stayed. The camp grew by the hour. Roman men called the whole situation madness. Roman women called it truth.

The priesthood split. The augurs could not agree. Some claimed her presence desecrated the sacred gates. Others fell to their knees after seeing her dance.

A Senator accused her of subversion. Another demanded a tribunal. One priest fainted during a sacrifice. Another tore off his robe, walked into the Tiber and drowned. His body was never found. Consumed by the river.

Albina used pressure gently, leaning against the edges of power without ever touching it. She never gave demands. Never sent a letter. Never stepped beyond the line of respect.

But each day the camp swelled. Each hour brought another woman, another voice, another pair of eyes watching the city walls. They carried baskets, babies, herbs, news. They came from every corner of Rome, Subura back alleys, senator's villas, temples, and brothels. They came alone, or in twos, or in lines that stretched down the hill.

And still she waited.

Waiting worked.

The priests whispered. The guards grew nervous. The matrons who'd seen her dance now spoke her name in soft reverence, calling her Sibylla. They lit candles at street corners. They poured milk at crossroads. Albina never asked them to. She didn't have to.

Inside the Curia, the senators began to argue. Crassus called her a distraction. Cicero called her a risk. Cato called her a foreign trickster.

But they had no answer for the pressure at the gate. No man dared send soldiers to disperse the women. No one could find cause to arrest her. No one wanted to touch the thing forming just outside the city's skin.

Even Caesar stayed quiet.

And so, the Sybil remained, untouched, unnamed, unstoppable, just outside Rome.

The Vestals kept silent as they visited the camp. The powerful and respected women of Rome advised Albina.

Still, she remained outside.

The Sybil of the East. The girl with long black hair. Her arms bare except for golden bands. Her bells still. Her face calm.

She waited.

And Rome trembled.

Chapter 62
THE MOTHER'S LIONS

N ews moved faster than horses in Rome.

By dusk, the priests of Cybele knew: Domina Marcia Tertia, widow of the late Gaius Cassius Labeo, one of Sulla's top men, had changed her mind. The looted statue, Kybele of Athens, chariot-bound, flanked by lions, carved of white marble and painted in vivid color, would not go to their temple on the Palatine slope.

The amazing statue would go to the foreign girl in the red veil. The Sibyl.

They gathered that night in their apartments. Five eunuch priests, heads shaved, fine robes dyed green and gold. Their residence stood three floors high beside the old temple of Magna Mater: marble floors, wide windows, cistern-fed fountains. They lived in comfort, well-fed, well-funded, and certain of their importance.

But the city whispered another name now. Not Cybele. Not the Great Mother. Albina.

The priests sent a delegation. Not at dawn, nor humbly. They came at noon, under full light, robes gleaming, rings flashing.

Albina's camp sprawled outside the walls, south of the Porta Capena, near the Camenae's sacred grove and spring. Silk canopies and linen tents stretched in rows, poles of brass catching sunlight. The smell of myrrh and olive smoke drifted heavy; chants and women's laughter rippled like waves. Albina's banner, deep red stitched with gold, snapped in the wind above the largest tent.

Guards met the priests first. Small, hard-eyed eunuchs in plain tunics, blades at their hips. The men of Cybele sneered. Roman law forbade them arms, but these eastern ones held short swords that they had ripped from the dead hands of their victims, as if they were born gripping steel.

The tallest priest stepped forward. His voice rang loud, meant for a crowd: "We bring words for the girl."

The guards said nothing. But a gap opened, curtain drawn, and Albina herself stepped through.

She came barefoot on the dirt, anklets still, veil drawn back to her shoulders. Black silk bound with a cord of gold hugged her frame. Her dancers flanked her, young faces hard with loyalty. The witches lingered behind, Zarmina tall, dressed in red dress, unsmiling. Nisaya pale, wearing black, ghostlike.

Albina's eyes, gold as flame, fixed on the priests. Her voice carried in the clipped, formal Latin she chose for such moments: "Speak."

The eldest priest cleared his throat. "We represent the temple of Magna Mater. The statue, taken in lawful war, belongs to the true shrine. The relic was promised."

Albina tilted her head. "By whom?"

"By the noble lady Tertia."

"Yet she wrote to me," Albina answered. "A letter sealed in her own hand. She dreamed the goddess spoke: 'Let the old be made new.' She said the statue waits at her villa. For me."

The priest's lips thinned. "Dreams shift with wind."

"Goddesses don't," Albina said.

The words cut sharp as iron. Women in the crowd edged closer, their faces intent. Slaves, patricians, freedwomen, whores, they all leaned in.

Another priest stepped forward, braver. "Return the gift. Rome's rites demand it. The Mother requires it."

Albina remained still. Her silence stretched. Then Nisaya moved.

The witch slipped forward, robes trailing like smoke. She carried a clay bowl. Without bowing, she placed it at the priests' feet. Ashes lay inside, still warm.

Her voice, barely more than breath: "Tell your master, the Mother has chosen."

Nisaya bent. Kissed the earth. Rose.

The youngest priest recoiled. The others turned sharply, robes hissing like dry leaves in the wind.

They left without blessing, without a final word.

By nightfall, the city swelled with rumor.

Three days passed.

The statue stayed sealed inside Tertia's villa in Herculaneum, wrapped in silk, guarded but untouched. Tertia issued no apology, no explanation. She waited, silent.

In his chambers near the Palatine slope, the high priest fumed. Old, rich, heavy with confidence, he rarely left his quarters. He had not joined the delegation; such insults were beneath him. But he wrote strongly worded letters. Sent messages. Plotted.

That morning, a woman saw him in the Forum. He bought figs at a stall. Wore a green sash. He told the merchant: "We will replace the eastern girl with one of our own. A Roman. A true vessel of the Mother."

He never noticed the woman with short hair in the gray shawl. She brushed past, left a coin in his palm. Nothing more.

By nightfall he convulsed on his chamber floor. His lips turned black. The priests found him with a half-eaten fig clutched in his hand.

At sunrise, a parchment lay at the temple's threshold. Folded once, written in red ink.

It read:

"She does not kneel."

No name. No seal. No hand identified. But everyone in Rome understood.

A priest of the Great Mother dead in his own chamber, without sword, without struggle, without witness.

Albina had spoken, without raising her voice. The message was not war. It was warning.

That evening, her camp burned red with torchlight. The drums did not play, yet women gathered anyway. They came not to worship but to learn.

Patrician wives, freedwomen, slave girls, they crowded nearby. They wanted to see the face of the woman who defied Cybele's lions and killed without lifting a hand. They wanted to hear her silence, to feel its weight.

Albina stood before them, still as carved stone, her dancers silent at her back, witches watching with half-lidded eyes. She did not raise her arms. She did not claim a crown.

And yet the women whispered the title, again and again:

Sybil.

The priests of Cybele retreated into their halls, whispering their own prayers, uncertain whether their Mother still listened.

Rome, meanwhile, leaned closer to Albina.

The city had seen power before, swords, gold, armies, crowns. But this, this was something older. A woman who did not kneel.

Chapter 63
FLAME RIDER

A black horse rode out from the hills above the Appian Gate.

Not a patrol. Not a senator's courier.

The beast stood tall. Muscles coiled under his shiny coat. Large hooves struck gravel like thunder. A thick mane, braided and ribboned, rippled like war banners in wind. The rider wore red: no laurel, no sash, no guard. Just a man. Tall. Lean. Upright.

Julius Caesar.

He came alone. No fanfare, no steel behind him. If you didn't know his face, you'd mistake him for a merchant or a patrician out for air.

The camp watched.

He stopped far enough not to offend. Close enough to see.

Albina stood barefoot in the grass. Veils loose. Anklets silent. Her gaze never dropped. Her arms rested at her sides, pale against the gold bracelets. Hundreds of women stood behind her watching him.

He said nothing. She didn't either.

The wind turned once, smoke from a brazier curling past her shoulder. A ribbon of red lifted from the carved box beside her.

Caesar's horse shifted. He didn't move.

He looked at her. At the girls behind her. At the pale-eyed guards. Then back at her.

She didn't flinch.

The witch in black, Nisaya emerged from the tent. Her face veiled. She did not bow. Did not greet. Just stood behind Albina and rested a hand on her shoulder.

The flame in the brazier flared.

Caesar blinked. Once. He turned his horse. No words.

The hoofbeats faded. And the camp exhaled.

* * *

He said nothing for a long time.

That night, in his large offices, he stared at the flame in the brazier. The guards kept their distance. He drank nothing.

A messenger brought word: the high priest of Cybele was dead. Poisoned. Found in the market, lips black.

Caesar dismissed the boy without comment.

His mother had warned him. He hadn't believed her.

She was right.

Albina hadn't entered Rome, yet already she ruled half its women.

The Sibyl was no mere girl. No harmless dancer. No temple toy.

She knew how to play politics.

He should've left her in the East. Let her be taken. Let her die in the mud. Or better yet, had her killed on the spot.

He just couldn't see past the pleasure of poking the Parthian king in the eye.

His damn pride. But now was too late.

He could not keep her.

To claim her would invite war from men and women alike.

To reject her would make an enemy of something old. Something eternal.

So, he sat. Alone. Staring into fire. And wondered, who to give her to.

Caesar needed a very loyal man who would obey his every command, and one who would not hesitate a second to end this damn dancing girl and her people.

But who deserved the curse?

Chapter 64
MATRON'S DECISION

Servilia's villa overlooked the Palatine slope. Close to power, far from peace. Polished stone floors reflected cold light. Slaves set a modest table: olives, dates, dark bread, fish paste. No wine: this was no feast. This was strategy.

Ariella arrived first, veiled in gray, her face unreadable. She carried silence like a weapon, using few words but cutting with each one. Caesar's mother. The servants stood when she entered. She nodded once. Enough. Servilia embraced her lightly.

"Thank you for coming."

"Rome depends on our understanding," Ariella said.

The others followed. Junia, the elder matron of the Latinus line, swept in with a sharp cane tap, chin high. Her voice cracked like iron striking stone, no patience for softness. Her sister, Rufus's mother, walked behind her, thinner now but eyes bright and unyielding. Fabia, the youngest of the five Vestals, moved without sound, her voice always a whisper, meant to be leaned into, never ignored. Several more filed in, old and respected names. Last came Domina Antonia, widow of Lucius Cornelius Scipio: her gaze lingered too long, her tone deliberates, as if she weighed every syllable for advantage.

When the slaves poured water and withdrew, the chamber sealed itself in silence. No guards. No men.

Servilia began. Her tone smooth, almost warm, yet edged with calculation, like a hand on a knife hidden under silk. "The girl waits outside our gates."

Junia's jaw tightened. "She draws crowds. Hundreds of women. Daily."

"Not Roman," Fabia whispered, her breath thinner than smoke. "Not one of us."

"We will have to visit her soon. She speaks to something older," Ariella said. "The Sibyl comes with veils and visions. Women feel her; men ignore her or curse her."

"Men shouldn't ignore her," Junia's sister snapped, words hot and quick. "That temple incident..."

"She didn't stab him," Servilia smiled faintly. "But he died."

The air cooled.

"Poison," Fabia murmured.

Ariella did not deny it. "He threatened what she was given. And so, he died."

"She sent a message," Domina Antonia said, her voice measured. "Not to him. To all of us."

Junia's cane tapped once on the floor. "She's dangerous."

"She's necessary," Ariella answered.

Silence pressed in, broken only by the hiss of a lamp. The Republic shook outside these walls. Pompey stretched his reach too far, Crassus moved coin like an avalanche, Caesar climbed faster than law allowed. And Albina drew eyes.

Servilia leaned forward. "Crassus would take her."

"He'd hide her in marble," Ariella laughed once, without joy, "and charge admission."

"Pompey?"

"He'd parade her."

"Your son Brutus?"

"Too clever," Ariella's mouth curled. "He'd try to own her mind."

"Cicero?"

"Too much law. Not enough blood."

"Then who?"

They all turned. Ariella held their gaze.

"Rufus."

Junia raised a brow, steel in her tone. "My nephew?"

"He earned the crown," Ariella said flatly. "And the scars to match."

"He's no patrician."

"He's Roman."

"He's brutal."

"He's disciplined."

"He frightens women."

"He also protects them."

Junia's sister leaned across the table. "He has no wife."

"We can arrange a wife. He has a name," Ariella replied, voice dropping to a blade's edge. "He has a record. He has coin enough now to silence the Senate. Caesar trusts him. And Albina's dancers watched him once, as if they already knew."

Fabia's eyes lifted, whisper steady. "The goddess chose her. But Rome will eat her without allies."

Servilia spread her hands, smooth and deliberate. "She needs one house. Strong. Rooted. Unbending... Rufus, huh? Interesting choice."

"She needs a man who won't touch her," Junia's sister said. "For as long as it takes."

Ariella gave no answer.

Domina Antonia tapped her cup against stone, words slow, heavy. "Let's stop pretending. We're choosing where to place the future."

"The priests hate her," Junia said. "That statue rewrote the rules."

"She never touched the thing," Ariella snapped. "The widow changed her mind. The priests overreached."

"And one of them died," Junia's sister reminded.

Servilia shrugged, smooth again. "They were warned."

Domina Antonia's gaze narrowed. "The eunuchs will not forget. But Rome will not care, so long as there is no chaos."

Ariella's words cut the silence. "Rufus will give her order, and steel. They won't dare touch her under Latinus protection."

Fabia folded her hands in her lap. "She's a spark. He is stone."

One nod passed around the table, then another.

Junia rose first, cane striking once. "Let it be done."

"No scroll?" Domina Antonia asked.

"No need."

"Then she must be watched," Junia's sister said. "Not harmed. Not followed. Protected."

"Agreed," Ariella said. She kept quiet about how Rufus would kill this girl if her son, Caesar ordered him to.

They stood. Robes brushed cold stone. Feet moved without sound.

History shifted. Not in the Forum. Not in the Senate. But here. In silence. Among women.

Rome's new center had been chosen. Not a temple. Not a crown. But a soldier's roof. A lion's eye. A woman's will.

Chapter 65
TIRZAH

Tirzah rose early. The floor had gone cold in the night, but she didn't mind. She covered her hair with the soft blue veil Rufus had gifted her and slipped out into the courtyard, where steam lifted from the fountain and the air smelled of lemon and evergreen.

She had the type of inner beauty that one appreciated the more you spent time with her. A few, like Rufus, saw her unique beauty and Judean grace instantly.

Two of his men waited, young, sharp-eyed, not cruel. They wore tunics under boiled leather, short blades on their hips. One nodded to her, respectful. Neither asked questions. They knew their orders. They knew the Dominus. They would do as he ordered.

She walked with them through the sleeping villa, sandals quiet on tile. Only the sound of the Dominus training and the sounds of a busy kitchen echoing in the distance.

Beyond the gates, Rome stirred.

The road to the Aventine curved past workshops and narrow alleys. Openings bled smoke into the brightening sky. Far ahead, sunlight touched the temples and tiled roofs like fire on bronze.

They passed a baker's stall. Tirzah waved to the old woman at the corner who always rose early to buy sesame cakes. The escorts let her stop. The woman handed her one, warm and sweet. Tirzah smiled, paid, and bowed in thanks. Rufus paid her a fair wage, but he gave her a small bag of silver every week so she could donate to her temple. They walked on.

She kept to herself as they moved uphill. She didn't speak to the men, never had, but she appreciated their presence. They let her breathe. They kept her safe. She thought of Rufus. His cruelty, yes. But also, his strange kindness. He had never struck her. He gave her clothes. Jewelry. Safety. He saw something in her no Roman had.

She didn't know if that made him good. She didn't pray for him too often. But she thought of him.

Past the last turn, the synagogue came into view, plain, low-roofed, with stone walls and narrow windows. Nothing like the towering shrines of the Romans. But the temple looked like it had always been there.

She paused at the entrance. One of the guards leaned close.

"We'll stay here as usual. Inside's yours."

She nodded and entered alone.

The holy place smelled of old wood and oil. A few others had arrived, an old man in a long robe, a mother with two sons, a man with scars who prayed while rocking.

Tirzah chose a place in the back. She didn't speak. Didn't move much. She just sat. Listened. Thought.

The voice of the elder rose, low and slow. A psalm. Not sung. Spoken. The words wrapped around her like a cloak.

He that dwelleth in the secret place of the most high shall abide under the shadow of the Almighty...

She closed her eyes. Not to sleep. But to feel.

The weight of the Roman world pressed heavy outside. But not here. Not for now. She let it go.

And when the prayer ended, and the scrolls were returned to their place, she rose and bowed her head, left her donation, and walked back into the light.

Her guards waited. She did not thank them. She never did. But she looked one in the eye, just for a breath. That was enough.

They turned. They walked. Rome swallowed them again.

The sun had lowered enough to soften the rooftops in gold. Tirzah stepped from the quiet of the synagogue courtyard, veiled again, her heart steady.

The Aventine felt cleaner than the rest of Rome. Fewer beggars. Fewer pigs. The air smelled like cut stone and baked bread. She knew the streets here, each crack in the walls, each crooked archway. An older woman waved from a stall selling oil and garum. Tirzah dipped her chin in reply.

They passed a small bakery. The smell of warm honey and chestnuts curled in the breeze. A boy called out something rude in Latin. One of the escorts stepped toward him and the boy ran. Tirzah said nothing.

They crossed a sloping street with worn stairs. She moved carefully, adjusting the basket on her hip. The fabric inside held the small prayer shawl her mother had sewn from scraps, years ago. A man stopped to look, saw the guards, and walked on.

"Not far now," one of the guards said in Greek.

Tirzah didn't answer. She rarely did.

At the corner before the alley, she paused. The sun threw long shadows between the buildings. A cat stretched across a rooftop. Somewhere, a child was crying. She listened.

Then kept walking.

Two more turns and the street opened to the edge of the market district. They passed a row of bronze workers. She nodded toward a Greek named Diodoros, who sold hinges and lamp bowls. He always gave her a smile and never asked her name. That made her trust him.

As they neared the villa, the guards relaxed. One unhooked his helmet and scratched his head.

Inside the gate, a slave girl met them. Tirzah handed off her basket, wiped dust from her hands, and stepped toward the inner garden.

She paused again.

The garden had changed. A new rose bush. A fresh coat of limewash on the statue base. Someone had swept the stone path.

Tirzah looked toward the upper window. Empty.

Not yet, she thought. Soon, though.

A priestess would come. A strange one. Tirzah had heard whispers from the kitchen. Foreign. Dancers. Gold and incense and blood. She didn't like the idea. But she would stay. She had no choice, yet. Except death.

This house gave her peace, food, and books. And the man who owned it had not once laid a hand on her if she didn't wish. He had placed her under the same protection as if a sister.

She owed him more than silence. She walked on. Up the stairs. Past the door with the lion carving. Into her large room.

She folded the prayer shawl once. Then again. Placed it gently under the pillow.

Outside, the sun dropped behind the hills. The guards posted themselves at the gate once more.

And Tirzah, Roman slave, daughter of Judah, watcher of winds, prayed without sound.

Chapter 66
HOUSE BENEATH HIS FEET

The Villa on the Caelian Hill

The white and tan cat of Mars slept near the warm stone lip of the atrium pool. He curled tight, tail over nose, ears twitching at the sound of water.

He knew the house.

He knew the hours of fire and silence. He knew the bowl where the cook dropped fat and meat. He knew where the mice lived, and the lizards. He knew the soft places and the warm places. He knew which door led to heat and which led to pain. He stayed out of the way, moved like steam, like breath, like things men forget.

He rose when the girl moved. The soft one. The one who never struck. Her steps meant warmth. She wore wool and smelled of cardamom. She left crumbs. The cat followed her until the man returned.

The tall one. Not loud. Not cruel. But full of power. Like storm clouds. He scratched his cheek when he thought too long. He stared into fire and made others wait. The girl watched him with wide eyes. The cat did too.

At night, the house quieted. That's when he moved.

Through columns and curtain, down warm halls. he passed slaves. They never touched him. He slipped into the kitchen. Waited. Stole what he could. Then back to the fire, where the girl sometimes let her curl near her feet.

She whispered once. He didn't understand the words, but he remembered the tone.

A soft creature in a house of lions. He understood that.

The back of the house stayed colder. Light barely reached it. The floor there held no fire beneath, only earth. Quiet lived there, a deep quiet, older than stone.

The white and tan cat passed under a wool curtain and strutted down the final hall. The air changed. Cooler. Still. He stepped across worn tiles, past a reed basket no one used anymore. The scent of fig and iron lingered.

At the end stood the wall. The tall wooden cross rose above a plain stool, bolted tight into brick and lime. The grain had darkened with years. No one touched it. It smelled of old death.

The cat sat.

He watched the cross like he watched the fire. Not for meaning. For mood.

He scratched once at the base. Just once. No one stopped him.

Behind the wall, nothing. Just silence.

He curled under the bush planted in the rear alcove, his second refuge. Soft dirt. Old leaves. It smelled of rain. he lay there sometimes when the noise got too loud.

Sometimes the soft girl with calm hands knelt nearby.

Sometimes Rufus passed it without a glance.

Sometimes neither came for days. He still returned.

A house has breath. It has heartbeat. Some men hear it. Others don't.

The white and tan cat heard everything.

At the far end of the house, where heat gave way to stillness and garden sounds faded, the cat crept on soft pads. His belly brushed mosaic. He moved like smoke. The hall narrowed. The air turned dry.

This place held no warmth. No cooking smells. No scraps. Just cool stone, quiet air, and a steady torch that burned low in its sconce, never out, never bright.

The cat paused at the doorway. Slipped in without a sound.

The old family shrine hung on the back wall, bolted to the stone. Old wood. Thick, weathered. No figure on it. Not yet.

He circled once, slow. Then crouched beneath it. One paw stretched forward. A claw clicked lightly along the grain. Then again. No sound. No mark. Still, he dragged his claws across it, as if to remind the wood: I was here.

He sat.

The room held its breath. Nothing moved.

He stayed that way for a long time, ears still, tail curled near his side, eyes half-lidded. At last, he stood and walked a slow lap along the base of the wall, stopping once to sniff where the stone met the floor.

Something had changed. Not here. Not yet. But the change was coming.

He felt it in the air, a pressure. Like the hush before a storm. Not the kind that broke trees. The kind that rearranged things. The kind that stayed.

His whiskers twitched.

He turned and left the room.

Down the corridor. Past painted walls and deep eaves. The sun had shifted. The wind smelled sharper. He passed a girl sweeping leaves. A boy stacking wood. Neither saw him. He wound past their legs and into the atrium.

He paused by the fountain. Watched the ripples. One fish swam in slow circles, one of the big ones. Tasty, not time yet.

The cat moved again, melting into shadow, tail low.

The house hadn't changed yet. But something had started. Something from outside. The kind of thing that never left once it entered. A power, an energy. He didn't understand it. But he felt it coming.

So, he walked the halls again.

He would know the moment change crossed the threshold.

And he would be watching.

Chapter 67
THE BRUTE AND THE PRINCESS

Caesar stood alone at the edge of the map room. Wind slipped through the open shutters, tugging at scrolls and silk banners. The air smelled of dust and parchment. Below the window, the Forum churned with sound, clatter, shouting, law, and heat. He watched without really seeing. His eyes were fixed on something else that wasn't there.

The girl.

She'd come from the edge of the world. Draped in red. Surrounded by myths and bodyguards. Her unseen dance burned in every senator's mind, every matron's whisper. Rome felt unsteady since she arrived. Women visited her daily. Men argued her legality. The priests could not agree if she should be blessed, banished, or burned.

He needed her out of sight, and out of mind.

He rubbed his temples. Ariella waited behind him.

"You cannot give her to Crassus," she said.

"I know."

"He'd bury her in marble."

"She is dangerous."

"She is necessary."

He turned to face her. "Then Pompey?"

"Worse."

He paced once. "Brutus?"

"He thinks too much. He'd try to master her."

"Cicero?"

"Too fragile."

Caesar exhaled hard. "Then what do you want me to do?"

Ariella met his eyes. "Give her to someone Rome fears."

"Fears?"

"Respects. But does not envy. Someone who will not use her. Who cannot."

He frowned. "There is no such man."

"Yes, there is."

He waited.

"Rufus."

He turned again to the window. "That brute is your choice?"

"My reading. She is a fire. He is stone. She needs someone who will not melt."

Caesar stayed silent.

Ariella stepped forward. "You owe him nothing. He'll ask for nothing. He is your loyal client. And he doesn't want her. So, if you ever decide that you don't want her around..."

Caesar smiled. "Does that matter?"

"That guarantees your future, one way or another."

Caesar nodded once. "Send a boy."

The boy ran through Rome.

*

At the Latinus villa, Rufus trained bare-chested in the courtyard. The boy waited near the gate. The steward brought him water. Rufus finished his forms, shield, blade, breath tight, legs set. When done, he approached.

"What do you want?"

The boy handed him the wax tablet. "From Caesar."

Rufus read it. Expressionless. His eyes widened.

"Who?" Rufus asked.

"The priestess"

Rufus looked confused, then angry.

"The one outside the gates?"

"Yes sir."

"What about her dancing girls, or her witches?"

"All of them sir. Caesar's mother requests your company."

"Now?"

"Now," the boy said.

He left his training gear. Washed quickly. Changed. And rushed out.

He would go to Caesar. Maybe, but not yet.

He went to Ariella as requested.

*

Ariella met him in her garden. Vines hung low. Shadows thick. She poured him water.

"I have to say no," he told her.

"You weren't asked."

"I don't want her."

"That's why you were chosen."

"She brings danger. And those witches"

"She brings power."

"I don't need power."

"She does. And she needs someone who won't try to steal it."

He drank. Set the cup down. "Give her to someone else."

"No."

He stood. "Then Caesar will hear from me."

She looked away. "He already knows, and by the way, don't even think about mistreating her or her people. Whatever they want, you provide it."

"Now, kiss my hand and go."

She didn't rise. She didn't need to.

Rufus stepped forward.

The room quieted.

Ariella extended her hand, bare, no rings, dry as parchment.

He took it lightly. Bent his head.

His lips touched skin that had survived civil wars, childbirth, and Caesar.

When he straightened, her eyes held him.

"You look like your grandfather," she said. "Now he is a handsome man."

He didn't answer. Didn't need to.

***

Rufus walked to his villa barely able to hide and control his anger.

Those nearby quickly got out of his way.

A sibyl.

He stared into the middle distance.

He hadn't once thought about her. Not a single time. Had no curiosity. No interest.

That foreign girl danced for gods, or snakes, or thunder, or whatever eastern nonsense made women cry and men grovel.

He fought lions. He stormed the walls of Jerusalem. He killed men with his bare hands.

And now this?

His house?

His roof over that circus?

Over witches and bells and holy whores?

***

Caesar sat at his table, scroll in hand. The boy returned and whispered.

Caesar smiled.

"Let it be done. May the Gods help him"

The boy left.

Caesar laughed deeply.

Chapter 68
ONE WALL AWAY

Albina sat alone in the tent. She had asked the witches and dancers to leave. The scroll lay beside her. She read it again. The name struck like a bell.

Gaius Latinus Rufus.

She smiled. Not soft. Not sweet. This was not a girl's smile. This came from deeper. Older.

She traced the letters again.

Rufus.

She knew that she should fear this young man, and she did. And she didn't.

The name burned low in her chest, like coals not yet gone cold. She had seen him, never in the flesh, never with her waking eyes, but in the dark places where the goddess spoke. She'd seen the lion's blood. The arc of his knives. His stillness before the kill. Always calm. Always alone. No prayers. No weakness.

He didn't beg the gods. He made them watch.

Now the scroll confirmed it. She would go to him. Just as the trance foretold. Just as the ache inside her had warned. Not hunger, not fear. Something different. A thread pulled tight, long before her birth. Long before his.

She didn't smile again.

There wasn't softness in her. Not now. The bruises hadn't faded. The inside of her thighs still wept at night. But her hands were steady. Her path was clear. Rome thought they give her to him, but they actually gave him to her. Rome thought it solved a problem, but Rome gave her an ax and laid their head on a stump.

They didn't know what they'd done.

She stood.

The witches entered again without sound. Her dancers followed. Barefoot. Silent. Alert. She gave the order.

"We begin."

They moved together. Step. Turn. Strike. They practiced the dance meant for one man. One chance. One future.

It was not sacred. Not holy. This was no offering to the gods.

This was for him. To stir his blood, his emotions, his thoughts.

Albina would dance to win him. To charm. To tempt. To control. He would belong to her when the dance ended. The women knew. The witches nodded. The guards approved.

He was the one the gods had shown her. In dream. In fire. In smoke. In the ache that never stopped.

He would never be tamed. So, she would not try.

But he would be hers.

He would provide. He would protect. He would give her a son, daughters. She would raise her son as a warrior of her people. Her daughters would continue her line.

He would never love another like her. She would make certain.

The dancers concentrated as they moved. Every gesture, every footfall, measured, exact. The dance would be performed only once. Her seduction could not fail.

If it failed, she would fail. Her war would fail. A Parthian temple would rise on the sacred ashes of her temple. Her people would vanish. The King of Kings would thrive. She had nothing but this. Only a dance.

The witches watched. One muttered a blessing. Another wept. Albina did not blink.

Her suite lay beside his. One wall away. She would sleep one wall from the man she must conquer.

The thought of him now knowing her name thrilled her to the bone, he was not happy about her coming to him. Such was his nature.

That would change.

The gods had chosen him. The gods had chosen her.

Now the time had come for her to act.

The mighty lion must submit.

Chapter 69
WITCH AT THE DOOR

The Villa, Caelian Hill, Rome

Zarmina the Red came alone.

She walked barefoot up the Caelian Hill, a blood-red robe clinging to her body. No escort. No smile. No sound but her steps. The city watched from doorways and shaded alleys, eyes tracking the small foreign woman who climbed as if the hill owed her ground.

At the Latinus villa she struck the great carved door with her fist, three hard blows that echoed through stone.

The steward unlatched the panel, opened it a hand's width, saw her face, and moved to close it again.

Her palm hit the door; she slid past him in one smooth shove.

"You cannot enter this door..." he started.

She lifted one hand. "I come from the Sibyl herself. I must see the rooms set aside for my Domina."

Her Latin came rough, as if the words scraped her tongue. The steward stepped back, off balance. She brushed past him into the atrium without waiting for permission.

The household shrine sat in its niche: Lares, Penates, a small bronze Mars. The flame flickered low.

Zarmina knelt. Touched her forehead to the cool stone. Kissed her fingers.

From the fold of her robe she drew a small wrapped object. She peeled the cloth away: a many-breasted woman crowned high, her face blank and old as caves. Artemis of Ephesus. She set the statue in front of the others, as if sliding a knife into a sheath that never expected it.

Then she rose.

The steward stared at the new figure; Zarmina stared at him. Judging. Testing.

He lost.

"You are expected," he muttered. "This way."

He led her down the eastern corridor. Marble floors under bare feet. Painted ceilings alive with gods and vines. Columns. Fresh flowers in bronze bowls. The house tried to impress her.

They stopped at a polished door.

"This room was chosen for her," he explained. "Dominus wants the best for her. The apartment holds every comfort."

Zarmina stepped inside.

A broad bed. Fine linen. A private bath carved from veined stone with running water. A dressing bench. A separate toilet. Closets for silks and jewelry. Lamps hung from gold hooks. A low couch, small tables, carved chairs. Clean air; faint rose oil.

She walked the perimeter once. Fingers grazed the wall, the chest, the rim of the bath.

She said nothing.

The steward's chest puffed. "This is the best room in the house."

"No."

His smile slipped. "What do you mean, 'no'?"

"Show me the rest."

He hesitated, then bowed slightly and obeyed.

They passed a nursery, clean, empty, swept, quiet. She glanced in, chin dipping once.

"Another nursery on the other side?"

"Yes, of course."

Dining hall next: open colonnade painted with lions and ships, a mosaic floor like a twilight sea. Beyond, the inner garden waited.

She stepped into the light.

Three fountains sang in the central pool; carved figures poured water from stone jars. White marble rails framed the space. A long ornamental basin stretched between columns, surface broken by carved jets. Gold fish slid in slow, lazy circles.

Two pairs of peacocks stalked the path, one white male trailing a train like snowfall. They scattered when she came near.

"This," she said, pointing to a shaded alcove under ivy near the eastern wall, "is where her shrine will stand. The Goddess faces east. The Sibyl speaks there at dawn."

The steward followed her finger. "It is a beautiful spot."

A ring of columns, more than two hundred, encircled the garden. The wind moved the leaves. The fountains answered with their own bright music.

Back inside, servants melted to the walls as she passed.

They came to another closed door. She stopped. "This?"

"The master's room," he replied.

Her gaze shifted to the next door. "And that one? Open it."

"The concubine's suite."

"Are you hard of hearing," she asked, voice flat, "or simply stupid? Open it."

His ears flushed. He unlocked the latch.

The concubine's suite lay smaller than the wife's, yet no less rich. A low bed with heavy blankets. Private bath and toilet. Painted walls and ceilings. Polished bronze mirrors. A soft rug underfoot. One connecting door stood between this room and the master's, bolted from Rufus's side.

Zarmina crossed the threshold. Stopped in the center. Breathed once, deep.

"She sleeps here."

The steward swallowed. "She..."

"Do not interrupt me again."

He locked his jaw.

"She sleeps beside the master," Zarmina went on. "She sees the moon from that window. She feels guarded, not caged. This room has breath."

His mouth opened, then closed.

"She requires seventeen rooms for her people," Zarmina continued. "She requires a nursery. She requires more slaves. A buyer from Alexandria will come; after he speaks with the Domina, the Dominus provides coin and transport. A very important statue waits in a city called Pompeii. The Dominus arranges its journey here at once. Instructions follow today."

Her gaze dropped to his belt.

"You sit lucky. Cut already." She flicked her fingers toward the inner wing. "No whole men, no uncut male other than the Dominus, may come near where she sleeps or walk that corridor. If any remain there, she acts. None of you will enjoy what comes next."

The steward swallowed again.

"She must not be touched for eight days after she enters this house," Zarmina said. "Not by the Dominus. Sacred law. Sacred timing."

She left him standing and walked on.

Through the kitchens: she smelled the bread, tasted water drawn from the pipes, tested the heat of the ovens with an outstretched palm. Into the slave quarters: counted cots, examined worn shoes, noted which blankets frayed and which did not.

She paused before a nine feet tall black crucifix bolted on the wall. She looked at it for a long heartbeat. Then moved on without comment.

Back in the concubine's suite, she sat on the bench near the mirror. The glass caught a thin slice of her face; the rest stayed shadow.

"Yes," she murmured. "This belongs to her now. The Jew must leave it."

She rose.

In the main hallway a tall painted vase brimmed with lilies. She lifted it with both hands.

And hurled it onto the stone.

Stained glass shattered across the floor. The sound cracked through the villa like a whip.

Zarmina turned on the steward and unleashed a torrent of Parthian, sharp, rolling words no Roman ear in the house could follow. The foreign language swallowed all other sound.

Rufus stormed in from the garden, bare-chested, breath still quick from sparring. Sweat ran down his arms; his hands stayed wrapped. Fury lit his face.

He stopped when he saw her.

Zarmina dropped to her knees. Forehead to stone. Arms stretched forward. Completely still. Submissive position, but not in any way submissive to a Roman.

"You," he snarled. "Who allowed you inside?"

The steward stepped in, shaking. "I tried to stop..."

Rufus's open hand cracked across his cheek. The man staggered, blood at his lip.

"You enter my home, smash my things..."

"She comes to prepare the way," the steward blurted, voice breaking.

"Silence."

Rufus glared down. Zarmina did not move.

"Speak," he ordered.

Her forehead remained on the floor.

"The Sibyl sleeps beside you," she said.

"What?" His jaw clenched. "No. Her rooms stand across the way."

"She will not touch you. On pain of death, you will not touch her. But she must sleep near you. Danger lives in distance."

"I said no."

Zarmina continued as if he had grunted at the weather.

"No male serves her unless cut. No whole man but you walks past her doors. The Sibyl sleeps next to you."

Rufus flung his hands wide, exasperated. "Fine. Move her where you want."

"The Jewess leaves that room at once," Zarmina added.

"Damn it. All right. Anything else, witch?"

"The Sibyl needs many slaves, new ones."

"She needs new slaves?"

"She needs what you promised. And the seventeen rooms for her people."

"Seventeen rooms?" His voice rose. "You stride into my house..."

"She needs a shrine."

"You can use the garden."

"Not the full garden. The ivy place. East wall."

He fell quiet.

"She needs seventeen rooms," Zarmina repeated. "She needs new slaves. Any male slave or servant near her wing must be cut. The statue in Pompeii must come to her. She must not be touched for eight days after her arrival into this house. My Domina will arrive in two mornings. Do you accept?"

He held her gaze at last; she lifted her head enough for their eyes to lock.

"She brings protection," Zarmina said softly. "She brings favor. Or ruin." A faint red glow from the courtyard flickered over her face. "Do you accept?"

Rufus looked at the broken vase. At the steward's bent shoulders. At the soft walls of his house. At the invisible line where his will had started to bend.

Old superstitions stirred like snakes under his skin. He had never trusted witches. Yet he had learned, again and again, to respect what stalked behind them.

A shiver ran through him.

He nodded once. "Yes."

Zarmina stood in one smooth motion.

She offered no smile. No bow. "You may prepare."

Then she walked out, bare feet silent on the cold stone.

Rufus watched her go, fists tight at his sides, breath still rough in his throat.

He looked at the steward. "Do everything she demanded."

"Yes, master."

Rufus did not move.

He stood in the center of his own villa, surrounded by his marble, his fountains, his painted ceilings.

The place no longer felt entirely his.

For the first time, the house felt like something else: a temple waiting for a goddess, and a trap waiting for him.

Chapter 70
RED WITCH EXITS

The Villa, Caelian Hill, Rome

Rufus stood in the entrance hall with his arms crossed, jaw locked hard enough to crack stone. The steward hovered behind him, cheek still swollen from the slap.

"Dominus," the steward said carefully, voice thin, "she left something at the household shrine."

Rufus didn't turn. "What?"

"A statue."

That earned a glance.

He followed the man toward the lararium. The lamps burned low. Shadows pooled under the carved niche. And there, at the center of Rome's household gods, sat a stranger, a dark stone figure, heavy-bellied, crowned tall, breasts stacked in rows like a brood.

The Artemis of Ephesus.

Eastern. Older than the Forum itself. Watching the room as if it judged every Roman breath inside it.

"You want it removed?" the steward asked quietly.

Rufus studied the idol. Too small to threaten. Too certain to ignore.

"No. Leave it."

After a while, Rufus cleared his throat and asked, "Are those... breasts?"

"That's how they carve her."

Silence dripped like wax.

"Furnishings arrived for the concubine's chamber," the steward added. "Linens, lamps, cushions. Enough to fill a merchant hall."

"Damn." Rufus rubbed his eyes. "Tirzah will need a new room. You handle it. She won't hear that from me."

He pointed at a quiet but luxurious guest chamber down the hall. The steward nodded, hiding a smile. Even he found it amusing that a war hero feared the reaction from a soft-spoken slave girl more than a man with a sword.

"More wagons come in the next few days," the steward continued. "Treasure from the women. Clothes. Furniture. Everything she demanded for her people. Her valuables will go to your strong room. Wagons and teams go to your farm."

Rufus exhaled. "How much?"

"Enough to fill those seventeen rooms."

"Seventeen?"

"For her dancers," the steward said, counting on his fingers. "Five blood relatives. Two witches. Six eunuch guards. Two apprentices. And two attendants, one with short hair who walks like a young soldier."

Rufus pinched the bridge of his nose.

"She expects a buyer to travel to Alexandria next week. She wants specific slaves. Only cut men. No whole male may walk past her chambers unless it's you."

Rufus snorted. "Good thing you're already cut."

"Yes, sir," the steward said dryly, as if the gods themselves had spared him a worse fate.

"And one more thing," he added. "There is a statue stored at Pompei. She wants it delivered here. You are to send a ship Immediately."

"A ship today?" Rufus asked.

The steward nodded.

A slow throb rose behind Rufus's eyes.

"She gave another warning," the steward whispered. "If any man touches her..." He drew a finger across his throat. "Castration first."

Rufus stared at the idol again. The room felt smaller.

"Eight days," the steward continued. "She said you cannot touch her for eight days after entering the villa."

Rufus didn't answer.

Eight days. Eight nights. Eight chances for rumor, for law, for gods to twist fate tight as rope. Orders from a general made sense. Orders from a witch in a red robe carried weight no soldier training could explain.

He looked at the foreign idol again. It waited in the lamplight like something placed during a siege. Those rows of breasts looked less like fertility and more like warning. She didn't just demand worship. She demanded space. She demanded sacrifice.

A prickling crept along his shoulders.

The steward cleared his throat. "She, and her whole group will arrive in two days. I'm sure a large crowd will gather. There will be a dance the moment she enters. In your honor. On the Gordian Knot mosaic and its hypocaust must be burning to heat the floors. Her dancers will join her. The guards will stand watch. No man may look at her with want. Only you."

"And if they do?"

"Dead within the hour."

The steward took a breath. "Also... another witch arrives tonight. Different from the first. A black one. She carries more statues. For the garden."

Rufus muttered, "She must have them stacked like grain sacks."

The steward scratched his chin. "Treat Tirzah gently, Dominus. She's my favorite."

Rufus walked away before he said something he regretted. The garden opened around him. Fish turned in the long pool with lazy strokes. A white peacock shrieked under the colonnade. The sunlight caught the marble lions, warm and gold.

He stood in the quiet, fists slowly unclenching.

She hadn't even crossed the threshold.

And already the house bent toward her will.

Already Rome shifted.

Already his life moved under a different star.

He looked back once at the idol in the niche.

The multi-breasted goddess watched him.

And he understood something Zarmina had not said:

Albina's shadow filled the villa long before her footsteps reached its floor.

Night settled soft over the southern fields, a thin blue dusk stretching between the city walls and the small foreign camp pitched just beyond the pomerium line.

Albina sat beside a low flame.

Her dancers huddled close, cloaks wrapped tight.

Zarmina ground herbs with a stone. A smile on her face brought by the memory of today's visit.

Nisaya supervised the loading of a wagon. She would enter the house of Rufus tonight.

The eunuchs stood at the camp's edge, led by Darak. Silent as carved obsidian, eyes sweeping every shadow.

Rome glowed in the distance.

Torches atop the wall.

Guards pacing.

A hum of life behind stone, drifting faint on the breeze.

Albina watched it all without blinking.

She could not cross.

Not yet.

A few more days she would enter the villa. Every detail planned and rehearsed.

The Senate's decree hung over the camp like a drawn bow.

After entering Rome, there would be no touching. Eight more days of waiting. Eight nights under foreign stars.

But even from here, Rome pulled at her.

The crescent under her wrist warmed once, a slow pulse. A promise. A warning.

Yamina sat beside her. "Domina... the city feels large."

Albina breathed in the scent of resin and cold grass.

"Large things crack," she murmured.

The dancers traded glances.

Tareeda drew her knees close.

Zermeh kissed the charm braided into her hair.

Nashti rubbed the mud from her ankles.

Mirae wrote a line of poetry with her finger in the soil, then erased it before anyone could read.

A distant horn called from the wall.

Zarmina looked up from her herbs.

"He feels the shift," she said.

Albina lifted her gaze toward the Caelian Hill.

The villa stood somewhere beyond that dark rise, warm lamps, polished stone, a man pacing through halls that carried her scent before her arrival.

Her voice dropped to a whisper.

"He feels me."

The fire snapped.

A cold wind rushed off the fields.

Nisaya muttered an omen under her breath.

Matineus, silent, guarded, watchful, leaned against a packhorse and tried not to stare at her in the firelight.

Albina felt that, too.

She said nothing.

Matineus would escort Nisaya to the villa soon.

The camp settled for the night.

Blankets drawn.

Blades placed close.

Guard shifts taken by men who had bled for her.

Albina sat alone a while longer, eyes fixed on the city lights.

The gate torches flickered.

Rome breathed.

The land waited.

Her pulse steadied.

"Let Rome learn to dream of me."

The fire sank low.

Behind the walls, the steady roar of a large mass of people settled.

Albina closed her eyes.

She was not inside Rome yet, but the city had already opened.

Chapter 71

RED RING IN THE ALPS

Somewhere in the Alps

Snow swallowed the ridge.

A crooked line of men pushed through it, bodies bent, breath ragged, faces raw from wind. Snow didn't fall; it slashed sideways, thin knives of ice cutting through skin and patience. The storm sent sheets of white roaring down the slope, grinding frozen grit into their cheeks.

Red Ring walked in front.

His black cloak snapped behind him, stiff with frost, a torn banner dragging through another man's legend. No saddle. No mule. No mercy. The horses had frozen days earlier, hooves locked, eyes clouded, ribs frosted solid. They cut strips of meat until the bodies turned to stone. Hunger tasted like iron now. The mountains cared nothing for oaths.

His brothers trudged behind him, four men built from ruin: one missing an ear, one whose jaw never closed, one who smiled at the wrong times, and one who walked silent and slow with a broken hand still tied to a spear.

Men shaped by punishment. Men who accepted cold the way others accepted prayers. They followed him because death meant less than failing him.

The wind snarled.

Red Ring didn't.

Each step wrenched at his wrists. Even wrapped in hide and layers of wool, pain crawled bone deep. The old scars never softened. Each ring, dark metal forged in his father's fire, dug into the thickened flesh of his fingers.

He remembered the chains.

White-stone walls scorched by sun.

A desert fortress where eunuchs held the keys.

A boy kept for leverage.

Iron anchored to bone.

Nights of clinking metal.

Dog-boy, they called him.

He remembered the older boy who laughed at his bleeding wrists.

He remembered pushing the chain around that mocking throat.

He remembered the guards' breaking rods across his back, rods that didn't break the boy he'd crushed.

When his father burned the compound, Red Ring didn't cry or run or thank him. He walked through ash on bare feet and never looked back. He forged a thick red ring the next year, dipped it into the blood of the first man he killed after freedom, then again after the next, and the next. The metal drank each life. The stain stayed, deep and old, darker than the rings of warlords.

He walked through the Alps now with that same heat in his chest.

Wind flayed him.

Snow crusted his beard.

Eyes burned raw and red.

Still, he never blinked.

Ahead waited Rome.

And in Rome waited a petite girl.

The Sibyl.

The dancer.

The fire-worshiper with the amber eyes.

The one the women adored, the one the men feared, the one kings whispered about.

His master wanted her dead now.

Red Ring wanted her broken.

He would cut down her guards.

He would rip through her dancers.

He would silence whatever power lived in her bones.

He would see her stare at him in terror before he closed her throat.

Snow thickened. A white wall smothered the ridge. Ice cracked under their boots. Frost crept into their boots until skin split at the heel. Still Red Ring pressed forward as if the storm pushed him rather than slowed him.

His brothers began muttering their oath, their voices raw and low:

"Blood for silence. Blood for silence."

He didn't hear them.

He heard only the clink of old iron in his memory.

The clink of chains from childhood.

The clink of the ring on his finger tapping against itself when he clenched his hand too hard.

The storm hissed.

Something else moved in the white.

The brother with the broken hand lifted his head. His breath stuttered.

The wind shifted.

Cold deepened, an unnatural drop.

Warmth drained from the air as if a mouth inhaled the world.

Red Ring slowed.

A shape formed in the storm ahead.

Small at first. Dark.

Then taller. Thinner.

Something long-haired drifted just beyond the snow curtain.

A woman's outline.

Bare feet on ice.

Her hands dangled at her sides, fingers dripping something darker than water. Her head tilted, slow, curious, as though examining a beast she had waited centuries to meet.

The men behind Red Ring stopped breathing.

Snowflakes curved around her body, as if the storm refused to touch her.

Red Ring felt nothing. Not awe. Not fear.

Only hunger sharpened by hatred.

He stepped forward.

His ring burned hot against his skin.

He believed he'd chosen this path.

He didn't understand the truth:

The Alps had not delivered him to Rome.

They had delivered him to her.

The woman drifted closer, lips dark with someone else's sorrow, eyes hollow enough to swallow storms.

The Blood Witch had found him.

And she never let prey climb out of the mountains untouched.

Chapter 72
BLOOD WITCH

High in the Alps

Snow crushed the passes.

Ice crystals attacked, a thousand needles slanting straight into bone. The wind hunted Red Ring's party down the narrow path, gnawing through wool, scouring their faces raw. Ice crawled into every seam.

Red Ring walked first.

Black cloak cracked behind him like a wounded banner. The ring on his middle finger tapped now and then, metal on metal, a counting of lives taken, a vow measured by sound alone. His brothers moved in a single file behind him, men pared down to hunger and tendon and spite. No horses. No supplies. Just boots, blades, and a hatred that kept their hearts beating.

They crossed the pine belt by dusk and saw the shack only because smoke fought its way through the storm. A roof sagged under old snow. A crooked door hung askew.

One brother dropped to his knees three times before they reached it; no one lifted him. Mercy froze early in the Alps.

An old woman waited in the doorway.

She shouldn't have been there, well-fed, round-faced, hair bound in a scarf patterned with moons. Her shoulders curled inward, but her eyes shone with a sharpness frost couldn't dull.

"You look hungry," she said kindly.

A brother checked for his knife but froze when he found nothing but numb fingers and leather. They followed her anyway. The cold had taught them obedience.

Inside, a pot simmered, steamed thick with fat and herbs. Meat floated in the broth. Vegetables softened to pulp. They ate without speaking. They slept without dreaming.

Red Ring woke up on stone.

The fire was out. His brothers gone. The shack stretched wider somehow, shadows long, wrong, bending like wet branches.

The old woman no longer stooped.

Her spine stood straight as a spear. Skin taut. Eyes pale as ash. Her shadow stretched across the wall, too large for her body, too sharp at the edges.

"You dream of fire," she murmured.

He tried to sit, but the cold pinned him. "What are you?" he rasped.

She smiled. The smile peeled twenty years off her face. "I feed on sorrow," she said, breath warm, voice soft enough to slip under the ribs.

Her fingers touched his chest.

The world cracked open.

A memory. His memory. Smoke in a courtyard. The boy he strangled with his own chain. The guards beating him until his back split like parchment. The prince's laugh when the iron rings were welded to the boy's wrists.

Red Ring gasped. She drank it in with a shiver, like tasting broth after famine.

"Name the one you fear," she whispered.

He clenched his jaw. His teeth ached. His throat tightened.

She waited.

"Albina," he finally forced out. The name scraped him from the inside. "The Sibyl."

The witch inhaled.

A deep breath of power.

Youth poured into her limbs; her cheeks flushed; her pupils widened. She moved in a circle, feet tracing serpents on the floorboards, hips rolling with the rhythm of something old and obscene. The rafters quivered. Copper charms clinked. Herbs overhead smoldered without flame.

She pressed a cold brand to his chest; antlers black as tar.

Red Ring screamed.

Then hands grabbed him, his brothers, hauling him up, voices muttering curses and prayers. The shack shrank to its old size. The pot was gone. The fire dead.

The witch nowhere.

Outside, snow fell softly.

At the threshold, the witch knelt by the cold coals.

"Now I know her name," she said.

She tasted Red Ring's grief on the air, salt of humiliation, rot of failure, the bitter tang of a father's disappointment. Her smile sharpened.

"Rufus," she breathed next. The syllables slid from her mouth like warm oil. "She will carry his seed. His blood will sweeten the hunt."

She outlined her plan for the coming years in the frost: weaken Rufus first by fear, then take Albina's power at the breast, then drink from the child. Power layered, harvested, hoarded.

She carved a lion's face into the lintel, horned, feral, smiling with too many teeth, and left it as her signature.

Then she walked north, toward the Rhine, where the wind would erase her passage and the mountains would hide her hunger.

The Villa - Caelian Hill, Rome

Night settled over the house like a heavy veil. Lamps trembled. Curtains breathed in the draft. Servants curled under blankets, dreams thin from the day.

Nisaya, her first night in the villa, knelt at the Sibyls' new shrine.

Cold stone touched her palms. She wasn't praying exactly, she listened. The water remembered what steps came near it. The stone remembered what ghosts had crossed its sisters in the north.

A tremor answered.

Then a scent like burnt rosemary. Then the faint sting of snow.

Nisaya's eyes snapped open.

She saw a scarred chest marked by antlers.

A woman whose shadow walked before her.

A mouth hungry for vows, not flesh.

A name whispered over blood: Rufus.

Danger, real danger, had stepped onto their board.

Nisaya rose. Fingers slid to the blade tucked under her sash, black iron, wrapped in old red wool, its edge holding a cold no hearth in Rome could warm.

She didn't panic.

Nisaya the Black looked toward the northern sky.

The air tasted wrong.

"Albina," she murmured, "a hunger walks away and walks toward you."

The pool rippled.

A door down the hall opened, Matineus shifting in his bed, sensing danger before dawn.

The witch turned her head.

The game had begun.

Chapter 73
THE HUNTER LEAVES

Matineus left at dawn.

No farewell. No bread.

Boots striking stone, breath sharp in the cold, a nod to the steward because anything more would break him open.

Behind him the Caelian villa stood quiet, smug, full of spaces Albina would soon fill. Rufus's house. Rufus's walls. Rufus's bed behind its door. He walked faster.

Down the slope. Past the river.

Past the baker's daughter who once winked at him; she stared straight through him now, and he let her.

His horse waited at the stables, hooves restless, winter steam rising around its chest. Matineus mounted without a sound, heels pressing hard, riding until the wind tore the tears from his face so he didn't have to wipe them.

Albina was coming.

To stay.

In Rufus's house.

The gods laughed, cruel and amused. Rufus didn't want her, never chased her, never trembled for her, and still the Senate set her beside him. Matineus felt the truth lodge under his ribs like a nail: Rufus would come to want her. Men always wanted the sun once it lay in their hands.

The family farm rose from the winter soil. Deep earth. Olive rows twisting like old fingers. Stone walls built by men long dead, moss in every seam. Dogs barked once, then quieted at his scent. He stepped inside the small house and drank warm wine from a clay jug, swallowing without tasting.

Two days, he hunted.

A stag broke from cover; the arrow took its throat clean. He gutted it on the spot, steam rising around his wrists. Fed the liver raw to the dogs, good meat for loyal creatures, while the carcass bled onto snow. He hauled the stag across his shoulders until his legs shook, refused to stop, dropped it on the butchering block and carved until his arms burned. Ate without salt. Drank until sleep hit him like a cudgel.

Nights came with women.

Not many. Enough.

Curious girls with spring laughter and coin-bright eyes: the smith's copper-haired daughter; a shepherd's niece with strong legs; another with gold at her ankles. Each came whispering his name, hoping for the man who had broken ambushes and carried Albina through fire.

They laughed when entering his bed.

Stopped laughing when he stayed silent.

Hands hard on hips, no tenderness, no lies, no lingering. They left quick, robes half-fastened, cheeks flushed with something close to shame. He never reached for them again. They tasted of nothing.

The nights lengthened.

He slept in the orchard, forehead pressed to the ground, the cold biting deep. Woke with leaves stuck to his cheek. Counted scars instead of sheep. Watched Orion crawl across the sky, each star a small wound he could name.

He split a fence post with his fist and left the splinters lodged inside the knuckles. Ate olives straight from the trees, bitter, tough, unripe, forcing them down so the throat burn could quiet the ache in his chest.

The farm took him in like an old soldier takes in a wound: without pity.

He mended stone walls. Cut dead branches until the axe slipped from sweat-slick palms. Carried river stones to fill an empty well. Worked until his breath rasped harsh, until his shoulders trembled, until exhaustion dragged him to his knees. No lantern lit. No fire sparked.

A sick wolf limped into the grove, ribs showing through fur. Matineus knelt beside it, blade in hand, and ended its suffering with one sure cut. Buried it under neat stones. The gesture felt like a funeral for himself.

When silence pressed too near, Albina returned.

Her eyes first.

Amber, alive with old gods and something deeper, something he wanted and was never meant to touch.

Her hands next.

Strong from knives and dance, guiding, commanding, holding secrets he would never hold.

Then her voice.

Soft as water when she wanted, sharp as flint when she refused comfort.

He saw her move through memory, her hips weaving through firelight, that long red robe swaying around her calves. Matineus felt the bruise of wanting her in the way men feel old breaks when storms come.

Food turned to ash.

Wine thinned to nothing.

He walked the olive rows until his legs buckled, until he woke on the ground with dirt in his teeth.

Pain kept him alive. Silence kept him sane.

The love stayed. Wouldn't leave.

He would live this way until something inside him healed.

If it healed.

And though each day hollowed him further, though his brother would take the woman he would have died for, Matineus loved her anyway.

Some vows break clean.

His did not.

Albina's shadow refused to let him go.

Chapter 74
HOUSEBOUND

Villa on the Caelian Hill

The villa moved. Not in noise or speed, but in weight. In waiting. Slaves whispered more. Girls walked faster. The air tightened around the door frames. Something sacred, or dangerous, or both, had been set in motion.

Tirzah moved through the change quietly. She passed the kitchen. Inspected the dates. Poured the oil herself. Tapped the amphora with her knuckle. Watched the golden liquid settle. She always checked.

Rufus never told her to. He never needed to. She knew what he liked. He liked control. Clean lines. Few words. The garden was trimmed; the floors washed in sea water. She saw to it all.

She passed under the household shrine. Stopped. Looked up at the new figure placed there. Female. Ephesus-style. Dozens of breasts. A crown that reached high like a tower. A foreign goddess with too many eyes.

The witch had placed the false idol there. Without asking.

She had seen the Dominus looking at it nervously. He didn't like the evil thing.

Tirzah lit a small lamp. Bowed slightly. She didn't worship the image. But she respected shrines. Even borrowed ones.

She heard the gossip. Everyone did. The Sibyl would come. The dancing girl in red veil. The foreign priestess. The storm. And she would come here. To stay.

Tirzah walked through the rooms again. Counted linens. Measured space. Set up trays of herbs where the witches might want them. Smoothed the bed she once used herself, in the concubine suite, now reassigned. She adjusted the lamps. Lit the incense. Then stepped back.

The room was perfect. Not hers. Not anymore.

She moved to a more secluded room separated from the others. Quiet and peaceful. Hers. One she could decorate as she wished.

The Dominus didn't want her to move, but he caved under the witch's gaze. Silly man afraid of such nonsense. Tirzah felt no fear of a witch; her God protected her from such things.

The Dominus felt bad when the steward told her she had to change rooms. He liked her next to him, and she liked being near him. She didn't cry.

She didn't love Rufus, not like a wife. Not like a girl. He never kissed her except when they made love. Never promised her anything. But he respected her. He listened when she warned him of bad omens, and bad men. He gave her silver. Good clothes. Plenty of good kosher food.

He had never asked what she needed, he just sent a servant under her command. The boy went to the Jewish quarter every third day with a pouch of silver and a list in his hand. Salted fish, lentils, oil pressed in clean vessels, lamb from a house where knives were washed in prayer. Rufus never questioned the expense. He gave orders. And the orders were followed.

She once overheard two slaves complaining about the trouble of it. Rufus walked past them. He didn't shout. Didn't slow. But both were gone the next day. To the mines.

He didn't hire a cook. He trusted her to keep her food clean, her hands clean, her soul between her and her God. He made space for her food, space in the storeroom, space at the hearth, space in a house built by Rome. That, too, was a kind of love. Or something close.

And once every seven days, with an escort of his choosing, he let her walk to the synagogue on the Aventine. No questions. No mockery. That mattered.

Tirzah carried her basket outside. Walked through the long garden. The white peacock shimmered near the columns. The other birds trailed behind like painted thoughts. She liked the garden best in the early light. When the air hadn't chosen yet between heat and cool.

She saw the slave boys. Saw the newly bought eunuch guards sparring in the side court. She noted who limped. Who slouched. She made mental notes for ointments, for corrections. She wasn't just a girl. She pulled levers. Whispered suggestions to the steward. Gave warnings that became policy.

That wouldn't stop when the Sibyl came.

Albina. The name felt soft in the mouth, but heavy in the house. Tirzah didn't fear her. But she would watch her. Always. The girl had power. Not from muscle. From belief. That made her dangerous.

Tirzah knew stories like hers. Girls from the east. Dancers who became queens. She would not fight her. Not openly. That was suicide. But she would find cracks.

One of the dancers would get sick. One of the witches would need herbs. Tirzah would offer the right blend. The right words.

She would listen. Stand in the shadows. Whisper to the guards. Feed the girls. Bind a wound here, give a name there.

She wouldn't be forgotten.

Let Albina dance in the garden. Let her place her bells and gods. Tirzah would be in the walls. In the schedules. In the private commands.

Rufus had built this house. But Tirzah made the home breathe. She would keep breathing.

Even with the goddess under the roof.

Chapter 75
THE CIRCUS

The Circus Maximus, Rome

The Circus Maximus trembled like a living thing.

Forty thousand voices rolled in waves, rising and breaking against the stone curves of the track. Color burned everywhere; green, blue, red, white banners twisting in the warm wind. Dust drifted in the sun, turning the air gold.

Rufus sat with his father, grandfathers, uncles, brothers, cousins, Latinus men packed tight on the stone benches, no armor, no rank marks, only family. The heat soaked through tunics. Sweat gathered at brows. Coins clinked as wagers changed hands.

His father lifted a hand.

"Green."

Their row thundered back the word.

"Green!"

Men stomped heels, thudded fists on knees. The Greens claimed Rome's wild hearts, the bruisers, alley-fighters, men who drank too much and swung first. Women watched them too; every charioteer carried a story whispered in bedchambers long after races ended.

Across the track, horses pawed the sand. Seven laps. Four teams. The drivers tied reins around their waists to free both hands for the whip. One crash could drag a man for half a lap before he reached his dagger.

Horns opened the sky.

Drums shook the benches.

Then the gates slammed wide.

The Circus erupted.

Chariots exploded into motion, wheels rattling, hooves slicing grit, whips cracking sharp as lightning across horseflesh. Rufus leaned forward without thinking. His breath sharpened. His brothers braced their legs and shouted until spit flew.

The smell hit him next: horses, sweat, smoke, old wine, crushed figs, oil on leather, and the unmistakable iron tang of fear. Vendors pushed through the crush with trays of bread and watered wine, shouting prices over curses. Somewhere behind him a woman prayed to Fortuna with both hands raised.

The Green driver tucked low and leaned back, almost part of the horses. The team lunged like a single raging animal. They scraped the first turn so close the axle shrieked in protest. The Blue driver whipped at them, eyes narrow, face streaked with grit.

A chant formed.

Spread.

Tightened.

Grew teeth.

On the third lap, the Red team clipped the metae. The crash tore through the Circus. A wheel splintered. The driver hurtled through the air and hit stone with a crack that silenced even the gamblers. His horses bolted, dragging his limp body until a slave severed the reins. A smear of red marked the sand.

One of Rufus's cousins laughed. Rufus's uncle cuffed him hard across the ear. Rufus's oldest brother laughed at his cousin's expression.

"Watch the race, fool. Death waits for all of us. Let the man keep his dignity."

The Greens surged again. The White team lost ground in a spray of dust. The crowd rose, thousands on their feet. Rufus felt their weight like a tide under his ribs.

The final turn came fast.

The Greens carved the inside line.

Wheels spun.

Hooves hammered.

Then the finish tore across the track.

Victory.

A roar swallowed the sky.

Rufus shouted until his throat burned raw. Men embraced, cursed, kissed their fists, lifted children onto shoulders. His father pressed a copper into his palm.

"Your first win," he said, voice thick with pride.

Slaves dragged the dead driver away. Dust drifted across the blood. The crowd thinned by degrees, every voice still humming with the wild pulse of the Greens.

Rufus stayed seated. The sand held his gaze. That dark smear lingered there, more truth than the cheering.

His father leaned close.

"This is Rome. Remember it."

Rufus listened.

"We chase speed," his father said. "Strength. Blood that spills clean. Glory that fades by nightfall. Men cheer a dead driver at noon and forget him by supper." He paused. "But what's coming to your house will not fade."

Rufus turned. His father's face carried a weight the Circus could not drown.

"That girl," he said. "The Sibyl. She comes under your roof. And with her come witches, dancers, guards, omens, relics, and the kind of power Rome pretends it cannot feel."

Rufus frowned. "She's foreign."

"All the more reason to mind your steps." His father's hand settled heavy on his shoulder. "Rome bends many things. But this one carries a spark older than our walls. Treat her with honor. Or the wound she leaves may bleed farther than you imagine."

Rufus swallowed. The roar of the crowd faded, replaced by something quieter, colder, the sense of a tide turning under him.

"She hasn't even arrived," he said.

His father stood slowly, knees stiff, cloak sweeping dust from the bench.

"And still, she moves Rome."

Rufus followed him out of the Circus, the smear of blood behind him, the weight of prophecy ahead. He felt the hinge of something shifting, an old life closing, a new one rising with the dust.

He told himself he wouldn't forget.

But the gods heard that kind of promise.
And they smiled.

Chapter 76
THE SHOW

The Villa on the Caelian Hill, Rome

Two days crept by on the Caelian Hill: long, restless, heavy with waiting. Rufus sent one ship south for the promised statue, another east toward Alexandria with coin sealed under wax and orders carved sharp: scribes, cooks, musicians, hair-workers, singers, and one scholar trained in the old rites. The villa hummed with anticipation, yet he slept like a man guarding a battlefield, light, alert, never truly under.

The steward woke him at dawn. Rufus rose from the cot, stretched until the scar along his ribs pulled tight. The sky above the open atrium shone hard and blue; a heat-day sky, the kind Rome loved and feared.

A runner bowed low. "Dominus... the street is full."

Rufus frowned. "Soldiers?"

"No, Dominus. Women. Noblewomen. A crowd across the road. Hundreds."

He scrubbed a hand down his jaw. "Across the road."

"Yes. They wait for the Sibyl."

He snorted. "Bring oranges. Water. Cool towels."

The runner sprinted off.

He dressed for the morning ritual, shaved smooth, hair trimmed by Tirzah's careful hand. She stood ready before he even called, braid looped high, a single strand loose against her cheek; dark indigo stola belted tight with bronze; the gold cuff on her wrist glinting like a small authority of its own.

"You look good," Rufus said, eyeing his reflection in her pupils. "Better than half the senators' wives."

Her mouth softened just barely. "You asked me to dress properly."

She shaved him steady as stone, no tremor, no wasted motion. Her breath feathered warm over his shoulder. The bowl smelled of clean water and mint; she caught the scar at his temple in the light, but she made no comment. She never did.

He ate quickly, bread, eggs, a splash of watered grape juice, and stepped toward the courtyard wearing only his subligaculum, tied high at the waist.

The noise hit first.

Across the street, the women of Rome had gathered in a sea; patrician wives in silk, freedwomen in linen, market girls, merchant daughters, foreign travelers with veils drawn low. The crowd rippled like a single living fabric. When Rufus stepped outside, every face turned.

He felt the heat of their attention settle on his skin.

He liked it.

He raised his hand; the women mirrored him in a wave of bracelets and bangles. A hundred smiles answered his grin. A soft gasp rolled across the crowd when he picked up the first javelin.

Then the show began.

He moved through the drills with his half-brothers, shields flashing, gladii cutting arcs through air, bodies twisting in clean, sharp violence. Stone echoed each strike. Dust leapt from the tiles. Sweat ran in clean tracks down his chest.

Women leaned forward without shame.

Every man in the yard tried to match him, no one could. Rufus moved like someone born for command: quick, sure, balanced on the balls of his feet, shoulders rolling with quiet thunder. His scars caught sunlight. His arms flexed. Muscle and discipline fused into spectacle.

Vendors pushed trays through the crowd, mint water, honey cakes, fresh fruit. Rufus passed out the oranges himself, cool towels as well. Women reached for them; some touched his fingers longer than necessary. He didn't pull away. He laughed and joked.

Tirzah walked among them with pitchers. Her stola brushed her calves with each step. More than one woman whispered about her, who she was, why she walked beside the dominus with such calm dignity.

Rufus trained harder.

He drove his brothers back; drove himself harder still. Dust turned to smoke around his feet. His breath came heavy now, though his face stayed iron-calm.

The crowd's silence held him.

Then he stepped up onto the stone portico, chest rising, breath sharp.

Tirzah approached again. Her movements smooth; her eyes down but aware of every gaze. She washed him in full view, cloth dipping into bowls scented with rose and mint. She ran it down his spine, across the lines of muscle under his ribs, across the long scar over his hip. He stood still through all of it, naked, unflinching.

Women watched without blinking.

She dressed him in deep blue: a tunic opened at the thigh, belted in gold, sandals wrapped tight. His hair combed back, face clean, skin scented with oil.

He sat beneath the portico then, ruler-still, reading scrolls, surrounded by scribes, signing where needed.

Across the road, whispers twisted.

That is the man she chose.

That is the warrior the Sibyl will stand beside.

Look how Rome watches him.

Wait until we see her.

Albina's name moved through the crowd like smoke through silk: soft, dangerous, translucent, impossible to catch.

The sun climbed higher. The air thickened. Women refused to leave. Rufus could feel the crowd building like a tide. Rome's women waiting for Albina, for the red priestess, for the witch's prodigy with amber eyes.

He waited too.

And just as the heat settled hardest on the street, just as the whispers peaked, a horn sounded far down the road.

Foreign.

Low, sweet, and carried on a rhythm that made every woman straighten.

Rufus closed his hand on the last scroll.

She had arrived.

Chapter 77
HER ARRIVAL

Rufus sat on the marble bench outside the gate, legs wide, scroll balanced across one thigh. The deep blue tunic stretched over his chest, every breath pushing against the fabric. Tirzah stood behind him, still, prepared; her indigo stola lifted in the breeze, gold cuff catching sunlight like a signal. She held the flask of mint water with both hands and watched the road.

Across the road, Rome's women gathered in rows that deepened by the moment. Veils low. Fans half-raised. Gems bright against their throats. They carried the nervous hum of a Senate chamber before a vote: whispers sharp, angled, restless.

The first sound reached them...

boom.

Low. Slow. Deep. Heavy as a funeral drum.

Another.

Then another.

The drums crawled up the Caelian Hill and pushed through stone, through Rufus's sandals, into the hinge of his chest. The rhythm claimed space, pressed the morning flat until even the birds quieted.

He stood.

Handed the scroll to his scribe without looking.

Whispers died. The whole street leaned toward the sound.

The litter came into view at the head of a long procession.

Eight pale men bore it, shoulders wide, blond braids swinging like ropes, red sashes tied tight around narrow waists. They walked in perfect unison. Exotic foreigners. Germans. Something carved with discipline older than legion drill.

Above them, a gold-thread canopy shifted in the breeze, each panel painted with black crescents against blood-red cloth.

The drums slowed.

The litter sank.

Silence.

Two witches stepped forward first.

Zarmina the Red, tall, pale, dressed in deep oxblood, moved with the gravity of a queen carved from cold stone. Her stare landed on Rufus without blinking.

Nisaya the Black, small, slight, all shadows, swept her gaze across the Roman women. Fans snapped shut. A few hands trembled.

The drums softened to a beating heart.

Two pink-clad apprentices emerged, anklets chiming in mirrored rhythm.

Then the dancers, five of them, saffron silk sliding over skin, bells in their braids and bracelets bright around long, hardened arms. Their bodies moved with a language of its own: hips slow, shoulders loose, breath synced to the drums. A seduction. A performance. A welcome wrapped in power.

Then came the guards.

Darak. Samut. Velkar. Teshun. Raevan. Khorun. The six eunuchs.

Small men. Silent men. White robes tight around ribs built for speed; blades curved like smiles at their sides. Eyes as cruel as wolves born in winter.

A single shift of a hilt made the air tighten.

Half-time.

A breath between beats.

The curtain of the litter stirred.

Albina stepped into the open.

One small bare foot touched marble. A scattering of gold bells answered with their soft ringing. The other foot followed. Red silk brushed stone. Bracelets chimed low around her wrists. Her black hair fell straight down her back, glossed, heavy, the kind of hair that held secrets.

She stood under the sun and lifted her head.

Amber eyes locked on Rufus.

A smile. A claim.

A wind curled through the street and tangled itself in her hair as she walked forward. The bells chimed with each step; the silk whispered along her thighs; her scent carried ahead, cinnamon, rose, warm musk, desert wind, the beautiful sweat of a dancer, smoke from a far shore.

Her size deceived, her presence did not.

She moved like a dancer teaching the earth how to turn.

Every step cut the distance until Rufus forgot to breathe.

He had seen priestesses chant by torchlight. He had seen men die in front of him without fear. None pressed on him the way this girl did. Something old traveled with her. Something that recognized him before he recognized himself.

The Roman women leaned forward, bodies drawn as if caught in a tide.

Albina passed her dancers, her witches, her guards. No one touched her. Even her shadow felt guarded.

She stopped three steps from him. Close enough for the warmth of her body to reach him, far enough to deny reach.

Her gaze dropped down the line of his chest and returned to his eyes. She held him there, still as a predator waiting for its moment.

The drums cut out.

Rufus's voice came rougher than he expected. "Water."

Tirzah stepped forward, offering the jug with steady hands.

Rufus poured a thin stream over the threshold, Janus's blessing. The silver splash echoed through the courtyard. Mint lifted into the air.

Albina watched every drop fall as if the water spoke.

He dried his hands, looked up, and met her gaze again.

"I welcome you, and yours, to my home," he said.

No reply.

Just her breath, quiet, measured, then a single, slow turn toward the villa.

She entered first.

Her dancers followed, bells soft.

The witches glided behind them.

The guards came last, steps precise; each man's hand hovered a finger's width from his blade.

Rufus stepped in after them, the door's shadow swallowing him whole.

Across the street, Rome's women surged forward, whispering, clutching veils, clinging to daughters. They tried to breathe in whatever she left behind. They failed.

They would remember this.

Behind the closing gate, Albina slowed.

She turned her head, not fully, just enough that the gold bells at her ankle chimed once.

She knew exactly where he stood.

And she smiled.

Rufus felt the ground shift under his feet.

He didn't know the word for the feeling.

He knew only that it had begun.

Chapter 78
HOOKED

T he door shut behind them with a heavy thud.

Outside, the street erupted, cheers, clapping, a rising roar of names shouted for her, for him. The sound climbed the walls like surf beating stone.

Albina never turned.

She crossed the threshold in slow, measured steps. Her heels kissed marble; the bells at her ankles murmured in answer. The heat of the portico faded behind her as the atrium swallowed her in cooler shadow. The air tasted of lamp oil, baking bread, and citrus; a faint thread of incense clung in the corners.

Two bronze bowls waited on the threshold stand, one bright with fire, one filled with clear water.

Albina lifted her hand over the flame. Heat licked her skin; she welcomed it. Then she dipped her fingers into the water. The surface broke in a small ripple that caught the lamplight. Steam rose. She touched her damp fingertips to her forehead, then to the center of her chest.

She turned to the shrine of Janus and raised her right hand in simple acknowledgment. Passage recognized. Gate crossed. House entered. A new home.

Then she stepped to the Lares. Small clay figures. Household guardians. Domestic gods. She touched each gently, the way one touches children left sleeping.

Last, she bowed before the dark idol her witches had placed days before, the many-breasted goddess in rough stone. Ancient. Powerful. Watching.

Whispered names left her lips. Three. None meant for mortal ears.

The bells on her ankles trembled though she hadn't moved.

Silence thickened around her. No slave chain rattled. No cat shifted. No breath from the gallery above. The house waited listening.

Albina rose.

She turned.

He stood framed in the archway.

The man from her visions: tall, red-haired, pale bronze skinned, the scars across his chest faint under lamplight. A clean blue tunic fell straight to mid-thigh, showing legs carved from war. His shoulders squared without effort. His stare bored through her, calculating, controlled, hungry in ways he hadn't recognized yet.

At his side stood the girl with the bowl.

Tirzah.

Dark hair braided tight, chin lifted just enough to hide the tremble at her throat. The water in her hands barely rippled.

Albina saw the truth in a single blink, Tirzah's fear, her loyalty, her place in this house, and the way Rufus failed to see any of it.

Albina stepped forward.

She didn't blink. Didn't look away. The fire and cat and girl dissolved into background; the world narrowed to one man standing in the archway.

She knew the breadth of him. She had seen it in visions, felt it in dreams. Yet the real weight of him struck harder. Strength lived in the scars, yes, but the danger lived in the stillness.

He watched her like a god deciding whether she deserved the truth of him.

She breathed once, deep and slow.

His jaw tightened. His breath hitched, a barely-there shift, but she caught it.

This was the moment the old women had spoken of. The moment the mountain rites promised. The kind of moment when two lines of fate dragged toward each other across centuries.

Albina stepped onto the warmed mosaic. The heat rising from the floor wrapped her feet, traveled up her calves, curled into her spine. Bracelets brushed. Bangles clicked. The air changed, thickened, hummed.

She felt his eyes.

Felt the weight of him seeing her.

The girl outside the gates, the caravan dancer. The petite girl with the large amber eyes and the long shiny black hair.

Her. Only her.

She crossed into the space between them. Close enough for shared breath. Close enough for a god to claim an offering.

"This morning," she said, voice soft, slow, edged with something old, "I prepared a dance for you."

From the left, Nisaya's voice drifted out of shadow, low, smoke-thin, rough, absolute:

"No other male may witness it."

Rufus didn't look at her. He looked at Albina. Only Albina.

He turned his head a fraction. "Leave."

Scribes, slaves, attendants slipped out in silence. Tirzah stepped back with a bowed head. The cat darted away. The archway emptied. The villa held its breath.

Albina took one more step forward.

A small smile, just the faint curling of her lips. Permission. Challenge. Invitation.

He swallowed once. A small movement. But the air between them shifted, tilted, caught flame.

She saw the moment he realized her size lied. Her beauty lied. Her softness lied. She could shatter him without lifting a finger.

His chest rose. His mouth opened, closed.

The bind snapped shut.

Recognition.

The giant bent before destiny.

Albina lowered her gaze to the center of his chest, then lifted it again. Slow. Deliberate.

Rufus smiled.

Just a hint.

But the gods felt it.

High above in the gallery, unseen, a single bell on a dancer's anklet chimed once, soft, sharp, and final.

Nisaya's breath caught.

Albina's fingers twitched.

They all felt it.

Something had begun, and something else had ended.

And Rufus... was already lost.

Chapter 79
THE FLOOR

R ufus nodded once toward the taller witch. "This way. To the floor she requested."

Albina moved behind him. Her guards formed a crescent around her, six small, scarred, golden-eyed men, quiet as blades. The largest stepped forward. Thick arms. Hard shoulders. Sleeveless tunic. A curved dagger rode his hip; the hilt worn smooth from devotion rather than use.

He blocked Rufus with a single step.

His Latin cut clean through the hall:

"No male touches the princess. Not servant, not guard, not family. Eight nights must pass; then only you, if she allows."

His eyes locked on Rufus, steady as iron pulled from a forge.

"No whole male walks near her rooms. Any man who looks with lust dies where he stands. Any man who touches her loses manhood, then hand, then breath."

A pause.

"No delay. No mercy."

He stepped back. Formation closed.

Rufus didn't blink.

He reached for a tall jar, poured spring-cold water into a clay cup. The sound rang through the atrium like a signal. Witches watched. Dancers leaned in subtle. Guards lowered their chins as if measuring distance. Rufus extended the cup, slow, deliberate.

A test.

Albina took it.

Their fingers brushed, barely, but the spark rose through both of them. A current. Recognition. A wordless oath neither had spoken yet.

She drank. Her amber eyes stayed on him, unbroken. In the mountains she'd seen him in visions, red-haired, scar-marked, fierce. Protector. Predator. The one the goddess had pushed toward her through fire and bone.

She lowered the cup. One of her young attendants caught it mid-fall without sound.

Rufus still watched her, no need, no heat, only a weight that told her he bowed to no mortal, but he would stand with her if she asked.

Bold, she thought. Good. I can work with bold.

They walked the corridor. Oil lamps spit and hissed. Painted frescoes flickered as bodies passed. Lemon wax clung in the air; smoke curled from bronze bowls lining the lower walls. Sandals whispered. Bells murmured. Stone offered faint echoes like a second heartbeat following every step.

Then the corridor widened.

Heat lifted from the floor in soft waves.

The chamber breathed.

No furniture, no clutter, just stone walls, oil light, and a warm wind rising from the hypocaust below the tiles. The entire room shimmered: a living hearth built for ceremony, for power, for binding.

Albina stopped at the threshold.

The floor filled everything. Thousands of tesserae locked into a spiral of red, blue, and bone-white, lines twisting, converging, fighting the pattern until surrendering to a single center.

Alexander stood at that center, forever young, sword lifted above the Gordian knot already split open. A moment captured the breath after destiny breaks.

Albina stepped forward.

Heat slid up through her soles, across her calves, up her spine. For the first time in weeks, warmth claimed her bones. Rain, mud, cold nights on the mountain, gone. This floor carried a pulse. A hum. She knew sacred ground when she felt it. The goddess approved.

She stood at the knot's heart.

Her guards moved to the walls. The dancers peeled to either side. The witch-es halted near the oil basin, their shadows bending long across stone.

Rufus leaned against a column quietly, arms folded, legs braced. A soldier at rest. A hunter waiting. Face unreadable.

A chair sat opposite the mosaic. The apprentices, the rose-draped twins, took his hands and led him forward as if he were a king walking toward judgment. He let them. He sat. Spine straight. Legs apart. Hands relaxed on his knees. No pretense. No fear.

Albina studied him openly now.

A young body carved by war. Scars thick across shoulders and chest. Arms that had carried shields, pulled men from death, killed in defense or command. But there was more beneath the skin, discipline, focus, something buried and silent.

This room would decide him. This moment would set the thread.

She rolled her shoulders back. Flexed her toes. Let her hands rise like feathers catching dawn. Every muscle aligned itself to purpose.

His gaze held steady. No flinch. No hunger. Only the slow shift of a man realizing this girl, small as a flame, held power older than any steel he knew.

Her breath deepened.

Held.

Suspended.

The bells at her ankles stirred, not from movement, but from whatever lived under her skin.

A drum sounded from the far wall.

One beat.

Another.

Her body answered before thought; ritual claimed her. The air thickened around her shoulders. The warmth underfoot rose through her thighs. Her fingers curved into shape. Her breath found the rhythm.

She stepped into the first arc of the dance.

The first gesture belonged to him.

But the power belonged to her.

Chapter 80
THE DANCE

Heat climbed through the marble and into her legs. The mosaic writhed beneath her feet, Alexander frozen mid-strike, the knot twisting like a living serpent below her shadow. Smoke dragged low across the tiles, cedar and iron braided in the air. She stood in the knot's center, breath held high in her chest, pulse waiting for its command.

If the goddess slept, her people would vanish. No graves. No names. No vengeance.

She carried that truth inside her ribs.

One breath. She buried the fear.

The hunt began.

A drum struck once, hollow, deliberate, the sound of a heartbeat echoing inside stone.

Her hips answered. A sharp drop. Another. Each motion claimed the floor. Red silk clung, peeled, clung again. Her arms carved slow arcs through the haze, wrists folding, fingers scripting old sigils in a language Rome never learned. She bent low, palms pressed flat, hair sliding over her shoulders like a beast lowering its head before the kill.

The watchers leaned closer.

Rufus with them.

The rhythm crawled forward, slow as a lion in tall grass.

She rose fast. Spine twisting. Hips snapping. The hem flared red, flashed gold, then settled back to blood. Behind her, the dancers wove through one another, Roksana steady as a prowler's shadow, Yamina baring her teeth in joy, Selka hungry for the beat, Tareeda silent as a knife, Zermeh devout as flame. They moved in her wake like wolves circling a queen.

But every gaze held to her alone.

The hunt's center.

The fire.

The threat.

The drums quickened.

She dropped to her knees hard, marble biting skin, the crack of impact running up her spine. Her back bowed in a long, breaking arc. Throat exposed. A lure before the strike. Heat rolled through her, ribs, hips, breath, a wave born in the mountains. Her hair brushed the stone behind her, shadow tasting flame.

Her arms opened wide. Froze for one slow heartbeat.

Then snapped back into rhythm.

Each hip-thrust met each drumbeat, claw against shield, blood against bone. Her breath came sharp, steady. The bells at her ankles hissed with each shift, chasing silence from the corners of the room.

The drums fell into a circling beat.

A trap.

Her head turned.

Amber eyes locked to him.

He sat braced on the bench, jaw tight, chest rising slow. One hand crushed the edge of stone, knuckles white. A pulse jumped along his neck. Around him, slaves whispered, dancers breathed hard, witches marked the air, but those sounds lived far outside the space binding the two of them.

His world narrowed to her.

She moved toward him, steps deliberate, dangerous. Anklets chimed. Wrists spiraled. Elbows led each ripple. The air stretched thin between them, thin enough to cut, thick enough to drown.

She circled him once.

Again.

Closer.

Silk brushed his boot, the whisper of a blade testing a shield.

Then the drums broke off.

Her knees bent. Anklets stilled. Arms lifted high.

Silence sealed the chamber. Breath for breath.

Eye for eye.

The space between them, ten feet, no more, held a promise:

war, hunger, surrender, survival, ruin.

Rufus breathed once, hard. A sound torn from the chest of a man who had faced siege walls, Syrian spears, desert ambushes, and never lost control. Until now.

The grooves his fingers carved into the armrest glimmered in the low firelight. Proof.

She held his gaze, unblinking. Felt the rhythm of his breath answer hers. Felt the room lean toward her as though gravity had shifted.

Her scent drifted into the silence, cinnamon, rose, musk, sweat. Heat moved with her. The floor breathed under both of them.

He didn't blink. Didn't swallow.

His world lived in her shadow.

She leaned forward, just a tilt, a shift of weight, the faintest sway of hips, yet the air changed, charged, bent around that single movement.

The smallest gesture of the night.

A promise.

A knife drawn but not shown.

The hunt had only begun.

Chapter 81
AFTER THE DANCE

S he stood at the center of the knot. Breath heavy. Skin damp. The bells at her ankles held still; even the metal seemed stunned into silence. Heat rose through the marble into her legs, a low pulse that felt like the floor still breathed beneath her.

Rufus hadn't moved during the entire dance. Not once. No shift of weight. No huff of breath. Not even a blink she could catch.

Now his chest rose, once, long, like a man surfacing after too long underwater. His shoulders eased, the exhale carving through the hush. He stood.

He stepped forward.

One pace.

A half more.

Then stopped.

His jaw tightened; words dragged behind his teeth.

"That was..." His voice scraped, raw from holding too much. He steadied. "No one dances like that."

He dropped his gaze for a heartbeat, then lifted it fully, into her, not past her. "Gratitude."

Albina nodded; she gave no bow. She had seen that look before, in kings who held the world, in priests who touched flame without fear, in hunters who knelt beside the kill and thought the moment belonged to them.

But in him the surrender had come from truth.

He was hers.

And despite every vow she had sworn, despite the goddess's cold demands... she was his.

No spell. No trick. No faltering ritual.

Forever. His.

Silence stretched between them.

Rufus turned and signaled a young woman from the wall. Tirzah stepped forward, small, steady, head bent. Her hands didn't shake, though the weight of this moment pressed on her harder than stone.

"You'll be shown to your rooms," Rufus said. His voice regained its soldier's calm. "You'll find what you need. Ask her" a tilt of his head toward Tirzah, "if you have any needs. Your statue is already on the road from Ostia. A ship has gone to Alexandria for the slaves you named."

Albina stepped off the knot. Her bodyguards flowed around her like closing hands. The witches followed, eyes bright and cold. Her dancers lifted their chins, bells whispering with each step, still trembling from the rhythm she had commanded.

Albina's gaze brushed the Jewish girl.

"Will she show me the house?" Albina asked softly. "Later."

Rufus looked to Tirzah. Only a glance.

Tirzah's nod carried no fear.

"She will," he said.

They moved down the corridor.

Shadows pulsed along the painted walls, red sea battles, blue storms, the old gods stalking across plaster. Lamps hissed from bronze brackets. Lemon oil clung to the air. The stone beneath their sandals had been scrubbed until it glowed. A quiet drip of unseen water kept time between footfalls.

Her girls whispered at the size of the halls; even the guards stared ahead with sharper breath.

Rufus walked in silence.

He didn't boast.

He didn't explain.

He gave the house as a warrior offers a weapon, without flourish, without lie.

They reached a carved door. The hinges swung open without a sound.

"This is your room," Rufus said. "Mine is next door. Your people are down that hall and on the upper gallery." A brief pause. "I'll leave you to settle in. Perhaps later we will break bread together."

Albina let a slow smile touch her mouth.

"I look forward to that."

The suite spread wide around her, heat held steady, the air thick and golden. High ceilings painted sky-blue arced overhead, clouds drifting in soft strokes. Walls washed in ochre glowed with afternoon light, vines curling in painted relief. Rugs thick as winter fur muffled her steps.

Flowers waited in niches, cut fresh, rose, hyacinth, iris. The scent lifted the air like hands raising a veil.

The bed dominated the space. Down filled. Wide. Draped in linen shot through with indigo thread. Gold trim caught lamplight and sent it climbing the wall. Pillows stood in four tall ranks, embroidered with vines and birds she did not recognize.

A cedar-lined wardrobe stood open, her clothing already stacked in order, folded crisp, waiting as if her hands had touched them first.

Two couches flanked the far wall. Wool covers. Bronze studs. A table between them gleamed with combs, pins, chains, glass jars of thick oils. A tall mirror captured the whole scene: the painted sky above, the rugs at her feet, the women behind her, the fire's reflection burning at her back.

A door to one side revealed a toilet room. A polished stone seat. Flowing water. No smell.

The dancers gasped.

One covered her mouth.

"Inside the house," she whispered, her voice cracking with awe.

Another chamber held the bath.

Steam climbed in soft spirals, scented with mint and rose petals.

Silver bowls stacked in neat lines.

Cloths folded in precise piles.

A dancer sobbed once, then laughed, trembling.

Nisaya pressed her palm to the painted wall and murmured in their own tongue. Words sharp. Words fast. Words older than Rome.

Albina stood in the middle of the suite.

Still.

Silent.

Letting the fire, the sky, the roses, the impossible privacy wash over her.

He had done this.

He had spoken with control while desire ran in him like a broken horse. He had given her warmth. Safety. Silence.

He had held himself steady when other men would have burned.

That restraint meant more than the room.

More than the dance.

More than Rome's eyes waiting outside the gate.

She would dance for him again.

He would step closer next time.

Much closer.

But now, she wanted a bath.

Heat still rose through her skin.

Her pulse had not settled.

Her breath carried the drum.

She loosened her bracelets.

Silk whispered down her hip.

The night waited.

She would bathe.

And later when the heat faded from her skin...

she would bathe again.

Chapter 82
THE TOUR

Tirzah arrived at sunrise.

Soft yellow dress. Clean lines. New sandals tied neat around her ankles. No jewelry except the gold cuff at her wrist, Rufus's mark, plain and quiet. The cat chased behind her, tail flicking once at the doorway.

The door opened for Albina the moment she approached. No command. Presence alone parted space.

Her witches followed. Nisaya drifted in last, shadow on shadow, eyes fixed on Tirzah as if studying a small flame in a dark room.

Tirzah bowed her head once.

Albina crouched and touched the cat. The small creature leaned into her palm. A welcome. A warning. Both carried in fur and breath.

The tour began.

The villa unrolled before them like a private city, stone bones, warm skin, a pulse of water somewhere deep beneath the floors. High painted ceilings, carved doors, heated tiles, the faint perfume of lemon oil burned in lamp bowls. No mold. No cracks. No forgotten corners.

They reached the kitchens.

Two of them. Plus a bakery. Baskets of bread. Bowls of olives. Figs stacked like treasure. Steam rose from copper pots, lamb and mint thick in the air. Cooks bowed low but stayed quick at their tasks.

Tirzah's voice stayed level. "Every eight days a wagon comes from the Dominus's farms. Meat, cheese, flour, wine, oil, honey, fruit, vegetables. The House of Rufus feeds itself."

Albina nodded once. The dancers whispered behind her, hands pressed to their stomachs. Relief pushed through their ribs.

The slave dining hall came next, long tables, smooth cushions, sunlight pouring through high vents. Order everywhere. No beatings. No fear in the air. Just work.

Then the baths.

Rows of stone seats, clean, private. Water flowing underneath, carrying waste away. Basins of rosewater for cleansing. Women's baths deeper and hotter; two large hot-water pools. And something new, shower baths where hot water rained from a bronze dish above.

One dancer gasped. Another covered her mouth, laughing through wonder. "Hot water inside a house?"

Tirzah allowed herself the smallest smile. "Rome grows strange."

Gardens opened around them: fig trees tied to arbors, ivy framing marble benches, fountains whispering among columns. Water everywhere, trickling, falling, feeding life. Birds perched on carved stone like they had always belonged.

Albina brushed a warm fig leaf with her fingertips. Living green touching living skin.

They passed musicians' halls, drums and lyres polished to shine. A singers' chamber with perfect echo, Albina tested it with a single hum. The walls answered back like silver bowls filled with sound.

The dance room drew soft gasps from her troupe, a wide chamber, high rafters, smooth floors meant for movement. A covered stage near the garden. Rows of seating for night performances. A grill where the household cooked meat under the stars.

Tirzah walked ahead. Never hurried. Never flustered. She did not turn when Albina spoke, but she listened. Always listened.

Albina studied the girl.

Long legs. Slim arms. A quiet sway in the hips. Perfect posture. Skin pale as milk in moonlight. Dark hair braided with care. Eyes full of depths that refused to spill.

Not a rival. Not a servant to fear. A woman shaped by obedience. Soft-spined but steady. And she carried Rufus's scent, on wrists, on breath, on memory. Albina marked it. Nisaya marked it more sharply.

They moved on.

Offices. Library. Trophy hall. Gymnasium. Guest quarters lavish enough for minor kings. Strong room sealed in iron. Storage rooms for olives, grain, textiles. A laundry large enough for a cohort's tunics.

They walked a quieter wing.

A narrow colonnade. Cooler air. Rows of small doors, bronze latches polished. No smell. No filth. Clean light. Order in every line.

Tirzah stopped at one door. She pushed it open.

Inside: a simple bed. One cotton blanket, one wool. A clay basin. A single chair. A carved shelf. A woven mat.

Her voice stayed steady. "These are the standard quarters. Every worker has one."

Albina stepped inside. The witches leaned in. The room held warmth and dignity. No cruelty buried in corners.

"There are over a hundred," Tirzah added. "Not full yet."

A beat passed, then the girl offered a thin slice of sarcasm, sharp as a reed:

"Your people's rooms are larger, nicer. Near the formal side."

Albina's eyes narrowed. Not offended. Interested.

Tirzah finished with a simple truth. "He built for growth. For years ahead. He expects the house to outlive him."

No pride. No bitterness. Just fact.

They returned to Albina's chamber.

Warm air swelled around them. Rose, mint, and steam drifted from the bathing pool. Towels waited in neat stacks. Oil glimmered in glass jars. Silver combs caught the lamplight.

Albina dismissed the dancers, the guards, even the witches with a tilt of her chin.

Only Tirzah stayed.

Albina turned to her.

Silence hung between them, thin, sharp, feminine. Not hostility. Not fear. Something older: two women measuring ground neither wanted to concede.

"What do you do for him?" Albina asked. Even tone. No cruelty.

Tirzah answered with no tremor in her voice.

"I bathe him. I shave him. I cut his hair. I serve his meals. I stay at his side in public. I obey his needs."

A pause.

"And I serve his lusts."

No shame. No triumph. Just truth.

She turned and walked away before Albina could speak again.

The cat followed her, tail low, glancing back once at the priestess.

Albina watched her go. Eyes unreadable. Breath steady.

Two women in one house. Two kinds of power. One future already bending toward collision.

Chapter 83
ECHOES

R ufus hadn't moved from the atrium.

The villa had gone quiet. Guards dismissed, scribes sent away, even the witches retreating to shadow. The oil lamps guttered low, smoke curling like black veins against the painted ceiling. Water trickled from a hidden fountain in the wall, steady and soft, the sound mocking his stillness.

He stood rooted, shoulders square, fists loose at his sides.

She had danced. And now she lived in his bones.

Not just the sway of her hips or the silk clinging to her thighs, but the gaze, amber and unblinking, claiming him as if he were already bound. She had seen him and knew. Not a slave. Not a concubine. Not even a priestess. Something older. Something sovereign.

He touched his jaw. Ache in the hinge where he had clenched too hard through the dance. His face burned hot, though the air had cooled. He hadn't spoken to Tirzah since. He would later, or not.

The scent still clung to him. Roses. Musk. Cinnamon. Sweet sweat under heat. Wood smoke woven through. She had left her fragrance like a scar in the stone. He breathed it again, hating it, needing it.

He turned at last, walking deeper into the dark halls. He needed a hunt, a fight, anything to burn her from his soul. Yet he knew he would not be rid of her. Not ever.

Albina entered the chambers Tirzah had shown her.

The Jewish girl moved through the villa with the quiet precision of one who knew every corridor, every chamber, every step where sound carried. Her braid swung across her back as she pointed out the carved doors, the painted ceilings, the polished floors. "This way," Tirzah had said, voice level, eyes lowered. No bitterness. No pride.

Albina had watched her, listened, remembered. This girl had spoken truth earlier without flinch: I serve his lusts. No shame, no heat, no fear. Just a plain sentence. That honesty lingered like iron on Albina's tongue.

Now, Tirzah left her at the chamber door. Albina slipped inside alone.

Steam rose from the wide basin sunk into the floor. Petals floated on the surface, white and red, the scent of rose sharpened by mint. Oil lamps glowed from iron brackets. The walls gleamed with fresh plaster, painted with vines and stags in flight.

She undressed without hesitation. The red silk slid down, pooling at her feet. Anklets chimed once, then fell silent. She stepped into the water. Heat closed around her body, kissed her skin, lifted the ache from her calves. Her hair spread across the surface like a dark fan, black ink on gold water.

She closed her eyes and sank deeper. Her muscles floated, her chest rose and fell with the steam.

She thought of the man.

He had not touched her. Not once. Not yet. He had only watched, silent, like a god weighing tribute. That silence carried weight more dangerous than hunger. His restraint had power.

Her hips still remembered the ache of the dance, the pull of each beat, the snap of each twist. She had given herself to the rhythm, not as priestess or pawn, but as woman. No other man would see that dance. No other would be given that power.

She pressed two fingers to her lips. They tingled. She had felt his breath across the distance, though he never moved.

The water shifted against her skin. Steam curled up around her face. She let it wash her; let it fill her.

She smiled once, faint, more a baring of teeth than joy.

This was no victory. No conquest. Not yet.

But the hunt had begun.

And she was not the prey.

Chapter 84
RULES OF HER HOUSE

Rufus studied the scrolls laid across his desk, but no words reached him. His mind stayed on the red-silk girl in the next wing, the scent of her, the scarlet shadow of her hips, the way she held silence.

A footfall whispered at the threshold.

Nisaya stepped inside.

She did not ask permission. Witches didn't. Her black robe brushed the floor, swallowing the morning light that spilled across the tiles.

Rufus didn't stand. "You wander freely."

"You must hear the rules of her house," she replied.

"My house."

Her eyes lifted, flat, bottomless, impossible to push. "Not anymore. You share it with her now."

A tension shifted in his chest, half anger, half something he refused to name. Nisaya glided closer, every movement slow enough to weigh the air.

"The Sibyl enters a binding period of eight nights," she said. "During these nights, no man touches her. No hand on her skin. No embrace. No breath on her throat. No male beyond the outer threshold."

Rufus leaned forward, hands braced on the desk. "Eight nights for what?"

"Her blood runs," the witch said. "Her goddess takes her. Her spirit must settle after crossing seas and mountains. The rites demand purity before union."

She paused, gaze narrowing. "Choose whichever truth keeps your pride steady."

Heat crawled up his neck. Shame? Anger? Both tasted the same.

"She slept near your room," Nisaya said, "but proximity is not permission."

His jaw clenched so hard the bone ached.

"There are more rules," she added.

"Of course."

"No whole male enters her hallway. No whole male approaches her chamber. Only those bound by oath or ritual pass her inner door."

Rufus laughed once, sharp. "I don't answer to witches."

"You answered to her last night without knowing it," Nisaya said, "before she spoke a single word."

The truth stung. His breath tightened. His heart kicked once, hard, then steadied.

"No whole male enters her hallway. No whole male approaches her door. Only those who serve as you do may pass the outer threshold."

He laughed once, low. "Serve?"

"You gave her warmth. Shelter. Restraint. That is service."

His laugh died.

"She will summon you when your presence serves her," Nisaya said. "Not before."

Rufus forced a breath through clenched teeth. "Are you finished?"

She considered him with a slow tilt of the head. "For now."

Nisaya turned as if finished, then paused at the doorway.

"One more thing," she said. "Your name vibrates around her. Sibyl does not hide that. The goddess hears it."

He froze.

Nisaya vanished down the corridor.

The moment she left, the office felt too small, too hot. The air tasted of smoke and irritation. He shoved the scrolls aside and strode out.

Down the colonnade. Past the shrine. Past the kitchen hall. Past the scent of mint rising from the bath chambers.

He reached the gymnasium.

Sand swallowed his feet as he stepped inside. Sunlight poured through the open roof. The walls echoed with the ghosts of a thousand blows.

He stripped off his tunic, grabbed the practice spear, and moved.

Thrust. Pivot. Drive.

Sand sprayed. His breath tore from his chest. Muscles burned. Sweat rolled down his spine. He trained like he had as a boy, when his father beat iron discipline into him, when every mistake cut skin, when the sons of centurions learned to breathe pain like air.

He pushed harder.

Faster.

Until his lungs clawed for breath and his vision thinned at the edges.

He swung again. Sand leapt. His body trembled.

He stopped only when his knees threatened to buckle. Hands on thighs, breath scraping, chest shaking.

Her face.

Her smell.

Her eyes holding him like a vow.

He cursed under his breath, straightened, and forced air into his lungs.

Eight nights.

He wasn't sure he would survive one.

Far from the sand pit, under a painted ceiling of cranes in flight, Sareph waited.

Short hair. Quick boots. A thin knife hidden in the fold at her spine. She kept no expression on her face; stillness was her shield.

Nisaya joined her.

"He accepted the rules," the witch said.

Sareph nodded once.

"You begin your work."

"What must I learn?" Sareph asked, voice low.

"His hallways," Nisaya said. "His guards. The paths he walks before dawn. Where he sleeps. How he breathes when he dreams. How long he pauses by the fountain. How many steps from his bathing pool to the rack of weapons. Count the distances. Listen to the silence around him."

Sareph's stance shifted, subtle. Ready.

"A day may come," Nisaya whispered, "when the goddess asks for his death. You must know the path."

A shadow flickered across Sareph's eyes, recognition, not fear.

Nisaya studied her. "You trained young," she said softly. "The elders whispered about you. A child who strangled a jackal with a cord of woven hair before she spoke her first prayer. A girl who learned poison by tasting it. A girl who learned silence by living in it."

A breath passed between them.

"You serve her now," Nisaya said. "But remember, the goddess may demand blood from those she loves."

Sareph bowed her head.

The corridor held still. Bells chimed faintly from Albina's wing, a soft tremor of gold.

Sareph turned toward the shadows, ready to study the man she might one day kill.

Far away, Rufus pressed his palms into the sand, breath raw, body trembling.

He didn't know someone watched the path to his door.

He didn't know a girl with short hair had already counted the steps from his chamber to hers.

He didn't know danger slept closer to him now than desire.

He lifted his head.

Tonight, would be the first of eight nights.

And the house no longer felt like his.

Chapter 85
A SILK WEB

Evening crawled in slow. The villa settled into that heavy quiet Rome knew after heat broke but before night claimed its rights. Oil lamps guttered low, smoke tracing thin black veins across plastered ceilings. The courtyard smelled of jasmine climbing the outer wall, thick and sweet as breath against skin.

Rufus had come from the bath moments earlier. Droplets clung to him, sliding in slow trails down chest and spine. His robe hung loose, linen damp and open at the throat. He sat on the stone bench in the peristyle garden, marble still warm beneath him; his skin cooled in the faint breeze. A cup of cold water waited in his hand.

He heard her before he saw her.

A single bell.

Small, precise.

A tap on the edge of silence, gentle enough to ignore, impossible to forget.

Another chime followed. Then another, spaced like heartbeats.

A shadow gathered in the archway.

Albina stepped into the courtyard. Alone. No dancers, no witches, no guards. Only her and the bells that moved with her body.

Her dress fell short on her thighs, silk pale as dawn light on water. Thin enough to cling. Thin enough to drift. With each step it shifted, revealing then hiding the long lines of her legs. Gold rings brightened her wrists, ankles, ears; each piece caught lamplight in soft flashes that danced along her skin.

She didn't greet him.

Oil gleamed along her collarbone, the inner curve of her throat, her arms, her legs. A foreign blend, rose, jasmine, musk, and something wilder beneath, rose around her with each movement. She reached the fountain, bent at the waist, dipped her hands into the stream. Water ran over her fingers, trickled down her wrist, slid along her forearm until it vanished beneath silk.

She still didn't look at him.

"Your home holds good heat," she said. Her voice struck the air with soft precision, every syllable shaped, every note clean. "It tempts one to forget she wears anything at all."

She turned her head.

Amber eyes met his, focused, deliberate, dangerous in their calm. Light caught at their center, where gold rimmed the darker flame beneath.

"But I never forget."

A tightness struck his chest. His grip on the cup slipped; water spilled across the back of his hand and down his wrist. He didn't wipe it. Couldn't. His lungs fought for rhythm as if something pressed against them from within.

She walked toward him.

Bells chimed in small, devastating sounds. Her perfume hit first, sweet jasmine warmed by skin, rose softened by body heat, musk coiling underneath it all. The air shifted with her, thickening, tightening.

Rufus tried to stand. His muscles ignored him. Heat pulsed through his throat, down his arms, into the knot at the base of his spine. The robe clung to him like a snare.

Albina stopped close enough that he could feel the warmth rising from her body. She leaned in, slow and sure, lips a breath from his ear.

"Seven nights remain," she whispered.

The words drove straight through him.

His pulse hammered. His breath scattered. His grip slipped on the cup again, and he had to use both hands to steady it. Muscles bunched along his shoulders, preparing for a fight that never came.

She lingered there, one long, punishing heartbeat, then her voice dropped lower.

"Try to survive them."

She didn't smile. She shaped something along her mouth that lived between promise and cruelty and walked away with the same steady control she had entered, bells marking each step.

The arch swallowed her shadow. Silence returned.

Rufus stayed carved in stone. He tried to breathe around the jasmine-heavy air, but it dragged slow through his chest. His pulse thudded against his ribs, a trapped fist looking for escape. Rage sparked under his skin, rage at her power, at what she could stir in him, at the helplessness he hadn't felt since boyhood.

And desire layered on top of it like heat against marble.

He drank the rest of the water. His throat stayed dry. He leaned his head back, eyes closed, breath uneven. The robe clung, suffocating. The stone beneath him felt too warm, too alive.

She had left.

And still she sat on his skin like heat.

Still, she moved inside his thoughts.

Still, she remained.

Chapter 86
BREAKFAST NOOK

Rufus sat bare-chested in the breakfast nook, one leg hooked over the stone bench, marble cool against his skin. The peristyle opened wide before him, fountains sighing like rain against the basin. Dawn stretched across the walls in pale gold. Birds called from the garden fig trees. The smell of wet leaves, lemon blossom, fresh herbs, and warm bread drifted through the arches in soft waves.

A scroll lay open, but the words refused to take shape. His thoughts swerved back to her: the bells, the scent that clung to his breath, the soft brush of her whisper against his ear. Red silk burned behind his eyes. He tore a fig and chewed, tasting nothing. His shoulders ached from morning drills; his temples throbbed from lack of sleep.

Tirzah had bathed him before sunrise. Silent as always. Quick. Precise. She laid the scroll, filled his cup, vanished like a shadow. She always sensed when he needed quiet, and perhaps she sensed it more today than ever.

Bread waited on the plate. Apricots. Olives. Dates arranged in a neat curve. A pitcher of mint water beaded with cold. He poured, drank deeply, hoping for focus.

Footsteps. Soft. Bare. Deliberate.

Not Tirzah.

He kept his gaze on the scroll.

Albina stepped into the archway.

She wore a deep green wrap, simple for her. No bells. No bracelets. Her braid hung heavy down her back, pulling her posture tall. Behind her, the witches lingered where tile met sunlight, two dark smudges waiting for breath.

"You eat like a lion," she said.

Her voice slid into the morning air like a fingertip tracing water.

Rufus lifted his eyes. She crossed the flagstones with the slow certainty of someone who owned her shadow and yours.

"And how does a lion eat?" he asked.

"With dignity."

She sat beside him without invitation. Reached for a date, choosing the softest one.

Rufus raised a brow. "Those belonged to me."

She bit into it, slow as honey dripping from a spoon. "Guard them next time."

A quiet laugh tore from him, quick, real, unfamiliar.

Her gaze drifted across the courtyard. "Your girls talk. Your slaves too. Even the ladies across the road." She lifted her chin toward the upper windows across the street. Drapes fluttered. Pale arms moved inside the shadows.

"They enjoy the view?" Rufus asked.

"Yes." Albina leaned back. "And you enjoy being watched."

He sipped his mint water, hiding a grin. "Sometimes."

Wind stirred the lemon leaves. A fountain splash echoed. One of her witches murmured behind the columns. Albina reached for a fig, rolled it across her palm, but didn't lift it to her mouth.

"Do you always eat alone?" she asked.

"Yes."

"That seems lonely."

"I prefer it."

"You'll adjust."

Rufus studied her. "You don't fear me."

She shrugged, the movement small and smooth beneath the green wrap. "Fear wastes time."

"Should I make an effort?"

Her amber eyes met his, direct, warm, clever. "Save your strength. I hear you outtrain your soldiers."

He leaned back, amused despite the heat building in his chest. "That spreads quickly."

Her hand hovered above the figs again. "I don't always wear bells."

"I noticed."

"And I don't always dance."

"Then what fills the time?"

Her lips curved, soft at the edges. "Listening. Studying. Dreaming." She leaned close enough for him to breathe the warmth off her skin, cinnamon, mint, rosewater, heat. "And sometimes, I tease lions."

A low laugh broke from him, rough at the edges. "Brave little thing."

She rose. Grace sealed every step. As she passed behind him, one fingertip brushed his shoulder, light as drifting ash, warm enough to leave marks invisible and permanent.

She paused.

"Or," she said, looking down at him with a smile small enough to be dangerous, "you're gentler than you pretend."

Then she walked away. No bells. No metal. Only the whisper of silk and the scent she left hanging in his lungs.

Rufus stayed seated, trying to breathe past the heat under his ribs. Mint burned his tongue. The air thickened around him, holding traces of her perfume like a hand cupped over his mouth.

Laughter rose beyond the garden wall, hers, bright as a struck bell. Girls giggled with her, their voices floating up like a secret shared between sisters.

Rufus didn't move.

The lion remained in his stone den, marked by the woman who had learned how to tame him without touching anything but the air.

And the day had barely begun.

Chapter 87
GARDEN SHRINE

Albina walked the gardens the next morning.

The air hung thick, orange blossoms, lemon rinds, crushed mint underfoot. Cicadas buzzed in the trees. Water trickled from three fountains at once. Heat rose from the stone paths. Shadows clung to the walls.

Her girls followed barefoot. Veils pinned up. Bracelets jingling. The witches moved behind them in silence. Guards flanked the outer path.

Albina stopped near the center courtyard. A curve of marble framed a small fountain shaped like a shell. Evergreen shrubs surrounded it. A breeze stirred the myrrh and rosemary plants. She knelt.

"Yes, here. Perfect."

One of the witches stepped forward.

"The place is strong," Zarmina said.

Nisaya dropped her hand onto the Empty One, then gasped.

The statuettes glowed.

Albina nodded.

"They approve."

The girls unrolled cloths. Cleaned the marble. Gathered small stones. The guards stood watch. The witches began to hum.

One girl reached down to place a stone. Her fingers brushed the surface, then pulled back fast, like it burned. She stared at Albina, wide-eyed. Albina gave her a small nod.

One by one, they placed the sacred figures in a circle:

The Sibyl's chariot. The Twins of Water. The Mother of Fire. The Moon-Maid. The Black Dog. The Bird King.

The Womb. The Blade. The Eye. The Old Child. The Thirteenth. And the Empty One.

When they were placed, Albina stepped back.

"This is the place. Their home. Our home."

She reached for a gold band. Slipped it from her wrist. Laid it before the center figure. The Sibyl on her lion-drawn chariot.

She kept them close, always. Twelve figures, carved in stone, each older than cities. The Sybil's Chariot stood at the center, newer than the rest, but sacred still. The chariot's lines etched sharp, her face intact. The others bore time's weight. Ten thousand years had worn them smooth. The Mother of Fire had no mouth. The Bird King had lost one wing. The Womb looked like nothing but a lump of pale stone, until the light hit right. Then the curve appeared. The eye. The hollow space inside.

Each stood about the size of a man's fist or a soldier's helmet. Not large. Heavy with memory. They must never be separated. Albina had known that since childhood. They whispered louder when together. They had traveled across deserts, buried in wool and fur. Across oceans, across blood. They were priceless, not in gold, but in meaning. They were the last of something old, something still breathing beneath the world. When she touched them, she remembered. When others touched them, she watched.

The bells on her ankle rang once.

Then silence.

Even the birds paused.

A whisper passed through the trees. They agreed.

The sacred space had been chosen.

The wind moved through the lemon trees.

Albina took the flame borrowed from the Vestal Virgins, a part of the Eternal flame they kept, and lit the bronze cauldrons fuel, including the charred sticks from the old temple at Valbena.

It burned proudly.

Zarmina stepped beside her. "It's done."

Albina didn't answer.

Nisaya knelt and pressed her palm to the warm marble. "She has marked this place."

Albina turned once. Looked toward the upper walls of the villa. Toward the chambers beyond.

Then she whispered something too soft to catch.

The guards didn't move. The dancers smiled. The witches bowed their heads. All prayed.

The house didn't know it yet.

But every stone and brick belonged to the Sibyl now.

Chapter 88

SOMETHING, CATALINA, SOMETHING

The Curia Hostilia, Forum Romanum

The Senate gathered in the Temple of Jupiter Stator, the hall of stone that had seen oaths broken and wars born. Morning light slid between pillars, but the air stayed cool, heavy with sweat and sacrifice.

At dawn a snow-colored pig had bled for the gods. Its throat slit, blood caught in a silver bowl. The altar still smoked. The augurs studied wings, wind, the line of smoke. A crow's cry, a hawk's shadow, omens shaped the day. Every senator touched flame and water. Rome bent her head before Jupiter, Janus, Mars, Quirinus.

Only then did the herald call the formula, sharp and ancient. Only then did the doors open. Sandals struck marble, lictors parted the way, and the white-cloaked Senate filed in under the gaze of statues older than their fathers.

The statues watched. Stone faces. Unblinking.

Cicero took the center. His robes perfect, his voice cut sharp into the chamber.

"How long, Catalina, how long will you abuse our patience?"

The words struck marble, cracked the silence, came back in echo.

Men leaned forward. Scribbles began on wax tablets. Lictors straightened.

Rufus sat near the side. Slouched, thumb grinding a groove in the stone. Eyes down.

Albina.

Her scent still clung to him, cinnamon, musk, rose, sweat, fire. Her wrist brushing his. The look that held him still as a chained beast.

Cicero's words rolled on. "How long will that madness of yours mock us? To what end will your unbridled daring hurl itself?"

The chamber stirred. Cato's arms stayed folded, his face a slab of Rome. Crassus leaned back, chin in hand. Caesar prowled with his eyes, measuring, waiting.

Rufus barely heard. He tasted her sweat on his tongue, saw her dress sheer with heat, silk plastered to her thighs. He had trained to exhaustion, run until lungs tore, poured cold water over his head until his skin burned, but none of it cut her from him.

Cicero raised his pitch. "O tempŏra, o mōrēs! The Senate knows, the Republic sees, yet Catalina lives!"

Men shouted back, some jeers, some calls for blood. Scribes scratched faster, points clicking like insects. Catalina sat alone now. His allies had slipped away, seat by seat, leaving him hunched and glaring, a single man ringed by marble and contempt.

It would be painted in centuries to come, Cicero's hand lifted, Catalina slumped, stone faces turned away.

Rufus didn't look long. He didn't care.

Her lips had whispered into his ear... Survive the nights, lion. He hadn't slept. Bare fruit at dawn. Tirzah found him in the courtyard still standing, back slick with sweat, eyes raw. The thought of Albina remained.

Cicero thundered: "There exists no crime you have not conceived, no lust you have not stained, no treachery you have not tried."

The chamber broke into roars. Fists on benches. Applause, hisses, oaths. Cicero rode the storm, voice higher, sharper.

Rufus sat rigid. His lungs refused him air. His wrist still burned with her touch. His chest strained, teeth ground tight. He hated her for it. Hated his own weakness. Hated the hunger that made his hands shake.

But he couldn't drive her out.

The vote came, lost in noise. Men rose together. Sandals struck stone. Cicero stood tall, Cato's jaw locked, Crassus wary, Caesar smiling with lips, not eyes. Catalina sat abandoned.

Rufus rose too. Filed out slow. He didn't speak. Didn't look at anyone. Only thought of her.

Chapter 89
FULVIA COMES

Rome, Villa on the Caelian Hill

Albina rose before the sun. She liked the world quiet when she opened her eyes.

By the time the light reached the eastern colonnade, her house already moved with purpose: dancers finishing their morning stretches, hair damp from the baths; eunuchs trimming fig branches with knives that glinted like fish scales; Zarmina tending the garden shrine; Nisaya grinding herbs on a red cushion, her fingers slow, her eyes unreadable.

As always, the gates opened for Rome's women.

Some entered with rings on every finger. Some entered barefoot, robes patched, children clinging to their hips. Some carried grief. Others carried envy. Some carried the ache of empty wombs. Albina sat with each. Touched their hands. Listened. Bound small threads around wrists. Let them wash in the bowl of water. They left coins, whispers, secrets, tears.

By midmorning the shrine floor warmed under the sun.

The statue had arrived hours earlier, white stone, lion-drawn chariot, arms outstretched exactly as the ancient texts described. The sculptors had carved the lions' manes with frightening precision. Even their stone teeth seemed ready to bite. The statue rested beneath a trellis of grape leaves, half in shade: a goddess waiting to be acknowledged.

Beneath it, the twelve sacred statuettes slept in their linen cradle. Women knelt before them one by one.

When the steward approached, his voice stayed low.

"There is a litter at the gate," he murmured. "Two noblewomen and their attendants."

Albina lifted her eyes from the statuettes.

"Names?"

"Fulvia and Sempronia. And their household."

Albina stood.

She smoothed her robe over her hips and walked barefoot toward the inner gate. The air changed when she moved. Even the slaves straightened.

Sempronia descended first, elegant, controlled, sky-colored gown trimmed in violet. Silver pins locked her braids in place. Strength settled around her shoulders like a mantle.

Fulvia followed.

Albina paused.

White hair. White brows. Eyes blue as cold flame. A beauty as startling as marble in bright daylight.

Behind her stood a quiet girl, barefoot, plain green tunic, thick black hair knotted tight. The girl kept her gaze on the stones.

Albina's attention lingered on her before shifting to Fulvia.

Sempronia spoke with the confidence of a woman used to doors opening.

"We ask only for a moment."

"I receive all," Albina replied.

They walked through the villa gardens, past dancers practicing slow hip rolls under the trees, past steam rising from the baths, past painted walls and the soft spill of water from a lion's mouth. Birds argued overhead in the branches.

At the shrine, Sempronia knelt. Fulvia knelt after. Neither touched the statue.

Albina washed their hands with a clay bowl, cool water trickling through her fingers. She offered each a square of linen.

"You may sit," she said, motioning to the stone bench beneath the pomegranate tree.

Sempronia sat like a matriarch carved into marble.

Fulvia sat like a girl raised to someday rule a household.

Her slave, Sura, folded herself on the ground beside her, hands in her lap, eyes lowered.

Albina settled opposite them. Her girls gathered behind her, silent as woven silk.

Sempronia began.

"My daughter has heard much of you. As have I."

Albina gave one slow nod.

"We've lived through Rome's changes," Sempronia continued. "Names rise. Names fall. Winds shift. But this..." her eyes swept the shrine, the dancers, the statue "this carries weight."

Albina let silence speak for her.

Fulvia lifted her chin. "I watched you dance at the Campus Martius."

Albina studied her. "And?"

Fulvia's voice softened. "You unsettle people. Because you take space without asking."

A faint smile touched Albina's lips. "Are you unsettled?"

"No."

Sempronia's gaze flickered, approval, worry, calculation.

"I believe you and my daughter must learn each other," Sempronia said. "Fates twist in ways neither of you control. They will bind you."

Albina waited.

"A marriage," Sempronia added. "Between the Dominus and the lovely Fulvia."

"We and the Latina's agree."

Albina's expression stayed unreadable. "And your patrician house accepts this future?"

Sempronia inclined her head. "It will not resist."

Fulvia spoke again. "We don't seek power from you. We seek it beside you."

Albina considered her. The girl's fingers moved with precision as she folded the linen, calm, practiced, promising a sharp mind. She would grow formidable.

A quiet moment followed.

Albina turned her attention to the slave girl.

She switched to Greek. "Your name?"

The girl lifted her eyes. "Sura."

"You serve her?"

Sura nodded.

Albina faced Fulvia again. "She carries strength."

"Yes," Fulvia answered.

Albina rose. Sempronia rose. Fulvia followed.

"You will come again," Albina said.

Sempronia dipped her head in respect.

Fulvia stepped closer and touched Albina's hand.

Albina allowed it.

Their gazes held, a small bridge forming, fragile but real.

Later, as the sun dipped to the western wall, Rufus returned from the farm. Mud on his boots, dust on his arms, fatigue on his shoulders.

He passed the shrine on his way to the baths.

Women knelt beneath the new statue. A girl from the Subura wiped tears with the back of her hand. Dancers swayed slow in the shade. The goddess seemed to watch him with her stone eyes.

Rufus paused. The lion's stone gaze met his shadow.

He nodded once. Small. Barely there.

Then walked on into the house that no longer belonged to him alone.

Behind the statue, where the grape-shadow thickened, a faint wind stirred the oil lamp.

The flame bent toward the hall Rufus had taken.

Toward the path Fulvia would someday walk.

Toward Albina.

The scent lifted, rose, dust, warm stone, and curled around the shrine like a whispered omen.

Somewhere beneath the marble, older powers shifted.

Three threads drew closer: warrior, priestess, future wife.

The knot tightening, patient, hungry.

Waiting for the moment it draws blood.

Chapter 90
NINTH NIGHT

For seven more nights, she passed near him.

Always barefoot, always scented faintly of smoke, cinnamon, citrus, and musk.

Once, he turned a corner and nearly walked into her. She bowed slightly; let her hand brush his chest as she passed. Never looked back.

Another time, she walked the edge of the garden after a bath in nothing but a thin rose robe. The wet silk clinging and coloring her naked skin. Her hair hung loose, still wet, droplets rolling over her collarbone. She said nothing.

On the sixth night, a red ribbon lay on his garden bench. No gift. No message. No explanation.

By the seventh, he avoided her or tried. He trained longer, hammered the javelin until his shoulder screamed, wrestled two men at once until they dropped. Ate alone. Slept poorly.

She never spoke the rules. Never reminded him. She didn't need to.

He counted the days by the way she passed him: a look, a brush, a silence.

Every night the pressure built under his ribs, heat under his skin. He woke drenched and angry. Wanted her. Hated wanting her. Tried to fight it with drills and cold water. It stayed.

On the ninth night, the house changed. The air itself felt heavier. No drumming. No girls. No visitors. Even the fountains whispered instead of sang.

Then came the sound.

A high, rising cry, piercing, rhythmic. Not loud but everywhere.

Ululation.

The sound of women from her homeland. A holy sound.

From the womb. From the throat. From a place older than Rome.

It curled through his ribs and set the blood moving faster. His chest tightened. His breath shortened.

Rufus sat up in bed. The sheet clung to his back. His palms felt slick. He rose and walked to the edge of the room.

The door opened without touch.

Albina entered.

She wore red.

Her smile was not just warmth but welcome.

Bare feet kissed the stone. Gold circled her wrists. Hair unbound down her back. Bells shimmered on her ankles, soft as breath.

Behind her came Zarmina and Nisaya, moving slow, each carrying a clay bowl of burning herbs. Blue smoke rolled from the bowls, sweet and bitter, curling toward the ceiling and sticking to his tongue. Behind them came the girls. Heads bowed, hands cupped around open mouths, shaping the ululation into something layered and deep. It rose and fell, a call and an answer, a wave beating against stone. His heart tried to follow the rhythm and failed.

They circled the bed once. Then again.

Attendants sat brightly burning lamps on every flat surface

Albina did not move at first. Then she stepped forward. Her step a dance.

Rufus waited. His jaw clenched until it ached.

The thin dress slid over her skin like poured water. Oil gleamed across her shoulders, down her arms and strong legs, catching the light of the oil lamps. The smell of frankincense and rose clung to her skin. His nostrils flared, dragging it in.

The dancers' hum bled into the walls, a low current he could feel in his ribs.

She came closer. Anklets sang once, then stilled. Her eyes never left his.

Shadows from the lamps wavered over her stomach. A pulse flickered in her throat. Each step felt chosen, deliberate: one for the goddess, one for her people, one for him.

Her hands rose. She undid the clasp of his tunic. The cloth fell to the floor without a sound.

No words.

Her palms touched his face, then his chest. Her fingers slid down his arms, leaving heat in their wake. His muscles jumped under her touch. He felt the warning from the guards like a knife at his throat, but none of them moved. None of them breathed louder than the song.

She leaned close and spoke in Latin, slow and precise:

"I am not your wife. I am not your slave. I am your fate."

Her breath on his ear was warm and smelled faintly of wine and smoke.

She lay down on the bed, arms open, gaze fixed.

The witches turned outward toward the walls, guarding the circle.

The girls knelt, hands still at their mouths, the cry now softer, steady as breath.

The bodyguards stepped inside, taking their places like carved figures.

No one blinked. No one breathed loud enough to hear.

The door shut behind them. Sealing them all within.

The sound continued.

Rufus moved. Not a lunge, not a rush, an answer. His skin felt too tight. The blood in his veins hammered against bone. Every sense sharpened: the hiss of the lamps, the resin of the smoke, the cold edge of the marble under his feet, her scent rising above it all.

He joined her.

No scream. No clamor. But something inside him broke, then softened, then burned, then built anew.

She moved like the dance she had given him before, so slow, deliberate, sacred.

Each motion a vow. Each breath a prayer.

Her hips rolled in a soft undulation, the same rhythm she had taught the girls but sharper now, intimate. Her arms curved in serpentine arcs, wrists folding, fingers sketching invisible runes. She slid from a standing backbend to a floor swirl, knees parting, hair sweeping over his thighs like ink across parchment. Every gesture a key turning in his chest.

Her breath matched his. Her body answered his, as if the answer had always been there, waiting for the question.

The lion met the fire.

The hunter found the altar.

He whispered her name once. It cracked.

She whispered his over and over, each time like a seal pressed into wax. The ululation shifted into a low hum, a drone of witness, until even that dissolved into the sound of breath and skin.

When the final tremor passed through them, she pressed her forehead to his chest and spoke in a language he did not know:

"You belong to me now. You will never harm me or my people."

Her breath warmed his skin. The words sank deeper than any blade.

He was hers now. Not Caesars.

And nothing in Rome would ever be the same.

Chapter 91
DAYS AFTER

A lbina radiated.

She moved through the house with the calm certainty of a flame that knew its own heat. Slaves lowered their heads as she passed. Scribes stepped aside. Even the eunuchs, not known for softness, straightened their spines.

She claimed no lover's privilege. Asked for nothing. But the villa shifted around her all the same.

She ate lightly. Slept little. In the marble practice room, she danced alone after dark, the bells at her ankles soft as breath, the oil lamps throwing long shadows that moved like spirits beside her. No one watched anymore. They had learned the cost of witnessing what belonged to the sacred.

One morning, Tirzah brought figs and honey to her chamber. She stopped at the threshold.

Albina knelt before the fire, barefoot, robe loose, hair unbound, murmuring in a foreign tongue. Her voice felt like smoke tracing stone. Tirzah set the tray down and backed away, heart thudding in her chest.

Albina never lifted her eyes.

That night, for the first time in years, Rufus slept without waking.

He didn't fully understand it. She had given herself, yes, but not in the way others had given themselves to him. She chose him without yielding to him. That difference pressed somewhere deep in him, in places even war had never reached.

He trained harder than usual. Drilled until sweat stung his eyes. Met with clients. Walked the farms. Sat in Senate meetings and courts. But every rhythm of his day carried her shadow: her scent lingering in the corridor, the faint chime of a dancer's anklet drifting through the atrium, the curl of incense from her shrine.

Even the cat, his cat, slept at her door more often than his.

Yet he felt stronger. More precise in every movement. His hand steadied on the gladius. His breath came deeper. His dreams, when he remembered them, were clean.

Whatever she had done to him, it strengthened him. It steadied him.

By the fourth day, her quiet rules had hardened into law. No one questioned them. The steward enforced them with a raised eyebrow, never a raised voice. The eunuchs followed Albina's will without a spoken order.

A young kitchen slave spilled water in the corridor.

Albina said nothing.

The punishment arrived before she looked up, seven days of silence, barefoot duties, scrubbed floors at dawn.

No one challenged it.

Rufus watched from a distance. He said nothing. She had brought order the way storms bring cleared air, unruly, then perfect. There was fear, the kind that sharpened rather than crushed.

And still she said nothing to him.

Days passed. She crossed his path only in glances, never enough, always too much. He felt the mark of her everywhere: in the scent she left on the stairwell, in the warmth of the marble she had stood on moments before, in the faint red thread someone found caught on the garden hedge.

After the ninth night, she wrapped herself in red and left his bed without a backward glance.

That silence worked under his chest.

Tirzah sensed it. He no longer spoke while she bathed him. No longer offered a word when she trimmed his hair or shaved him. He endured the ministrations, then rose and left as soon as she finished.

She accepted it without complaint.

But one night, she set a perfect pomegranate on his table.

A small act. A quiet truth.

A man claimed by another woman.

A woman claimed by none.

He ate it with a soft smile he did not show her.

Outside, the wind shifted.

Albina stood in the garden, robe brushing her ankles, bare feet in the cool earth. The eastern sky glowed faintly, the first sliver of dawn catching on the marble walls. She held her hands across her lower belly, not possessive, not expecting, only aware, as though listening to a whisper beneath the soil.

Something moved there.

Something old.

Something rising.

The cat wound around her legs and looked toward the horizon as if it understood.

Albina exhaled once, long and slow.

Whatever waited for her had begun.

Chapter 92

THE BOY IN THE QUIET ROOM

The house held a strange silence after the ninth night.

The house waited and watched for the inevitable changes the came with a new woman.

Something heavier, like stone cooling after fire.

Anticipation.

Albina walked the upper hallway barefoot; bells muted at her ankles. The scent of sacrifice still clung to her wrists. The slaves lowered their eyes when she passed; even the guards moved slower around her.

Zarmina guided her toward a side room she had not yet entered.

"He's inside," Zarmina murmured. "The middle brother."

Albina paused. "The genius?"

Zarmina dipped her head. "Yes. Lucius."

Albina pushed the door open with her fingertips.

The room was spare: one long table, jars of wax, thin metal rods, a bowl of water clouded with clay, a half-carved ship-model, a stack of scrolls covered in markings she didn't recognize. The air smelled of dust and lamp smoke and something cleaner, cedar shavings.

Lucius sat hunched over the table. One leg straight, braced. The other tucked. Shoulders narrow; spine curved like a drawn bow. His hair hung in a loose fall that brushed the top of one cheek.

He didn't hear her at first.

His hands moved fast over a wax hull, reed-tip sketching channels along the underside, the lines of a river no one else in Rome could see.

Albina drew closer. Quiet as incense. Watching the patterns of his breath, how it changed when the reed touched water, how still he became when an idea took hold.

He looked up.

Golden-brown eyes. Not like Rufus's steel blue. Softer. Brighter. Lit from inside, as if flame lived behind the pupil.

He froze. The reed trembled.

"You're her," Lucius whispered.

Albina stepped into the lamplight. "And you're Lucius."

He swallowed once. "I'm... Lucius."

Lucius's gaze dropped to the wax model. His fingers twitched. He adjusted the hull by a hair.

"You build rivers," Albina said.

He blinked. "Rivers?"

She nodded at the model. "You make them move where you want. Or let them." Her tone softened. "It's a rare mind that listens before it commands."

Lucius stared as though she had spoken a secret he didn't know he kept. The reed slipped from his fingers into the bowl.

Albina reached out. She picked up the reed and set it beside him.

Behind her, soft steps.

Tareeda entered without knocking.

A shadow of a girl, quiet, graceful, slim as a reed herself. Her dark hair braided with three tiny brass charms that chimed faintly when she breathed. She carried a small clay pot of warmed oil.

Zarmina must have sent her. Tareeda, one of Albina's dancers, obviously had feelings for Lucius. Good.

Tareeda hesitated when she saw the priestess so close to the genius. Then she lowered her gaze, bowed slightly, and approached the table.

Lucius tried to rise, but his braced leg shook.

"No," Tareeda said softly. "Let me."

Albina watched the girl kneel beside him. No fear. No pause. Her hands worked with a gentleness that belonged to nights, not days. She lifted his braced leg, loosened a strap, tested the stiffness of muscle with her fingertips.

Lucius went rigid. "You don't have to..."

She brushed the words aside. "I know."

Something passed between them. Quiet. Barely born. But alive.

Albina felt it like a change in wind.

Tareeda warmed the oil between her palms and rubbed it into the scar that ran along the outer edge of Lucius's calf. He winced. She didn't stop. Her touch found the stiffness, coaxing it loose inch by inch.

"You walk too long when you're thinking," Tareeda murmured.

Lucius flushed. "I don't mean to."

"I know," she repeated.

Albina stepped back, letting the room shift around the gravity forming between them. She watched how Lucius stole glances at Tareeda, as if unsure he deserved her nearness.

Tareeda pretended not to notice. Girls always noticed.

When she finished, she wiped her hands on her skirt and adjusted the brace with small, precise motions. Lucius watched her fingers like they were solving a puzzle he'd never seen.

Albina broke the silence. "Lucius."

He startled. "Yes?"

"Rufus trusts you," Albina said. "So will I."

He looked at her, uncertain.

"You see patterns before others do," she went on. "Your mind is a doorway. Some dare open it. Some don't."

Lucius swallowed. Hard.

Tareeda rose to her feet, standing now close enough that her hip brushed the table. She rested one hand lightly on Lucius's shoulder without thinking.

Albina caught the touch. So did Lucius.

But neither spoke of it.

Albina's voice softened. "Your brother loves you fiercely."

Lucius's mouth tightened. "He thinks I'm strong."

"You are," Albina said. "Strength isn't measured by swords alone."

Lucius stared at the wax ship. "I can't protect him."

Albina stepped closer until she stood on the other side of his table. "You already do."

He blinked, confused.

"You give him the world he walks on," she said. "Bridges, boats, temples, roads. A man fights better when his home stands firm."

Tareeda's hand pressed a little firmer on his shoulder. "And when someone waits for him to return."

Lucius's breath caught.

Albina saw the truth spark in his face.

Good.

She would need the boy, his mind, and the quiet strength that came from being loved without asking.

Albina turned toward the door.

"Priestess?" Lucius called.

Albina stopped.

Lucius hesitated, then asked, "Will you... dance again soon?"

A small smile touched her lips. "For Rufus, yes."

"And for the house?" he added, voice shaking.

"For the house," Albina said, "I will never stop."

Tareeda bowed as Albina passed, and the priestess touched the girl's shoulder with two fingers, acknowledgment, blessing, warning.

When the door closed, Lucius let out the breath he'd been holding.

Tareeda leaned close to his ear.

"Don't fear her," she whispered. "She sees you."

Lucius looked down at his hands.

For the first time in years, they trembled not from pain, but from hope.

Chapter 93
DUST AND CHAINS

The caravan arrived at midmorning.

Dust came first, a pale, choking cloud rolling ahead of it, the color of old bones ground thin. Wheels groaned under the load. Oxen strained, heads low, their breath steaming in the heat. Chains clinked with each turn of the axle, a slow metallic heartbeat. Flies circled in a thick ring around the cages. A barefoot boy walked in front, ringing a cracked brass bell with red, split knuckles.

The Latinus gates swung open without a command.

Rufus stood at the top of the portico, bare-chested, arms crossed. Sun caught the scars across his ribs. Sweat gathered at the base of his throat, ran down the line of his sternum. He didn't move.

The cat hovered in the doorway behind him, tail low, ears flattened, staring hard at the cages as if it recognized something inside them.

Below, Albina stepped out from the garden.

She wore a black veil that hid her face completely. The same furs she had escaped the mountains in, now cleaned, brushed, and gleaming like liquid shadow, draped her shoulders. Even in the heat, Albina hid her form with thick clothing. Zarmina and Nisaya flanked her. Her five dancers followed with hands folded, bells wrapped in cloth. Tirzah came last, quiet, apart from all of them.

These were not sacred Alexandrian specialists.

These were Rome's daily slaves, broken, branded, bartered.

The merchant dismounted quickly and bowed until his forehead touched the dust. "You summoned stock, Domina."

Albina did not bow. Her voice came soft, exact, velvet.

"Open the cages."

Bolts scraped back. Hinges groaned. Chains rattled like metal serpents slithering across stone.

The smell hit first, sweat, fear, iron, dried blood. Sharp enough to sting the back of the throat.

One by one, the slaves climbed down. Ankles raw, necks collared, eyes hollow or defiant or dead. Dust streaked their cheeks. Some limped. Some fell. Most kept their gaze pinned to the ground.

Albina walked the line without pity.

Without warmth.

Without hurry.

She didn't touch.

The witches did, Zarmina running rough fingertips over bones, Nisaya checking wrists and teeth. Their murmured tongue rose and fell like distant wind against ruined stone.

The merchant opened his mouth to explain, then shut it.

Albina stopped before a girl no older than twelve. Matted hair. Swollen cheek. Thin as a sparrow, but her eyes held ground.

Albina touched her brow with two fingers. "This one."

She moved on. Stopped at a boy with thin legs and long fingers, shoulders set high like a fledgling hawk preparing to fly. She circled him once.

"This one too."

Then an older woman, gaunt, bitter, a scar roping across her temple. She refused to kneel. She hissed something in a dead tongue.

Albina answered in the same tongue.

A single curse.

Cold. Precise.

The woman's eyes widened.

Fear. Or recognition. Or both.

"Take her," Albina said. "She will break, or she will rise."

Near the back stood a shape that dwarfed all others.

A tall woman.

Black-skinned. Barefoot. Muscled like a warhorse.

A collar at her throat, no chains on her wrists. She stood with the stillness of stone. Calm eyes. A nose long-since broken. Shoulders broad enough to carry a large billy goat.

Albina stopped.

"What is her name?"

The merchant swallowed. "Makara. From Numidia. Hurt two overseers. Refuses commands. Won't speak. Eats too much. My Dominus will send her to the mines."

Albina stepped forward. She had to look up.

Makara looked down.

Their stillness matched.

No flinch.

No fear.

Albina lifted her hand and placed two fingers on the woman's chest, right over the sternum.

"This one is mine."

The merchant cleared his throat. "She's dangerous, Domina. She'll..."

"I said," Albina murmured, "she is mine."

He hesitated. "As you wish, of course, but she costs dearly. Very dearly."

Zarmina watched Makara with the intensity of a hawk sizing an equal.

Tirzah's eyes narrowed, unreadable.

Even the dancers leaned to see.

Albina turned to the merchant. "Three more. Girls if possible. Strong backs. Clear eyes. I will send for boys another day."

"Yes, Domina."

"And the ones I marked?"

"Whole, yes."

"Fix them. Bleed them clean. Return what lives."

The man bowed lower, slower now.

"These are not your slaves anymore," Albina said. "They are mine."

She turned. Her dancers followed. Chains dragged across the dirt behind them, long and heavy, like the tail of an ancient beast waking from sleep.

The sun burned against Makara's shoulders. She watched Albina walk away.

Didn't blink. Didn't shift. Didn't break her stare.

Then she stepped forward, quiet as shadow, steady as oath, and followed.

Chapter 94
WORMS

T he mosaic floor still held her scent.

The chamber where Albina first danced belonged to her now.

Albina removed the white furs and Sareph took them from her. Albina wore black silk.

She stood near the center, gold rings on her fingers, bare feet planted wide. The new slaves lined the wall, backs straight, eyes lowered. The Nubian woman towered above them all, shoulders rising like a carved pillar.

Zarmina watched from the shadows. Nisaya sat cross-legged by the water bowl, her gaze cold and patient. The dancers stood behind Albina in a perfect line. Two eunuch guards flanked the doors, hands steady on hilts.

Albina moved down the row, slow, exact, measuring each face.

"There is your sleeping hall," she said, pointing with a finger heavy with rings. "You eat before dawn, at midday, and after dusk. You work until dusk. You obey."

She stopped before a girl whose hands trembled.

"If you lie, we'll know. If you steal, we'll know. If you gossip outside this villa," she said, lifting a brow, "we will know."

A few swallowed. None dared look up.

Her finger swung toward the far wall where Crassus's blackened cross hung, bolted deep into stone. Nine feet tall. Thick. Silent. Its wood remembered everything.

"That cross came from the Spartacus revolt," Albina said. "A rebel died on it. He hung until even the flies forgot his name."

A breath moved down the line, thin, sharp, frightened.

"It stays as a reminder."

She turned to the Nubian.

"Makara," she said. "You enforce the rules."

Makara nodded once. The nod felt like steel striking stone.

Albina faced the line again. "You obey me. You obey the witches. You obey the girls. You obey the guards. You obey Dominus."

The silence that followed was deep enough to taste.

"Follow me."

They obeyed.

They moved through carved arches into the formal gardens. Light flashed off white marble. Perfumed water spilled from lion mouths into small pools. Frescoes of gods and victories watched in fresh color. Two peacocks strutted near a fountain. The cat, Mars's gift, lounged on a warm ledge, eyes amber and ancient.

Albina walked ahead, her black dress sweeping the path. Zarmina and Nisaya flanked her. The eunuchs matched stride. Behind them, dancers and apprentices glided in silence, every step precise.

The new slaves stole glances at statues and flowers. One flinched when the faint bell at Albina's ankle chimed. The youngest whimpered at the cat's stare; the animal blinked once, slow, dismissive, and turned away like a small king.

They reached the back of the house. Mosaic floors gave way to plain stone. Heat thickened in the air, woodsmoke, grilled meat, bread, hot oil. Dogs barked. Chickens scattered. Slaves hurried with baskets and pots, eyes down.

Rufus stood near the food tables. Uninterested in the slaves. Inspecting the roast. The kitchen smoke curled around him. Tirzah waited behind him, silent. Menon watched from the corner, arms folded.

Albina halted the line. Her eyes narrowed.

"You smell like beasts."

Sweat stained their necks. Dust clung in thick strips along their arms.

"Your old clothes burn tonight," she said. "You will be washed. Scrubbed. Given garments and shoes. Keep yourselves clean. Keep your sleeping space clean. If your work soils you, bathe again. Take pride in yourself and this house."

The dancers shifted, quiet shadows behind her.

"Do not let me smell you twice."

She walked the line slowly; bodies stiffened as she neared.

"You're full of worms," Albina said. "You'll take medicine monthly. It tastes foul. You swallow it anyway."

A small, ugly sound escaped the youngest. Zarmina's eyes snapped to her. The girl froze.

"You will call me Domina," Albina said. Her head dipped toward Rufus. "You will call him Dominus."

She turned to Makara. "You are my hammer. If any lie, steal, gossip, disobey, strike until they scream. If any eye lingers where it must not," She pointed at Rufus, " drag them here."

Makara inclined her chin. A promise.

The cat stretched against the vertical beam of the cross, claws scraping wood. A long, dry rasp sliced the air. The slaves flinched. The cat stared at them with thin, yellow fire.

Albina's voice didn't rise; the calm made it lethal.

"You touch him," she pointed at Rufus, "you die screaming. You dream of him, keep it to yourself. If your eyes linger, gouge them out."

She lifted her hand. Sun cut through the colonnade and lit the cross.

"If you disobey," she said softly, "I'll hang you up there."

The shadow of the cross spilled long across the yard, stretching like a tongue of black fire. One of the dancers made a small sound, Nisaya glared once; silence returned.

Albina let the shadow settle over them. Let them feel it.

"You obey my witches, my dancers, my apprentices. You obey Dominus." Her smile barely rose. "You never gossip outside this villa. I hate gossipers. I will know. And if you speak," her voice thinned into something older, "I will cut the tongue from you."

A few heads bowed. A few nodded. Fear folded itself into obedience.

Albina nodded to the guards. "Bathe them. Deworm them. Then assign rooms. They start work in the morning. The African rooms near us."

The guards moved in quietly. Makara stepped forward, her shadow falling long over the tiles.

Rufus sniffed the air, satisfied with the roast, and said nothing. He heard the scrape of sandals as the new slaves were led away.

Albina did not look back.

The cross cast its black shadow like a warning. The cat dug claws into the wood again, ritual, memory, claim.

The beam remembered the rebel of Spartacus.

The air remembered his scream.

Rome remembered everything.

Chapter 95
WHISPER LINES

The House of the Fulvii, Quirinal Hill

Fulvia stood at the high window with a half-eaten fig resting in her palm. Its sweetness clung to her fingers. Below, the caravan crossed the street in a slow, controlled line. Dust trailed behind the wheels. Chains sang a dull rhythm. The guards moved with a farmer's patience, steady as oxen. The whole procession shifted toward the Caelian Hill.

His hill.

"She's building something," Fulvia murmured.

On the couch, Sempronia did not lift her eyes from the scroll balanced across her knee. "She already has."

Fulvia finished the fig and licked the juice from her thumb. Her gaze followed the tallest shape in the line, a woman built like a temple column, dark skin bright in sunlight. Behind her, others shuffled barefoot, thin, bruised, heads down.

"She's too beautiful," Fulvia said, almost to herself.

"In her fashion," Sempronia replied. "A foreign blaze. But you, daughter, are Rome's beauty."

Fulvia let that sit. A breath. A ripple of pleasure. A hint of envy.

"She moves like she floats," Fulvia said. "Doesn't make a sound."

Still Sempronia read.

"She doesn't speak like us," Fulvia added.

"She isn't us."

"But the women follow her. Every class. Every color of veil."

"Women gather around a flame," her mother said. "Men, sooner or later, gather around the smoke."

Fulvia rested her cheek on her hand and watched the last wagon turn the corner. Dust settled. A dog barked at nothing. A gull drifted low, pale wings flashing.

"What if she leaves?" Fulvia asked.

"She won't."

"You sound sure."

"She has no world but the one she just claimed."

Fulvia's fingers traced the cold stone of the sill. "She frightens me."

"Good," Sempronia said, crisp as snapped papyrus.

Fulvia turned. Her mother's tone held no comfort, only fact.

"She blocks everything," Fulvia whispered.

Sempronia finally lowered the scroll. Her gaze landed on her daughter with the weight of a verdict. "She doesn't block anything. She opens the path. That's different. And your future remains yours."

Fulvia swallowed. "I want him without her shadow."

"You'll get him," Sempronia said. "Patience sharpens a girl faster than war."

The house creaked with the early heat. Shadows of fig leaves slipped across the walls. Two slaves passed beneath the window with baskets of dates; their bracelets clinked once, then vanished into the courtyard arch.

Fulvia whispered, "She'll change everything."

"She already has," Sempronia answered.

A servant entered with a lamp. Flame rose with a soft whoosh. The shadows stretched long and thin across the mosaic floor.

Fulvia faced the glass again.

"She's staying," she said quietly.

Sempronia rose, smoothed her gown, and touched her daughter's shoulder with a single, precise hand.

"Yes," she said. "She's home."

Chapter 96
THE GIRL IN GREEN

Tirzah stood still in the heat. She had not moved since Albina left.

She inspected the cross. The scent of cinnamon and body odor lingered even after the line of new slaves passed.

Tirzah kept her head down, hands folded.

She had never seen anyone command like that. Not even him. Not with that kind of stillness.

She glanced up once. Albina had already disappeared through the back colonnade, her witches close, her girls behind, her guards like wolves.

But Tirzah saw one thing they didn't.

Rufus's hand, gripping the edge of the table, just a little too tight. The veins in his wrist stood out. His knuckles blanched.

That was how she knew.

Albina hadn't stolen the house.

She'd been handed it. Dominus gave the house to the witch Albina.

Rufus gave the house away with his silence. With that stillness. With the kind of deference that no Roman man gave without cost. Especially not to a foreign girl with bells on her ankles and knives at her side.

Tirzah watched him from the shadow of the arch. She had stood where Albina stood now. She had poured the water. Taken the orders. Warmed the bed.

But this was different.

This girl, the one in black silk and bracelets, hadn't just taken a place in the house. She was the house now. Tirzah could feel it in the air. A shift. Something permanent.

She hated her. But part of her still wanted to kneel, and that was worse.

She muttered something low. Half-prayer. Half-curse. Something about witches. About painted eastern girls who dance and eat the pigs that God forbids.

Tirzah swore she would find a way not to have to obey this foreign devil. Only Rufus.

She spat lightly, three times to the side, as her mother taught, to keep curses from clinging to the tongue. Then she turned toward the direction Albina walked, eyes hot, throat tight.

Chapter 97
OSTIA

Albina began sleeping beside Rufus because the bed felt safe, wide enough for breath and silence. They grew close in the small ways first, shared laughter, soft jabs, the warmth of her foot brushing his shins at dawn. The villa changed around them. Rhythms formed. Ritual tightened. Her presence turned stone halls into something alive.

The specialty slaves arrived from Alexandria days after. They came cloaked, clean, shoulders straight. Not common slaves. Sacred. Chosen for skill, not labor.

The eunuch cook came first, a broad-shouldered Egyptian with blade-scarred forearms and a voice rough as gravel. He carried the scent of cumin and lamb smoke. He had once fed a wealthy Jewish family, and he bowed only to the statue of the Sibyl, never to men.

The musicians followed, two slender brothers and their sister, faces veiled, fingers ringed in gold. Their drums and lyres looked older than marble. They tuned by firelight and played only after nightfall. Music clung to their hands like magic.

Then came the silk master, long lashes, thin wrists, gender blurred like heat over sand. A eunuch, yes, but something else too. His fabrics whispered as he moved. He dyed with indigo dark as seawater, reds that looked wet. When Albina wore his cloth, draped over one shoulder, low at the hip, the house held its breath.

A perfume-maker came next. Oils in glass no thicker than dew on a leaf. She spoke little, mixed only by moon cycles, her hands always stained with resin and jasmine.

A eunuch hair-and-makeup artist followed. Brushes wrapped in black silk. Seashells filled with colored powders. His hands hovered like a priest's over the girls' faces, reshaping shadow and line until they looked carved.

Last arrived the hawk handler. Young, sun-browned, more girl than woman. Leather gloves scarred by talons. A Saker falcon rode her arm with the elegance of a prince. She walked the bird at dawn; the household made room for her without being told.

Each slept apart. Each answered only to Albina. They had been sent from Alexandria before she ever stepped foot in Rome, because Albina had always known what she would become.

Rufus asked nothing. He paid. Watched. Adjusted. Let her carve the villa into something sacred.

His brother Lucius stayed at the villa most days now. Albina's dancer, Tareeda, cared for him. A beautiful love grew between them.

Tall despite his limp, thin from years of pain, he stood in the doorway of the inner garden drawing invisible lines in the air with his finger. Patterns. Ratios. Curves. He studied the fountain's spray as if measuring its fall.

Tareeda, quiet and observant, knelt behind him on the tile and warmed his hands between hers. She adjusted the wrap on his bad leg. Pressed a fig into his palm. Spoke to him in soft fragments. He blinked, listened, and murmured back, voice low and precise, naming the distance between the fountain stones.

Albina passed by.

She stopped.

Lucius did not look up. He drew a new shape in the air, something like the bow of a ship cutting water.

Tareeda noticed Albina and lowered her gaze. Albina stepped closer, watching Lucius's fingertip cut a perfect arc through the air.

"What does he see?" she asked.

Tareeda answered softly, "Everything."

Lucius finally looked at Albina. His eyes were pale, sharp, full of geometry. He lowered his hand, shy, but he didn't look away.

Albina inclined her head. Respect met respect

One warm morning, Rufus said,

"Come with me to Ostia."

No flourish. No persuasion. A simple command softened by something almost like hope.

"I bought a private loft above a seafood theater hall," he added. "You'll like it."

She lifted one brow.

"I've got a house there," he said. "Quiet. Lucius designed it. We'll stay a few days. I've business. You can walk the markets."

She agreed. They left at sunrise.

The litter rocked gently as it rolled down the road. Thick curtains blocked the sun. Albina leaned into padded cushions, fingers trailing along carved wood. Her eunuchs marched tight around her, knives hidden beneath robes. Her dancers rode behind in a covered mule-cart. Laughter and foreign tongues floated between them like bright ribbon. A pampered Lucius rode with them. A smile on his face. Tareeda laughing as she massaged his knee.

Rufus walked ahead of the litter. Bow slung across his back. The small hawk handler followed, her falcon catching more rabbits than he did. He nodded once, impressed. Menon led a packhorse behind them, bags loaded with scrolls, gear, and Rufus's black-iron weapons.

Albina hadn't left Rome since her arrival. Rome smelled of dirty bodies, sewage, crowds. Ostia smelled of salt. Pine. Wind.

At Rufus's seaside house, she bathed for an hour. Steam rolled from the deep tub. The witches oiled her skin until it gleamed. The dancers dressed her under the silk master's eye; the makeup artist shaped her face with strokes as light as breath.

When she rose, hair falling in black waves held by gold thorns, eyes rimmed in kohl, lips stained berry-red, she looked like the queen of some lost coast, carved from heat and shadow.

Rufus waited in his small office, already dressed, boots polished, tunic dark.

She entered. The scent of blue lotus and frankincense reached him first.

"You're beautiful," he murmured.

Albina smiled, slow and dangerous.

"Let Rome gossip," she whispered. "I am yours tonight. And I want the world to ache for what it cannot touch."

They laughed together and crossed the garden. Peacocks strutted like jeweled soldiers. At the gate, guards lifted Albina into her litter, curtained, gilded, her girls following behind. Rufus led on foot. Lucius and Tareeda sat in a seperate litter focused on each other.

Ostia at night buzzed with life: fish frying, torches flaring, merchants calling out in Greek, Latin, Egyptian. Perfume, salt, wine, all of it washed together into a single breath of the port.

They reached the restaurant, a scandalous place in Rome, permitted only because Rufus was young, powerful, and dangerous enough to ignore opinion.

Albina stepped down. Black silk clung to her shape like water. Gold bracelets gleamed at her wrists and ankles. A single red gemstone burned at her throat.

She vanished inside the building, quiet, controlled, leaving only the ghost of her scent behind.

Inside, the place looked like a theater. Lanterns swayed. Bodies pressed shoulder to shoulder. A stage glowed below. Upper balconies held private viewing boxes draped in heavy curtains. Behind those curtains, patrons drank, feasted, schemed.

Rufus's box was the highest, largest. Cushions piled in a half-circle. Low tables set with fruit, cheese, and wine.

The witches placed smoking bronze bowls near the cushions, the scent a blend of hemp and sweet herbs, soft enough to warm the edges of thought.

Albina kicked off her sandals. Sat cross-legged, a queen in shadow-light. She poured her own wine, lips curving.

Rufus tasted everything, rare for him, cold fish in herbs, grilled squid, clams in broth. Hour after hour, new dishes came in on trays. The feast never stopped. Music never stopped. The sea wind drifted through cracks in the shutters, carrying the scent of salt and lantern smoke.

Albina leaned back, eyes half-lidded.

"Let them see me like this," she said. "Let them think they understand."

Rufus didn't answer. He watched her. Watched her drink from a bronze cup. Watched how the lamplight slid along her cheekbones. Watched her dancers sway in rhythm. Watched his brother and the beautiful dancing girl touching, kissing.

Music thickened. Smoke curled. The dancers moved around them, anklets chiming. Witches clapped softly, keeping time.

Albina drew closer. Her fingers brushed his knee, light, deliberate. Her hand lingered at his chest. She leaned into him, her hair falling over them both like a dark curtain.

The dancers circled. The music deepened.

Albina whispered near his ear, "We are gods here."

She didn't climb atop him. She didn't undress him. She didn't need to.

She rested her forehead against his collarbone, breath warm, scent curling against his throat. Her fingers traced his jaw, slow and certain. The touch alone felt like a vow.

When she finally leaned back, her eyes glowed through the lamplight.

She whispered something in her ancient tongue, a name, a blessing, maybe something more. The sound slid into his chest like a seed taking root.

Then she laughed. A soft, quiet, private sound.

Rufus drew her close, and for a long moment they simply remained, breath against breath, heartbeat against heartbeat, while music rose and crashed below their balcony like waves.

Outside, the crowd cheered a performer's fall.

Inside, the world narrowed to the space between them.

And held.

Chapter 98
CRUCIFIXION

The girl's name slipped out of the house before the light faded.

Young. Pretty. Wheat-colored hair. A soft voice. A gift from a grateful merchant when Rufus returned from the east.

They found her behind a curtain, knees drawn tight, clutching a knotted cloth filled with sixty silver denarii. Coin meant for bread, oil, and Tirzah's sacred food. Coin meant for the house.

Nisaya didn't shout. She simply lifted her hand and called for Zarmina.

The guards came next.

But Makara closed the gap.

The Nubian's arm locked around the girl's throat, steady and cold, while her free hand tore the pouch away. No struggle lasted long against her.

Albina arrived last.

She didn't raise her voice. She didn't ask why.

A single finger lifted.

A single finger dropped.

That was the sentence.

The girl's tunic came off. Iron snapped around her wrists. Chains fixed her to the courtyard wall. The wind touched her bare back. Other slaves gathered at the edges, pulled by something older than curiosity, judgment had gravity.

"One lash for each denarius," Albina said.

The whip was plain leather, dark with memory. The eunuch who held it had carved meat for years; he understood how to cut without killing too quickly.

The strokes came steady.

Ten.

Twenty.

Thirty, her voice thinned into ragged sobs.

By forty, her legs buckled.

By fifty, her breath shook in shallow bursts.

By sixty, she hung slack against the wall, her back marked in straight, bright lines.

Albina's nod gave the next order.

They lifted her arms. Pressed her wrists to wood. The nails drove through with a single heavy strike each. The sound cracked the yard, a sound everyone knew, even those who had never heard it before.

The crossbeam rose. Fitted into the waiting post bolted to the rear wall. The girl hung high, above eye level, where every slave would pass daily. Her toes scraped at nothing.

She lived. Barely. Held aloft by pain more than breath.

Rufus returned through the service gate, a crust of bread in hand, tunic open at the chest. He saw her. Stopped.

She raised her head. Blood touched her mouth when she spoke.

"Dominus... please..."

Rufus stood still. The yard held its breath. A dog barked somewhere near the stable. A chicken scratched the dirt. Nothing else moved.

He finished the bite. Wiped his hand.

Stepped around the blood.

Gave Albina one slow nod.

She didn't smile.

He didn't ask.

That night, Albina took the pantry keys. The wine room. The strongbox. She checked every lock herself. By week's end, Rufus placed the strongroom key in her hand without a word.

From that day, the house belonged to her: the coin, the silence, the order.

No one stole again.

No one tested a boundary.

No one whispered her name cheaply.

The girl died before dawn. Her body was removed before the first bell. The courtyard was washed clean. But the cross kept its stains. And the flies remembered.

By the next market day, the story had already changed.

Some claimed Albina called for a hundred lashes.

Others swore the nails came from Parthian iron.

A few whispered that the wind died when she raised her finger.

And the boldest, always women, said her gaze could pin a person to the wood without a hammer.

They began to say her name with both reverence and warning:

"She crucifies."

The cross stayed bolted to the rear wall.

Black wood. Tall shadow. Watchful as any guard.

And in that villa, nothing moved without her notice.

Even the flies obeyed.

Chapter 99
THE RED THREAD

The coin came in quietly. Small pouches. No markings. A few denarii, sometimes a silver ring, sometimes gold. Left in baskets of figs. Slipped into folded cloth. Always from women. Always by hand.

Albina didn't ask for a single denarius. The women gave generously anyway.

The money filled a locked chest in her room. Then another, and another. Most had to be taken to the strong room. Nisaya sorted each coin by weight and date. Zarmina said nothing. Just watched. Albina stood barefoot on the warm mosaic tiles, eyes on the floor, listening.

She had a nearby empty room turned into an office. A reed mat. A low writing desk. One stone from her homeland beneath the shutters.

"We begin," she said.

They lit no lamps.

That night, six letters were written. Two to Egypt. One to Rhodes. One to Hyrcania. One to Coptos. The last, short and sealed in wax, went to Neapolis. Zarmina handed the letters off to the right girls; relatives, loyal ones. Albina spoke to each before they left.

"You serve me. But you serve the goddess first."

They knelt. Kissed her hand. Vanished before dawn.

Across Rome, the flow of information shifted. A silk seller in the Forum began whispering about Parthian tariffs. A dockworker from Ostia delivered dates but asked questions in Greek. One of the eunuchs, bare-chested and silent waited on the roof at night, eyes trained east.

Rufus asked nothing. That mattered.

The money she gave was hers to give. He saw no ledgers, no names. Just chests, or bags carried out one by one. And each time he asked if she needed anything, she smiled.

"I have everything," she said.

But her dancers trained longer. The eunuchs trained them in the use of blades. The witches spoke less. The shrine grew heavier with old statues, gifts from the women. And late at night, alone, Albina stood with her maps. Maps off Rome and Italy. Of routes. Sea and land. Nile to desert. Desert to sea. A red thread stretched from Rome to the far edges of the Parthian Empire.

She touched the thread. Tension pulled in her fingers.

The war had already begun.

The men who owed Albina blood or birthright began to move.

Her high-born Arabic relatives, and her command of their language gave her a secretive and powerful ally right in the middle ground between the two worlds.

One left a merchant ship in Cyrene. Another disappeared from a spice caravan outside Petra. Three more, all sailors, all Hyrcanian, vanished from a Parthian patrol near the Gulf. Their names never reached Rome, but their silence did.

Albina had written nothing down. She had spoken only to the old one with the cracked voice, Nisaya the Black, and to the dark-eyed silk master who had sewn her new red dress. Even Menon, Rufus's steward, didn't see the money leave the house.

But the gold and silver moved. Quietly. Heavy coin and thin bars, some stamped with Rome's seal, some with Albina's crescent moon, others not stamped at all. All made their way south. First to Alexandria. Then down the Nile.

Where the river narrowed, Albina's agents bought mules. Sand guides. Camel drovers. They passed through the desert crossing and arrived at the Red Sea ports, just as the spring winds shifted.

They called the sea Yam Suph. The Sea of Reeds. Rome called it Arabia. But to Albina's people, it was older than all names. Her spies found places no

Roman had ever stood, coastal shrines, deep inlets, storm caves carved by wind and tide.

At the docks, her people worked with the grain keepers and spice counters. They paid the pearl divers well. Gold and wine for secrets. A song for a map. A knife for a lie. Every man and woman placed in position knew what they served: the slow undoing of the king who had destroyed their homelands.

All had a sacred duty to do as their last remaining sovereign needed.

By summer, messages passed on salted hides. Inks that vanished in sunlight. A mark on the toe of a sandal. A braided thread in a sash. Albina never saw the senders. She didn't need to. The chain stretched now from Egypt to Babylon.

One fisherman swore he'd seen the Parthian king's barge gliding down the Tigris. Another, a kitchen slave in Seleucia, smuggled out a recipe for sweet-bread, and a list of noble names attending court.

Albina read them by lamplight. She memorized each one.

She circled a name.

And breathed, "Soon."

Men died in the east, and Rome never heard the sound.

A horse trader drowned in the Euphrates. Two scribes disappeared outside Susa, left behind only a coin etched with an eye. An oil merchant in Palmyra seemed to slit his own throat after a visit from a foreign girl with golden earrings. All these deaths traced back to Albina, but no one in Rome could have followed the trail. That's how she wanted it.

Her war needed silence. Her coin bought the silence but not sleep.

The Goddess wanted blood. But first she wanted patience.

The Red Sea ports now pulsed with energy. Albina's agents didn't wear Roman togas. They wore robes bleached by desert sun, tunics dyed deep with crushed beetle and salt, cloaks pinned with coral teeth. Her funds paid for ink, papyrus, bribes, replacement sails. They controlled three harbors outright, and the harbormasters knew who truly held power.

From these ports, small ships moved east. No banners. No horns. Some carried olive oil. Others, wine. All carried words.

Albina's network, her Red Thread, followed every rumor of the Parthian king's court. They learned who was building palaces. Who was hoarding grain. Who fathered bastards with temple girls and who whipped his slaves in public.

They learned what frightened him.

And slowly, Albina learned too.

Back in Rome, she said little. Her dancers trained. Her witches brewed. Her eunuchs cleaned their blades. She took her pleasure in the shadows and walked the garden after dark.

Rufus thought her at peace.

But each night, she knelt before the twelve statuettes. She whispered their names, one by one, and traced the worn stone of the Sybil's Chariot. Her favorite. The newest.

"Let him choke on dust," she whispered to the Blade.

"Let him see only fire," she said to the Eye.

To the Thirteenth, she said nothing. Only placed her hand.

That night, a eunuch placed a small, wrapped bundle on her floor. No one saw him enter. No one saw him leave. She unwrapped it by candlelight. A signet ring. Blood still in the grooves. The crest broke. Parthian. Albina didn't speak. She placed it on the cold stone near the Sibyl's Chariot and let it rest there, an offering, a warning, a promise kept.

"A good start," she whispered and smiled.

The temple they meant to raise atop her homelands ashes now lay in limbo, delayed, disordered, cursed before the first stone.

Far from Rome, her spies carved a map into the inside of a folding fan. On the fan were no cities, only tides, and winds, and names that had not yet died.

Albina would see them dead.

And the Parthian king would never see her coming.

Chapter 100
THE KNIFE BENEATH THE TRADERS BELT

They came silent. With knives.

No names. No gods. Just blood still owed.

They dressed as traders. Mud-stained tunics. Broken sandals. Beards left unwashed. Leather belts heavy with hidden steel. Resin packs stank of oil and poison.

They crossed land by foot, by bribe, by fire. Through rivers and mountains. Heat and dust. Rome pulled them in.

Above Clusium they bought a guide with a single silver coin.

Two miles later, they cut his throat and rolled him into the ditch.

By the time they neared the city they looked like ghosts. Thin, scarred, hollow-eyed. Yet their strength had returned since the Alpine passes. They slipped among the hundreds arriving daily, farmers, traders, beggars, freedmen.

No nobles. No banners. No greetings.

Just men bent on one target.

They entered separately. Four gates. Four false names.

No one looked twice.

In a back alley near the Aventine, they reunited. A boy waited. Paid days before. He led them to a house, small, walled, quiet, with a hidden cellar.

They moved in that night.

The next morning the birds did not sing.

Red Ring sat alone at the table, hunched over his wax map. A black needle for each of her people, guards, dancers, servants, vendors. He traced the marks with a fingertip, eyes fixed, muttering names under his breath.

His brothers scattered into the city.

One took work near the market.

One limped along the aqueduct.

One shadowed the butcher's boy.

One bribed a house slave.

The noose tightened.

They stole a gold ring from one of Albina's dancers, cut her satchel, spilled the contents into the street. They wanted her to feel the shift.

That dusk, Nisaya stirred. The dark one. The quiet one. She froze in the courtyard, face tilted, as if listening to something no one else could hear. Her voice, thin and sharp, slipped from her lips:

"Beware the jackal's walk in man's skin."

The guards at the gate stiffened. One rushed to look, but by the time he turned, the alley was empty. No one there.

Zarmina frowned. Albina's bells gave a faint chime as she passed, gold eyes narrowing. They spoke no more of it, but the omen hung in the air.

Red Ring already knew where she slept. Where Rufus trained. When the girls danced. Who brought the wine. Where the water flowed.

He wanted her to see ash before she died.

His brothers whispered dreams.

One wanted to gut Rufus in the Forum.

One spoke of wild dogs tearing flesh.

One kept sharpening his blade, saying nothing.

They would wait. But not long.

Rome watched Albina. Rome adored her. Rome sang her name.

No one watched the shadows.

Red Ring came soundless.

And Rome never saw the knife beneath the trader's belt.

Chapter 101
BLOOD ON THE PORTICO

The woman at the herb stall noticed him first.

She always did. She knew the beggars, the limping veterans, the mothers who whispered to stone gods for luck. Their smells, their rhythms, their sorrow. She fed them figs when she had extra.

But this man wasn't one of them.

Thin, foreign, wrong.

A beard too neat for a beggar; hands too soft for labor; eyes too sharp to ignore.

He sat outside Rufus's street for three days without asking for coin.

When the woman finished packing her herbs, she made the slow climb to the Caelian Hill. She didn't wait for permission. Albina saw her the moment she stepped through the gate.

They spoke without riddles.

Albina took her hand. Called for wine. Pressed a gold ring into her palm.

The woman gave her the location.

Albina sent someone she trusted to follow him, Sura, a slim, quiet girl on loan from Fulvia. Temple-born. Quick-footed. Loyal. Fulvia trusted her with secrets; Albina trusted her with danger.

Sura followed the man through the market, down the side streets, past the butcher stalls. She saw him speak with a trader. Circle twice. Then vanish into the alleys.

She went after him.

She should not have.

The dog howled first.

The baker's boy saw the body next.

Then the guards.

Sura hung from the portico beam by her wrists. Rope burned her skin. Her stomach lay open; her insides draped the steps like wet rope. Flies thickened the air. Blood soaked the white stone.

Zarmina and Nisaya arrived.

Albina followed them into the morning light.

She didn't flinch. Didn't cry.

She crouched. Dipped two fingers into the pooled blood. Rubbed it between thumb and forefinger as if testing grain.

Then she stood.

"He's here."

Her witches nodded.

Rufus appeared at the gate, tunic half-laced, knives in hand.

He stopped when he saw Sura, shock, rage, breath turning to fire.

He scanned the street. Every face. Every window. Every shadow.

"Cut her down," he said.

Albina didn't look at him.

She whispered one word.

"Red."

She turned and walked inside.

The doors closed like stone.

The news reached Fulvia by noon.

Sempronia read the letter twice before speaking. "She's dead."

The wind pushed the curtains inward.

Fulvia stood at the window, silent, rigid. Tears ran without trembling.

"They hung her from his portico," Sempronia added. "Entrails on the steps."

Still no reply.

"She followed the beggar," Sempronia said. "Alone."

Fulvia turned. "She followed Albina for me. That makes her ours."

The words shook nothing in her face, but her hands closed slowly, deliberately.

Sura had grown up in Fulvia's house.

Seven years old when her father brought her home.

Fulvia eight.

Two girls given honey to calm them, led through the same gate, hands brushing in shyness.

They learned letters together, Latin, Greek, old Phoenician.

Fulvia protected her from cruel tutors.

Sura braided her hair each morning.

Fulvia held her during fevers.

Years of secrets shared under blankets and lamplight.

And when Fulvia asked her to spy, Sura didn't hesitate.

Not for coin.

Not for fear.

For love.

Fulvia's voice came low.

"She trusted that house. Someone is testing it."

Sempronia lifted her ink brush. "Your lion won't like this."

Fulvia kept her gaze on the window. "He'll wait."

"And you?"

Fulvia exhaled, slow, steady.

"I'll bring roses. And fire."

Across the city, in a piss-stinking alley, Red Ring crouched in shadow.

He watched the patrol torches fade.

They had seen his message.

Good.

Sura's death should have bought them time. It hadn't.

The priestess moved too quickly.

The witches hunted.

Rufus hunted harder.

He didn't understand how they had discovered him, not yet.

A beggar's whisper?

A coin dropped where it shouldn't?

A woman selling herbs?

It didn't matter.

The four brothers met in the cellar, damp stone, no lamp, only breath.

One wanted to strike again. Another wanted to stay hidden.

Red Ring cut them off.

"We go. Now."

No argument.

They vanished from Rome that night, slipping through goat trails, moving without fire. A wolf crossed their path once; it looked, then walked on.

They crossed the Tiber before dawn.

Days passed in a shack hidden by rock and spring.

They lived like hunted animals: silent, watching the wind, burying whatever trace they made. Once they saw tracks, fresh, heavy, armed. Twice they smelled smoke.

Word reached them in broken whispers:

Rufus furious; guards doubled; bounty posted; slaves questioned.

Albina veiled and listening everywhere.

Rome boiled; the trail ran cold.

Red Ring waited. Recorded each breath. Counted each heartbeat as if it belonged to someone else.

He replayed the girl's death again and again, searching for the mistake.

He didn't see it yet. Didn't understand that Rome's eyes had shifted. That its women were no longer silent. That Albina now ruled the whispers.

He only knew one thing:

He would strike again.

And when he did, Rome would remember her name.

Albina.

Priestess.

Witch.

The woman whose house smelled of blood on the portico.

Chapter 102
THE COIN

The litter stopped at the gate of the Fulvian house.

No guards opened it. A slave girl did. Young. Careful. She blinked when she saw who stepped down.

Albina wore black. Veiled. Barefoot. Gold bells at her ankles. Her arms bare but ringed in copper and gold.

Only one figure followed her, Nisaya, the dark witch, hooded and silent.

No dancers. No guards. No fanfare.

Albina had only left the villa to travel within the walls of Rome once since she arrived. Until now.

They were shown through a quiet atrium. Painted walls. Polished tile. Statues of serious ancestors. A dozen wax masks of ancestors. The smell of honeyed wine and lavender smoke.

Albina moved slow, eyes steady. This house held ghosts, and she knew better than to speak carelessly in front of the dead.

Fulvia waited in a side room. She stood when Albina entered.

No one else came. No one else stayed.

Albina bowed. Then knelt. Her bells rang once.

Fulvia didn't speak.

She untied a leather pouch from her waist. Full. Heavy. She set it down on a small table between them. The silk cord still held the knot.

"I bring this with sorrow," she said. "Enough to buy three Suras."

Fulvia looked at her, face flat.

Albina reached into her robe and placed one coin on top of the pouch. Not Roman. Old gold. A lion's head stamped deep.

"I come to ask forgiveness." Albina lowered her eyes. "Apologies."

Fulvia didn't sit. Didn't touch the disc of gold.

"She was mine since I was little," Fulvia said. "She braided my hair. She knew every scar on my feet. She knew my sleep sounds. She knew my silences."

Albina didn't look up.

"She followed you," Fulvia said. "And she died for it."

"I know."

"I sent her to help you."

"She did help me."

Albina raised her eyes.

"She followed without question. She was brave. She was loyal. She was kind. I did not protect her. And for that, I ask your forgiveness."

Fulvia stepped forward.

"She was cut open like a goat. Hung up like a chicken at the butchers. They meant her to be a message."

Albina nodded. "And it was received."

Stillness thickened the air.

Fulvia stared at her. "What do you plan?"

"I will find the ones who did this. I will know their names. I will feed them to the Goddess."

Fulvia studied the gold again. Turned it over.

"Where's your guard?" she asked.

"I brought none."

"Why?"

"To show you, my sincerity. And my grief."

The space between them held.

Nisaya hadn't moved.

Fulvia finally sat.

Albina remained standing.

Albina didn't sit. She had not come in strength. She had come in shadow. And shadow must never rise above the wounded.

Fulvia picked up the coin. Weighed it in her hand.

"I forgive you," she said.

Albina closed her eyes. "Gratitude."

Fulvia added, "But forgetting her, never."

"I don't ask you to."

Fulvia set the lion-marked token in her lap. Her fingers closed around it.

"Swear it," she said. "I want that beggar killed."

Albina did not blink.

"I swear," she said. "By the twelve stones. By the lion. By the water and the fire and the name beneath my name."

Fulvia nodded once.

"Then go," she said. "And let me mourn."

Albina bowed. Deeper this time.

Then she and the witch turned and left.

No one followed. No voices rose behind them.

By the time the litter pulled away, the coin still sat warm in Fulvia's hand. She didn't move for a long time.

Sempronia found her in the tablinum. The foreign coin sat on the desk. Fulvia hadn't moved in a long time.

"She came in black," Fulvia said.

"I heard."

"Veiled. No guards. Just one witch."

Sempronia crossed the room. She didn't sit. "Dangerous."

"She knows."

Sempronia looked at the pouch still unopened. "Did you count it?"

"No."

Sempronia studied her daughter's face. Fulvia's hair was pinned high, but a strand had fallen loose. She hadn't fixed it. Her fingers rested near the lion-marked gold, not touching it now.

"She bowed," Fulvia said. "She knelt."

Sempronia said nothing.

"She swore by her gods. By her name. She took responsibility."

Sempronia finally sat. "Good."

"She asked for my forgiveness."

"Did you give it?"

Fulvia looked up.

"I said I forgive her. But I told her I won't forget."

Sempronia nodded once. "That was correct."

A pause.

Fulvia's voice lowered. "She brought no guards because she knew it would offend me."

"She brought no guards," Sempronia said, "because she knew no one would touch her."

Fulvia was quiet a long time.

Then: "She loved her. I saw it."

Sempronia replied, "She rules her house. Love or not, that death weakened her."

"She won't show it."

"No," Sempronia said. "But it's there. Grief has its uses."

Fulvia stood. Walked to the window. Rome burned under the sun, tile, smoke, the hum of the street.

"She looked different today," Fulvia said. "Not like a goddess. Like a woman. A woman who had lost something."

Her veil had clung to her face when she entered, still damp from the walk. Not from rain. From sweat. From heat. From mourning. Her ankles bore dust. Her eyes, rimmed dark. Not painted. Real. Fulvia had never seen her look small. Until today.

"And so have you."

Fulvia turned from the window.

"I want to help her."

Sempronia raised an eyebrow.

"I mean it."

"I believe you," Sempronia said. "But wanting and helping aren't the same."

"She's sworn vengeance."

"So have we," Sempronia said.

A silence.

Fulvia returned to the desk. Picked up the token, again. Held it flat in her palm. She looked at her mother.

"Then let's make it cost."

Chapter 103
THE SENATE ERUPTS

C old light poured through the high windows.

Marble underfoot. Red hems at every bench. Eyes everywhere.

No laughter. Only the scrape of sandals and the low grind of voices.

Caesar entered first with Rufus just behind him. Crassus followed, the chain of command glinting like a drawn blade. They took their seats. Silence rippled through the Curia like a tide pulling back before the break.

Then Cato rose.

The same black mourning toga. The same clenched jaw that never softened, not even for wine.

His hair hung uncombed, eyes narrow and cold, as though fixed forever on some invisible horizon where virtue still breathed.

No one expected what came next.

"I rise not to speak of war or taxes," he began, "but of infection. A rot housed inside the very walls of this Republic."

The senators shifted. Murmurs broke like insects scratching in dark corners.

"A foreign woman lives among us," he said, lifting his chin. "Not here by merit, but by decree. She comes from the edge of the earth, where barbarians bow to idols, and women trade prophecy like bread. She keeps witches. Eunuchs. Painted girls. She dances, smokes, deceives the weak with trinkets of fire and song. The blood of Eastern monarchs stains her veins. She calls herself priestess..." His lip curled. "But to a false goddess."

A hiss of air. Heads nodded. Others watched Caesar. Others watched Rufus.

"She hides behind holiness as if it were armor," Cato continued, pacing. "Wears a red cloak to mask a red lie. She gathers our women, our citizens' wives, our daughters. She poisons them with talk of freedom, of female divinity." His voice rose. "This harlot they call Sibyl! This Clodia reborn! A snake in silk that makes herself the altar upon which our women kneel."

The Curia went still.

"She has bewitched one of our own," he said, voice sharpening to a blade. "A hero of the state. Rufus, the lion of the East... now keeps company with liars and whores."

Dozens of eyes turned.

Rufus sat motionless. Shoulders wide, face carved from restraint.

Caesar's gaze flicked sideways. Waiting.

Cato stepped down from the dais. "He is not to blame," he said, softening his tone like oil over a flame. "They say he slew lions, broke shields, defended the eagle at Dyrrachium. A soldier's soldier. But now?" His mouth twisted. "Now he sleeps under silk. Watches dancers instead of the horizon. A pet lion, tame and soft, feeding birds and cats like a widow."

Laughter cracked through the chamber, short, nervous, cruel.

Cato pretended pity. "We forgive him for his delusion. Soldiers are simple. They see loyalty and call it love." He swept his hand toward the benches. "But we, who swore oaths to this Republic, know better."

The murmurs swelled. Cicero whispered to Crassus. A young senator laughed too loudly, then froze when Caesar's eyes touched him.

Rufus's fingers brushed the bench edge. Once. Twice.

His jaw stayed locked. His silence louder than any roar he'd ever loosed in battle.

Cato pressed on, relentless. "She has gold. Spies. Witches. If she bears children, they will be born above the Senate itself. Sons who suckle on blasphemy and claim the sword with one hand and the altar with the other."

His fists trembled. For a heartbeat, it looked like madness instead of virtue.

Crassus coughed. Cicero looked away.

The chamber shifted, no longer laughter but unease.

Eyes slid toward Caesar, measuring how far the old lion had gone.

Caesar didn't move. Stillness was its own verdict.

Cato's voice cracked. "This is what happens when men abandon duty for comfort. When our best warriors kneel to foreign flesh. When Roman virtue lies under Eastern perfume. I call for her expulsion from Rome. I call for the cleansing of this corruption..."

He drew breath for another strike...

and Rufus stood.

The sound was small, a man rising, but it cut through every whisper.

Cato turned, startled.

Rufus's voice came low, steady.

"Cato."

The chamber froze.

Even the pigeon high in the rafters stopped cooing.

"You speak of infection," Rufus said. "Of rot. Of foreign women and lost virtue.

Tell us... how well did you preserve yours?"

A pulse moved through the benches. Cato blinked, thrown.

Rufus stepped forward one slow pace.

"Or have you forgotten Atilia?"

The name struck harder than any sword.

Atilia, his first wife. The one he divorced for infidelity.

Every man in that chamber knew.

"You condemn my house, yet could not hold your own," Rufus went on.

"I house wild women, yes. But I do not drive them to another man's bed. I keep her in mine."

A gasp. A nervous chuckle that died halfway out.

Rufus's gaze did not waver. "You preach of virtue because you lost it, and the echo is all that answers you back."

Cato's color rose, hands shaking.

Rufus leaned slightly forward, voice sharp enough to draw blood.

"He who cannot rule his own house," he said, "should not speak of the Republic's, or mine."

The silence afterward was living, breathing, watching.

Cato's mouth opened, then closed.

He turned away, face raw with fury, every inch of him trembling.

Rufus sat again. Calm. The marble under his palm cool and solid.

No one moved for a long time.

Caesar's gaze found Cato's.

No words, just the kind of silence that marks the first cut.

Cato's voice came again, shaking, desperate to recover the high ground. "If Rome forgets her virtue, she dies!"

No applause.

Only parchment rustle and the scrape of a sandal leaving the floor.

One senator stood and left. Another followed.

The rest looked anywhere but at Cato.

Above, the pigeon cooed again.

Cato turned away, unaware he'd already been condemned, not by decree, but by patience.

Caesar and Rufus left the Curia in silence.

The sun hit the marble steps like a forge.

Senators spilled out behind them, whispering, robes brushing stone, sandals scuffing.

Caesar walked with hands behind his back, head bowed slightly.

Rufus followed, jaw tight from everything he'd swallowed.

At the foot of the steps, Caesar stopped. The noise of Rome pressed close, hooves, shouts, the ring of hammers on bronze.

"You did well," Caesar said.

Rufus said nothing.

"He wanted you to roar," Caesar continued. "To give him his martyrdom. You denied him that."

Rufus's voice came cold. "He called Albina a whore."

"He calls everyone a whore," Caesar said. "That's his virtue, the only one left to him."

Wind carried dust from the Forum.

"Patience, Rufus. I told you once, our enemies always hang themselves if we give them enough rope."

Rufus nodded, slow. "How long do we wait?"

"Until he climbs high enough for the fall to break every bone in his body."

Rufus laughed.

They started walking again. Two shadows long over the stones.

Behind them, the Senate guards closed the great bronze doors.

The sound echoed like a tomb sealing.

Rufus looked back once. Cato still inside, arguing with a clerk, finger stabbing at the air.

Caesar's voice came low. "Let him talk. Every word feeds the fire under his own feet."

They reached the fork at the Basilica Aemilia.

Caesar turned uphill toward his house. Rufus faced the winding street that dropped toward the Subura.

"Go home," Caesar said. "Spend time with her. Keep your temper. We'll have our turn."

Rufus nodded once.

He would.

But first, he had dinner plans at the house of Claudius.

Chapter 104
HUNTRESS

Palatine Hill, Rome

Cato's fury still clung to Rufus's skin when he stepped out of Caesar's shadow and crossed the Forum. The stones held heat from the day; arguments and insults drifted like smoke behind him. He kept walking. Past marble. Past murmurs. Past hands pointing at the young hero Rome claimed to own.

Claudius's villa rose ahead, lamps low, columns sweating resin, laughter spilling out like cheap wine. Servants in the doorway stiffened when they saw him. A soldier's stride at a dinner table always carried something sharp, even with no steel in hand.

Inside, the air tasted of smoke and half-spoiled grapes. Incense struggled against the sweat of too many bodies. A brazier snapped in the corner; sparks licked upward and died.

Claudius sprawled across his couch, tunic sticking to his ribs, hair damp, cheeks flushed from wine that dulled his tongue more than his fear.

"Rufus!" he shouted, lifting a goblet he could barely hold. "Tell me, how many Parthians lie under your feet now? Ten thousand?"

Rufus sat straight. Back unyielding. Toga folded clean. He rested one hand on his knee and let silence answer for him. A soldier used his voice sparingly; words carried weight.

Across the room, Claudia leaned forward on her elbow.

Her beauty struck like torchlight.

Oiled arms. Gold stacked from wrist to elbow. Hair lifted high with pins sharp enough to wound. Her eyes caught his.

"They whisper you fight like Mars," she said, voice pitched low, intimate. "But do you dance?"

Rufus didn't blink and smiled. "I never required it."

Claudia smiled, slow, hungry. "Then you've never lived. A dance shows everything: where a man weakens; where he hungers."

Claudius slapped his leg. "I swear, girl, you'd rule the Senate in a week."

Rufus's lips moved barely a breath. "My hunger sits elsewhere. War; Albina; silence."

"I could teach you all three," she murmured.

She stood, letting the room watch the line of her body. She drifted behind him. Her perfume, myrrh and honey, brushed his breath. Her fingers hovered above his shoulder before making contact, light as a promise.

Claudia carried the kind of beauty poets lied for. Skin pale as temple marble. Eyes sharp with calculation. A smile that wanted to own, not charm.

"Perhaps the lion wants softer prey tonight," she whispered. Thumb brushing his collar, testing boundaries.

Lucullus coughed, old general, old scandals, eyes faded from too much wine and too much regret.

Rufus looked at him once. A soldier's glance. A reminder of what he'd never become.

He said, "I chase my own prey."

Her hand slipped away; her smile sharpened.

Claudius raised a brow. "She's brought senators to their knees. Even that little Egyptian princeling. No one ignores her."

"I hear her," Rufus said. "And I choose otherwise."

The room tightened around the answer.

Fulvia, Claudius's wife, lifted herself on one elbow. Her beauty quiet as winter water. Her voice precise enough to cut silk.

"Careful, Claudia. Your tongue wins applause in your brother's atrium, but this still belongs to men."

Claudia leaned closer to Rufus's ear. "I speak where I'm heard."

Fulvia rose without rush, dropped a curl of orange peel into the brazier. Sweet smoke rose, twisting between guests like a ghost.

"My cousin, who shares my name," Fulvia said lightly, "adores our soldier. She plans to wed him."

Rufus didn't look up from his untouched cup. "I plan no such thing."

"My cousin always gets her wish."

Claudia's eyes flicked, interest sharpened into strategy. "The one Antonius begged for? The girl who refused him? She's young. Clever. Beautiful." A pause. "And she hunts well."

Rufus met her gaze. "So do I."

Claudius lifted his cup. "To the lion. May Rome never tame him."

Rufus didn't drink.

He rose before the cup cooled.

Outside, the street smelled of figs, horses, and night soil. Moonlight pooled along the stones. His sandals struck a slow rhythm as he walked, heat easing from his chest.

During the meal, Claudius had let something slip, too loud, too drunk, too careless.

Antonius had whispered poison into Cato's ear.

The same poison hurled at him in the Senate.

Rufus thought of the girl who had refused Antonius. The one Fulvia mentioned. A huntress with a will sharp enough to bend Rome itself.

He allowed himself one breath of amusement.

Then it faded.

Rome bred hunters, from senators to sisters to girls with bright eyes and dangerous futures. Some hunted with gold and silk. Some with knives. Some with words sharper than steel.

Every hunter's name mattered.

He exhaled into the dark.

"Fulvia."

Chapter 105
ANTONY

Near the Temple of Tellus, Upper Esquiline Hill, Rome

Across the city, another man trained.

The girl he wanted belonged to someone else.

The man who shamed him once now walked Rome untouched.

And the fire in his chest refused to die.

The sun dragged long amber across the Antonius training yard. Heat clung to the stones. Flies circled. Sweat darkened the dust beneath Marcus Antonius's feet. He stood bare-chested, muscles slick, hair stuck to his forehead. His wooden gladius hammered the practice post in savage, tireless rhythm. Straw burst with every strike, drifting like husks of crushed bone.

Gaius leaned against the wall, arms folded, face carved from shadow.

Lucius lounged on a bench, tossing grapes into the air, missing half.

"You'll kill the post," Gaius said, voice flat.

Marcus didn't stop. "Shut up."

Lucius snorted. "He's right. That dummy died hours ago."

"He hasn't," Marcus growled. "He still walks."

The name hung unspoken.

It didn't need to be spoken.

In the Antonius house, his shadow lived in the silence.

Gaius spat dust. "Years have passed. Let it go."

Marcus struck again, harder. Sweat sprayed. Breath tore from his chest. "Did you forget how he made us look? Humiliated us in front of Pompey's son, in front of the Juli..."

"I remember my nose breaking," Gaius said. "I also remember the wine. You threw the first punch."

"And the second," Lucius added. "And the third."

Gaius shrugged. "Rufus threw the last."

Marcus hurled the gladius. It slammed into the post and dropped like a dead limb. "There were three of us."

"Doesn't change the truth," Gaius said. "We picked a fight we never should have picked."

"We were drunk," Lucius added. "He wasn't. He wakes up at dawn and trains hard every day like the gods owe him something."

Marcus glared at the post until the edges blurred. "He made us a joke."

"We made ourselves the joke," Lucius said. "He just refused to laugh."

Silence thickened.

Lucius cracked another grape between his teeth. "You know who's not laughing? Clodius. His sister tried to snare Rufus."

Marcus looked up.

Lucius grinned.

"At that party on the Palatine," Lucius said. "Claudia, the pretty one. Oiled arms. Gold everywhere. She pushed herself at him."

"He stepped away," Gaius said. "Fast."

Marcus's jaw tightened.

Lucius tossed another grape. "You'd have taken her. Don't pretend otherwise."

Marcus didn't answer. He didn't need to.

He remembered something else, the first time Clodia had chased Rufus years ago on the Campus Martius. She hated him for turning her down, and still wanted him more. Marcus never forgot the look in her eyes.

Two nights ago at Lucullus's dinner, Marcus watched her again, married now, still venomous with beauty, and saw the moment she slid too close to Rufus. The light hand on his wrist. The smile that promised anything.

Rufus never moved.

Never blinked.

Never cared.

And then Fulvia.

Marcus once dreamed she might choose him, white-haired, blue-eyed, born from a line older than half the Senate. He watched her once across the Forum and imagined her hand on his arm.

Then she saw Rufus.

And everything ended.

Fulvia told her brother she had no interest in Marcus Antonius.

None.

She had already chosen. Quiet. Firm. Final.

Marcus felt every word like a blade pressed under the ribs.

He sat later at the fountain, breath shallow, gladius beside him. The post stood broken in the yard, straw spilling like entrails across the ground.

His tunic reeked.

Borrowed. Torn in a brawl two nights ago.

Once, he wore purple trim.

Tonight, he wore another man's sweat.

Gaius's voice still echoed.

Lucius's laughter still stung.

Every memory gnawed him from inside.

His father's words pulsed like poison:

Antonius blood commands; it does not kneel.

If that were true, why did Rome kneel for Rufus?

Rufus with his Civic Crown.

Rufus with the lion pelt.

Rufus who walked like a war-god and made the streets part without speaking.

And Fulvia never even looked at Marcus now.

Marcus lifted the gladius, set his stance. His breath steadied. His muscles shook from hours, but he forced them into rhythm.

He didn't train to kill Rufus.

Not yet.

He trained so that when Rufus saw him next, he would see someone equal.

Or someone worse, someone shaped by hate instead of honor.

He trained because Rufus had taken something he never wanted... until someone else wanted it more.

At dinner, Gaius passed wine without looking at him. Lucius flirted with the oil girl. Marcus stared at his plate until the torches blurred.

Their mother watched him across the table.

Once she had called him her lion.

Now her gaze slid past him to the wall.

He rose before the meal ended and stepped into the street.

Lamps kindled along the Via Sacra, flames trembling in the wind. Boys played legionaries near the basilica, reenacting battles in the dust. One wore a ring of oak leaves and shouted:

"I'm Rufus!"

Wooden sword raised.

Victorious.

Admired.

Marcus didn't slow.

Didn't turn.

Didn't breathe until he reached the shadows beyond the lamps.

They would remember his name one day.

Not because he was Antonius.

But because he would burn down anything that blocked his path.

Even gods fall when men have nothing left to lose.

Even Rufus.

Even Fulvia.

The night seemed to watch him as he walked.

And the dark felt suddenly very awake.

Chapter 106
THE BONA DEA

The scrolls came sealed in wax, hand-delivered by temple runners. The summons carried no softness: the women of Rome, to the rites of Bona Dea. No men. No exception.

Albina read the line twice. Old Republican script, elegant and controlled. She warmed the seal over a lamp; red wax slid, one narrow river down the lifeline of her palm. The pain felt right: a mark for the goddess.

That night, she prepared.

White linen. No gold. No bells. Hair bound hard and high; a crown of black rope pinned tight. Her girls wrapped her without song. Zarmina watched from the corner; Nisaya crushed herbs in a stone bowl until the air held bitter smoke.

Rufus waited near the inner gate.

"You don't have to go," he said.

Her gaze met his; steady, level. "I do."

He accepted that with a sharp nod; stepped aside. No more words.

She entered the litter. Curtains dropped. The house fell behind.

Caesar's villa burned against the hill like a low, contained fire. Torches along every wall. Laurel hung thick. Smoke of myrrh and pine resin rolled through the colonnades.

The Rites of Bona Dea.

Women filled the place wall to wall: patrician matrons, senators' widows, priestesses, Vestals, young wives, old crones, girls barely blooded. Sandals whispered over stone. Bangles chimed. A thousand small prayers moved like a hush under the roof.

No male sandal crossed that threshold. No male slave. No male animal. Even the household statues of gods carried veils over their carved faces.

Albina stood inside the inner ring. Bare feet on cool stone. Her witches and dancers stood near. The altar ahead: garlands, bowls of grain, a covered image of the goddess. The air tasted of wine and crushed laurel. She felt something old and coiled wake inside the house; the goddess liked crowds.

Purification first: hands in water, smoke over hair, a simple chant. Voices braided together.

Then the music: flutes, soft drums, the slow chant of women who carried Rome's future inside their ribs.

The first shift came as a ripple; heads turned, voices dropped.

A stranger in the press of bodies. One more white gown; one more braided head; one more soft-voiced "sister." Yet the rhythm around her warped.

Too tall. Shoulders wrong. Hands wrong. A jaw that didn't sit easy above the throat. Feet that worked the floor like a soldier, heel first.

Whispers crawled through the hall.

Who?

Do you know her?

Whose cousin?

Then a voice cut high and sharp. "Uncover her face!"

Hands grabbed at the stranger's veil. Cloth tore. A wig slid sideways. Lamplight hit rough stubble; fear widened eyes that knew no birth bed, no monthly pain.

He did not belong.

Publius Clodius Pulcher, wrapped in stolen silk, stood before the altar of a goddess who received only women.

The hall split.

One woman screamed. Another lunged. Cups flew; sacred wine spattered the floor. A priestess clawed at her own cheeks until four women held her arms. A Vestal dropped where she stood; another tore at her veil as if fire crawled inside it.

Albina didn't move. She watched him fully.

A man walking upright under a roof that had never accepted a man. A smirk half-formed, already turning to panic. Perfume clung to his throat, male sweat under it, cheap powder on top. A small, sour smell of fear worked through the incense.

Someone hurled a bronze cup; it struck his jaw with a flat ring. He flinched, grabbed the torn gown, stumbled sideways. Hands reached; nails raked; curses in Latin and Greek and older tongues slammed into him. He fought like a trapped dog and burst through a side door, scraped himself over a wall, and vanished into Caesar's garden.

Silence did not fall.

The silence shattered.

Women sobbed. Some fell to their knees, retching. One cried, over and over, "She saw him, she saw him, she saw him," meaning the goddess, meaning the altar, meaning something inside herself now soiled. A circle of matrons huddled around the covered image, arms outstretched as if rival shields.

Albina stepped forward until she stood within arm's length of the altar. Her heart hammered; her face remained still.

The smell in the room changed: incense, sweat, terror, shame. A private sanctuary ripped open by a laughing mouth in borrowed silk.

She reached out. Her hand hovered above the altar cloth, then closed back into a fist. No touch. Not tonight.

In her own language, under her breath: "He has walked on your blood. I saw. I remember."

The goddess listened.

Albina returned before dawn.

Rose light licked the Caelian hill. The gates parted; the villa's courtyard lay hushed.

Her robe hung crooked, one shoulder bare; dust darkened the hem. Her hands had gone raw from the washing basins at Caesar's house; cold water, hot water, more water, none of it enough. The skin on her knuckles cracked red where she had scrubbed.

Rufus stepped from the shadow of a column. "Albina..."

She passed him like smoke.

Past him, past the girls waiting with questions, past Zarmina and Nisaya with their bowls and herbs. Her footsteps carried straight to her suite. The door shut.

The bolt dropped once; the sound rang through the quiet like a hammer on stone.

No one heard her voice for two days.

A jug shattered once: sharp crack, then ceramic rain. A low sound followed, pain or prayer, cut off halfway. Then nothing.

Rome held its breath with her.

News thickened the air in the streets.

Caesar sent Pompeia away with one line: A wife of Caesar must remain above suspicion. No trial. No long speech. Just that, and the marriage cracked.

Clodius stood before a court soon after; accusations flew; witnesses shouted. Money moved in the dark. Juries swayed. Verdict: acquittal.

No guilt, they said.

The women of Rome heard that and understood; guilt had no vote in that chamber.

Pain settled over the city in a slow, choking veil. Midwives whispered of sudden losses; of women who had carried children full term once and now couldn't hold them a month. Temples found more foundlings at their gates; small bundles left before sunrise, nameless, silent, some breathing, some already beyond reach. Old superstitions crawled up from the dirt: children conceived that night carry a stain; better no child than a cursed one.

No one counted. No one could.

But every courtyard carried at least one woman who stared at her own belly with dread where joy had lived before. The fear moved through Rome's womb like a sickness: doors shut; curtains stayed drawn; songs for newborns fell quiet.

The wound reached further than law. It cut into the one place Rome had guarded for women alone and showed them a man's laugh behind a veil.

That scar would sit under the city's skin for a lifetime.

On the third day, Albina came out.

The garden air tasted of rosemary and damp earth. The twelve ancient statuettes waited in their place; the new stone Sibyl, lion-chariot, outstretched arms, watched from her niche.

Albina walked barefoot to the altar. Hair unbound, falling in a black curtain down her back. Eyes ringed dark; not from paint. From wakefulness.

She set a small carved figure beneath the Sibyl's wagon: a lioness, ribs scarred, standing anyway. Driftwood, smoothed by years of water. The grain caught the first beam of sun.

Albina knelt. Smoke from Zarmina's brazier curled over her shoulders.

She spoke in her desert tongue; each word landed like a stone in a bowl.

Zarmina gave the Latin after each short phrase, voice steady:

"No stranger shall cross holy ground again."

"Only those marked, those we know."

"Only those the goddess accepts."

"Men who seek entry must change; flesh and soul; or stay outside forever."

A long, rolling ululation rose from the witches; the sound shook the leaves. Then silence dropped hard.

Rufus watched from the far portico. He did not step closer; distance suited this. His fists stayed clenched so tight the knuckles blanched. Veins stood in his forearms like cords.

He listened to each translated line; stored them like orders.

He would remember.

Later, under the Senate roof, Clodius tried to walk like a man in control again.

He joked. He smiled. Words oiled his tongue. He pushed blame toward servants, toward shadows, toward misunderstanding; anything except his own feet in that forbidden house.

Rufus moved through the crowd of togas without hurry.

No drawn steel. No raised voice. Just a man with a Civic Crown's right to speak and a soldier's right to judge.

He stepped into Clodius's space: close enough to smell the cheap wine under the perfume, close enough to count the pulse at his neck.

Clodius's sentence died halfway; lips still shaped sound, no air behind them. His eyes climbed from Rufus's chest to his face and met a gaze that had looked down from ships at hordes of cut throat pirates, from ramparts in the East, from the line between life and death a hundred times.

Rufus said nothing.

No curse. No warning. Just that quiet, measuring stare.

Around them, conversations tangled and thinned; more heads turned. Men who had laughed at the acquittal now watched the space between the two like a drawn bow.

Clodius stepped back first.

He swallowed; his tongue worked along his teeth; a brittle smile tried to grow and failed. Wine sloshed against the lip of his cup.

Rufus turned away; toga whispering along the floor; no backward glance.

In a city drunk on words, that silence carried more weight than any public threat.

Albina had promised the goddess memory. Rufus carried the other half of that vow in his bones.

Not every knife cuts skin; some cut futures.

Chapter 107
THE STORY OF OTIS

A light wind passed over the courtyard. Albina stood in the doorway of the garden room, arms bare, breath shallow. She hadn't eaten since the sweet bread at dusk. Her stomach twisted, not pain yet. Just a tightness she couldn't explain. A heat in her chest. A pull behind her eyes.

Zarmina the Red lit three sticks of incense near the lion mosaic. One bent slightly. Bad sign. Nisaya snapped it in half and threw the omen into the brazier.

"Go lie down," Zarmina said.

Albina didn't answer. Her body still bled each month. Regular. Strong. But now, nothing. Two nights. Then three. Her hands felt strange, full of pressure. Her ankles stayed warm long into the night.

A girl approached from the corridor. She carried a wooden bowl. She stepped forward.

"From the dock," the girl said.

Inside the bowl, mud, straw, a crude clay idol the size of a cat's head. It had no eyes. No mouth. But the hair had been pressed into place with care. Someone had added bits of green glass to the surface. A tiny handprint marked the back.

She took the delicate statue in silence.

Zarmina approached from the shadows. "His name is Otis. We keep him?"

Albina looked down at the figure.

"Not in the shrine," she said. "Not near the girls."

She turned and handed it back.

"But somewhere close."

Tirzah stood nearby, watching. She didn't speak, but her brow creased.

Zarmina noticed.

"You don't know him," she said. "That's Otis."

Tirzah looked from the idol to Zarmina.

"Dock gods. Boat gods. Poor people carve them from firewood, stone, whatever they have. The most beautiful one I've seen was made from fish bones. Truely magnificent. They carry them in sacks, sleep with them in their arms. Not Roman. Not Parthian. Older."

Tirzah looked again at the statue. "Is it dangerous?"

"No," Zarmina said. "But it remembers. And it watches. That's enough."
    There, in the servant's area, embedded into the wall, an empty shrine sat head high. Zarmina placed Otis there and left a silver coin as tribute.
    The next morning, a warm crust of bread was added by someone.

Without speaking, Albina moved slowly to the corner couch and sat. Her hand rested just below her ribs. Not pain. Not yet. But something. A tightness she couldn't name.

She leaned her head back and closed her eyes.

Outside, smoke curled above the brazier.

The dock women had left flowers.

Zarmina crushed three seeds in a stone bowl and added oil. Nisaya the Black began the chants.

Albina heard none of it.

She drifted, breathing slow.

From her fingers, the smallest drop of blood had begun to rise.

It wasn't time. Not yet.

But something had changed.

Chapter 108
THE OLDEST STORY

The oldest story. Before Rome. Before Troy. Before fire caught the first dry grass.

She walked barefoot, alone, carrying twelve stones and a black cloth.

Each stone held a name no man could speak. Each name, a goddess that once ruled the earth.

She hid the stones in a cave where no sun reached. She sealed it with her blood.

Then she waited.

She aged backwards. Hair blackened. Bones straightened. Eyes lit like twin torches in smoke.

When men first came, she met them at the edge of the forest.

They bowed. They begged. They gave her their sons, their silver, their secrets.

She gave them one thing: a voice.

The Sibyl does not speak for gods. She speaks as one.

In firelight, she told them their futures. By moonlight, she tore open their past.

She danced on ash and made it holy.

Kings fell at her feet. Queens kissed her hands. Slaves called her mother.

Warriors carved her name into shields.

When armies marched, she vanished. When they died, she returned.

Each generation, a girl is born with her mark. Eyes of amber. Hair like night. A voice that cuts.

No school. No scripture.

She is not taught. She remembers.

The twelve stones call her. She answers.

Her name is Albina.

And she is pregnant from a lion.

And she could not be happier.

Chapter 109
TRIUMPH

The Via Sacra, Rome. 61 B.C.

The sun rose over Rome like a new gladius, sharp and gleaming.

For two days, Rome exploded in color, noise, and ritual. Crowds pressed into every open space. Columns were wrapped in garlands. Trumpets sounded from balconies. Every road and alley flowed like blood toward the Forum.

A Triumph.

Pompey Magnus, conqueror of the East, entered in glory. No one staged a spectacle like he did. He oversaw every detail.

They came first, the floats, painted scenes of battles and faraway places. Then the wagons. Hundreds of them.

Filled with gold, armor, ivory, scrolls, statues. Caged tigers. Painted slaves. Incense. Draped carpets. Broken thrones. Prisoners marched in chains, eyes lowered, walking behind signs that bore their names and crimes. Spoils of empire.

Then the generals.

Then the standard-bearers.

Then came Rufus. Proud and glorious.

He stood tall on his own float. A gift. A statement.

He wore his full aquilifer uniform; the lion-skin mane cascading over his shoulders, gladius sheathed at his side. The Civic Crown sat above his brow, framed by bronze and sunlight. His float bore painted panels: one showed him raising the eagle standard on a battlefield; another showed him climbing a wall through fire. A slave holding high the famous shield impaled by a hundred arrows.

Rufus held a small bow in one hand, a quiver of colored arrows at his side. Each arrow bore a silk ribbon.

He began to fire them into the crowd. The ribbons unwound and left streamers of colors.

Many red. Many green. Many gold. One after the other.

Then, one blue.

Only one.

Rufus found the ribbon in his mother's workshop. The perfect blue. The color of that white-blond haired girl's eyes. Made in case she was there.

Fulvia stood in the front row, lifted on a polished wooden platform with her mother, Aurela, and Julia. Her dress was white with deep blue embroidery. Her hair braided high.

Rufus saw her and fired.

The blue arrow sailed high then down toward her like a dart from the gods. She caught it mid-air.

Gasps. Smiles. Julia elbowed her gently. Her mother whispered, "That was no accident."

Fulvia didn't speak.

She held the ribbon and smiled.

For a breath, he forgot the crowd. The noise fell away. The float seemed to glide in silence.

Rufus gave a small smile, nodded at her, and waved.

He wanted to acknowledge her, and to be acknowledged by her. Afterall, she had traveled with him, in his mind, every step of the way. Her memory had calmed him and kept him warm a thousand times. The ribbon was a small gift of thanks.

Far above, on the balcony of the Caelian villa, Albina stood with Zarmina and Nisaya.

She wore a pink robe loose around her belly. Her hand rested there.

She saw the float glide through the crowd. Watched Rufus. Noticed the flick of his eyes, and his wave toward the raised platform where Fulvia stood.

Albina said nothing.

But her fingers tightened on her belly.

She turned from the railing and stepped back into the shrine chamber.

There, in silence, she placed a carving, a lion cub, at the Sibyl's feet.

"He will walk these streets," she said. "And they will not forget him."

Pompey came last, riding a chariot drawn by four white horses.

He wore a golden cloak. His laurels flashed in the sun. Behind him stood a slave, whispering into his ear; "You are only a man. You are only a man."

Pompey waved to the crowd. He passed Caesar's private viewing perch and saluted. The Senate rose.

As his chariot rolled past Rufus's float, Pompey turned slightly and nodded once.

Rufus did not nod back. He smiled instead.

He stood still, holding the empty bow.

That night, Fulvia sat at her dressing table.

She opened a cedarwood box and placed the blue ribbon inside.

She closed the lid.

Across the city, Albina stood alone in the shrine.

She lit a single flame.

She whispered to it, "He is already here."

And Rufus?

He fell asleep in the atrium chair. His boots still on, head back, the sounds of the crowd still echoing in his ears.

Two women dreamed of him.

A lion stirred in the belly of Rome.

And Rome would never forget.

Chapter 110
THE LION CUB

Caelian Hill, Rome

The morning after the Triumph, the villa felt quiet but not still. It listened.

Albina rose before the sun. She moved without sound through the halls, her bare feet on polished tile, long robe trailing behind her. The villa had been built for Roman men. But it had changed. It breathed her scent now. Her colors. Her people. Her Goddess. Her voice. This was her home.

Into the garden shrine, before the dawn, barefoot.

The marble still held the chill of night. A faint curl of smoke rose from the bronze basin where oil had burned low through the evening. The statue of the Sibyl loomed above her, arms open, lions pulling her chariot. Twelve figures rested in the cradle, ancient, worn smooth with reverence.

Albina knelt. One hand touched the mosaic floor. The other moved to her belly.

She didn't need a test. Or Zarmina. Her body had spoken.

The moment Fulvia caught the ribbon, something shifted, not injury, not pain. Just a soft break inside. the visions had begun take form. As the women planned, the marriage would happen.

Albina felt a jealous surge.

***

Zarmina entered moments later.

She carried a cloth bundle of dried flowers and cut fennel. She did not look surprised.

"It's a boy," she said.

Albina nodded. "Yes."

No tears. No smile. Just stillness.

Zarmina placed the bundle near the flame. "The gods chose this house."

"No," Albina said. "I did."

Zarmina smiled and said nothing.

***

The steward found himself summoned at dawn. One of her newly arrived specialty slaves, the eunuch knew the ways of Albina's people.

He bowed deeply, adjusting his tunic. Albina stood before the fountain, wet hair clinging to her shoulders, wrapped in a purple robe trimmed with lion fur.

"You will commission a larger basin for the garden," she said. "Marble. Eastern style. Twelve steps around it, for the sisters."

He nodded, scribbled notes.

"Double the storage in the herb room," she continued. "And a second bathing chamber. It must be warmer, with cedar."

"Anything more, Domina?"

She looked at him without blinking.

"Yes. Begin clearing the old wine room. That will become the birthing chamber. Have the roof opened. Sunlight must reach the floor."

He hesitated. "The room's layout? It should be Roman squares, yes?"

"No," she said. "Round edges. Not Roman. Let it breathe."

"Yes, Domina."

He left quickly.

***

Inside the eastern wing, Nisaya the Black ground bone ash into honey.

Her hands moved like a ghost's, silent, fluid, precise. She prepared three mixtures. One for strength. One for pain. One for protection.

Zarmina the Red prepared the birthing bed herself.

They spoke in their native tongue.

"She is calm," Nisaya said. "Her spine rests different. Her steps changed."

"Yes, already her dreams have shifted, closer now, to blood, flesh, water."

"She is no longer becoming. She is." Zarmina added.

"No child born in this house will die young. All will reach adulthood. All mothers will survive childbirth."

"Yes."

***

Later that day, Fulvia returned.

She came quietly, alone.

Albina met her in the garden.

Neither spoke at first.

Fulvia unwrapped a small carved box of olive wood. Inside lay half of the blue ribbon folded twice.

"I caught it," she said.

Albina nodded.

Fulvia closed the lid. "The other half stays with me."

"Of course."

They stood under the arbor beside the statue.

"Rome is watching," Fulvia said.

"They always were," Albina answered.

Fulvia's gaze lingered on her for a moment.

Then she stepped forward, placed the ribbon box at the feet of the Sibyl, and bowed.

Albina did not smile. But she did not look away.

The two young women, as different as day and night, stood proudly looking at the other. Battle lines were drawn.

A gust of wind blew dust and dried leaves across their feet and lifted their dresses around them.

***

Rufus trained with his shield brothers that morning.

He broke three javelins on stone and cut open his forearm on a sharp-edged target. He didn't notice.

He had begun thinking of Fulvia. Just a little. The blue ribbon. Her quiet hands. The look on her face when she caught his gift.

But that was all.

He hadn't seen Albina's eyes on him from above. Hadn't felt the power behind that silence.

He didn't see the movement, Romes's women already circling, already hunting. The women had begun their war. He didn't know that Fulvia's family had spoken with Aurellia. He didn't know that his mother and aunt spoke with her as well. Or that a dozen marriage alliances now curled around his name like vines on a fence.

He trained. Ate. Bathed. Slept.

And the rest of Rome moved around him.

***

In the shrine that evening, Albina burned a new mixture. Sweet, bitter, earthen.

The girls danced without sound. Their feet barely touched stone.

Fulvia watched from the portico, quiet. The rhythm was different here. The gods were not Roman. She realized as she left that his house followed someone else's law now.

Nisaya rubbed oil on Albina's feet.

Zarmina sat nearby, sharpening tools and counting days on a carved stick.

Albina stared into the flame.

"I want more watchers east," she said. "To Parthia. Armenia. The Caspian shore."

Zarmina nodded. "Already done."

"I want new girls from the ports. Smart ones. Watchful. Loyal."

"Yes."

"I want to know what happened to his brothers."

Zarmina finally looked up.

"We will find them."

***

The next morning, Albina walked along the edge of the fountain. The sun lit the garden gold. Her robe trailed in the water. She stopped beside the Sibyl's statue and placed a new figure in the cradle:

A lion cub.

Carved from rosewood. Small, perfect. Strong.

She knelt. Placed both hands on her belly.

"You will have his blood," she whispered. "But you will live by mine."

The girls bowed behind her. The witches watched.

And above, from the upper portico, Rufus stood, half in shadow, silent.

He didn't speak.

He didn't know.

But something in him stirred. Not a warning. Not yet. But something.

The Goddess would whisper to this child, but the mother would answer first.

The lion slept. But the lioness moved.

Chapter 111
THE FIRST WORD

The sun hung low over the Caelian Hill, washing the courtyard in pale gold. The air carried figs, olive oil, and crushed mint from the garden beds. Cicadas rasped in the trees. Rufus sat on the stone bench beside the pool, sharpening a blade against his thigh. The sound came steady and dry, a rasp of steel over whetstone, a sound that could lull or kill, depending on his mood.

He had fought half his life and still found peace in that rhythm, the pulse of steel.

Albina stepped from the shadows into the light.

Barefoot. Calm. The robe around her hips hung loose, tied once at the side. The color caught the fading light, red deepening toward black. Her eyes held something different, a new calm that he hadn't seen before. He stopped sharpening, rested the knife across his thigh, and looked up.

She didn't speak.

She crossed the courtyard's smooth stones, the sound of her steps light, unhurried. Her long hair brushed the silk at her back. When she reached him, she took his calloused hand and set it flat against her stomach.

He blinked once. Then again. The pulse in her belly met his palm.

Her voice came soft, almost lost beneath the sound of the fountain. "I carry your child."

The whetstone slid from his lap and hit the ground.

He looked at her, silent. The courtyard itself seemed to hold its breath.

"You're certain?" he asked at last.

Albina nodded, eyes unflinching. "A son."

He stood so fast the bench creaked behind him. His hand stayed where she had placed it, over the warmth of her belly. His eyes searched her face, found only truth.

"A son," he said again, testing the word as if it were a blade newly forged.

She smiled, faint and knowing. "That is what I believe."

He gathered her into his arms. His chin brushed her hair; his hands framed her back, her waist, her stomach. The scent of figs and pine clung between them.

"I will protect you," he whispered. "Both of you."

Albina's hands rested against his chest. "You already do."

He pulled back enough to look at her belly again. His voice lowered to a rough laugh. "My first child. My blood. My son."

His smile radiated brightly.

"Yes, well, we do not yet know for certain if it's a son" she said.

"Yes," he murmured. "We do. Or you would not have said it."

Her smile widened slightly. For her, that was joy in full.

When night came, he returned to the Latinus compound in the Subura, the old home of his line. Smoke from the hearth curled through the roof beams. His uncle and two cousins sat cross-legged by the fire, tossing knucklebones. His grandfather stirred a pot of lentils, muttering at the slow boil. Rufus entered without sound, then stood in the doorway until the firelight caught his face.

"She's with child," he said.

Every sound stopped. The dice froze in mid-air.

His uncle rose first, grinning. "Albina?"

Rufus nodded.

His grandfather set the ladle down, poured a cup of wine, and thrust it toward him. "About damn time," he said. "Double the guards before word spreads. A woman like that carries more than a baby; she carries enemies."

Rufus lifted the cup. "To my son."

The old man smirked. "Or daughter."

"Either way," Rufus said, "my joy breathes."

His father barked a laugh from the far corner. "And your balls work."

The room burst in rough laughter. The sound filled the old walls, shaking dust from the beams. For once, no one mentioned Caesar or the Senate or war. They drank until the pot burned.

Later, back at the villa, Rufus found Albina in the small shrine off the peristyle. A single oil lamp burned before the lioness carving. The flame caught the gold at her wrists and made her robe glow from within. He paused in the doorway, watching her move, small, measured gestures that seemed part of something older than Rome itself.

He came to her quietly, set his hands on her shoulders, feeling the warmth through the fabric.

"I told them," he said.

"I know," she replied without turning.

"They're proud."

"Are you?"

He smiled. "More than proud. I didn't think joy could weigh this much."

She turned to him. The flame painted her face in amber light.

"There will be dangers," she said.

"There always were." He hesitated, thumb tracing her collarbone. "Now they frighten me."

She placed his hand over her stomach again. "Then walk beside me unafraid."

He looked at her, thinking of the fields where men had died beside him, of the noise and smoke, and how all of Rome's blood now felt small compared to what stirred under his palm.

Albina whispered, "The goddess will bless him."

"She already has," Rufus said.

They stood together in the glow, the oil lamp sputtering, the air thick with scent of myrrh. Outside, the garden wind carried the faint ring of her dancers' bells.

He pressed his forehead to hers. Neither spoke. The silence held more meaning than any oath.

That night Rufus Latinus slept with both arms around her. The sound of her breath matched his own.

For the first time since his boyhood, he dreamed not of war, not of lions, not of the dying.

He dreamed of a child's laughter echoing down marble halls, and of a world he might one day leave whole.

Chapter 112
THE MOTHERS DECIDE

The olive trees swayed in a quiet rhythm. A breeze carried the scent of oranges and thyme through Caesar's shaded garden. Aurella sat across from her son, her hands folded neatly in her lap, as if she'd been waiting for years to speak this one truth.

"Fulvia's ready. As is her family."

Caesar poured wine, though he would not drink the sweet white. He swirled it and let it breathe.

"So is Rufus's family."

"Then don't wait," she warned. "Before your consulship ends. Let this be done."

He smiled.

Rome would have its symbol. He would bind the lion to the heart of the city.
***

The garden at Julia's house was louder. Fulvia, Julia, Calpurnia, and the daughters of senators lounged in a ring of cushions beneath a fig tree. A platter of olives sat untouched. Half the girls were barefoot.

Fulvia wore a simple white dress. Around her wrist, tied with care, was a thin strip of blue ribbon.

Julia reached over and tapped it.

"Always carrying that?"

Fulvia smirked. "He made a good shot."

"He didn't miss."

Calpurnia leaned forward. "And he will marry you?"

Fulvia shrugged. "He hasn't asked."

"He doesn't get to," said Julia. "Caesar does. So do our mothers."

The girls laughed, but they all knew that simple fact was true. Usually, patrician girls didn't get a choice.

So, Rufus not having a choice didn't concern them in the least.

***

The shrine garden glowed in the early morning haze.

Albina sat beside the fountain. Fulvia stood near her, arms crossed, watching the steam rise off the heated stones.

"You love him," Albina said.

Fulvia didn't answer.

"I knew before you did."

Still silence.

"You love him as well," Fulvia said.

Albina leaned forward, placed a lion cub figurine in a bowl of scented oil.

"I was never meant to keep him alone."

For a moment, her eyes darkened. Not just with jealousy, but something older. She had known since the first vision. Known what loving him would cost. But the Sibyl did not choose her path. She walked it.

Fulvia looked at her then. "I won't pretend to be what I'm not."

"Good, pretending doesn't last long in this world."

Fulvia lowered her gaze, not in shame, but in something close to reverence.

"We have to make this work." Fulvia stated.

Albina nodded in agreement.

They sat together. The fountain bubbled. The shrine watched. The shrine listened.

***

Rufus sat at his desk, shirtless, sweat on his arms. Tirzah brought a bowl of chilled mint water and set it beside him without speaking.

The steward appeared in the doorway.

"A scroll has arrived."

Rufus gestured. The man brought the message forward and left.

He recognized the seal.

Not Caesar's personal ring. The family mark.

His mother's. Aurella.

He broke the wax and unrolled the parchment.

You are summoned to the house of senator Gaius Fulvius Flaccus in three days. Go clean and dressed in Roman senatorial white. You are to marry his daughter. Caesar and your mother expect you to do your part.

Rufus leaned back. Exhaled. Looked up at the ceiling.

"What!"

"Jupiter's nuts."

He looked down at his hands. Callused. Scarred. Built for war, not marriage. He had dreamed of battlefields, not bedsheets and banquets. But Rome did not care for his damn dreams.

"And who is this girl I am to marry?"

***

He found Aurellia in her personal study. She was writing letters by lamplight, the shutters half-closed against the heat.

"You arranged it?"

She did not look up. "I did."

"Without asking."

"You would have said no."

"I still might."

Now she looked up. "You won't."

He paused. "I'm not ready."

"No one is. But she is. And so is Albina."

"I don't even know this girl."

"Oh, yes you do."

He stared at her.

Aurellia stood, crossed to him, placed her hand over his.

"You've been bred for Rome. This is Rome. You're the lion. She holds the key."

"Now, kiss my hand and go."

Rufus obeyed.

***

Aurellia stood still after Rufus left her study.

She stared at the scroll, still curling like a serpent. And then, quietly, she laughed.

She remembered the boy.

Years ago, when Rufus was small, she had kept him at her house for a few hours now and again. It was tradition for the patron's wife or mother to care for the children of loyal clients. But Rufus had been different.

He hadn't feared her, even though his father warned him of punishment if he misbehaved.

He asked questions no other child did. He'd once built a miniature siege tower from twigs and leather cord and tested it against her herb garden walls. She could still see his serious little face and red hair as he launched dried chickpeas at imaginary Gauls.

At the time her son, Caesar was being held for ransom by pirates. The worry had increased her melancholy.

She had known, even then, what would become of young Rufus. His destiny. His doom.

He would die alone, in pain and blood, laying in the cold mud of a ditch, far from home for the glory of Rome.

She'd wept once, silently, as he played in the dirt, unaware of her sadness.

Now he towered over her. Sharp-jawed. Muscled. Almost as striking as Caesar himself. As handsome as the rest of the men in his family.

***

The next day, Caesar summoned Rufus and his father.

They entered his chamber, lined with maps, weapons, and marble busts.

Caesar didn't stand.

"I've arranged your marriage," he said. "Congratulations. You're the last to know, and no, you can't fight your way out of this one."

Rufus blinked.

"I've heard, but Caesar, great one, I don't want to be..." he began.

His father's hand struck him hard across the cheek.

"You will always do what our honored patron commands."

The sting meant nothing. He'd taken worse in training. But the shame cut deeper. In front of Caesar. In front of his father. And he couldn't speak, not because he obeyed, but because he understood.

Rufus wisely kept quiet. Muttering only, "Apologies."

Caesar grinned. "For your impertinence, and your big mouth, I'll assign you to bring great gifts to both your bride and her mother."

The matter was settled.

***

That night, Rufus sat in the bath. Tirzah scrubbed his back.

The scroll rested on the marble ledge beside him, curled again, like a serpent.

Steam curled around his shoulders.

He stared forward, jaw tight.

Behind him, Tirzah's voice, soft, but sure.

"You're troubled. I'm here, I always am."

"Are your people's women as troublesome as ours?"

Tirzah gave a rare laugh.

"Every bit as troublesome."

Rufus smiled and whispered, "remove your dress and get in here with me."

Tirzah obeyed.

Chapter 113
THE HOUSE OF FULVIA

The House of the Fulvii, Quirinal Hill, Rome

The gates of the large and old money Fulvian estate opened in silence.

Rufus entered with his two half-brothers, both large, both silent. One carried a curved gladius, the other a short, thick staff. Both sword and staff given to the door man. Behind them came a young scribe and an assistant, each holding a sealed wooden chest. The rest of his large escort waited at a nearby tavern.

No one spoke as the men honored the household gods.

The sound of their boots against polished stone echoed down the corridor, heavy and deliberate, like war drums softened only by leather.

He wore pure white, his finest senatorial formal. His face unreadable.

The guards led them through the long corridor toward the atrium. Marble cooled under his feet. Water trickled from a lion's mouth at the center basin.

Fulvia's father, the great patrician Marcus Fulvius Naso, waited. A tall man, lean, blond. Whatever his thoughts were, they never reached his face.

So did her mother, Sempronia. The daughter of Lucius Sempronius Atratinus and Aemilia Paulla, both high patricians.

And her older brother, Gaius Fulvius Naso.

"Please, have a seat."

***

Rufus bowed slightly. "Gratitude for receiving me," and sat.

The mother offered a nod, formal, composed. The brother leaned in, elbows on knees.

"You've made an impression," the Naso said. "In Rome." The brother was tall, thin, and blond. He knew him, he grew up with Rufus's oldest brother.

Rufus said nothing.

"The crucifixion of that slave girl... bold." He picked at his nail. "The incident with Marcus Antonius years ago... memorable."

Still, Rufus said nothing.

The brother leaned back slightly. "Still quiet after all these years. Even when Marcus Antonius bled in the street, you kept quiet."

Rufus held his gaze. "He shouldn't have touched my sister."

The brother raised a brow. "And Claudia?"

"What about her? I didn't touch her."

"That's the point."

Rufus didn't respond.

"The girl you crucified?" Naso pressed.

"A thief," Rufus answered. "She stole from Albina."

"Oh yes, what about this Albina?"

"She's under my care."

"Care, is that what it's called?"

The brother had a disgusted look on his face.

Rufus looked down at his feet uncomfortably. Avoiding looking at this Naso. To hide his sudden rage at the brother's wasted attempt to shame him.

Silence returned.

The father cleared his throat.

"We've received Caesar's letter," he said. "And Aurellia's. And your mother and father's. My wife and I discussed it with our children. The match has been made. Fulvia's dowery is settled at three hundred silver talents. I will oversee its investment."

Rufus nodded once.

"Her role in your household, shall be second to no other female, including this Albina or any other. She shall manage your household, as she's been well trained to do, and as is expected. She will hold the keys. Her children with you shall be first heirs to your entire estate. You will draw up a will including these demands, and I and Caesar will witness. She must become a matron of high status. You will provide for all her needs, slaves, clothes, whatever."

"No objections," Rufus said.

The gifts remained in the background; unopened, unspoken.

***

A sound.

Light footsteps.

Fulvia entered the room in black, her long white-blonde hair braided down her back. She held a blue ribbon in her hand.

Rufus turned, saw her, and his eyes widened.

"You?" he murmured. No anger. Just surprise. Recognition. Then joy.

Fulvia smiled softly and teased. "You?"

He blinked.

You're the Fulvia?" He smiled open relief covered his face.

"I am, " Fulvia laughed.

She added. "The triumph. The arrow. The Campus Martius."

He nodded. "The horse race around the wall. I never knew your name."

"I'm also your sisters' best friend."

Fulvia sat next to Rufus. She smelled of herbs and spices. She filled out the black silk in exactly the right places. Her smile was infectious. Rufus forgot about her brother.

They talked and laughed. Time blurred.

***

The father gestured. "You may walk the garden."

They moved side by side beneath the arching green. The house faded behind them.

"You knew?" Rufus asked.

"Not at first. Then I hoped. Then I prayed."

They passed a fountain shaped like a boar.

"I didn't think I wanted to marry," he admitted. "But now..."

"You still don't," she replied. "But I do."

He smiled at that. "Good, because you're mine."

Fulvia smiled.

She lifted her wrist. The blue ribbon still tied.

"This was the only blue one," she said.

He touched it lightly. "Yes, I chose it. From Aurellia's collection. It was my mothers. I saw the color and thought of your eyes."

Fulvia looked up. "I know. Albina told me."

Rufus asked, "did she tell you that I think you are the most beautiful girl I've ever seen?"

She smiled.

They laughed.

***

They returned.

The chests were opened.

One held a carved box of sapphire jewelry; irregular and ancient, raw and beautiful. The other held a set of gold pins and brooches with crushed blue stones from the eastern desert. Rare. Definitely unique. The sapphires shimmered unevenly, like sea glass stirred from the bottom of an ancient tide. Albina had chosen this jewelry, from his vast collection taken from pirates, for their imperfections, for the way they caught the light without ever giving it back whole.

Both sets were priceless.

The mother gasped and put her hand to her chest.

Fulvia took the ribbon from her wrist and tied it to the lid of the first box.

"These are unbelievably gorgeous. Gratitude," a stunned Sempronia smiled.

Fulvia ran to Rufus, her ample breasts bouncing, and gave him a strong hug and kissed him deeply and with just enough passion to promise more soon.

"Gratitude my love," Fulvia purred.

"Fulvia... behave," her father warned with a hidden smile.

***

The family spoke longer that evening.

The mother praised his courage. The father admitted his doubts, then his respect.

"I know my blood is not good enough for your house," Rufus acknowledged. "Yours is too good. But the match matters. To Rome, and to me. I will do whatever is needed to insure Fulvia's well-being and our two family's future."

The father nodded. That was enough.

The brother said nothing.

***

Rufus returned to the villa long after dark.

The halls were quiet. One lamp still burned in the atrium.

Albina sat by the shrine, crushing herbs in a shallow bowl. She didn't look up.

The shrine smelled of basil and crushed fig leaves. A flicker from the oil lamp danced in Albina's amber eyes, though her gaze stayed fixed on the bowl. Whatever she was making, it mattered.

He crossed to her and knelt.

He placed a kiss against the round of her belly.

"Gratitude," he whispered. "For making this happen. They loved the jewelry you chose."

She said nothing.

"I love you," Rufus said.

But her hand touched the back of his neck.

And stayed.

Chapter 114
HIS ENEMY

The garden held its breath.

Rufus walked the narrow path between the trimmed myrtle hedges, past the still pool guarded by marble lions, past the bronze brazier that hadn't seen flame since spring. Last light clung to the walls, turning stone honey soft. Water spilled from the lion's jaw into the basin with a faint hush, cool enough to touch the air.

He wore a loose dark-red tunic, linen light against his skin, nothing on his feet. Warm stone pressed through bone and muscle. His left hand brushed his chest as he walked, habit, not vanity. His fingers found the two red chevrons stitched over his heart: the stripes of the Sons of Centurions. Old thread, rough under his thumb.

He hadn't worn that tunic in months.

Fulvia's brother, Naso, would have known the symbol at once. Would have stared. Would have hated what it meant.

Rufus moved to the stone bench beside the fountain and sat. The carved Mars sword spouted water into the pool, catching the last sun in a thin gold stripe. The air smelled of jasmine and pine resin, a clean scent, but never harmless.

He had learned long ago that beautiful places became dangerous places. Quiet places hid ghosts.

Tonight felt like both.

His fingers pressed the worn stitches again. Stretched fabric softened by years of training, sweating, bleeding. He had earned those marks young, first in drills, first in trials, first to kill, first to bleed.

His grandfather had pinned the stripes to this very tunic the day Rufus dragged an armed cavalryman off his horse in front of a Senate tribune. The arena roared. Rufus never looked at the crowd. He had only one focus in one place.

His grandfather's hand, calloused, heavy, warm as a brand, landed on his shoulder. A single nod. No praise. No lecture.

That silence had mattered more than an ovation.

He felt that hand still, some nights. Felt its weight. But the old man watched from a distance now. As if waiting to see what shape Rufus would take when Rome cut him open.

And Rome would. Soon.

He thought of Marcus Antonius.

The memory rose like heat from stone, three boys, older, drunk, circling his little sister, Latina, during a feast. Their words sharp. Cruel. Cowardly. Rufus had stepped in. Fifteen, unafraid, already forged.

He threw the first punch. And the last.

Lucius Antonius spat teeth. Gaius staggered with a broken nose. Marcus took one good elbow at Rufus's ribs, then Rufus lifted him clean off the ground and hammered him into the marble tiles hard enough to rattle lamps. Two fists to the temples. Fast. Brutal. Over.

No roar. No victory.

Rufus had walked away while the Antonius brothers clawed for breath.

Now Marcus climbed through Rome like rot through timber. The defiler, Clodius, at his shoulder, his own older brother Sextus eager for a fight, and Naso whispering poison in whatever ear leaned closest. A pack of ambitious jackals circling power.

Rome loved men like that.

But Rome feared men like Rufus.

He shifted on the bench. Watched a moth circle the torch by the gate, flutter, swoop, suicide. The flame bent, then straightened. The night thickened.

Albina would be in her chamber. Perhaps asleep. Perhaps in trance. Her witches had warned him weeks ago that the city stirred in ways that had nothing to do with politics.

He looked at his hands, scarred knuckles, faint burns from training, a new blister from reins. Hard hands. Earned hands. Hands that killed and built and steadied.

Lucius's hands, the crippled genius brother, were nothing like his. Long fingers, ink-stained, trembling when touched, brilliant when left alone. Lucius could sketch a ship's hull, calculate weight and drag faster than most men signed their name. Rufus thought of him now, bent over a wax tablet somewhere in the house, working by lamplight, lost in numbers. Fragile. Necessary. His brother. His responsibility.

Rufus pressed his palm over the old stripes again.

They were a warning to lesser men. Men that grew up to be lying cowards. Men like Marcus Antonius.

He stood. Turned toward the villa. Stopped once more in the dimming garden.

The light had gone. The fountain whispered. An owl called from a neighbor's roof. Somewhere far down the hill, a dog barked and fell silent. Rome never slept, but it breathed slower at this hour.

Somewhere in the city, Marcus Antonius drank, plotted, dreamed of blood.

Rufus touched the twin chevrons over his heart.

He remembered.

And the chevrons remembered too.

Chapter 115
THE WEIGHING

The women gathered first.

Fulvia sat beside the bronze table, eyes lowered, hands clasped in her lap. The jewelry lay between them, two matching sets; deep blue stones streaked with silver veins, heavy as truth. One for her. One for her mother.

Her mother's fingers hovered above the earrings, then drifted to the necklace. She touched the stones like they might speak.

"This came from the eastern provinces?" she asked quietly.

"Taken from a pirate's vault," Fulvia answered. Pride shaded her voice. "Or so he claimed."

Her mother's lips curved. Her aunt leaned in for a better look, bracelets chiming as she moved. Patrician women, they carried iron spines in public, but the glint of rare stones could soften them into girls again. Gold did that. It caught the eye the way sunlight caught water.

"Well, you would never find such work in even the best local shops." The aunt said.

"Very fine work," her mother murmured, turning the necklace. "Fit for a daughter of the Fulvii."

"Even if he's not," Fulvia's brother said from the archway.

Her father didn't turn. He stood behind his chair, one hand resting on the carved back, gaze fixed on the vine-covered wall beyond the garden door. Cool dusk light pooled over the marble.

Fulvia looked at him. "He's not of our blood. But he's bled for Rome. For Caesar. For Pompey."

Her brother snorted. "He also shares a bed with a witch. Lies with her as if she were a Roman wife."

Fulvia's head lifted. Sharp. "She is no witch. She's the Sibyl. She's the Oracle of Rome. She has the women of Rome in her hands."

"That's the trouble," her brother muttered.

Her mother glanced between them and placed a gentle hand on her daughter's wrist. "We know what he's done. We know what she is. But what do you want?"

Fulvia hesitated.

"I want what holds us together," she said finally. "What makes a house stronger. What protects children. He does that. And I..." Her breath slipped. "I like him."

Her aunt raised a brow.

"I like how he moves," Fulvia added. "I admire how people move when he enters."

The room tightened with quiet understanding.

At last, her father turned from the garden. "I've met him. Twice. He stood straight. Looked me in the eye. Spoke little, but wisely. Strong hands. Good eyes."

"Like a slave," her brother said.

Her father didn't blink. "Like a Roman. You need to learn the difference."

He stepped closer to the table and lifted the heavier bracelet. "Men like Rufus don't appear from dust. His family built half the roads and bridges in southern Latium. His grandfathers fought under Marius. His father under Sulla. That's old blood, even if it's not noble blood."

"But not senatorial," her brother pushed. "And his own brother, Sextus, thinks he's not fit for my sister."

"But his star is rising, ours has settled."

Her mother lowered her gaze to the necklace again. "And we will be remembered as the ones who brought him into our circle."

"Brought him in," Fulvia said, "and tied him to us. Which ties Albina, and her goddess, to us."

That drew her aunt upright. "You think the girl will last?"

"She'll endure," Fulvia said. "The women love her. And Rufus listens to her."

Her brother laughed. "Then why not marry Albina?"

Fulvia's voice cracked like a whip. "Because I'm Roman. And Albina is not."

Silence settled, thick, full of old truths.

Her father sat at last. Slowly. With weight.

"The Antonius boy," he said, "is too wild. His hands shake when he talks. His mind runs too fast. He drinks too much, gambles too much, lies too easily. And he remembers the beating."

Fulvia blinked. "You knew about that?"

"I saw the bruises. I saw the shame. He shrank after that fight. Turned bitter. Dangerous. Small."

He turned his gaze to his son with a scowl. "And even with your friendship, I would never let that Antonius boy marry your sister. He's not good enough."

He nudged the bracelet toward Fulvia with two fingers.

"Rufus is not small," he said. "And he is good enough."

Fulvia picked up the bracelet. Held it to the lamplight. Blue fire shimmered inside the stone.

"I do want this," she said.

Her mother smiled. Her aunt followed.

"Eastern work," the aunt murmured, tracing the clasp. "This came from royalty, not a merchant."

She tapped one of the stones with her nail. "This stone is absolutely flawless and as big as a pigeon's egg. Priceless. Fit for Fortunas fingers... If he lied about pirates, he's the best liar in Rome. Which makes him perfect for you."

The jewelry sparkled, triumphant.

Her brother muttered, "It's just jewelry."

Her aunt didn't even look at him. "Nothing is just jewelry, dear boy. It's a ledger worn on the body."

Her mother added softly, "It's proof of a woman's power."

Serponia, who had watched silently from the far corner, touched a bracelet with reverence. "Like the oak leaves on Rufus's head."

Fulvia's pulse warmed.

Yes.

Some symbols changed the room.

Some changed Rome.

Chapter 116
THE HOUSE PREPARES

T he villa held a different heat now.

Every room felt tighter, heavier, full of breath that wasn't there weeks ago. Dried lavender hung over lintels. Bowls of vinegar soaked the corners. Oil lamps smoked. Voices floated behind curtains. Bare feet whispered across polished stone. Garlands swayed whenever the doors opened.

Albina sat in the garden atrium, leaning back into a silk cushion. The wrap around her shoulders hung loose, thin from the heat. Her belly sat like a hill carved from sunlight. She had not danced in weeks. Her ankles ached. Her back ached.

Zarmina the Red walked behind her, muttering in their tongue, a low river of words. Nisaya the Black followed, carrying a bowl of crushed herbs. The room smelled of mint and clay and storm-light.

When a young slave dropped a pitcher, Albina snapped, words flew from her mouth that would shock a sailor. A sound sharp enough to crack the air. Even she flinched. Her fingers tightened, then loosened. She smoothed her wrap as if a gentler hand could erase the moment.

Along the far corridor, Tirzah swept the marble, quiet as a prayer. A simple dress, clean. A silver bracelet on her wrist, Rufus's gift. She moved with a grace she didn't claim. Albina noticed her. Always had. Tirzah walked by and left a question hanging in the air, unspoken.

Fulvia arrived near midday with her mother's midwife and a sealed scroll of dowry lists. Her white gown pulled at the sides to let air in; her face held that calm patrician assurance, but her eyes went straight to Albina's belly, then to the carved lion cub on the shrine ledge.

"You're strong," Fulvia said.

Albina raised one eyebrow. "I'm tired."

Fulvia smiled, a soft thing. "They'll remember you like this. Women remember who carried life with courage."

They did not speak of Rufus.

Not directly.

Fulvia slid a small ring box across Albina's lap. Inside lay a gold band, a bracelet carved with ivy leaves, old work, older than the Republic.

"My grandmother's," Fulvia murmured. "I'm wearing the other."

Albina held the precious object, thumb tracing the leaves, no words offered. The bracelet felt warm, as if Fulvia's hand had left something inside it.

"If it's a girl," Fulvia said, "she will live in both houses. Raised by both names."

Albina nodded once. "If she's a girl, I'll let you name her."

Fulvia blinked. "If she's a girl? You think... a boy?"

Albina's eyes narrowed, "I'm not wrong often."

They parted quietly, two women carrying different futures. Neither had slept through the night in weeks.

At dusk, Matineus arrived.

Dust on his shoulders. Sword at his hip. A jar of honey under one arm. He nodded to Menon, the steward, and spoke in the clipped tones of a man who did not waste breath.

"Your half-sister is ill," he told Rufus. "She'll recover."

He stayed only hours. Ate little. Spoke even less. His eyes tracked shadows the way hunters track wind.

Before he left, Albina called him into the garden.

"You look thin," she said.

He met her gaze. "You look heavy."

A dry laugh escaped her, pain pulled through it, but it came anyway.

"Take care of yourself," she said softly.

"I do what I must."

He left before nightfall, boots silent on the stone.

That evening, Nisaya rubbed oil into Albina's calves. Zarmina counted herbs. A storm built over the hills; thunder pressed low in the air, not yet sound, just weight.

Albina exhaled hard through her nose. "I'll kill someone soon. No reason. Just to feel better."

Tirzah passed behind her carrying folded linens.

"If you need help," she whispered, "call me."

She vanished into the shadows of the hall.

Zarmina watched her go.

"She means it," Zarmina said quietly.

Albina turned her head.

Zarmina didn't smile. "The quiet ones are loyal. The others chase noise. Watch that one."

Albina didn't answer. But her gaze lingered on the hall, long after Tirzah had disappeared.

At dawn, the dowry was finalized.

Fulvia's mother signed her name beside Menon's. Rufus trained in the yard, feet on stone, breath steady. A scroll arrived from Caesar confirming the match, the seal still warm from the courier's hand.

Albina stood alone in the garden before the shrine.

She wore white. Her hair unbound. Her belly brushed the edge of the marble as she leaned closer to the carved lioness. The sun caught her skin, her breath, the curve of her new world.

She placed both hands over the child.

"You're not ready," she murmured. "Neither am I."

A wind moved through the archway, soft, cold, like a finger across the spine.

Somewhere inside the villa, a bell rang.

Albina didn't turn.

She listened.

The house prepared.

And something else listened back.

Chapter 117
BIRTH OF THE LION'S CUB

Albina's water broke at sunset, during a thunderstorm pounding over the skies of Rome. The witches rushed her into the birthing chamber, stripping her of rings and cloth, laying her on linens soaked in myrrh and vinegar. The contractions came hard. They came fast.

The sky above Rome turned black with stars. Inside the Caelian Hill villa, every torch burned. Lamps lined the halls. Women gathered by the gates, some kneeling, others humming under their breath.

In the birthing chamber, Albina gripped the edge of her bedding, sweat pouring from her face. Zarmina and Nisaya stood over her. The girls fanned her. The room glowed red with flickering oil.

From far off in the villa, a sound came low and steady. Male voices humming in unison.

Rufus sat in the great dining room. He jerked at every scream. Around him, seated in wide concentric rings, were all his male kin. Dozens of them; legitimate sons, half-brothers, cousins, uncles. Soldiers, builders, farmers. Latinus men.

In the center of the room stood a towering statue of Mars, carved long ago by their own ancestors' hands.

An old priest from the Alban Mount homeland stood barefoot before the god. He wore wolf pelts; his arms tattooed with red spirals. He raised one hand.

The falling rain steadied. Flashes of lightning and the boom of thunder rumbled over the atrium.

The room fell to stillness.

A boy softly beat a drum.

Then they swayed.

Sitting upright, they twisted to the right as one, forming a slow-turning tide of muscle and bone. North, east, south, west, as the heavens turn, as time flows. As their fathers had turned before them. As the hills turned above the Alban Lake. Their hum deepened into a dirge. Ancestral. Ancient.

This was the rite of birth and blood. A welcoming to the newly born... or a farewell to the mother. It had not been performed since the birth of Rufus's youngest half-brother was born nearly two years before.

From above, they could hear the cries of Albina.

Then silence.

Then a child's voice.

In the birthing chamber, Albina fell back onto the linens, barely breathing. Nisaya leaned close to her ear.

"A boy," she whispered.

Albina opened her eyes. Her voice was weak but calm.

"Take him... to his father. Naked. Place him on the stone at his feet."

Zarmina the Red nodded and took the child, so pink and strong, still slick with birth. No swaddling. No incense. No chant. Only flesh, blood, and judgment.

Barefoot, she entered the hall, stepped between the rings of men.

No one moved.

As she reached the center, she stopped just before Rufus.

She knelt and laid the child on the wet stone directly at his feet. She ignored the statue.

The god watched from stone. But the man would choose.

Then, in broken, rough Latin, she spoke:

"Your son and heir, Dominus."

She didn't move. Head bowed, hands crossed on her waist. Rufus met her eyes. Just an instant, a breath between them, no words. No need. Her nod was slow. Certain. Albina would be fine. His shoulders eased. The fire behind him cracked once. Then the boy cried.

She remained there, head lowered.

The room held its breath.

Rufus looked down.

A moment passed.

But only a moment.

Thunder rumbled in the distance.

Then he bent.

Rufus inspected the baby's hands and feet. His privates. His eyes. Perfect, no flaws.

He picked up the boy, slowly, carefully, with both hands.

Rufus held him high above his head.

A gentle rain splashed the baby.

Lightning. Thunder.

Mars beheld the infant. The family god approved.

Rufus turned to face the clan, his voice rising:

"My son."

"Gaius Latinus Leo, the Lion!"

He roared the family war cry.

The room erupted. Dozens of men rising and joining in, fists raised, voices howling in celebration.

The baby cried once, strong and loud.

In the birthing chamber, Albina heard it.

Nisaya moved to help her lie back, but Albina held her wrist.

"Let me see," she said.

They turned her toward the open doorway, where shadows danced with firelight and lightning.

Rufus held her son high, the men all reached to touch him, yelling the war cry as he cried.

She whispered:

"If he had not lifted him, the boy would not be his, the boy would be nothing. Not in the eyes of Rome. Not in the eyes of the gods. He would have been left in the rain to die. It is their oldest law."

She closed her eyes, smiling faintly.

"But he lifted him."

She exhaled, long and slow.

In the heavens, above the thunder and lightning, the gods and goddesses looked down and celebrated the birth of the Sibyl's son.

"The lion cub lives," Albina smiled.

In the great hall, the lion roared back.

Chapter 118
THE VILLA CHANGES

T he mornings shifted after the birth.

The garden softened. The air moved easier. Even the guards kept quieter by the gate, as if sound itself respected the new life inside the walls.

Albina rested in a sunlit corner near the atrium; the baby nestled against her breast. Her feet tucked beneath her. Her hair brushed clean and shining. One girl fanned her with a palm frond: another kneaded oil into her aching calves. The child, tiny, warm, perfect, suckled, then drifted to sleep with hardly a sound.

Zarmina and Nisaya had worked through the night. Stones warmed by fire laid along Albina's spine. Bitter roots pressed beneath her tongue. Charms tied at her wrists. Whispered chants old as dust. The labor had torn her small frame, but the witches coaxed her body back together with stubborn, sacred skill.

Rufus watched it all. At first from a distance. Then closer. Always silent.

Now, each dawn, he trained in the courtyard, bowstring creaking, spear shaft cracking wood, and returned to find Albina sitting upright, her eyes clearer, her body healing faster than anyone expected.

"You're walking, it improves," he said once.

"I walk well," she answered. "I just bled out a god."

He smiled at that, slow, private, true.

The nursery sat in the room beside hers. Warm. Painted with bright clay figures. A lion cub carved in low relief above the doorway. Tirzah had chosen the cloth for the cradle, deep red trimmed in white. She lit incense every morning, cleared the air by noon, moved quiet as a cat. She sang sometimes, soft and low, never when she knew others listened.

Albina noticed everything.

"She is careful," Albina murmured.

"She watches everything," Rufus replied.

Albina adjusted the blanket over the child. "She has seen more than she speaks. And she loves you."

Rufus said nothing. He didn't have to. Albina understood the shape of his silence.

Midweek, Matineus arrived.

Dust on his shoulders. Sword at his hip. No smile. He brought a jar of honey from home, handed it to Menon without ceremony, and sat beside Albina for a moment. He held the baby, awkward, reverent, then gave the boy back as if passing off a relic.

"You'll train him?" Matineus asked.

"If he wants it," Rufus said.

"He will. He has your wrists."

Matineus stood, nodded to the witches, and left. Albina watched him go.

"He mourns," she said.

Rufus nodded once. "Yes."

The garden saw them most. Albina walked barefoot in the grass when the baby slept, humming low melodies in her mother's tongue. She wore soft red linen now, looser, easier. Her figure had returned, but fuller, richer, like earth after rain. Rufus sat on a bench, sometimes with a scroll, sometimes with nothing, always watching.

Once, she placed a fig in his palm.

"Eat more," she said. "You forget when you think too hard."

He smiled and obeyed. She laughed, one bright, aching note that stirred the whole garden.

The steward arrived one morning with scrolls tied in blue cord. Dowry terms. Guest lists. Arrangements for the wedding. Fulvia's household sent updates daily.

Albina read over Rufus's shoulder. "She will be a fine Roman wife."

"Yes."

"I will give her the keys," Albina said. "And you must buy her new slaves."

Rufus glanced at her, amusement softening his stern face.

"You're not afraid?" she asked.

"No," he answered. "Are you?"

She looked down at the child. Placed her right hand over her heart. "No. I will keep what matters."

She kissed the baby's head. "Everything else passes."

That night, the house gathered in the great room: Rufus, Albina, the child, Tirzah, the witches, the dancers, and a smiling Lucius. He felt a special bond with his newest nephew.

Music drifted from a corner, soft, slow. They ate roasted lamb, mushrooms, warm bread, honeyed cakes, watered wine. Firelight painted the walls gold.

No one spoke for a while.

Rufus shifted, settling the baby in his lap. Albina leaned against his side. Zarmina stirred the coals. Nisaya braided charms into fresh cord. Tirzah sat cross-legged on the floor; eyes fixed on the slow-moving shadows above.

Albina whispered, "We are a family now."

Rufus answered, "Yes. I love us."

She looked up at him. "I want more children."

Tirzah's head turned, just slightly.

Rufus raised a brow and winked.

Albina smiled. "Not yet. But someday."

Outside, Rome murmured in the dark.

Inside, the house; blood, breath, stone, and hope, held perfectly still.

Chapter 119
FULVIA MARCI FILIA FULVIA

The day began before sunrise.

Outside the house of Fulvius Flaccus, torches burned low and steady. Inside, women moved in silence. Fulvia sat tall on a carved stool, wrapped in a pure white stola, her hair parted into six braids by a matron with salt-and-iron hands. A bridal veil, flammeum red, bright as fire, waited on the cedar box behind her.

She wore no jewelry. Only a simple woolen sash tied around her waist with a single knot. The nodus Herculeanus. The Knot of Hercules. No one would untie it but her husband.

Her mother placed a hand on her shoulder. "Today you become a Roman matron. So, do try not to appear too eager."

Fulvia said nothing. Smiled.

At the Latinus villa, Rufus stood bare-chested in the garden. His shield-brothers had already rubbed his arms with oil and laced his sandals. He put on a white tunic with purple edging, freshly laundered. Around his neck, a bronze charm shaped like a boar's tooth, a gift from his uncle, swung once before he tucked it away.

His father approached, eyes sharp. "Remember: this marriage is not for her.

Not for you. This is for Rome. For the family."

Rufus gave one nod.

By mid-morning, ten guests gathered at the Fulvian atrium. All Roman citizens. All witnesses. The bride stood under the family lararium, the household shrine. Her father placed her right hand in Rufus's left. The dextrarum iunctio. The joining of right hands. The oldest form of Roman marriage.

A priest of Jupiter murmured prayers in perfect Latin. Then a sacrifice, a small pig, throat cut cleanly, the blood caught in a shallow bronze bowl.

The augur examined the entrails. "Fortunate."

Fulvia did not blink.

At noon, the coemptio was performed. A mock sale. Rufus weighed out bronze coins onto a balance scale. Fulvia's father accepted them and struck his staff to the ground. She passed from one house to another, by law and by ritual.

The veil was lowered.

Then came the pronuba, the married woman chosen to lead Fulvia to her new home. Her aunt. Stern-faced, tall, unflinching. She tied Fulvia's hand to Rufus's with a woolen cord.

"Hold fast," she said.

The deductio began. The procession.

Flute players walked ahead, followed by slaves bearing torches, flowers, and bowls of fruit. All surrounded by guards. Lots of guards.

Fulvia walked beside Rufus, her veil glowing red in the sunlight. Children threw flower petals. Women sang old songs, half prayer, half bawdy jokes.

Bystanders watched from rooftops. Some cheered. Some spoke.

"She's beautiful. What a fortunate man."

"Her blood is among the best in Rome."

"Rufus just holds out his hand, and the gods pour gold and beautiful women into his palm,"

"She marries the one who took the Sibyl in."

"And beat Antonius in the street."

"Did you see the gifts? Eastern stones. Pirate spoils."

"Rome is changing."

At the Latinus villa, the doorway had been scrubbed with wolf's milk and bay leaves. A garland of laurel hung over the lintel.

Rufus carried Fulvia across the threshold. Her veil caught the light one last time before vanishing inside.

She touched the hearth. Placed a coin by the fire. Passed her hand through the fire. Wet her hand in the water bowl. Whispered to the household gods.

The guests ate honeyed cakes and drank watered wine in the atrium. The air buzzed with approval.

That night, after the crowd thinned, Rufus stood at the window, arms folded. He wore nothing but a thin tunic, the bronze boar's tooth, and a hard look.

Albina passed behind him. Quiet, steady, unreadable. She did not speak. Her white dress brushed the floor. Her eyes touched his back for a moment, touched his hair, then vanished down the hall. She would not cry.

Tirzah watched Rufus from the distance. Even though her chest hurt, she felt something like pride that her... Dominus... could marry such an incredibly beautiful and high borne wife.

In the bridal room, Fulvia sat alone on the edge of the marriage bed. Her hands rested over her lap. The red veil lay folded nearby.

She waited.

The door opened. Rufus stepped inside.

No words. Just breath. Just weight.

He stood before her. She rose.

She wore the girdle, the knot of Hercules, tied high around her waist, its folds sharp, deliberate. A mark of virtue. Of legacy. Of Roman law.

He stepped close and touched it.

Not with hunger. Not yet.

The knot didn't resist him. It gave easily, like it had waited eagerly.

No words passed between them.

He let his tunic fall off.

Fulvia kept her eyes on his.

She didn't breathe until her dress was gone.

Then she let her hands fall to her sides, loose now. Open.

He'd expected awkwardness. Distance. Something arranged. But in the silence, he found none of that. Just her. Steady. Beautiful. Willing, but not soft. Not delicate. Fulvia had entered the marriage the same way he had, by choice. Her choice. Not by fire. Not by fate. But by will.

"By the gods, you're beautiful."

He didn't rush her. Didn't need to. Her eyes told him everything. Not fire, not worship, not mystery, just truth. The kind a man could reach for without being pulled under. She was his wife now. Not a prize. Not a rival. Just a woman who had waited and now was ready. She stepped into him with no hesitation, only breath.

He placed one hand behind her neck. She reached for his chest.

Their mouths met.

Later, Fulvia would remember how he touched her like a warrior who knew every weak point, every hidden path. How he did not rush. How he did not falter.

How he did not once speak Albina's name.

And how Rufus whispered her name. Only her name. Again, and again.

Chapter 120
THE ORACLE OF ROME

Night fell hard on the Caelian Hill.

The garden held the last of the heat. Torches burned low along the colonnade. Smoke drifted in thin blue ribbons, tasting of clove and wet stone. The fountain murmured behind the figs. Lizards clung motionless to warm marble.

Albina stepped barefoot onto the heated mosaic circle.

Her body felt different now, healed, but softer, fuller, marked by the birth. She wore only a thin wrap of red silk tied at the hips. No gold. No bracelets. No bells. Tonight, the Goddess asked for a woman, not a queen.

Behind her, the dancers arranged themselves in a crescent. Her blood-kin first, legs coiled, hair braided tight. The two apprentices took the edge of the pattern, breathing fast, watching every shift of Albina's shoulder. All dances began with Albina. All dances returned to her.

The sky above turned violet, thickening toward night.

Zarmina the Red stood by the shrine, hands folded, her robe heavy with resin smoke. Nisaya the Black crouched in the dirt, grinding something green and wet between her fingers, something that clung to the air like grief.

The smell rose: sweat, myrrh, woman.

Near the fig tree, Tirzah rocked the baby against her chest. Leo slept, face pressed to her collarbone, while she hummed the soft mountain-song her grandmother once sang. Albina had never asked for it. Tirzah offered it anyway.

Zarmina lit the resin.

Nisaya whispered the words.

Albina lifted her arms. One hand open to the sky, the other pressed to her ribs, a gesture older than Rome.

A single drumbeat rose from below the garden floor, deep, slow, the heartbeat of the house.

Albina circled the mosaic. Once. Twice.

Her hips rolled. Her spine arched. Fingers carved the air like blades. Her head tipped back. A long breath left her. The bells she didn't wear still seemed to answer.

Her body remembered.

She danced.

Heat gathered at her skin, pulled tight along her bones. The world narrowed to rhythm, stone, breath. The Goddess moved through her feet, through her ribs, through the hollow beneath her throat. Albina sank into it, deeper, deeper, until her eyes fluttered shut.

The dancers hummed.

Then Albina's body went rigid. Her head snapped back.

The trance fell on her like a predator from a tree, sudden, silent, absolute.

Everything stopped. The girls froze where they crouched. Fire became a single still flame. The drum struck once more, then fell silent.

Albina spoke. But the voice that came from her chest was not her own, rounder, older, edged with sand and thunder.

"She comes with wind in her mouth," the voice said. "And teeth in her prayers."

Zarmina's head rose sharply.

"She wears no red," Albina continued. "Her skin is ash. Her breath cuts."

One of the younger girls whimpered.

"She walks behind kings," the voice said. "And feeds on queens."

Albina's eyes rolled back until only white showed. Her hands pinned themselves to her sides. The wrap around her hips did not stir. Even the torches leaned away.

"The fire will dim," the voice warned. "The sky will forget our names. And daughters will not dance."

Nisaya stood as if yanked upward. The crushed resin on her fingers smeared across her robe.

Albina's breath shook.

She saw the false one.

It's face and named blurred. A shape. A hunger pretending to be a calling. A woman who copied power the way a jackal mimics a lion's roar. A crown of gold that hovered above her hair but never landed.

A lie made flesh.

Albina saw women kneel, not in devotion, but in want. Saw gold replacing truth. Saw the echo of a forgotten goddess dragged out of her grave and twisted into worship.

The usurper walked where the Goddess once walked. Her feet never touched blood, yet the soil behind her dripped with it.

A thousand women cried out in the vision, none strong enough to speak her true name.

Albina stood before the pretender, not priestess now, not queen, but witness.

And as the vision cracked, the pretender turned. And smiled.

Albina screamed.

Zarmina shouted, "Enough!"

The trance snapped. Albina collapsed. Nisaya and Zarmina caught her before her skull hit stone. Her body shook once, hard enough to rattle her teeth, then stilled. Breath returned in short, fast bursts.

The girls broke and sobbed.

One crawled to Albina's side. Nisaya held the girl's hand tight. Zarmina brushed Albina's cheek, face unreadable.

"She saw the Second," Nisaya whispered. "The usurper."

Zarmina nodded. "The rival. The false flame."

"We must prepare."

At the far end of the colonnade, Rufus watched.

He hadn't moved once.

His back pressed to a marble column, arms loose at his sides, jaw clenched. The shadows around him thickened, bending at the edges as if pulled by whatever had filled the garden.

He tried to steady his mind, weight, breath, distance, the soldier's trinity. But none of it held.

Because Albina was not on the floor anymore.

For one breath, maybe two, she had hung above the mosaic, an inch, maybe less. But above it. No jump. No push. No arc of muscle.

Her body had simply risen.

The air had thickened around her, pushing the torches back, bending sound. Time staggered. He blinked, thinking he had imagined it, but the garden still shivered with whatever had touched her.

He had seen men leap from towers. Seen acrobats dive through rings of fire. Seen priests' fake miracles with careful strings and clever smoke.

But he had never seen this.

Albina's powers, and this was power, were real.

His hand drifted toward the sword he did not carry tonight.

Albina lay breathing again.

But something old had moved with her.

And Rufus knew this night would mark everything that came after.

Chapter 121
AFTER THE FIRE

The night held its breath.

Frost clung to the tiles. The torches guttered thin, their smoke drifting low across the garden like a warning. The trance had broken, yet the air still trembled as if Albina's scream kept echoing through the stone.

Rufus stood beside the brazier, arms crossed, shoulders set hard. Heat licked his skin, but he felt none of it. His gaze fixed on the dark beyond the flame, jaw tight, breath shallow. He had seen battlefields, ambushes, the eyes of dying men. Nothing in those places had made the hair rise along his arms like what he had seen tonight.

Floating.

No push.

No leap.

Just lifted.

He hated the part of himself that could not explain it.

Above the colonnade, a shutter opened and closed. Lucius stood there for a moment, his thin frame outlined in weak lamplight. His damaged leg trembled under his weight. He leaned against the wall; eyes narrowed in concentration. Curiosity. Calculation. He watched the brazier's flame split and bend. He watched Albina's shadow sway on the inner wall. Then he slipped back inside without a word.

Something in Rufus eased at the sight of him. His brother's strange mind could measure things Rufus could not.

But even Lucius could not measure what Albina had called down.

Inside the villa, Fulvia paced before the hearth, one hand pressed against her lower belly as if guarding some fragile possibility. Her gown brushed the floor like water. She tried to hum to steady herself, but the tune died again on her lips. The house had swallowed music tonight.

In the nursery, the infant slept. One soft sigh. One flutter of lashes. Then stillness.

Further down the corridor, Tirzah paused with a folded cloth in her hands. She had come to adjust the coals in the brazier. That was the reason she whispered to herself. Yet her feet would not move.

She had heard Albina's voice split open into something older than stars. Words that did not fit in Roman mouths. A sound her faith had no place for. She felt it still, like a trembling thread stretched across her ribs.

She prayed under her breath. Her God would hear. He always heard. But tonight, even prayer felt small.

A vase cracked from the cold. Rufus flinched. Fulvia gasped. Tirzah pressed her fingers to her lips.

Inside the inner chamber, Zarmina closed the doors and knelt beside the Sibyl.

Albina had collapsed but, she had not fainted. She knelt exactly where the vision left her, hands on her thighs, eyes open but unfocused.

Zarmina did not touch her. She simply sat close, enough for breath to mingle, enough for presence to pull Albina back inch by inch.

After a long silence, Albina tilted her head and whispered, "She moves."

Zarmina nodded once, grave.

"She moves," Albina said again, slower. "And she wears another woman's faith like a mask."

At the chamber's threshold, Nisaya slipped in with a bowl of dark resin. She placed it on the floor, the scent rising like bruised honey.

Zarmina spoke first. "We must prepare."

Nisaya's voice rasped like sand. "She gathers names. And names gather power."

"She gathers lies," Zarmina answered.

"She gathers women," Nisaya whispered.

Albina's throat tightened. "I saw them kneel."

Zarmina looked to the flame. "Not to a goddess."

"To a shadow," Nisaya finished.

They shared a glance, the kind that held dread and duty tangled tight.

Far from them, the baby stirred once and quieted, as if some unseen hand soothed him.

Albina's breath slowed. Her shoulders dropped. Her palms pressed into the cold mosaic.

"She is in Egypt," Zarmina murmured. "But she grows."

"Not this year," Nisaya added. "Not next."

Albina closed her eyes.

"But soon."

Outside the doors, Rufus leaned against the jamb, listening without meaning to. The torch beside him hissed, its smoke rising straight, unbroken. He felt the weight of something vast settling over the villa.

He would face Marcus Antonius.

He would face Clodius.

He would face men.

But this...

This was not a man.

Rufus had just learned a new type of fear; heavy with the helplessness and hopelessness that comes when faced with the wraith of the gods themselves.

Inside the chamber, Albina lifted her head. Her voice came soft, raw. "She will come for women first."

Zarmina nodded. "And the women will decide the victor long before the men ever see the field."

Albina lowered her gaze to her hands. They still trembled.

For the first time in months, she did not think of Red Ring. His shadow vanished like smoke behind a greater, older danger.

The house fell silent.

Rome breathed.

And the night prepared.

Chapter 122
THE MUD COAST

R ed Ring Never Forgot

The city spit them out like gristle.

Red Ring and his three surviving brothers fled the Caelian Hill without pattern or plan, burned, hunted, bleeding from every edge. They took the sewer road first. Then the salt path. Then no road at all. Only dark fields and animal trails and the places Rome forgot.

For weeks they moved like feral things.

Sleeping in goat pens.

Eating roots torn from frozen ground.

Drinking from hoof prints.

One brother coughed blood.

Another wrapped his leg in stolen linen until it stank.

Red Ring never slowed.

At dusk, long after hunger had scraped them hollow, they reached the coast north of Ostia, an ugly ribbon of dark sand and silt. Wind whipped salt and cold through their cloaks. Smoke curled from a rough camp nearby: driftwood fires, tar pots, meat pits. The smell of men who had chewed through their own pasts.

Pirates. Smugglers. Escaped slaves. Knives-for-hire.

Fifty of them, maybe more.

Red Ring walked straight in.

Did not blink.

Did not bow.

His brothers followed. They found a spot near a low fire and sat like they had always belonged. No one questioned them. Men who lived by the blade recognized their own.

The brothers built a decent enough shelter from scratch.

They stayed.

Days bled into weeks. Long enough for wounds to close. Long enough for whispers to start.

Red Ring watched everything, who commanded with a stare, who folded under it, who killed for food, who killed for fun.

The camp learned his silence. Leaned away from it.

On the third night, the boy arrived.

Thin. Filthy. Eyes hidden under a strip of rag. He crouched at the edge of the fire's reach with a knife too long for his hand. He did not speak. Did not ask. Only watched the flames.

One pirate cursed him.

Another kicked at him.

Both bled for it.

He wiped the blade on his sleeve, unbothered. Then shifted closer to the fire.

He wasn't child fast.

He was killer fast.

By dawn, he had eaten from someone else's bowl without permission. No one stopped him. They watched him the way they watched Red Ring, careful, measuring distance, deciding whether to test or obey.

He never spoke a word.

But by the end of the week, he rose when Red Ring rose, sat when Red Ring sat, ate after Red Ring ate. Always three steps behind.

No oath. No request.

He simply chose.

And Red Ring let him.

They still had gold, enough to hire killers, enough to move men who feared nothing but hunger. He kept it quiet, hidden in belts and boots, guarded by the weight of their reputation.

Then, one moonless night, Red Ring made his offer.

Twelve men.

The worst of the worst.

Big, fast, and silent.

No homes.

No loyalties.

Nothing left but rage.

The boy stood among them, knife glinting.

They said yes.

The rest of the camp?

They died in their sleep.

Throats opened.

Bellies carved.

A few tried to run.

One climbed a tree and screamed until someone cut him down.

One ran into the sea and drowned in the first cold waves.

Only one man lived.

By accident.

He had wandered off to piss behind the dunes, old knees, slow feet. When he returned, the sand was slick with blood and death still warm in the air. He hid behind the rocks and watched Red Ring hand out weapons, watched the twelve mount horses, watched the silent boy nod once, blade wet, face unreadable.

He heard the plan.

Back to Rome.

Not for vengeance... for annihilation.

Albina.

Her dancers.

Her witches.

Rufus.

His brother Matineus the Cunning.

Even the newborn.

The house had a weakness already inside it.

A child. Trusted. Loved.

Ready to pour poison as sweet as honey.

The survivor waited until the hooves vanished. His breath scraped his throat raw. When silence settled, he crawled from hiding and searched the bodies for coins, rings, anything worth keeping.

He found enough to fill his pockets. Enough to fill his courage.

He looked toward Rome.

"I know the lion," he whispered. "I know his fortune. He has people in Ostia."

He spat into the sand.

"They forgot me once."

He stood, straightened his cloak, and limped toward the road.

"They won't forget me again."

Chapter 123
OSTIAN WARNING

The informant waited until Red Ring and his men were long gone. When the last of the troop disappeared on the ridge above the camp, he moved with the desperate speed of a man who had nothing to lose.

He ran to Ostia by midmorning; sand still clung to his calves, sweat crusted around his collar. The port smelled of fish and tar and the thin sick smell of stale wine. Boats nosed against roped piles; sailors shouted in a dozen tongues. He did not stop to barter or plead; he pushed through the market, past the granaries, past the painted sign of the Latinus shipping house; two lions biting the same boar; the emblem had once been bright; now it was salted with time.

He refused a prefect's escort. He refused a guard. He said only one thing: "I must see a Latinus. Urgent." No name. No story. Plain words, hungry eyes. The steward at the gate frowned but obeyed the urgency in the man's throat. The steward sent the message to an older Latinus cousin, a man who ran grain contracts, who kept ledgers by night and made bargains by day.

They met at the wharf, where gulls fought over stale bread and children skipped stones into black water. The cousin came with two porters; his hands were thick with rope-callus; his face cut by sun. He listened without surprise. Men like him hear bad news every month. He kept coin for bribes; he kept knives for thieves. But when the man spat the name, Red Ring, his face went small and sharp.

"They're coming," the informer said; his breath ripped, his chest hollow like an emptied jug. "A dozen. One-eyed, burned across the face. He hates the Sibyl; hates her child; hates the hero who keeps her. He's paid men with gold; he's bought steel; he's bound poison to the hand of a youth. He's going to strike in Rome while the city sleeps."

The Latinus watched the docks, watched a rope swing free, watched the slow rhythm of oars; his jaw worked. He asked a few cold questions; who rides with him; what corsairs; a name for the boy. The informer coughed, coughed out a boy's color, the tidings as if they were bile.

"He brought a child," the man said; "a boy tucked in his train. And there's a boy inside the hero's villa, left as a slave. The poison comes by bread, by cup; it comes in sleep."

The grain-man's fingers closed on the coin the informant offered; the silver sang in his palm like a small, obscene bell. He gave the man a fat purse; the man's eyes widened; his knees trembled.

"Gratitude for coming to us."

Then the Latinus did something the waterfront had long learned to expect and never speak of: he drew a small knife from his belt and slit the man's throat with one smooth motion.

The body dropped with a wet sound. The purse thumped to the soaked planks. The Latinus reached; he took the bag; the coin against his palm felt heavier with blood. He did not look away; he never looked away. The porters stared and looked to the sea as if the horizon might reply.

"Go," he said to a slave standing near. "Fast horse. Tell Rufus: the red one returns. He brings death; he brings a boy and poison. Tell him: make the household ready."

The slave vaulted to the saddle; a thin sound of leather beat as he rode off, already bled onto the roads. The Latinus did not watch him go. He turned to the two porters and pointed. "Drag him to the dump. Strip him. Keep whatever fills his pockets. Slit his belly. Let the dogs feast."

The two men obeyed like men who had been given a sensible order. They dragged the corpse across the planks, the sandals sticking, the skin slack; they stripped the ragged tunic and threw it into the water where the tide would claim it later. One slit the belly; the other reached into the dark opened belly and tore free the informant's small purse; he found the coins already damp with blood and the cloth clotted in dreams.

The Latinus crossed his forearms and mouthed a prayer to the household gods; his lips formed the old syllables without feeling, an act of muscle and habit. He called down blessing on the nephew who lived under Rufus's roof; he whispered for the lares and penates to keep the boy safe. He had ledger books and grain leases; he had a sharp hand. He had no illusions that gods answered every whisper. He had no illusions that his nephew's life would be insurance enough.

When the slave left, the Latinus did not wait for the slow council of elders or for the magistrate's permission. He went to the stables and pulled men who knew sails and swords: crew from a letter-ship, sailors bred to speed; a half-dozen of the Latinus household retainers who drank their own ale and kept their knives bright. He gave them money and instructions that left no room for argument: fast horses; heavy arms; orders to follow hard; no gates would bar them; no magistrate would scrawl a halt; no question would be asked.

He selected a captain who had fought in the Tiber skirmishes; a young man with a scar across his brow and an eye that did not forgive. "You ride for Rufus," the Latinus told him, voice flat as a whetstone. "You find his house. You take no counsel. If there is hesitation, if there is talk, cut the talk and ride. Heed this: the red one keeps a child. He keeps poison. Protect the boy. If the red one seeks the house, kill him."

The captain bowed; his hand touched the hilt as if asking permission to begin. Men bundled up cloaks; they strapped water skins; they checked straps; a man took a small jar of grain rolled in cloth, antidotes, the Latinus hoped; the captain folded them into his saddle.

They moved out of the port like a wedge of shadow: horses, oarsmen turned riders, a few heavies carrying long spears. They threaded lanes, passed under arches, slipped around customs. Merchants cursed under their breath. An old woman watching from her doorway crossed herself and spat into the alleyway; the horses' hooves smacked old stones.

The warning had gone out. The hunt had begun.

Behind them, the corpse lay face down among the gull-gnawed refuse. Men came to the wharf and took note of the fallen and then turned away; old news accumulates quick in Ostia, like salt, like rot. The Latinus stood where no one would bother him, hands folded; the coins warm in his palm. He had paid for sleep; he had paid for speed; he had paid for answers forged in the same coin the red one had spent to buy poison. In the end, the city would keep its market and the household would keep its children. That was how bargains worked. That was how men survived.

Outside the gate, a rider pushed his mount into a trot toward the hills. Farther inland, another horse took a road toward Rome. The sun slid down. The harbor smells thinned; gulls returned to their quarrels. The Latinus crossed himself again and turned for the ledger he always kept in the back room, where names could be added or crossed out and no magistrate could see. He would write the night's losses later: a purse, a man, a promise. For now, the family awaited; men were moving who would not be questioned. The city hummed along; under its breath, a different animal stirred: the hunt.

Chapter 124
POISON

Latinus Villa, Caelan Hill, Rome

The villa had fallen into rhythm. Fulvia slept on the left, Albina on the right, Rufus between. The baby was brought to them in the second hour after midnight, fed by a Latinus wet nurse, then curled between the women until morning. The three of them woke together, bathed in light.

Fulvia talked more now. Albina laughed more. Rufus had begun to hum.

Each day held its shape, walks in the garden, a visit from Caesar's men, a few business matters with Rufus's uncles.

A few trips to Ostia that Albina loved and Fulvia enjoyed. The two women started to like and enjoy each other more. At least on the surface. However, there was mutual respect. They valued what the other brought to the household.

Rufus loved watching them dance together and drink and inhale the witch's smoke.

He enjoyed the love making.

The boy grew stronger. His fists clenched when Albina touched his cheek. Fulvia sang to him in Greek. The eunuchs watched from doorways, knives hidden in sleeves.

The household quieted in the evenings. Meals turned simple. Rufus's sister visited both Albina and Fulvia, they braided each other's hair on the steps in the garden. Fulvia's mother sent figs and salted nuts. The baby began to sleep through the night.

No one thought of Red Ring.

* * *

The first sign came with the dogs.

They howled just before dawn. Not a bark, howls. Long, stretched, wrong. Then silence.

The giant Nubian slave woman, Makara, caught the boy near the kitchens. He moved too quiet. His eyes darted. She grabbed his arm. He fought back. Bit her. Then tore a vial from his tunic and drank the clear liquid.

The poison worked fast.

He dropped to the ground, clutching his chest. Blood spilled from his mouth. Then his nose. Then his ears. He convulsed, spasmed hard and his eyes turned red.

They tried to stop him, but it was too late.

Rufus, Albina, and Fulvia showed up and stood over him as he convulsed, suffered, and eventually he stopped.

He was gone.

* * *

Rufus stood barefoot in the kitchen courtyard. The boy's body lay at his feet. The blood had soaked through the gravel. Flies had already come.

Albina held the baby close, staring. Fulvia stood behind her. Neither spoke.

The Nubian woman bowed her head. "He said nothing. But he knew what he was doing. He wanted to die."

Zarmina stepped forward. "The vial smelled of ground metal. He carried it for days, weeks, months."

Nisaya's voice followed. "He was loyal. Or scared."

Albina turned. Her eyes locked on Rufus.

"He's back," she said.

Rufus didn't answer. He bent and picked up the boy's body.

"I hate poisoners."

* * *

Rufus burned the boy's body outside the house. No songs. No coins. No name.

The smoke and smell of burning flesh signaled the failure of the poisoner and sent a message to Red Ring: I'm hunting you.

Rufus ordered the villa locked down. No food left unguarded. No visitor unmarked.

He sent for Matineus, and others. Many others.

He gathered a dozen tough men at every gate out of the city. He sent out feelers, offered huge rewards, and called in every favor to find this Red Ring.

Albina used her network of women to watch and inform.

***

Rufus entered the chamber near dusk. The fire had burned low. The boy's body had already been burned, quietly, without spectacle. No one in the villa spoke of it, but the tension lingered like the smoke.

Albina stood by the carved table, her back to him, reading a short scroll. She didn't turn. Didn't speak.

He crossed the floor and stopped beside her. Her eyes stayed on the parchment.

"This war of yours," he said. "Against the King of Kings."

A pause.

"I want in."

She looked up then. Her face didn't shift, but something behind her eyes warmed.

"My ships," he said. "My coin. The mail carriers. My men, if you want them. Tell me what you need. I won't pretend the threat isn't real anymore."

Her silence wasn't hesitation, it was calculation. She'd hoped for this. Now she had Rufus's help.

"I will need more sea access soon," she said. "And speed. Reliable messengers, those who can cross the desert and come back alive. Some already do, but I want more. And stronger. I will give you names. And letters."

He nodded.

"Pepper... many things, even silk come across the desert between the Nile river and the Red Sea. Perhaps you could send an uncle or half-brother to oversee that area, to exploit opportunities, to build a Red Sea fleet, and act as someone close to make quick decisions in our war with our enemy."

"And if you wish," she added, "there is a man in Alexandria you could speak to. Quietly. He trades spices and camels, but that is not what he truly moves."

"I'll send someone," Rufus said. "I have just the man in mind. I could go there personally, with you, if you wish to set it up."

She smiled at that, not with mischief, but with trust.

"Not yet," she said. "You're much too visible, and too famous. And I have powerful enemies there, caution is required."

"I'll hide and stay behind the wall, then."

She reached for his hand. Held it. Briefly. Then let go.

"I knew you would offer. But it still pleases me to hear you offer."

A sound behind them; leather over stone. Rufus turned slightly.

Makara stood, among the eunuch guards in the shadows of the rear column, arms crossed, face unreadable. She had not been invited into the room, but no one had stopped her either. Her eyes never left Albina.

"She doesn't trust the walls," Albina said, not looking at her. "Neither do I."

Rufus nodded once. He didn't trust walls either.

Albina set the scroll down and reached for a wax-sealed letter on the table.

"This man in Alexandria, he's called Kophar. Officially, a trader. In fact, his offices are in the office building two doors down from your warehouse. Unofficially, he manages a series of coastal safehouses east of the Nile. He pays tribute to the Red Sea princes and arranges passage for... unspoken things."

She handed the letter to Rufus.

"I need someone to take this to him. It must not be copied. It must not be intercepted, but before we send it, first we must kill Red Ring."

He studied the seal.

"Then I'll send Matineus."

Albina's eyes lit, not with joy, but recognition.

"Your half-brother, perfect choice. The one who moves like a shadow."

"As you know so well."

She nodded. "He won't go through Rome. He'll pass under it. That's good."

Rufus looked again toward Makara. She still hadn't moved. Still watched every word.

"Should she go with him?" he asked.

Albina shook her head. "She stays with me. I need someone the slaves fear. And someone the enemy never sees coming, if there's another attempt within our villa."

Makara blinked slowly, approval or obedience. Maybe both.

Albina picked up a small pouch from the edge of the table and pressed it into Rufus's hand. It was heavier than it looked.

"Silver. For Kophar. And for your brother's needs along the way."

"He doesn't have needs; I'll provide the silver for him."

"Good. Best too much than too little."

Rufus pushed the pouch back to her. "I got this. He will take my gold instead of silver. I want them to know that I'm involved now."

He didn't ask what the letter said. She didn't offer.

"We'll send him the moment after the Parthian's death."

Albina stepped close. Laid one hand against his chest.

"I will burn Parthia from the edges in," she said, soft as prayer. "And you will help me carry the torch."

Rufus kissed her forehead. Then stepped back.

"Everything I have is yours to use as you wish. I will even work within the senate."

Makara finally moved, just one step forward. Still silent.

The deal was done. The war moved forward. At full force.

None of them looked at the fire. The fuel was already burning.

***

Albina washed the baby herself that night. Fulvia helped.

Neither smiled.

Rufus spoke and planned quietly with trusted family.

Outside, in the street, a black-cloaked man stepped into a wine shop. He said nothing. Just drank. Then smiled.

An exhausted rider from Ostia rode up to the villa. Knocked and entered.

The black-cloaked man left the wine shop without seeing the dozen riders arrive shortly after.

Chapter 125
RED RINGS RETURN

The word spread faster than fire. Red Ring had returned. Gold flowed. Names had been spoken. A quiet contract now hung over the Latinus name.

Rufus didn't wait.

He met with his father, uncles, cousins. They lit a brazier in the family courtyard and swore an old oath, one from before Rome's founding. By fire and steel, blood answered blood. Within hours, the Latinus hunt began.

And death followed.

The first came easy. Two hired blades laughing in a wine shop, bragging about the storm to come. Matineus slit one's throat from behind the curtain. The other drew a blade but didn't get far, good Latinus steel punched his ribs. Both bled out on the floor, wine mixing with blood.

The next died near the baths. He followed a noblewoman too closely. Didn't see the boy servant watching him. When he stepped into the alley to relieve himself, three cousins closed in. One took his legs. One his arms. The last cut his throat and left the body on a heap of trash.

By nightfall, two more lay dead.

One, Red Ring's youngest brother, tried to hide in a cheap taberna near the market. Rufus walked in alone. Sat beside him. Asked questions. Ordered food. Then drove his knife through the man's hand, pinning him to the table. Before the screaming finished, Rufus opened his neck and cut his head off. No one stopped him.

Rufus took a bar towel and wiped the blood from his face and hands. He dropped gold coins, commented on how good the food tasted. He ate the roasted dates wrapped in pork fat as he walked out the door. He tossed the head to a half-brother who dropped it with a wet thud. Rufus laughed and continued eating.

The owner would boast about this for the rest of his life. He even commissioned a painting mural on the wall depicting Rufus cutting off the assassin's head. That mural would be seen there for hundreds of years.

Another ran. Fast. The family chased. All of them. Across rooftops, through fruit stalls, past shouting women. He threw jars. Kicked dogs. Scaled a wall. None of his efforts mattered. A javelin took him through the back. He died on a butcher's table, pigs hanging above him.

The Latinus clan left gold coins where the bodies fell.

Gold always opened eyes.

Payment for the mess. Rewards meant to be remembered.

They kept count.

Five more remained.

One tried the temple district. Hid under a portico with other beggars. A cousin found him there, nose twitching. He waited until the man lowered his hood to eat, then struck. The beggar screamed. Others scattered. The assassin died with blood on his teeth.

Another tried the river. A warehouse near the Tiber. He didn't expect four men waiting in silence. Oil lamps flickered once, then the fight. Fast, ugly. He wounded one cousin before Matineus crushed his larynx with the pommel of a sword.

The last three broke off. Thought to vanish into crowds.

One never made it. Fell in love with a whore who sold him out.

One walked into a restaurant and saw Rufus smiling and already sitting at the table. He ran. Didn't get far. His body hung from a bridge by morning. Missing its head.

One killed himself after being hunted down and trapped in a rented room. He left a note in bad Latin: They never stop.

Now only Red Ring and the boy remained. His brothers all dead.

They waited in the alley. Just off the main road. They had knives. They had hatred. They had nothing else.

Red Ring sent a message. "Come get me."

The city slept.

But the Latinus clan came.

And the gods held their breath.

Chapter 126
ALLEY OF RED RING

R ain from the late afternoon still slicked the stones; gutters hauled black
water toward the Tiber; the dye-vats had stained the walls purple where
their ghosts seeped through plaster. The alley behind the warehouses constrict-
ed to a throat; one way in, one way out. Lantern light guttered in a crooked
bracket; smoke crawled the bricks; the smell of old wine and human waste lay
heavy. A tavern door thudded somewhere beyond; laughter died as if the city
held its breath.

Red Ring waited at the far end. Cloak thrown back; curved blade in hand;
one eye bright as an ember. He did not move like a man fleeing; he stood like
an animal that had been cornered and had accepted the fate the Gods gave. His
brothers had given him bites of ritual and slaughter; the alley held their names
in the hush between droplets. Now he wanted this moment to be an answer.

Rufus stepped from the mouth of the lane. Caligae laced tight; subligaculum
blood-red; oil dark on chest and arms. Two blades rode his hands: a thin long
for reach; a thick short for breaking bone. Lightning flashed behind him. He
took the stone underfoot as counsel, where to plant, how weight crossed a man,
which swing would trap the light. No shout left his throat, no oath. Matineus
moved to his left, a shadow that kept roofs and windows honest, ivory-hilt
gladius held low. Caesar's gift gleamed like a promise in his hand. Behind them
a few family members melted into the dark, shields angled to drink surprise.

Red Ring laughed; the sound had lost any humor. "You don't know what
you've done," he spat.

Rufus tightened his grip. "I know exactly. I killed your brothers. I killed your people. I counted. One by one. Only you and that snot nose lives." He let the knives swing easy, wrists loose, motion shaped heat.

The Parthian charged.

Steel kissed brick: sparks spattered; the first blow screamed off stone. Red Ring's curved blade sought the soft seam above the belt; the place men kept their lives; it skidded along masonry when Rufus angled left; the shock chased the attacker's arm; Rufus answered with a fast upward slash across an inner thigh. Blood drove out hot and quick; the Parthian did not pause. He fought like a boar trapped under a net; slash, shove, bite; there was no finesse left in him, only the blind hate of insanity.

Rufus yielded a pace and read rhythm: inhale, high swing; step; shove. He punched the scarred jaw; teeth cracked; his knee hit gut; blade nicked ribs; Red Ring staggered, spat dark and bright. Still, he smiled through blood, madness keeps some men upright.

"You don't get to end me," Red Ring snarled.

"I already did," Rufus said, flat as a blade.

The Parthian lunged again, desert feints nested in the arc. Rufus slipped the left hip, elbow finding jawbone; the man's knee buckled; a quick rake beneath the ribs opened another warm seam. Red Ring's legs trembled; he bowed to gravity; he fell toward the cobble like an animal finding a place to die and then refusing.

From shadow behind a shutter a boy moved, red hair, narrow shoulders, a knife gripped like a promise. He slid forward without a breath: close, high, the blade seeking spine. Matineus moved first; his motion blurred because practice breeds' speed. One step, one turn, one swing; the small head left the neck clean. The act made no show: a single flat whack, a wet sound, a small face striking stone. The body folded, twitching as if learning to fall.

Red Ring saw the knife wake and skittered; he reached with hands wet and useless. Rufus drove the pommel into the scarred temple; the bar of metal cracked bone. The Parthian tried to crawl; wrists found nothing. Rufus drove a gladius up under the ribs, angle, twist; heat spilled, black and sweet. Blood braided with gutter-water; steam lifted faint and obscene.

Rufus knelt; he did not hurry. A man's end deserves care: one clean cut, one angle that leaves no clinging shame. He pressed his heel to the sword-hand and smashed the wrist; the blade clattered. Then he reached for the final arc.

"This is for the dancer, my lover, the Sibyl," Rufus said. "For the girl on my portico. For every market you burned because you could."

He lifted the long knife and pushed under the right flank finding the liver; the steel went home; he twisted. The Parthian sobbed a raw sound; old wars and new regrets braided in it. He tried to rise; he failed; the alley took him down.

Rufus's hand found the mutilated middle finger where the man wore his iron ring. He sliced that finger clean and held the ring. It felt heavy; the metal tasted of rust and oath. He dropped the finger into the gutter; a wet knock answered. He slid the red metal onto his own middle finger and flexed: the iron sat like a cursed promise.

Rufus held his hand up and wiggled his fingers showing off the ring under Matineus's nose and smiled. Matineus nodded his approval and admiration.

Matineus watched the gutter; the men of the Latinus family closed the mouths of side lanes; no one moved to praise; the city seldom made noise for this kind of justice.

Silk whispered at the alley mouth, no hurry. Albina came veiled in black; Zarmina flanked; Nisaya's hand already found a knife. They crossed the muck with the silent certainty of women who had learned to weigh a life and strike deep. No surprise, no fear, only the cold work of finishing accounts.

Rufus stepped aside. Albina knelt beside the ruin without pretending reverence; the torch painted her gold. She touched the Parthian's face the way a midwife might examine a newborn: quick, unromantic, final.

"You tried to break me," she said, voice low. "You tried to end my name. You snuffed the eternal flame and burned down the Goddesses Temple."

Red Ring rasped, "Yes... I extinguished your flame."

"You spat on something you do not own." Albina's hand left a dark smear across his hair. She unwrapped a small cloth, precise, practiced fingers, and with Nisaya's silent help she took the parts he had tried to keep: a tongue, ears, the eyes, his manhood. One by one they left the human where it had lived: dropped into the drain. The gutter took them, and the city swallowed them without ceremony.

"Your sons," Albina looked at Red Ring, "are doomed."

Red Ring screamed and keened as if noise alone might ransom him. Albina listened with a grin. She did one last small thing, she set the ritual knot, a blood-bound twist of black silk meant to bind a man's ghost, on the lip of the grate and let it fall. A splash answered, the sewer ate the sound.

Red Ring died.

"They will remember," she said. "Every last pulse that remains. After that, no sight, no voice."

She found a brand on his side: antlers burned into skin, proof of the fraternity that had made this man. She cataloged the mark with a glance, then nodded to her witches. Two guards hauled what remained and shoved it toward the grate. The rotten weight sunk into the sewers of Rome and vanished; rats answered with tiny teeth.

Matineus exhaled like a bell released. Rufus rolled his neck; sinew popped with the habit of the man who expects pain. He looked at the red ring on his finger and knew this alley would hold its hush for a long while, rumor would do the rest.

Albina rose. She did not look satisfied; satisfaction is for simpler things. She looked at Rufus with arithmetic shading her face: debts tallied; dangers measured; a future trimmed. "We leave now. It's stinks here." she said.

They filed out slowly: family men first, shields against shadow; Matineus last to pull the grate home where teeth clicked iron; the torch burned low. Outside, Rome resumed the ordinary: a woman hauling water, a drunk praying for a softer bed, a child chasing a moth with cupped hands. Beyond those small things the Tiber moved on, indifferent.

The alley held steam and the smell of brass; it kept the echo of a head that had hit stone. The cat that had hissed earlier sat on a cracked amphora and blinked; the city breathed and turned the night into rumor. Rufus did not wash the ring clean that night. The ring would be mounted in his trophy room.

They left the alley the same way they had come, silent, practical, complete. The claim had been collected. Rome would continue on.

Chapter 127
JOY

R ome

The world slowed... for once.

Caesar had gone west to Spain, crushed debtors and bandits, sharpened his blade for what everyone knew would come. He returned lean, rich, and famous, narrowly escaped disqualification, forfeited his triumph, ran for consul, and won. Five years of rule in Gaul waited. Riches. Empire. Legend. Until the summons came, Rome held its breath.

Red Ring's body had hardly cooled when Albina sent word east. Not directly. Through whispers and caravans, through spice merchants and silver-fingered traders. The message cut like a scar.

One of yours came west. He failed. He died. More will follow. Beware your own blood.

In the royal gardens of Parthia, the King of Kings read the scroll, broke the seal with his thumb, laughed once, then crushed the letter under his heel. Courtiers pretended not to hear. Tension spread like fire through silk. Messengers doubled. Spies withdrew.

A second scroll arrived a week later. Unsigned. Silk-wrapped, tied in red twine. Inside, a burned scrap of cloth and a single lock of hair.

He didn't laugh this time.

Matineus returned from Egypt, skin burned dark, eyes older. He carried no letters, only a list of names: shipmasters, desert guides, trusted ports. Routes from Alexandria to Pelusium, then east beneath moonlight. Two new Lucius designed ships waited on the Red Sea, long, narrow, and fast. Crews trained in silence, blades oiled, sails trimmed to run like wolves.

Albina called it tribute. It was preparation. Gold sealed in clay jars. Medicines. Sacred tools. Passphrases whispered between witches. A network built not of soldiers, but believers.

Rufus didn't ask for details. He trained, sparred, built muscle on muscle. She asked; he gave. He offered; she took. Between them, something that felt like a kingdom formed, half flesh, half faith.

The Senate pretended not to see her. Behind closed doors, senators spoke her name like a superstition. Some laughed. Then they stopped.

The Latinus villa changed. Into their home.

Fulvia's belly rose, first soft, then proud. Rufus kissed it each morning, whispering to the child inside.

"A boy," the midwives said. "Strong. Loud. Ready for battle."

Albina's second child sat lower, still and quiet.

"A girl," Zarmina said. "One who listens before she strikes."

Rufus moved among them like a god grown gentle. Barefoot through mosaic halls. Kissing each woman in turn. Lifting his son high until laughter filled the courtyard. The boy chased doves across the tiles, shouting curses the guards swore they hadn't taught him.

They held small dinners. Senators and philosophers. Their wives, curious and silent. Fulvia led the talk. Albina steered the rhythm. Rufus watched and listened. Rome's great men sipped his wine and feared his silences.

Every month they traveled to Ostia. Sea wind tasted of salt and hemp smoke. Slept late in the seaside villa. The theater balcony where Albina danced became ritual ground, red silk, bells, torchlight. Food. Wine. Smoke. Fulvia clapped to the rhythm of the music. Tirzah laughed and ate and danced. Lucius began kissing the dancer, Tareeda as she rubbed oil onto his leg. She was in love with him. Rufus sat back, cup in hand, whispering to no one:

This is what life should be.

Sometimes they sailed far from shore. Slow. Moonlit. Oars steady. Fulvia slept below deck; Albina leaned on the railing, hair black against the stars. The brother, Lucius, studied the waves and how the ship moved. He drew plans for a better, faster ship. Tirzah let her hair blow and remembered her earlier voyage on this ship. Rufus trained in his subligaculum with the longbow, the creak of seasoned yew mixing with the sea's breath.

He bought land near Vesuvius, where ash sweetened the soil. The slope dropped toward the bay. Olive trees curled in the wind. The volcano slept then, green, calm, but Rufus loved its danger.

"A place worth dying near," he said.

The new villa would face the water. White columns. Bronze lamps. One courtyard for silence. One for song. One for the goddess.

Matineus brought gold charms for the unborn. Crassus sent an ebony-and-ivory cradle. Aurelia, Caesar's mother, sent violet-wrapped clothes that once touched Caesar as an infant.

They began calling Leo, Lucian, Albina's fathers name. Lucian grew fast. Two languages before he turned two. He rode the household dog like a warhorse. Called Matineus "Uncle Lion." Called Fulvia "Second Mother." Called Rufus "Father" whenever proud or tired.

Every eight days they held a feast of joy. Braziers flamed under olive branches. Musicians played eastern strings. Albina danced first, her girls flowing behind her. Fulvia joined, slower but radiant. Rufus watched them, drink forgotten, eyes bright with the fire.

Rome paused around that villa. The Subura still stank, the Senate still schemed, but none of it crossed their threshold. The gods had given them a season of peace.

But the summons came.

Caesar had secured Gaul. Five years of conquest.

He sent for Rufus.

No one cried. They had long known this moment would come.

The official letter lay on the table two days before Rufus opened it. The wax bore Caesar's eagle. The message was short:

You will ride with me the north. We take the men. The gods have chosen us.

That evening, Albina lit lamps in the courtyard. Fulvia brought wine. Tirzah stood by the fountain. Lucius sat on a bench. None of them spoke.

Rufus looked from one beloved face to the next. For the first time, peace pressed heavier on him than war.

They would have one more season. One spring. One harvest. One final year.

They would hold every minute tight as a fist.

The garden filled with laughter again.

Lucian splashed in the fountain.

The unborn stirred.

Anklets chimed on the stone.

The house smelled of myrrh and roasted figs.

The mountain slept above the bay.

The sea turned silver under the moon.

And for that year, they lived.

Chapter 128
A FORM OF EQUALITY

Tirzah entered with the tray balanced on her hip.

The breakfast nook held its silence. Morning light crept along the wall, thin as parchment. Rufus stood half in shadow, arms bare, jaw rough, the scent of steel oil and leather rising off him. The bread cooled untouched on the plate.

She set the tray down. Silver trembled against her wrist.

"Tirzah."

She paused. His voice carried no command this time, no cold edge.

He looked her over, fully, as someone who mattered to him, as someone he needed. "You're coming with me."

She blinked. "To Gaul?"

He nodded once. "I'll need eyes that see behind words. Around corners. Someone who reads hunger and fear in a face."

Her breath caught. Praise from Rufus always weighed more than gold.

"I trust your instinct," he said. "You move like someone who survives."

She steadied her hands. "You want me there?"

"I do. I've thought on it long enough. Please come. I need you."

She turned slightly, unsure how to stand.

"But I want more than silence from you," he said. "Speak when you see truth. Don't wait to be asked."

She faced him again. "Yes, Dominus."

He frowned a little. "Good. And please, no more of that Dominus business."

"Yes, Rufus."

The name settled between them, heavy as a vow. Outside, the fountain dripped once. A fly circled the figs. Neither spoke.

Then she lifted her chin. "If I go with you, I want a better room when we come home every year. Not the one by the stair. Albina's guest room, the painted ceiling, the river-God mosaic. I don't ever want to be moved again. You promised a bath, toilet. Build it."

He tilted his head.

"I want more silver," she continued. "Mine. I want to serve only you. Not Fulvia. Not Albina. No one else."

Her voice held steady now.

"And if you die in battle," she whispered, "I want to be free."

Rufus stepped forward. Not to threaten, only to close the space.

She didn't retreat. "And my father's gold. You said it still exists. I want it. And his house in Jerusalem. That's my right."

His mouth curved. "You'll have it."

He didn't move for a long while. The silence between them pressed flat.

No jewels on her. No paint. Just her truth.

He reached and took her hand.

"I remember Rhodes," he said. "The market. The boy with ink on his ear. You warned me."

"I was so young."

"You saved me trouble."

"I watched him lie before he opened his mouth."

"You still do."

She liked that he remembered.

He walked around the table. Close enough she smelled salt, wool, clean sweat. No perfume. No mask.

"I want you near me in Gaul," he said. "Not with camp followers. At my side. My rank has privileges."

She met his gaze. "Then treat me like someone who stands there."

He grunted. Approving. "You've changed."

"You taught me to."

"You'll advise me?"

"Yes."

"You'll speak when it matters, not when I think it does?"

"Yes, Rufus."

"Good. Watch everyone. Especially the ones who smile too much."

"I already do."

He brushed her hand again. "You're mine," he said, quieter now. "But not like before."

"I know."

"You're not a concubine. Not a wife. You're..."

"A partner?"

That surprised him. Almost drew a laugh.

"You'll have the room. The gold. The house. Freedom when I fall."

"You won't fall."

He didn't correct her. He let her keep that.

She turned for the curtain. He watched her walk, head high, hips steady. The girl he enslaved in Jerusalem now moved like a woman who owned her own fate.

"Tirzah."

She stopped. Turned.

He crossed the room with measured steps, warm breath touching her cheek. "You were right. You should've spoken sooner."

She didn't bow. Didn't soften. "Then listen."

He waited.

"I want a good horse. Not a mule. Strength and speed. I ride beside your guard."

He nodded.

"I want thick clothing, fitted, warm. Not slave rags."

"Done."

"I want a Latinus knife of my own. No... two."

An eyebrow rose.

"You'll teach me."

"I will."

"I'll cook for you. Shave you. Wash your back, your linens, your wounds. I'll keep your boots dry. You'll never call for help again."

"Done."

"I don't serve the women anymore. Only you."

"Alright."

"I want a share of the loot," she finished. "One percent. Gold, cattle, captives... it doesn't matter."

He studied her.

Then stepped close enough she felt the heat of him. "You'll get two."

Slow breath. Her hand brushed his sleeve, quick and soft and alive.

He didn't stop her.

At dawn, she stood in the courtyard. Marble still cold. Four horses waited under the arch. Big ones, fresh-shod, restless.

Rufus watched from the portico.

She walked the line, touching each neck. Feeling warmth. Feeling strength. The third horse tossed his head and stamped. A fighter.

"I'll take this one," she said.

The groom looked to Rufus. Rufus nodded.

She mounted smooth, unassisted. Sat straight. Let the horse test her. He settled first.

A guard carried two blades wrapped in leather. She unrolled them, tested weight, balance. Drew one. Steel hissed.

A small, sharp smile.

Rufus said nothing. But the way he watched her, he understood what she had become.

She dismounted, wiped the blade on her tunic, sheathed it herself.

"Pack your things," he said. "We ride within the week."

"I'm ready now."

He believed her.

She led the horse to water. Sunlight caught the braid over her shoulder.

The courtyard bells rang first hour.

Rufus turned and walked inside.

Behind him, Tirzah stood in the rising light, horse at her side, two blades crossed at her hip, not a servant, not a possession, but the shadow of a warrior yet to come.

Chapter 129
THE QUIET GENIUS

Lucius Latinus Maximus traced the grain of the cedar board with one finger, slow and precise, following every ridge as if reading a poem written in wood. Morning light caught the curls of shaving on the floor. Dust floated around him like gold drifting through water.

He didn't look up when Rufus entered. He rarely did. Lucius never greeted anyone until the thought finished in his mind. Today, that thought lived inside the curve of the hull he was sketching.

Rufus waited.

His brother's hand paused, lifted, then moved again, one long, perfect sweep of charcoal across the plank. The line arched like a bow drawn to its limit. He exhaled softly, pleased.

"A new yacht," Lucius murmured. "Yours."

Rufus stepped closer. The drawing stretched across three boards laid edge to edge, precise measurements, angles, weight distribution, thickness of ribs, position of oars, curve of keel. He could see the water already moving around it.

"You designed this for me?"

Lucius nodded once. "Silent. Fastest yet. Maneuvers smoothly. Strong. Cuts through wind. Cuts through the river. Cuts through the sea."

Rufus smiled. "It's perfect."

Lucius frowned and tapped a small mark with his finger. "Not yet. Need better cedar. Longer. The Cypress cedars would be best."

"I'll order a shipment," Rufus said.

Albina entered the workshop with the dancer Tareeda beside her. Lucius brightened when he saw the dancer, his fingers tapping his thigh three times, his greeting. She gave him a small bow.

"You're early," Albina said to Rufus, brushing her hand across his back. Her belly rose beneath her white gown. The scent of rose resin followed her.

"I wanted to see him," Rufus said.

Albina smiled at Lucius. "He's been out here since dawn."

Lucius nodded again. "Thinking. The whole night. The boat came to me in my sleep."

He tapped his head once with the charcoal.

Dreams held equations for him. Shapes. Distances. Silence.

Tareeda moved to his side, gathering the scrolls he had left scattered across the table. Drawings of arches, aqueduct channels, tension rods, weight loads. She understood none of them, but she protected each sheet like a rare jewel.

"He didn't eat yet," she said softly.

Lucius touched her forearm in thanks. That touch meant trust, rare, deliberate, sacred.

Rufus looked between them. "You take care of him."

Tareeda nodded. "Always."

Albina stepped closer, her hand resting lightly on Lucius's shoulder. He didn't flinch. He leaned into it. That ease was her gift, she never pressed, never startled him, never forced her presence. Lucius responded to her calm the way animals did instinctively, wholly.

"You'll stay here," Albina told him gently. "When Rufus goes north. This is your home."

Lucius didn't react at first. His eyes stayed on the cedar plank. Then slowly, his lip trembled.

"I know," he whispered.

Albina's hand stayed firm on his shoulder. "He must serve his legion. But you stay. You build. You design. You keep this house alive."

Lucius stared at the plank again, as if the wood steadied him.

Rufus moved closer. "Lucius..."

His brother turned, finally, eyes wide and wet but unfallen. Lucius rarely cried. He felt too much for tears.

Rufus placed a hand on his shoulder, the same gesture their grandfather once used. "I'll come back. And when I do, I expect this boat ready to launch."

Lucius sniffed once, nodded hard. "I'll build two."

Tareeda covered her mouth to hide a smile.

Albina stroked his hair. "He now has purpose. Fear leaves when purpose enters."

Tareeda brushed the curls from Lucius's forehead. "He draws all day. Talks to the cat. Plays with little Lucian. He will not be alone."

As if summoned, a soft meow drifted from the doorway.

Gift of Mars stretched lazily on the threshold, long and lean, fur black with one streak of white like a scar from a god. He strutted toward Lucius, tail curled, and jumped onto the table without hesitation.

Lucius lifted the cat gently and placed him against his cheek. Mars purred deep, almost vibrating.

Albina laughed softly. "He loves you most."

Lucius whispered into the cat's ear, "Stay. Guard."

A command wrapped in affection.

Later, in the garden, Albina sat with her legs curled beneath her, watching Lucius walk the length of the path, counting silently under his breath. He touched the hedge every ten steps. Paused. Turned. Began again.

Rufus watched beside her. "He's preparing."

"For what?" Albina asked.

"For my leaving."

Lucius paused at the fountain. Gift of Mars followed him, tail flicking like a metronome. The cat brushed against his leg, steadying him.

Albina whispered, "He feels everything. Even when no one speaks."

Rufus nodded. "He always did. Even as a boy, he knew when someone was afraid before they did."

Lucius knelt by the fountain. His fingers traced the carved lion's mane. Then he looked up at Rufus.

"Will you fight?" he asked.

"Yes."

Lucius nodded once. "Don't die. I don't want to start over."

His voice cracked.

Albina covered her mouth with her hand.

Rufus crossed to him and knelt. "I won't die."

Lucius leaned his forehead against Rufus's chest. A rare gesture. Pure trust.

"You will come back," Lucius whispered.

Rufus held him. "I will."

Tareeda watched from the shade, eyes soft, hands clasped. She had woven new charms into Lucius's belt, red thread, shells from Ostia, a strip of cedar bark. Protection, she said.

Albina approached and kissed Lucius's head. "Your mind builds what armies cannot destroy."

Lucius blinked, unsure how to answer praise. He looked at the ground instead, then whispered, "I will finish the aqueduct."

Rufus laughed quietly. "I know you will."

That evening, Lucius sat with Gift of Mars on his lap while Tareeda fed him honeyed milk and bread dipped in olive oil. He ate slowly, precise, savoring each bite.

Albina watched from the doorway.

"He is Rome's purest soul," she whispered to Rufus.

Rufus nodded. "He is."

"And one day," she said, "his work will outlive all of us."

Rufus watched his brother stroke the cat, whispering numbers under his breath, calculating a future only he could see.

Lucius looked up suddenly and said, "Your boat won't sink."

Rufus smiled. "I never doubted it."

Lucius returned the smile, small, crooked, perfect.

He whispered to the cat,

"We'll wait. And he'll come home."

And the house held that promise like a blessing.

Chapter 130
HOME

R ome – Early Spring. 58 B.C.

Caesar arrived at dawn.

No litter. No horn. No show of rank.

Only dust, hooves, and the crisp silence of a man carrying the weight of continents in his chest.

The villa still slept when the riders came through the gray haze. Iron clicked softly against bit. Hooves struck stone. Caesar rode first, cloak thrown back, breath white in the cold. His eyes fixed on the courtyard as if he had already crossed Gaul and returned again.

Rufus waited armed.

A wool cloak wrapped tight over his sword arm. Leather creaked at his waist. The smell of oil, steel, and cold morning sweat rose from him. He looked carved from the same stone that held up the villa.

Caesar dismounted without speaking.

They faced each other, the aging lion and the young one.

"As I mentioned," Caesar said, loud enough for every ear in the courtyard, "five months. Then Rome will call you back."

Rufus nodded once.

"I've settled it with the Senate. You'll return each October, elections, votes, the planting season. You'll ride north again after the rains."

"May," Rufus said.

Caesar's mouth curved. "Yes. You'll be home longer than you're gone. Make everyday matter. And remember, here or in Gaul, you remain one of my weapons."

The courtyard stilled. Even the fig leaves stopped stirring.

Rufus turned toward the villa.

Albina waited in the archway. A thin black veil draped over her hair, clinging to her breath each time she exhaled. Small and still.

Fulvia stood beside her, hand on her rounded belly, gold glinting at her wrist. Morning light caught her profile, strong, patrician, unafraid, Roman.

At their feet, little Lucian, hair wild, cheeks flushed, pushed his carved lion cart across the tiles, unaware of the weight gathering in the air.

By the gate, Tirzah waited with her horse.

Her hair bound high. Linen layered for travel. Eyes sharp beneath the hood. The armor boy stood beside her, bare-armed in the cold, two mules loaded with gear packed by Maccus: spare bows, oiled arrows, rope, field tools, whetstones, wrapped bundles that smelled of cedar, iron, and war.

Rufus moved among them without wasted motion. He checked buckles, straps, girths. Ran his hand down the horse's neck. Listened to the air for signs of rain.

Caesar watched from the fountain, still as a statue in a square of rising light.

At last, Rufus walked toward the women.

Albina stepped forward first. Her small hand found his arm, her touch like a brand of heat.

"Come back whole," she said. Her voice soft, but the command inside it iron.

Her eyes finished the sentence she didn't speak:

Come back to me.

Fulvia followed. She lifted her face and kissed his cheek. "And clean," she murmured. "Don't track Gaul into my house."

He almost laughed. Almost.

Albina's fingers tightened. Her gold rings left faint marks in his skin. "The Goddess watches you," she whispered. "Even where other gods forget their names."

He met her gaze. "Tell her I'll keep the flame."

Fulvia cupped his face a heartbeat longer than was proper. "Our child will know your stories before he knows your voice."

"Then tell them true," he said.

"I'll leave out the cruel parts."

He kissed her hair, light, reverent, then knelt to the boy with the wooden lion.

"Guard them," Rufus told him.

The boy straightened, proud as a miniature centurion.

Behind them, saddle leather shifted. Caesar mounted. Riders adjusted reins. The smell of dust and cold earth lifted as horses stamped the stone.

Rufus's father stepped forward, his arms around a silent Lucius, cloak around his shoulders, beard silvered. His voice traveled like a centurion's decree.

"Go with honor and come back with honor... or don't come home."

Rufus met his father's eyes. "Yes, Father."

Then he turned slowly, taking in the courtyard, the worn marble steps, the trembling fig leaves, the mosaic of the river god shining by the pool. Every corner carried a memory: Albina's dance, Fulvia's laughter, Tirzah's quiet tasks, Lucius sketching, the baby's first cry.

He turned back one last time.

Albina's veil moved in the cold breath of dawn.

Fulvia stood straight, spine unbroken by fear or pride.

The boy clutched the lion cart.

Tirzah watched from her saddle, eyes dark, steady, and loyal.

Rufus climbed into the saddle.

His horse shifted under him, alive, eager, aware.

Caesar raised his hand.

The riders moved.

Dust rose in soft clouds behind them. Olive branches brushed their cloaks. The road beyond the gate opened into dew-wet fields and a horizon colored like steel.

Rufus looked back once.

Albina raised her hand, slow and deliberate, a movement older than Rome, a gesture of blessing or warning, no one could say. Fulvia lifted her chin beside her, a matron of the future and of the now. Tirzah bowed her head once.

He faced forward.

The city waited beyond the hills, half-awake. A bell rang near the Tiber. Smoke drifted from the bakeries. The breath of Rome thickened in the cold.

Caesar rode ahead, cloak snapping like a war banner.

Rufus followed.

Behind him, the women watched until the dust under the umbrella pines swallowed him whole.

The lion cart lay overturned by the fountain, its wooden wheels still spinning.

The sacred fire inside the villa burned low, its smoke a thin ribbon curling upward like a prayer.

Albina whispered a word no one else heard.

The wind carried it east.

Rome seemed to pause.

And the ages remembered the morning Gaius Latinus Rufus rode out from the Caelian Hill.

Chapter 131
THE FLOW

R OME - FALL, 58 BC

The villa on the Caelian Hill slept.

Life there flowed along it's path.

They had just returned from the sea, salt wind still in their hair, sun still warm in their bones. The seaside always gave them days where breath felt easy, where the world loosened its grip.

Tonight, the air smelled of myrrh and wood smoke. A thin early frost silvered the roof tiles, but the cold felt deeper than season. A northern kind of cold, the kind that breathed on the back of a man's neck. The kind Rufus now felt on his ride home.

Outside the walls, Rome murmured through its autumn hush. A dog barked once. A cart rolled, then vanished into silence. In three market cycles, elections would begin. Any day now, Rufus would be home again. He would do Caesar's bidding in the senate and the city. She would sleep in his arms again.

Inside, the villa held its warmth.

The boy slept under a wool blanket, clutching the carved wooden lion Matineus had shaped by hand. His lashes trembled with dreams of ships and horses.

In the cypress basket, Albina's daughter, Seraya, stared up at the rafters, quiet, alert, ancient in some small way no one could name.

Fulvia dreamed in the outer room, hand cupping her belly. Midwives promised a boy. Her heart whispered for a girl. Both hopes curled in her sleep like warm breath.

Albina walked barefoot through the hall.

Her shadow crossed the mosaics like a shadow. She paused at each room, the nursery, the hearth, the family shrine, before she slipped into the small temple chamber.

The air inside felt different.

Sharper.

Listening.

She inhaled once, slowly. The desert lived in the back of that breath, dust, wind, the long red horizon of her birth. Crowns and stolen power, a whisper from somewhere deep murmured. She pushed it aside. Not yet.

She knelt before the shrine.

The statue of Cybele towered above her, lions carved mid-snarl, eternal in their stone fury. Before the goddess stood twelve older idols. Crude. Heavy. Carved by hands that never knew Rome. The Sibyl's lineage. Mothers of mothers. Eyes hollowed by centuries of worship and warning.

Albina reached into her red silk pouch.

A lock of Rufus's hair lay inside, bound in silver thread. She had cut it herself the spring morning he rode north, using the black iron knife passed down through Sibyl-priestesses for a thousand years.

She pressed it to her lips.

Then slipped it beneath the oldest idol.

"He will soon return," she whispered. "And he will be more than he was."

The flame wavered. Shadows leaned closer as if to hear.

Somewhere deep in the villa, a wooden beam creaked softly, cautious, as if the house itself listened.

Zarmina the Red entered with a cup of mint and honey tea. She set it down quietly, bowed to the idols, and left without a word. The older woman knew when silence belonged to the living and when it belonged to the gods.

Albina stayed.

She thought of snow on iron, blood freezing on leather, the scream of winds from a world of bones. She thought of false Sibyls rising in the southern heat, weaving lies in silk, gathering shadows like courtiers.

She thought of Rufus, his breath, his promise, his silence.

And the fire inside her lifted its head.

She touched the flame.

Let it burn her fingertip.

Did not flinch.

"This is not the end," she said.

The lamp hissed back, as if agreeing.

A wind stirred the courtyard.

The torches danced.

Somewhere, a shutter tapped.

Rome slept.

The gods did not.

Far north, under snow older than any mortal name, something stirred. A voice shaped like a woman's breath whispered from stone... a blood hunger waiting.

Far south, beyond burning sands and the Nile's bright coils, the usurper gathered power, her hands clean though the ground behind her bled.

Albina rose.

Light traced her cheek like a flash of gold. Her red silk robe whispered as she walked through the villa, past the cradle, past Fulvia's sleeping form, past the chamber where Rufus's scent still clung to the linen.

At the threshold she paused.

The night sky above Rome shimmered with cold stars. Northward, beyond hills and forests and frost, Rufus carved his name into the world.

Rome dreamed of order.

Albina dreamed of fire.

One day, those dreams would meet.

And the world would tremble.

Epilogue

T he years unfolded like silk.

Rufus grew gray, then old. When pain took his throat, breath shortened, he chose his own death... standing, not kneeling, as a Roman should.

Fulvia followed in quiet dignity, her laughter tucked between the stones of their home.

Tirzah prayed, walked, and finally faded, her life burned bright and honest.

Their children rose in their places, builders, warriors, statesmen. Some led legions. Some held offices. Some loved too fiercely. Some died young. Their daughters married kings. Their sons fathered dynasties.

And Albina watched it all.

Decade after decade, the Sibyl of the Eastern Sea walked among them. Her step slowed; her hair paled; her skin thinned. Yet her eyes stayed bright. Her steps stayed sure.

The goddess still whispered when she slept.

Sometimes in her own tongue.

Sometimes in none at all.

Visions came like storms.

She saw temples rise; temples fall.

She saw a new god born under a wandering star.

She saw his sign spread across marble, stone, flesh.

She saw her blood kneel before it.

She saw kings fall to dust and slaves rise to power.

She saw a fire that outlived memory.

In her last year, her one hundred and fourteenth, Albina sat before the flame she had tended all her life in Rome.

Her robe faded.

Her hands thin.

Her back unbent.

The twelve idols glowed red in the lamplight.

Old mothers. Old warnings.

She smiled.

Not at the past, but at what waited beyond it.

She saw popes wearing her bloodline.

She saw empires whisper her name.

She saw the old goddess slip beneath the new world like a hidden river, still running, still alive.

She saw the man she loved once more.

She was priestess.

She was princess.

She was the Sibyl.

The flame flickered once and steadied... eternal.

Rome turned.

Empires rose.

Empires crumbled.

But somewhere in the shadow of time, a red flame burned.

Because she had walked here.

Among heroes.

Among gods.

Among the unforgettable.

And the world dreamed her name.

Afterword

Stories don't end. They circle.

Rome will forget names, but not the blood that built it.

The Sibyl will walk its alleys long after temples fall, and somewhere a soldier will still whisper a prayer to her flame.

Rufus rode north into mud and fire, and men followed.

Albina watched from Rome and waited.

Their children would rise, fight, love, and die in the shadow of their names.

That's how legacies work, not in marble, but in flesh.

I wrote this book to remember that the Republic was never a clean idea. Life then was short, cheap, and cruel. It was hunger, hope, and human hands shaping power out of dust. There were laughter and love and dancing. The old gods still watched. The new ones were not yet born.

Their story continues in Rome's Warpath.

But for now, let them rest.

-D. Amon Hume-

Acknowledgements

Oracle Publishing LLC
  oraclepublishing@zohomail.com

About the author

D. Amon Hume is a former U.S. Navy servicemember from Kentucky who now lives near St. Louis, Missouri. A lifelong student of ancient Rome, classical warfare, and forgotten religious cults of the Mediterranean world, he blends rigorous historical curiosity with mythic imagination in his fiction.

His work explores the collision of empire and prophecy, faith and power, soldiers and priestesses, stories rooted in archival-style mystery, political intrigue, and the dangerous aftershocks of antiquity that echo into later centuries.

When not writing, Hume researches Roman engineering, military campaigns, early Christian history, and the ritual traditions of the ancient Near East, building immersive worlds where legend and scholarship blur.

Flame of the Oracle; A Mythic Ancient Roman Romantasy, marks the beginning of his epic series, The Oracle of Rome.

D. Amon Hume has been signed with Oracle Publishing LLC since 2025.